THE ARMAGEDDON CHRONICLES

A Mafia Epic

COURTNEY SUTTLE

ISBN 1-886225-55-9
Library of Congress Card Number: 99-69621

Cover design by BJ Taylor

Note: This is a work of fiction. Characters, names, places, and incidents are the product of the author's imagination and are used fictitiously. Any resemblance of this work of fiction to actual persons living or dead, corporations, institutions, events, or locales is coincidental or is common knowledge.

Dageforde Publishing, Inc.
122 South 29th Street
Lincoln, Nebraska 68510
Ph: (402) 475-1123 FAX: (402) 475-1176
email: info@dageforde.com
www.dageforde.com
Printed in the United States of America
10   9   8   7   6   5   4   3   2   1

Acknowledgments

I would like to thank the following people for their love and support. St. Mark's faculty members Mario Foster, Elva Eichenwald, Paul Weadon, Ted Whatley and Ken Owens, whose love for teaching transcended the classroom. Dr. Jack Robbins MD, friend and mentor who continually teaches my mind, heals my body and enlightens my spirit. My good friend and mentor Dan Stanton and his wife, Kelli, who provided me with work, food, shelter, guidance, and love during the completion of this project. Adele Caruth, Karla Adams, and Kimberly Kuehler for nursing me while I lay at death's door. Dr. Fraser and the ladies at the Presbyterian Asthma Clinic, Felicia, Kim and Denise for all their care and consideration during my illness and rehabilitation. Mary Pat, Stacy, Mary T and DC for scaring me into being a better bartender. Zenon, Tony Martin, Joe Ricco, the Savoicier twins, Doc, Rusty, Charlie and my boys at Charlies on SPI; Power Jack, Hollywood, Craigy D and all my brothers at Trees; *mi hermano* Jesus, Spoda, Vince, Jam, Juan, Dixon, Skippy, Berto, Alex, Evaristo, G Alvarez, Joel, Holly, Eddy Metten and yes, you, too, Kenyon, from my other home at the Red Jacket in Dallas and all the hammer bartenders it has been my pleasure to drum or be drummed by during my career. My readers Jennifer Newman, Amy Beisel, Penny Carr, and especially Alan Hayslip, whose final read helped more than I can say. My initial readers June Hoey and Carol Sawyer who were the first believers in this book. BJ Taylor for designing the incredible cover and Chris Howell for the cover conception and cover photo. Linda Dageforde for her expertise, support, and hard work. As for my editor, Tiernan Alexander, I cannot begin to list her contributions to this novel. I can tell you that I am a better writer and a better person for having known her. And finally, Nate Stinson, the ramrod behind the publication of this book. I wrote the first sentence of *AC* on his old Brother typewriter eleven years ago and finished the first draft six years later as his roommate. He has long since moved beyond being my best friend and I now know him by only one word— brother.

Author's Note

By the twentieth century the only major world power left using the Julian calendar was Imperial Russia. At the time of the First World War the Russian calendar was thirteen days behind the rest of the world. For the sake of the reader I calculated all dates in the chapters of *The Armageddon Chronicles* taking place in Russia during 1917 using the Gregorian calendar.

To God and the fellowship
for saving the life I almost destroyed

1959

Parkland County Hospital, Dallas, Texas, September, 1959

When the door opened and light fell across the doctor's face, it felt hot, like rays from the sun. Voices spoke to him from afar. His body began to rock as if he were in a boat speeding across a lake. The voices nearby became louder and more focused as they rushed toward him. The boat hit a rock tossing him into the water and with a fearful start Turturro awoke.

The young doctor sat up and rubbed a hand across his face. It felt numb and heavy. He smacked his lips, a foul taste in his mouth.

"Wha—?" he muttered and realized the door had shut leaving the room in darkness.

"We need you to come with us, Doc," a voice commanded, urgently. "Now!"

"Thought I was the only wop in Parkland," Turturro muttered, commenting on the street-wise Italian accent. "Is it Mrs. Posen?"

"We don't know any Mrs. Posen and we ain't from the hospital, Doc."

Turturro tilted his head trying to place the voice. "Then what do you need?"

"*Ha poche esigenze,*" the voice uttered in a sinister whisper. His needs are few.

Nature flipped a switch and any sense of sleepless exhaustion was zapped out of his system by an adrenaline-spiked rush of fear.

Turturro fumbled for the bedside lamp, knocking his stethoscope to the floor. "What do you want?" he asked two hulking figures revealed in the dim light.

"A small service for *tu famiglia.*"

"My family's in New York," Turturro offered, feigning ignorance.

"Your family is wherever *he* is."

Turturro paused trying to think. Finally accepting the inevitable, he asked, "What is it you need? Has someone been hurt?"

The men exchanged a glance. *"Non occorre dirgli tutti i particolari,* Carmelo," one said to the other.

"What do you mean I don't need to know anything? If someone's injured I'll need instruments, drugs."

"There's plenty of that where we're going. All you need to do is come with us... *subito!*" the one called Carmelo barked at him.

The men leaned over and yanked him out of bed. "We don't have a lot of time, Doctor. Put on your shoes and let's go."

"I need to let the nurse know..."

"That's been taken care of," Carmelo interrupted him.

"Well, can you tell me where we're going?"

"Not far," Carmelo answered as they hustled him out the door.

Carmelo spoke the truth. After jumping into a waiting car they drove five blocks to a small medical complex. Most of the tenants were family practitioners.

Carmelo drove the car into the underground garage and pulled up next to the service elevator.

"Hurry, Doctor," Carmelo said, yanking him out of the car and into the elevator. He pressed the button for the third floor.

When the door opened, he said, "Down here."

They ran to a door marked PRIVATE and entered without knocking. Carmelo led him down a narrow hall and into a waiting room.

"You made good time, Carmelo. Thank you." The voice came from a nondescript man of average height and thinning hair seated on the far side of the waiting room.

"Don Busambra," Turturro gasped, astonished to see *him* so far from New York.

Don Bennedetto Busambra smiled at him. "I need your help, Leon. Can I count on you?" he inquired with urgency.

Turturro croaked, *"Sí, padrino mio."*

"You sure he's up to this?" a stern voice asked from across the room.

Turturro turned. "Dr. Danielson?" he asked, completely befuddled.

Dr. Victor Danielson's intelligent eyes observed Turturro disdainfully. "Yeah, he'll fuck it up," the surgeon concluded disgustedly. Though his face was deformed by anger, he was incredibly handsome. Tall and solidly built, he was dressed in a hand-tailored silk suit. His tan face was framed by thick, dark hair.

"Dr. Turturro," Don Busambra snapped.

Turturro's head whipped around. *"Sí, Don Busambra?"*

"Ignore Dr. Danielson," Don Busambra commanded. "All you need concern yourself with is my request. Do you have a problem with fulfilling your duty *a tu famiglia?"* Don Busambra asked, pointedly.

"No, Godfather. I am happy to serve you," he mumbled, unsure of himself. "What is it you wish of me?"

A bloodcurdling scream froze the room. Don Busambra, unperturbed, steepled his fingers and eyed his godson. "The service lies beyond that door. What I wish from you is that you not fail me, Leon." He parted his hands and raised his eyebrows.

Turturro crossed the room quickly and took Don Busambra's right hand. He kissed the blood-red stone. "It is as you say, *padrino mio."*

Turturro turned at the sound of another scream. He followed painful moans down a hall to a room marked EXAM 2. Taking a deep breath he turned the knob and pushed open the door.

Strapped to the table was a young woman. She looked at him, terror on her face. Between her legs, a man in surgical scrubs held a scalpel glistening with blood.

"What are you doing?" Turturro demanded.

The man turned. His arms and chest were covered in blood. Drops of blood spotted his mask and face.

"Get over here now!" he ordered.

The woman screamed again. Tissues tore and a blood vessel burst further, drenching her assailant in blood. Feeling metal tearing her flesh again, she shrieked, *"El dolor! El dolor!"*

But the pain was necessary. It would become her child.

The man yanked the mask off his face. "I'm losing her, Leon. No time to scrub. There's gloves on the counter."

Turturro snapped on the surgical gloves and leaned over the patient. "Dr. Rabinowitz." Another surprise, he thought. Jacob Rabinowitz was one of Dallas' leading internists and a lecturer at Southwestern Medical School. "What the hell is going on here?"

"Breech birth, Leon. A bad one."

"I can see that. It *is* my specialty," Turturro explained.

"And that's why you're here. It's definitely not mine."

"Obviously, Doctor," Turturro remarked, observing the carnage. He probed the birth canal. "All right, Dr. Rabinowitz. Out of the way. I'll take it from here."

Rabinowitz moved aside.

"Run it for me, Doctor," Turturro ordered. Rabinowitz gave a brief medical history of the patient, the specifics of the labor, her current vitals and the medication he'd administered.

"It hurts," the woman gasped, in English. "Please help me," she begged.

"I can't give you any more pain medication," Turturro responded, giving Rabinowitz a disapproving look. "Dr. Rabinowitz has given you too much as it is. Any more could hurt the baby."

She nodded and lay back. "You are right," she gasped. "Mustn't hurt the baby."

Turturro looked at his patient for the first time. Even with her brown hair plastered to her sweaty face, she was beautiful.

She is a brave one, he thought. Most women would sell their souls at this point to stop the pain.

"Jesus, Dr. Rabinowitz!" Turturro exclaimed as the hemorrhaging continued. "How did you let it get this far?"

6

"I did my best," he replied. "There were no indications, no symptoms…"

"I'll need Dr. Danielson," Turturro said, interrupting. "Get him scrubbed."

"That's impossible," Rabinowitz stated.

"Why?" Turturro asked angrily. "He's the best surgeon I've ever worked with. He should have been in here from the beginning."

"Fathers don't deliver their children," he replied, simply.

Turturro looked up, stunned. He'd met Danielson's wife several times at medical functions. This woman was a stranger.

"Concentrate on your patient," Rabinowitz admonished Turturro. He handed him some fresh gauze, which immediately soaked through.

"We need to get her to a hospital. Now, doctor." For all his training, Turturro began to panic.

"Impossible," Rabinowitz stated, flatly.

"Why impossible?"

"You know who is out there and yet you ask me why?" Rabinowitz looked at the young doctor with concern. "What he commands is what you do, Leon, or had you forgotten?"

Turturro hadn't forgotten, he just didn't like to think about the bargain that had been forced upon him years ago.

"I have heard of your predicament, Signor Turturro," Don Antoni Busambra stated. "Your son, Leon, has had to quit school to care for you and your children. Such a shame a brilliant young man must work as a grocer when he could have given so much to our community."

"Sí, Don Busambra," Nico Turturro replied, "a great shame. But Leon's duty is to his family. What other choice does he have? His brothers and sisters must eat."

"I agree, Nico. A man's duty is to his family. My son Bennedetto will use his education to serve his family and his community. If only I could be as sure of Leon's sense of duty as I am my son's…"

"My son is an honorable man, Don Busambra. If you were to honor us with your help, he will do as I wish."

"And as I command, Signor Turturro?"

"Sí, Don Busambra. He will do as you command."

"She's too far along to perform a C-section," Turturro concluded quickly, shaking off the old memory. "If we don't get this baby out soon it will suffocate, but if it comes too quickly the mother will bleed to death." As he made another attempt to turn the baby, he spoke quietly, "We might lose one."

Rabinowitz spoke into his ear. "We sacrifice the mother to save the baby if absolutely necessary. I know, but Don Busambra wishes that they both live."

"Then pray, Doctor, because we need a miracle."

Turturro got the baby out as quickly as he could. He handed the newborn infant to Rabinowitz. Looking at the torn flesh he grabbed a clamp.

Where do I start? he asked himself. He heard Rabinowitz pounding on the baby's back and realized he was on his own.

Turturro applied the clamp and began to work. The mother weakened and he began to lose hope.

"I'm losing her!" Turturro shouted. "Too much blood loss. I just don't know."

"Stop the bleeding as best you can," Rabinowitz said as he struggled with the newborn. "The baby's lungs are clogged. As soon as I'm done, I'll hook up another unit of blood."

"It might be too late," Turturro explained, working furiously.

"Don Busambra never makes a mistake, Leon. You wouldn't be here if he didn't have absolute faith in your abilities. Now work. Honor the commitment he made to you and your family and save this woman's life!"

Rabinowitz spoke the truth.

Don Busambra saved my family from poverty and gave me my dream, he thought. I have become a doctor because of his trust. And because of that it is my duty to serve, never to question, and if necessary to sacrifice my life for my *padrino*.

This sacred trust bolstered the doctor's confidence. Determined not to fail the don, Turturro concentrated on saving the woman's life.

The baby cried out as his lungs cleared. "The baby will live, Leon!" Rabinowitz exulted.

"And so will the mother, Dr. Rabinowitz," he answered, confidence returning.

An hour later Turturro tied off the final suture. He sat back exhausted.

"Good work, Doctor," praised Rabinowitz. "You've got good hands, my friend, some of the best I've ever seen."

"We were lucky, Dr. Rabinowitz."

"Luck is nothing without skill, Leon," Rabinowitz replied.

Turturro removed his gloves and dropped them in the wastebasket. "Who is she?" he asked, finally.

"You should know better than to ask," Rabinowitz replied.

Turturro sighed. "How is the baby?"

"Fine, Dr. Turturro. You saved them both, no thanks to me."

Turturro placed a hand on Rabinowitz' shoulder. The man was shorter than Turturro. The only outstanding feature the man possessed was a large nose set on a kind face, a face that displayed a worldly wisdom far beyond his forty-seven years of age. "You're a great physician, Dr. Rabinowitz. A great teacher. You have nothing to be ashamed of. You kept the mother alive until I arrived and saved the baby. Most doctors would have failed to do that."

"You are kind, Leon. Thank you."

Turturro looked at Rabinowitz. He was disturbed by the man's presence. This gentle doctor obviously knew Don Busambra, but how well and for how long?

"I am confused, Dr. Rabinowitz," he began, searching for the words.

Rabinowitz looked at him. "Why, Leon?"

"I know why I'm here, Doctor. I'm Italian," he explained. "I grew up in the same neighborhood as Don Busambra and I owe my education to his generosity. But you and Dr. Danielson? How do you come to be here in this office, in this city with the don? Don't you know who he *really* is?" he asked, voice falling to a whisper as though he might be overheard.

Rabinowitz hesitated to answer. He did not want to endanger the young doctor. But after saving the mother and her child, he felt he owed Turturro something. Besides, the look on Turturro's face showed that he was genuinely concerned for his safety.

He smiled, trying to put Turturro at ease. "Do not worry, Leon. Many years ago my father performed a great service for the Busambra family. I am quite safe."

Leon hesitated to ask but his inquiring gaze prompted Rabinowitz to speak.

"My father delivered a baby. Another breech birth. And he saved them both as you have done."

That explains your connection to Don Busambra, Turturro thought. But why is Dr. Danielson here? They both turned to look at the mother and her child.

"It is funny how history repeats itself," Rabinowitz said to himself. "Forty-two years," he muttered. "Forty-two years."

Coming out of his reverie he turned to Turturro. "Time for you to get cleaned up, Doctor. There are fresh scrubs in the office. I will tend to our patients."

Turturro grabbed the scrubs and left for the shower. Questions that would remain forever unanswered buzzed in his head. When he returned he noticed the woman was awake and holding her son. Dr. Rabinowitz had cleaned them both up and was smiling at the small miracle she held in her arms.

"Thank you, Doctor," she spoke in a whisper. "Thank you both."

"You and the baby are lucky to be alive," Rabinowitz stated. "God was with us today."

The woman beamed as she held the baby. Rabinowitz let her have this moment. There wouldn't be many more.

"It is time, Madam," Rabinowitz spoke softly. "I must take him to Don Busambra."

The mother gave her son a last hug and with tears in her eyes handed him up to the doctor.

"It is best, Doctor? I am doing the right thing, am I not?" she asked, fighting back her tears.

"It is best for the child," he lied.

"A boy, Benjamin," Rabinowitz announced, addressing Don Busambra.

"God is great, Jacob. Bring the baby to me."

Rabinowitz placed the infant in his arms and backed away respectfully. "The baby?" Don Busambra asked.

"Healthy. It has a strong heart."

"As it should. And the mother?"

"She suffered complications. Severe hemorrhaging," Rabinowitz explained. "But Dr. Turturro saved her life."

"Leon?" Busambra said, turning to Turturro.

"She should recover fully, Don Busambra."

"I owe you a great debt," he offered sincerely.

"Bullshit! I still think we should get rid of her," Danielson spoke from across the room. He paced back and forth smoking a cigar. "It could be bad for us."

"You mean bad for you, don't you, Victor?" Don Busambra commented.

"That bitch tried to blackmail me, Bennedetto," Danielson snapped. "She could still take us both down."

"Nonsense. She was only protecting the baby, Victor," Rabinowitz spoke. "I'm glad you finally listened to reason. I would have never forgiven you had you acted rashly."

"He didn't listen to reason, Jacob," Don Busambra said. "He listened to me. Killing without exhausting every other resource first is bad for business. My father didn't tolerate it and neither will I."

"Though you hate her now, Victor, you once loved this woman. In time you will love the boy. And when you come to your senses, you'll thank me. I have killed enough to know that you can regret it."

Rabinowitz walked over and looked at the baby. "He has your eyes, Victor," he observed. "Come and look."

"Yes, Victor," Don Busambra agreed. "Don't you want to look at your son?"

Danielson hesitated before striding across the room. He looked suspiciously at the baby boy. The infant gurgled and Victor Danielson choked on his cigar smoke.

"Ach, Victor. Get that nasty thing away from the baby," Rabinowitz chastised his friend. Danielson walked to the couch in disgust and sat.

"Well, Jacob. We have our bastard," Don Busambra remarked, looking at the child.

"Yes, Benjamin. But what do you plan on doing with him?"

"I will see that he is educated well and protected." Victor scoffed, but the don chose to ignore him. "And when he is old enough he will serve us, Jacob. He will serve his godfathers. It is the way things are done."

Jacob shook his head sadly and walked away. Don Busambra continued to stare at the child, mesmerized. He began to play with the baby, making cooing sounds and sticking his finger in the infant's tiny hand.

Turturro watched, enjoying the sight of Don Busambra as he played with the baby. The godfather was not a demon, not as cruel as his enemies would have the world believe. But he was powerful.

Even now, standing at a distance, Turturro could feel the man's power. It transformed him into a force to be feared and admired. Don Busambra's father, the first *"tuti capo di capi,"* had taught his son to wield his birthright in a fair and unassuming manner. The don had learned his lessons well and at thirty-five commanded the respect of the older, more established, bosses.

"If you are through with me, I will take the baby to the mother one last time," Rabinowitz spoke quietly.

"Not just yet, Doctor. Tend to the mother, but let me have another moment with the child."

"As you wish, Benjamin," Rabinowitz said. He left the room, taking Turturro with him.

"So it is just you and me, my small friend. Few will know how you came to be," Busambra confessed to the infant. "You will never know who your real mother is, nor will you know your heritage through her. In this way, I will assure your safety as well as hers. Please forgive me."

Il capo di tuti capi gently held the baby at arm's length, smiling mischievously. "I have chosen you for great things. Our families fought across the expanse of time and thousands of miles to create a new life for us in this country. A slender thread indeed has held us together through many violent and dangerous times. Our survival, your survival, is proof that God has chosen to watch over us. I wonder if you have any idea how lucky you are?" he asked. *"Bastardo mio.* My godson."

The baby coughed, spit up, and began to cry. Maybe the child knew more about his destiny than the godfather.

Later that night, the boy was separated from his mother forever and bundled off into the dark and an uncertain fate.

PROLOGUE

Ice

SS New Zealand, *North Atlantic Ocean, November 13, 1917*

Lightning ripped through the night sky, exposing the convoy of ships struggling through fifty-foot swells. Gale force winds hammered the fleet as it groped its way toward New York and safety. The admiral commanding the convoy worked frantically to keep the mixed convoy of US, UK, Greek, and Italian ships together, safe from the German U-boat fleet. His efforts were wasted as the tight formation was slowly pulled apart by the storm. The admiral prayed that the storm would end suddenly, as it had begun, leaving him time to coordinate his forces before the Germans struck.

Captain Richmond Masden watched the violent rain lash the bridge of the SS *New Zealand*. Even with all the precautions, the journey had not been without tragedy. Masden had lost one crewman, washed overboard as he tried to secure a lifeboat. Unfortunately, convoy discipline forced the captain to leave the man behind. To stop and search would have left the *New Zealand*, a cargo-passenger ship, vulnerable to torpedo attack from U-boats known to be lurking in the area.

Masden gripped the rail and caught his balance as the ship rolled into a deep trough. The storm was a tiny force compared to the maelstrom they had left behind. American forces were just now trickling into the trenches, too late to stop the Germans' fall offensive. In Russia, the Bolsheviks had just overthrown Kerensky and were threatening to pull out of the war. The British Imperial General Staff suffered nightmares at the prospect of facing eighty new German divisions pulled from a peaceful Eastern Front. The future seemed grim. But for all the bad news Masden found himself cracking a brief smile.

The captain loved being at sea in any circumstances. The storm made the chances of a U-boat attack remote. If he survived the trip Masden was looking forward to a long overdue shore leave in New York City and the possibility of making the acquaintance of one or two attractive American lasses. And besides, the bloody Yanks might make a difference in the war after all.

See, not everything's to rot, mate, Masden thought. Mother always said "Hope springs eternal."

The captain's smile widened as the *New Zealand* plowed on through the rough seas.

Ecstasy! Oh, what wonderful pleasure, his mind sang as he whipped the belt across the naked child's buttocks. I am the Lord of Tankenshire and you are mine to do with as I please.

Sweat popped out on his forehead and his engorged penis pressed against the fasteners of his trousers. He wanted the release—*NOW!* But, experience, delicious experience, told him his pleasure would be increased if he waited. So he raised the belt again, exulting in the muffled screams of the gagged and bound boys.

The smaller of the two boys was nearly insane from fear. The pain, although terrible, paled next to the terror. It was worse than the rats and the fire he'd left behind. So he prayed. He prayed for his aunt to forgive him for sneaking off to play on deck. He prayed for his uncle to come and save him and take him back to Russia. He prayed for his uncle's Sicilian friends to come for him, especially the big one with the broken nose who played with him. He could hurt this bad man. Streva could hurt him until the bad man died. He continued to pray but the fear grew worse.

The larger boy, receiving the more vicious blows, was also afraid. He also cried. But something unknown was turning his fear to rage. Rage at his father for letting him fall into the clutches of this crazy man. Rage at being forced from his village and almost killed. And, most damaging of all, rage at God for making his people different.

He'd seen all his friends die for being different. His family had barely escaped the slaughter. And in his terror he came to see he was being tortured for that difference. His rage focused on his God, and on himself, for being what his persecutors called him—a filthy Jew.

While his cousin prayed to God for salvation he prayed to anything but God for the chance to change and be anybody but who he was.

As the English lord raised his belt to administer another lash two men crashed through his stateroom door. The man in front, a burly peasant, held a wicked-looking knife in one hand. His companion, tall and gaunt, wore a battered military greatcoat, shabby boots and a Russian army officer's cap. Before the Englishman could react, the peasant moved. In all his life the lord swore he'd never seen anyone move faster.

Alistare, the lord's batman and bodyguard, stepped in front of the charging bull. The peasant ducked the first punch, rolling under the extended arm, and hammered the bodyguard in the kidney. As Alistare's head dropped, the peasant snapped his hand up and caught the man under his chin, dropping him to the floor with a loud thud.

Meanwhile, the lord of Tankenshire released the belt and swiftly retrieved a derringer from his waist. By the time he raised the small pistol the peasant had vanished. Surprised, he turned to his left in time to see the peasant spinning close to the ground, left foot shooting up, kicking the derringer toward the door where the startled Russian grabbed it out of mid-air. Still spinning, the peasant brought his knife down on the Englishman's skull, splitting skin from scalp to forehead. The Lord, stunned by the blow, reeled into the bulkhead.

16

The Russian watched the lord collapse and slowly turned his gaze to the bed. He took a step forward and stopped, not believing the horror spread before his eyes.

The peasant snarled and looked at him. He shouted orders at a huge man lurking just outside the stateroom in the gangway. "Streva, get the boys out of here." The giant moved to the bed and untied the whimpering boys. They were lost in his massive arms as he carried them to safety.

"Finish it, Emil," the peasant ordered the Russian. "Hurry up, goddamnit!"

Emil didn't comprehend. He just stared at the now-empty bed, too numb to act.

"I've seen men torn to pieces, gutted, frozen stiff in the snow...I've fought disease, infection, I...I've killed...blood spurting in my face. But this...this...this is insane!"

The peasant watched Emil quivering and shook his head in disgust. Out of respect, he gave the former soldier a minute. After all, the man had saved the life of his sister and her child. But, if his friend didn't recover soon he would finish it himself.

The peasant grabbed Alistare off the floor and pitched him against the dresser. He pressed his bloody knife against the man's throat. The ship pitched violently in the winter storm and the knife bit into Alistare's flesh as the peasant struggled for balance. Blood dribbled down Alistare's neck, staining his starched white shirt collar.

"Mind the blade, Laddie," the bodyguard rasped in English heavy with a tough East End London accent.

The peasant, ignorant of the English language, kneed the man in the groin. "Shut up!" he growled as the man slumped to the floor, groaning. Turning to Emil, he barked, "Finish him and let's get the hell out of here."

Emil stared a moment longer and then his eyes narrowed. The boys, he thought. He hurt my boys. He strode across the room and knelt beside the lord, trying to contain his rage.

If he killed this English noble his dream for a new life in America would be over. The English were allies and the Russians traitors. No one would believe the story about the boys. No one would give a damn. But his lordship might not know that.

"My friend, Antoni, is displeased, to say the least," Emil began evenly, his English tainted by a thick accent. "I can't tell him what to do because I don't speak Sicilian, so it's probably best not to do anything stupid," he explained, holding up the small derringer. "I'll keep this in case you get stupid again." He dropped the pistol in his pocket.

"You're dead, you son of a bitch," his lordship answered in the highbrowed tone of England's upper crust. "I'll have the captain arrest you for attempted murder and, when we get to America, you and your friend will spend the rest of your lives in jail."

"Not unless you bleed to death first," Emil responded. "You'll be all right if you get some stitches. Wouldn't like to see the scar though. It'll look very nasty."

"Not as bad as when I get finished with you, you bastard." The soldier's calm evaporated.

"You will do nothing. You will not harass us, and you will not call the captain. Not if you appreciate your standing in society. I don't think your peers would respond too well to your appetite for buggery."

His lordship's eyes blazed, but he kept quiet.

"Remember this, if you try to harm me, my family, or that man," he said, jerking his thumb toward Antoni, "or his family, I will kill you with my hands. Slowly. You understand me?"

The man's lips curled in defiance. "Bugger off!"

Emil whipped a knife out of his belt and brought it a millimeter from his lordship's naked eyeball.

"I asked you if you understood, you bastard!"

After a moment his lordship relented. "Yessss," he hissed.

"That's better," Emil said, releasing the Englishman. "Your kind are going to have to learn some manners. The Bolsheviks just threw Kerensky out and they're going to pull Russia out of the war. Your king could be next. Times are changing, I'd be aware of that."

He backed away and motioned to the peasant. "Let's go."

Antoni looked confused. He was amazed the soldier hadn't killed the English bastard after what he'd done to the children. In his country…but, he wasn't in his country. Sicily was a long way off. He kicked the bodyguard in the face and backed toward the door.

The defiant look on his lordship's face had been replaced with a blank expression. Antoni paused and looked into the Englishman's eyes: empty tunnels leading to a deep, black abyss. Dead eyes. His mother had told him about Satan's spawn on earth. They had dead eyes and would steal your soul and destroy the world. He'd never believed her—'til now.

"A fucking peasant and a Russian deserter. A bloody Jew from the looks of him," the lord said softly. The peasant didn't understand the Englishman, but he was mesmerized by the tone of voice and the empty eyes. "The army took my command, the King took my lands, then Scotland Yard took my freedom and now you people take my pleasure." He dragged his right arm across his face and curled his crimson hand into a fist.

"It bloody well ends here, you ignorant, peasant bastard," he continued as he curled and uncurled his red fingers. "I can't hurt the King or the army. At least not yet. But you will pay. You and the Russian Jew. For all their sins. For all those who have transgressed against me. You will pay for it all. I won't kill you." The hand clenched and unclenched, the eyes as cold as ice. "Too painless." Clench and unclench. "But I'll make you suffer. You will watch your children suffer, and their children. Unending suffering. And the pain will go on and on," he chanted as his fist formed and relaxed, clenched and unclenched. "On and on. On and on."

Emil shivered. He spat on the floor, made a sign to ward off evil and hurried out the door.

The peasant found Emil down the gangway huddled in a stairwell. The soldier was hugging the two small boys, who were crying quietly. Streva stood watch over them.

"Good job, Streva," the peasant addressed the giant. Antoni bent over the soldier and placed a hand on his back. The soldier looked at him, his face wet with tears.

"We must go back and kill him, friend," he spoke softly, earnestly. "His kind is very dangerous if left alive. He has a black soul. Please, we must go back while there is still time," he pleaded.

Emil shook his head sadly, unable to comprehend.

Wind

Bilwaskarma, Nicaragua, January 20, 1989

They had come at night, black figures emerging from the trees like demons from the jungle. The sleeping villagers had been caught completely by surprise. Herded into the middle of the village they had watched helplessly as the marauders ransacked the village searching for food and valuables. The *campesinos* stood by quietly until the mercenaries began to separate the women and children from the men. Several fistfights erupted as husbands and fathers fought to hold onto their families. Then...gunshots, screams, silence.

And two men lay dead, their blood seeping into the ground.

José Urcuyo ran through the jungle, tearing his way through the undergrowth as he raced ahead, desperate to get to his village. Fishing in the early hours of the morning he'd heard the shots echoing up the banks of the silent river.

They've come again, he thought, as he stumbled and fell. Picking himself up he hurtled forward to get to his home.

And to his father.

Vines tore at his clothes and his flesh but he paid no heed.

Father, he asked himself. Who has come, father? Sandinistas or Contras? And why have they come at night? That was the question that terrified him the most. Sandinistas, Contras, they were both the same to young José. They came during the day so as not to alarm the villagers. They smiled, made their speeches and then selected several of the younger, healthier men to conscript into their respective armies.

But they never shoot their guns, José thought. Because they don't want to frighten the *campesinos* and make them enemies.

And they never, ever, come at night.

José tripped over a root and slammed face first into the ground. Dazed, he rolled onto his back and grabbed his rapidly swelling ankle. Struggling to sit up he heard a sound which sent goose bumps rippling across his flesh.

Shrieks. Women screaming in terror and despair.

They never touch the women, he thought. Why? What is happening?

Terror on terror. José stood up and began to run and fell back to the earth. His ankle hurt too badly to support his weight so he began to crawl through the dirt and thick jungle mist toward the sounds.

I must get to father, he thought. If they do that to the women then what will become of the men? Stark terror stopped him from completing the thought.

As he reached the edge of the jungle the sounds ceased. José peered through the mist into the village. Black figures, demons with painted faces, barely visible in the ghostly light of a few kerosene lamps, herded sobbing women and children out of the village and into the jungle. More women stumbled out of the one-room schoolhouse clutching torn clothing to battered bodies and joined the others streaming out of the village.

In the center of Bilwaskarma, surrounded by the demons in black, stood the men of the village. A shouted curse and the men were silently herded north at gunpoint toward the Coco River and Honduras.

José, frightened at the prospect of being left all alone, searched the subdued, shuffling mass for his father. For a moment his spirits soared as he thought he might have escaped and just as quickly they crashed as his eyes saw the truth.

There, in the rear of the column, a man limped. It was a distinctive limp, evidence of a farming accident that happened years before José was born. Only one man in Bilwaskarma walked like that, his father, Pedro Urcuyo.

José, all his attention focused on his father and his despair, at first dismissed the sound traveling on the wind from the jungle but slowly his head turned into the breeze and the sound of the terrible keening. Women and children, crying, praying, pleading for their lives.

"*Qué es?*" he asked aloud, as the eerie sound reached a crescendo.

Gunfire. Screams cut short in the night. And a terrified thirteen year old began crying quietly as a wide-awake nightmare engulfed him.

Tears blurring his vision, José watched paralyzed as black figures emerged from the mist and raced through Bilwaskarma toward the river only to be swallowed by the darkness on the far side of the village. The demons appearing to float in the air before they disappeared, leaving him utterly alone in the night.

Fire

Caribbean Sea, August 24, 1994, 4:43 A.M.

The Libyan freighter *Saracen Star*, lolled off the eastern coast of Panama. Her captain, Mohmed En'ghazi, stared off the starboard bridge toward the evening lights of Colón. The captain sweated profusely in the heavy, humid air of the summer tropics.

En'ghazi cursed the complete lack of breeze, the overbearing Libyan Secret Service policeman who had ordered him on this cruise and, finally, his bigoted South African passenger. The Afrikaner, who introduced himself as Kruger, had joined them shortly after passing through the Strait of Gibraltar. He and his men, a lethal-looking platoon of mercenaries, had arrived by seaplane.

The mercenaries never ventured out of their quarters, even for exercise. En'ghazi wondered what kind of men could lock themselves away for weeks in a cargo hold. No sun, moon, or wind, just four walls. En'ghazi shuddered and prayed for merciful Allah to deliver him from such fanatics.

The bridge door opened, spilling out a momentary glow of red, and just as quickly closed, leaving the captain and his new companion in the dark. En'ghazi cursed again as he realized it was Kruger.

Kruger was the only one of the infidel foreigners who ever left their self-imposed prison. He subjected the captain to short, curt questions as to their position and progress. The mercenary had even requisitioned his personal launch for tonight's mission without bothering to inform him. Although he was master of his vessel, En'ghazi felt like a hireling in Kruger's presence.

Why Qadhafi and the Revolutionary Council would do business with fascist infidels was beyond his knowledge. He had never been asked to perform this kind of mission, but as a servant of the revolution he accepted whatever orders he was given. En'ghazi also accepted the largest fee of his life.

Kruger lit a cigarette. In the glow of the lighter, En'ghazi observed the granite face, colorless eyes, and the scar extending from the right corner of his mouth to just under his ear. Abruptly the flame went out and the Afrikaner spoke.

"Have we heard from the boat, yet, Captain?" Kruger asked, staring at the luminous face of his watch.

"Yes. We should be hearing the motor any minute now," En'ghazi answered.

"Good. Have the ship prepare to get underway," he ordered.

"I have already done so. As soon as the launch is brought aboard, we will sail. May I ask our heading so that I may give instructions?"

Kruger didn't answer. Instead, he cocked his head to one side and said, "There it is. Do you hear it?"

"Yes, over there," he said, pointing toward the southeast. A light flashed on and off from the bow of the approaching launch. One of En'ghazi's deck hands answered the signal.

After the launch was brought alongside the freighter, more mercenaries climbed aboard. A moment later, one of Kruger's men came out onto the deck. In the glow from the bridge, En'ghazi saw that the man had a stubby machine pistol. He did not acknowledge the captain in any way. Kruger asked a few questions in Afrikaans and, after hearing the replies, spoke to En'ghazi in English.

"What time do you have, Captain?" he asked, looking at his watch again.

En'ghazi looked at his watch and answered, "0500 hours."

"Anytime now," Kruger muttered.

Anytime now for what, En'ghazi asked himself.

A hellish white light, brighter than a hundred suns, followed seconds later by a deafening thunderclap was his answer. En'ghazi watched dumbfounded, as the white light flickered to orange and climbed skyward. The crew poured onto the deck to gaze at the night sky turned day. The sailor on aft-watch was on his knees screaming in pain as he rubbed his eyes.

En'ghazi heard the sound of an onrushing freight train and ducked as a hammer blast of hot, compressed air tore over the ship. Sailors were knocked off of their feet. Anything not tied down was blown off the deck. And just as quickly as the hurricane had come, it disappeared, leaving injured crewmen stumbling about in a daze. The mercenaries, braced for the blast, calmly gazed at the panic-stricken crew.

Sailors fell to their knees shouting prayers to Allah. Hatches slammed as others hurried below in fear. The huge mushroom cloud rumbled as drops of rain fell on En'ghazi's skin. He looked at Kruger bewildered.

Kruger smiled devilishly. "The sea water closest to the blast evaporated in the intense heat, traveling upwards in a huge cloud of steam where, hitting colder air, it condensed back into liquid and— *voilà*," he said, extending his hand into the unnatural rain.

"Merciful, Allah," En'ghazi muttered. "What in the hell have you done?" he screamed at Kruger, "Are you mad?"

"Not mad, you bloody *kaffir*," he cursed as the smile left his face. "Just following orders."

Kruger pulled out his pistol and shot En'ghazi in the face. En'ghazi's hands flew up as his body hit the deck.

"All of them, Kurt. Every bloody one of them," Kruger ordered his sergeant.

The bridge door flew open and red light spilled onto the deck. The first mate stepped out and stumbled over En'ghazi's body. Looking down, he saw his captain lying in a pool of blood. As he shouted and turned back to the bridge, Kurt shot him in the back and moved on to the bridge spraying gunfire into the unarmed bridge crew. Finishing off the last man, he went to the communications center to find one of his men emptying his pistol into the radio operator.

Kruger stared at the mushroom cloud as he listened to the sounds of the massacre. It didn't take long to kill unarmed men. Moments later, Kurt returned to the bridge deck with a slight smile on his face.

"Like shooting *kaffirs* in a corral, Major," his man reported.

"Have the charges been set, Sergeant?" he asked.

"Yes sir, Major. Should I call for pick up?"

"Yes, Kurt. And muster the men. Let's get the hell out of here."

"And, Kurt," Kruger added, "bring along five or six bodies of the crew."

"Yes, sir," the sergeant answered, smiling at his commander's ingenuity.

A few minutes later, the men assembled, stripped down and hurriedly put on diving gear. They dumped the gathered bodies into the ocean and then stepped off the ship into the water.

They swam away from the ship, dragging the bodies with them. Two hundred meters from the freighter a buoy broke the surface with a pop. A small strobe light attached to the buoy flashed eerily in the inky blackness. The diving party swam to the buoy.

"All right, men, turn the bodies loose. They'll surface in a few days and give the Americans something to chew on," Kruger ordered in a quiet voice.

The mercenaries released the bodies and disappeared below the surface until only Kruger was left. He peered to the south toward the thinning mushroom cloud and the slight orange glow that remained of the fires. He smiled as he gazed upon his dark work.

Kruger pulled an electronic detonator from a small pouch in his wet suit and, aiming it toward the *Saracen Star*, depressed the trigger. A series of dull thuds sounded as the explosive charges his men had set detonated and ripped the bottom out of the ship. The Libyan freighter slid silently underwater.

After a last look at the inferno Kruger wrapped the cord from the buoy around his arm and punctured the float with his combat knife. He cut the buoy free from the cord and watched the flashing light diminish as the buoy sank below the surface. When he could no longer see the flash of the strobe, he deflated his vest and grabbing the cable began his descent. Without a ripple, the mercenary disappeared below the surface following the cable to the submarine waiting below.

PART I
Prodigal Son

1

Dallas, Texas, April 9, 1988

"Hey, Scarface. When do we go, *Mon?*" asked the Jamaican, motioning to the two men standing behind him.

Scarface didn't answer immediately. He stared instead at the water rushing into the storm drain across the street. The clear evening had been interrupted by a sudden, violent thunderstorm. It disappeared as quickly as it started, leaving in its wake slick streets and a heavy, humid smell. He had heard about the weather in Texas, as unpredictable as the Jamaican, he thought.

Scarface turned and looked at the chief enforcer of the New Rebels Posse, a powerful, Houston-based cocaine ring. The Rastafarian wasn't nervous or anxious. Just bored.

"In a little while, Juju. We have to wait for the last of the customers to leave."

"*Mon*, I don't give a fuck 'bout no customers. If they git in the way, what do I care?"

"It goes off like we planned," Scarface hissed. He almost added "you bloody *kaffir*" but thought better of it.

The New Rebels were crazy. They enjoyed the killing that came in their line of work. And Kruger knew that anyone who enjoyed killing had to be handled carefully. He preferred working with more trustworthy people, but the scenario his employer had mapped out specifically called for lowlife like Juju and his companions.

"If the op' doesn't come off as planned, you won't get the rest of your money. You understand that, *Mon?*" Kruger added sarcastically.

"Yeah, *Mon.* I understand. But don't be going and making fun of the way I talk, Scarface. 'Specially with that scary accent you got. You dig, *Mon?*"

Kruger ignored the remark. His concentration was focused on the cafe across the street. A woman was letting out the last of the help. As she told them goodbye a couple of cars drove by. Other than that the street was deserted. The employees splashed through puddles to their cars and drove off leaving Kruger and Juju alone.

After locking the door, the woman stared through its glass straight at Kruger. Buried in the shadows of an alley between two buildings he was invisible but it gave him an unsettling feeling nonetheless.

"Hey, Scarface. She stared right at you, *Mon.* Spoooooooky," Juju said, laughing.

"Shut up, Juju," Kruger said, checking his watch. 2:43 A.M. "OK. You know what to do. And Juju, don't fuck it up. You dig, *Mon?*"

"No problem, Scarface. We goin' to have fun now. You watch what we do to the little lady. Maybe you learn something." Juju's companions laughed as they started toward the restaurant.

Kruger watched them disappear behind the building and pulled a phone from his jacket. The number he dialed was answered on the first ring.

"Ready?" Kruger asked.

"Yeah. I'll start rolling as soon as they get set," the man drawled.

"Don't miss anything. We only get one shot."

"Hey, Kruger, relax. I'm a professional, unlike those Jamaican clowns you hired. If they don't fuck up, we'll be fine."

Kruger hung up without answering. He watched the couple in the bar as they went about closing up. The woman came to the front and closed the shutters, blocking his view.

Pity such a beautiful thing has to die, he thought. He lit a cigarette and walked down the street.

Xavier Daniels sat at the bar doing the books. His wife, finished with the shutters, walked up behind him and gave him a hug. He looked at her reflection in the mirror behind the bar and saw her beautiful, smiling face. Smiling back, he thought about how lucky he was.

"Hey, Honey. It's been so busy tonight I haven't had a chance to give you any attention."

"You were too busy flirting with our female clientele to even notice me. I'm getting used to it, though. It's what happens when you marry the best-looking man in Dallas."

"Thanks, Min. You're great for my ego." Xavier didn't think about his looks one way or the other. His wife found him attractive, and that was all that mattered. That and his health.

Xavier ran every afternoon and worked out at a martial arts *dojo* each morning. His skin was bronzed from the sun that lightened his dark brown hair. He would never be in *GQ*, but his nonchalant attitude and his healthy physique made him attractive.

Min rubbed his three-day growth of beard with a soft hand and said, "If you shave this off tonight, I'll give you something that will make you extremely happy."

"What? Some money?" he asked.

"Smart ass. You won't get anything unless you finish those books."

" It seems to me that you should be doing the books considering you minored in math at that hoity-toity college you graduated from."

"Vassar is not hoity-toity. It's one of the best universities in the country. Unlike that primitive state-sponsored institution you attended," she said, jabbing him in the ribs.

"You make it sound like a correctional facility. Texas A & M is the best university in the world. Our football team could kill yours on any given day," he said proudly.

"Vassar doesn't have a football team," Min replied.

"That's what I mean. Who would want to go to a school that doesn't have a football team? Now that's primitive."

"Don't start with me, Mr. Marine," she said, as she jabbed him again. "Just get the books done so we can go home before sunup."

Xavier watched her walk away. "Hey, Min. I love you."

She turned and looked at him, a smile on her lips. "I know you do. You can't help it. Don't forget to blow out the candles behind the bar. We wouldn't want our business to burn down. I'm going to make a grocery list for Amy. Maybe she'll even read this one," she sighed, walking through the kitchen doors.

She's right about one thing, Xavier thought. I can't help loving her.

Xavier looked at a picture of them stuck to the mirror behind the bar. It was from their honeymoon in Cozumel. She was in his lap at Carlos 'n Charlie's, laughing. It was the time of their lives. They dove Palancar Reef all day and made love all night. Another picture next to it showed them at the wedding with his best man, Uncle Jake. Since Xavier's father passed away, Uncle Jake was the only family he had. His mother had used his court martial as an excuse to end an already strained relationship and keep what remained of his father's fortune.

The newlyweds were broke, but Jake had come through with the Cozumel trip. He had also loaned them the money to start their business. Jake's contributions were an expression of the love he had for his godson.

Xavier looked at the picture of him in his Marine Corps dress blues. Min had it prominently displayed over the register. He hated her insistence on hanging the photograph. Xavier was still bitter about his forced discharge from the Marine Corps. It had been a hard pill to swallow after six years of loyal service and outstanding evaluations. But Min was still proud of his military service and his combat record; proud enough to show the whole world.

As he watched the candles wink in the mirror, he remembered how they met. A month after his court martial he was drunk in a bar not far from the restaurant they now owned. Always a heavy drinker in the Corps, as were many Cobra helicopter pilots, he'd gone over the deep end after his career was destroyed. He was well in his cups when she walked up to him and said, "You're cute. I've been watching you. You're also quiet. I like that. Will you buy me a drink?"

He'd looked up at an Asian beauty with thick, coal black hair reaching to her buttocks and sparkling almond eyes. Her lips were thicker than most Asian women and her straight teeth shone pearly white. Her skin was smooth and glowing. She wore no makeup and seemed so clean. He was astonished she wanted anything to do with him. For once, he didn't turn on the chopper jock charm and was painfully honest. It was the smartest thing he could have done.

"Lady, you're obviously real nice. And I'm obviously real drunk. So before I say or do something stupid that offends you and makes me look like a fool, I'd suggest taking a rain check."

"Quiet and honest. Now I really like that. Not quite the image of a pilot." He looked at her with surprise. "The haircut and the flight jacket, silly. When you call this number, you'll find, among other things, that I'm very observant." She stuffed a cocktail napkin in his jacket pocket and walked out the door.

Xavier was stunned. It took him four days to work up the nerve to call. He was glad he did.

Min was caring and honest and wonderful. He opened himself to her completely. It was a new experience for him. She didn't judge him. She believed his story about the trumped-up charges that forced him out of the Marine Corps. Min helped him to begin a new life.

Until meeting Min, Xavier's shame had prevented him from telling Jake about the court martial. Her love gave him the strength to call his uncle and ask for help. Between Uncle Jake's wisdom and Min's love, his spirit began to heal.

Most important she didn't nag at him about his drinking. He gave it up on his own. Shortly after that, they were married.

And here we are, he thought. A year ago I was a failure at the only thing I'd ever wanted to do in my life and was drinking myself into an early grave. Now I'm married to the most beautiful woman in the world and I'm the owner of a successful business. What more could a guy ask for?

Xavier looked at the ceiling and said a small prayer of thanks. God, you do work in mysterious ways. But for whatever reasons, I got the luck of the draw, thanks.

He heard Min come out of the kitchen and turned to tell her he loved her again, but was shocked to see a black man in dreadlocks walking toward him. The man held an automatic pistol in his right hand. It was pointed straight at Xavier's head.

"Well, *Mon*. What we got here?"

Xavier dropped his pen as one word formed in his mind. Min!

Thibodeaux Dixon was a happy man. Surveillance was his passion, and he'd perfected it to a fine art. He was pleased he'd found a legitimate job in which to practice his craft. He was even more pleased when he got a chance to moonlight as the pay was better. Tonight Dixon was ecstatic. Tonight, he was moonlighting and doing his job at the same time.

Dixon leaned back in his chair and lit a half-chewed cigar as he watched the monitors in the van. Dixon didn't notice the acrid smoke that quickly filled the tiny space. He'd been smoking cigars since he was a twelve-year-old boy in Lafayette, Louisiana. The back door to the van snapped opened and Kruger stepped in.

"Put out that damn cigar," Kruger ordered, waving his hand in front of his face.

"It's no worse than your cigarettes," he drawled but stubbed the butt out in an ashtray. He swiveled to face Kruger and scratched his large belly. Kruger wondered how anyone could let himself get so out of shape.

"As you can see, they're in," Dixon said, pointing to the video monitor.

"Then it's time for you to leave," Kruger said.

"Don't you think we ought to give them a minute?"

"Not a good idea. The Jamaicans are not reliable."

"You're telling me," Dixon added, as he leaned up out of his chair. "You sure you know how to work the equipment?" he asked, hesitating to leave his state-of-the-art electronics in the hands of anyone besides himself.

"Trust me, Dixon. Just go do your job," Kruger ordered.

"Duty calls," Dixon said, exiting the van and slamming the door behind him.

Kruger watched the monitor. Dixon had placed his camera well. He watched as the transaction was completed and willed Dixon to hurry up before the Jamaicans got out of hand. Viewing the monitor, he realized Dixon was going to be too late.

"Where's my wife?" Xavier asked, as the Jamaican approached.

"Never mind that, *Mon*," he answered smiling. "She's perfectly safe with me boys. Move over to the table there. It's time we got down to business."

Xavier moved slowly to a table and took a seat. The Jamaican turned a chair around and sat in it backwards. His automatic rested on the back of the chair, pointing at Xavier.

"Now then. Listen up, white boy. Name's Juju and I'm here to do some business."

"Where's Min? Where's my wife, asshole?" Xavier demanded.

"Control yourself, *Mon*. When we done, you'll get her back. But you gotta cooperate one hundred percent. You dig?"

Xavier nodded his head slowly.

"That's better. What I want you to do is to go to your safe and get out the $5,000 in emergency funds you keep there..."

"How'd you know about that?"

"What I know about you, white boy, could fill a book. Now you got to be listening. My patience is wearing thin. And that doesn't do your beautiful woman any good." The smile vanished from the Jamaican's face. "Go to the safe and get the money. Now!"

Xavier got up from the table and began walking to the back office. When he passed the Jamaican, he slowed and looked over his shoulder. Juju was staring at the front door, his back turned to Xavier.

"*Doan* be so predictable, white bread," Juju said looking straight ahead. "I got two of my meanest boys with your pretty lady. And I tell you right now they both got eyes for her. Listen up. They're brothers, *Mon*. They don't mind sharing. You take my meaning?"

Xavier's blood was rushing. He was barely containing his anger.

He hurried to the office and opened the safe. He searched desperately for a weapon. Envelope opener, pens, Min's nail file. Xavier's twenty years of martial arts training bolstered by six years of hand-to-hand combat courses in the Corps enabled him to use most anything with a point or edge.

But can I afford to do anything 'til I know about Min? he asked himself. Hell no. Maybe if my gun was back here, but it's behind the damn bar...

Damn, damn, damn, his thoughts raced. How did they know about the money? Only Min and I know about it.

He retrieved the cash and headed back to the table, glancing to his left as he passed the kitchen. Juju calmly smoked a cigarette. Xavier took his seat and tossed the money on the table.

"There. You've got what you came for. Now give me my wife and get the hell out of my restaurant."

"Not so fast, *Mon*. I'm a good businessman. You always get what you pay for." The Jamaican turned his head toward the kitchen. "Trudi," he shouted, "Bring the good *mon* his stuff."

It was hard for Xavier to keep his seat when Juju turned his head. He knew he could have taken him and broken his neck. The Jamaican was too confident. But he could afford to be confident. Xavier couldn't make his move until he knew his wife was safe.

Juju turned back to him smiling. "You need to learn how to relax, *Mon*. All that stress gonna kill you."

Trudi came through the kitchen doors. He was huge. His dreadlocks hung down to his chest. His eyes were obscured by a dark pair of sunglasses. An Uzi hung from his shoulder.

When Trudi arrived at the table, he took a package from one of the large pockets in his coat and placed it in front of Xavier. Grabbing the money Trudi stuffed it in the same pocket. He then took up a position behind his boss and unslung the Uzi. Trudi pointed the weapon at Xavier's chest.

"Open it up, *Mon*, and see what Santa Claus brung you."

Xavier did as he was told. The package was wrapped in brown paper. He tore the paper off, revealing a shoe box. Lifting the lid he peered inside and saw three cylindrical bundles wrapped in plastic.

"What the hell...?"

"Check all three, *Mon*. I guarantee you it's righteous stuff. The best your money can buy."

"I'm not checking anything, You have my money and I sure as shit don't want your drugs." Xavier was alarmed. This was much more than a simple robbery. He was off balance and losing control.

"Trudi," Juju said, holding out his free hand. Trudi reached in his jacket and pulled out a stiletto. He handed it to his boss. The Jamaican thumbed the switch and the blade shot out. He twirled the lethal-looking knife for a minute and then slammed it into the table. The knife quivered between them.

"You'll check it now or I'll have your pretty lady not looking so pretty, *Mon*."

"Fuck you, Juju," Xavier said, coming out of his seat. Trudi took a step forward and raised the Uzi menacingly.

"Sit," the Jamaican ordered. Xavier eyed Trudi, daring him to pull the trigger, but slowly sat back down.

"Since you insist on being a stubborn fool, you lady gonna suffer, *Mon*. She gonna suffer bad. Cubby, bring her out."

The kitchen doors burst open, and Min and her captor emerged. Cubby had a muscular arm under her neck and half-carried her into the restaurant. He stood well back of the Jamaican, but even from this distance Xavier could see he had a gun to her back. The terrified look on her face magnified Xavier's barely controlled rage.

"All right. Don't hurt her. I'll do as you say."

"Wise choice. But just in case you want to go and be forgettin'. Cubby!"

Cubby lifted her off the floor by her neck and jammed the gun into her back. Her windpipe closed off, Min croaked in pain. He lowered her to the ground and eased his choke hold. Min began to retch.

Xavier fought the urge to attack. It took all his self-control to keep his seat.

"What am I checking?" Xavier asked, pulling the stiletto out of the table and stabbing it into a bag of white powder.

"Coke, *Mon*. Pure as the driven snow. You gonna like this stuff, white boy."

Xavier pulled the knife out. "I wouldn't know good coke from bad coke."

"It don't matter, *Mon*. Just have a taste."

Xavier lifted the knife to his nose and looked at his wife. Even in her predicament there was concern in her eyes.

I'm doing this for us, babe, he thought. Just trust me.

Xavier had all three men in the same room. And his wife was in his sight. He could make his move soon.

Xavier closed one nostril as he had seen it done in the movies. He let out his breath and then sniffed the powder into his nose. The coke blew up his nasal passage and exploded in his head. Xavier could feel his throat go numb and his heart begin to hammer.

"How's the stuff, *Mon*?"

"Fuck you," Xavier replied slowly.

"Coke makin' you uppity, *Mon*. I said you gotta relax. Now check the rest of it."

"I've done all I'm going to do."

"I don't think so. Cubby!" the Jamaican shouted.

Instantly Cubby lifted Min off her feet. He jabbed the gun into her back forcing her stomach away from his body as his arm closed over her throat. Her feet jerked helplessly in the air as she tried to breathe. Xavier quickly stabbed the last two batches and snorted the samples. As soon as he was done, Cubby lowered Min to the floor. She hung limply on his arm as she tried to catch her breath.

The mixture of cocaine and adrenaline was having a strange effect on Xavier. He felt calm, full of rage, and confident at the same time. His fear had left him. Xavier looked at the Jamaican with a smile on his lips.

"What you be smiling for, white boy?" the Jamaican asked.

"I'm thinking about how I'm going to kill you and your friends," Xavier answered.

"That coke gone and made you think you got big balls, *Mon*. Make you think you real tough. Best to know what is and what isn't," he said. "Now put the knife on the table."

Xavier slammed the knife into the middle of the table. Instead of reaching for it, the Jamaican smiled.

"Now comes the fun part. Cubby, Trudi. The bitch is yours."

Xavier came up out of his seat only to find the Jamaican's pistol pressed against his forehead. Min shrieked as Cubby walked to her and ripped open her shirt. Sweat popped out on Xavier's brow.

"Sit down, white bread. If you want to see her alive you'll sit down." Xavier sat. "Now if you go trying to be a hero, *Mon*, Cubby gonna cut her up real good. You either get her back used or you get her back dead. It's up to you."

Xavier sat with clenched fists as Cubby fondled his wife's breasts. "I love you, Min. It's going to be all right. Just remember that I love you," Xavier said, steadily.

"Take her to the back," Juju ordered. "No sense in him seeing what a real *mon* gonna do with his woman."

The brothers dragged her back to the kitchen. She struggled with them as they tried to drag her through the kitchen doors.

"I swear to God that I will find you and kill you when this is over," Xavier promised.

"*Mon*, the only thing you're gonna be finding is thin air," the Jamaican said, laughing. "When my boys get done with your wife, you gonna be too busy putting her back together to be worried about where old Juju is."

"Your boys're already done," came a drawling voice from the kitchen.

Xavier looked over the Jamaican's shoulder to see the brothers backing out of the kitchen dragging his wife. The kitchen doors swung open to reveal a balding, overweight man in an ill-fitting suit. He held a gun in one hand and a badge in the other.

Xavier relaxed and smiled at the Jamaican. "Maybe I won't have to wait to come kill you."

The Jamaican didn't move, didn't even flinch. He just kept on smiling. "Oh, I see. You think the cops have come to rescue you, white bread. If I'm thinking correctly that be a fat man coming through the door, name of Tibby."

"Fuck you, Juju," the cop said. "The little lady's not supposed to have a mark on her."

"What do you care, *Mon*? She's dead anyway." The smile left Xavier's lips and the fear came roaring back.

The cop put his badge in his pocket. With his free hand he grabbed Min away from her captors and walked her to the table.

"The man said it was to go down one way. And one way only. You could have fucked us all out of our bonuses."

"You worry too much, Tibby," Juju said, shrugging his shoulders.

"Working with you I don't worry enough. He done the coke, yet?" Tibby asked, pointing at Xavier.

"Yeah, *Mon*. He flying high as a kite. That shit come from my personal stash."

"Good. Let's get on with it. Trudi, get the man's gun."

Trudi went behind the bar to the cash register. He pulled a glove out of his pocket and opened the drawer under the register. The Jamaican pulled out Xavier's automatic, checked the clip, and yanked on the slide, jacking a bullet in the chamber.

"Get over here, Trudi. Cubby, take the girl," Tibby ordered. Cubby walked behind Min who was looking at the ground as she clutched the tattered remains of her shirt to her chest. Trudi stationed himself a few feet behind Xavier.

Freed of the girl, Dixon moved beside Xavier. He rested his gun hand on the table and the other on the back of Xavier's chair. When he leaned over, Xavier could smell the cigar tobacco. For some reason, he thought of his father.

"Please understand, Mr. Daniels, this is business. Nothing personal."

Xavier looked up into the beady sunken eyes, the fat face, the tobacco-stained teeth.

Nothing personal, he thought.

"I'm here to arrest you. I've got the whole transaction between you, Juju, and Trudi on video tape. Unfortunately, the tape ran out. Which means Juju's escape isn't recorded."

"Unfortunately, *Mon*," Juju chimed in.

"Shut up, Juju," Dixon said, hanging his head. When he looked up, Xavier was staring at his wife.

"The rest of it goes like this. I catch you in the act. You're loaded on coke..."

Xavier tried to convey a look of love with his gaze.

"...you're also in possession of a major amount of illegal narcotics. Enough to get you ten years without parole..."

She stared back at him and seemed to calm somewhat.

"...but when you find out your wife was the one who turned you in..."

Their eyes locked.

"...you shoot her down in cold blood with your gun that you had hidden on your person."

"Min!" he cried.

Cubby let go of Min and stepped away. Trudi raised Xavier's gun and fired twice. The first round hit her in the chest. The second round hit her in the throat. Her limp body was punched through the air and onto a table that crashed with her to the ground.

Xavier moved. He yanked the stiletto out of the table and jammed it into Dixon's wrist up to the hilt, nailing it to the table. Dixon screamed and slumped to the floor pulling on the knife. Xavier grabbed the cop's gun and rolled to the floor in one motion.

Juju, caught by surprise, reacted too late. He fired, hitting Trudi in the stomach. The bullet smashed through Trudi's spinal cord crumpling him like a piece of wet paper. Juju threw himself out of his chair and onto the floor, firing as Xavier leaped over the top of the bar.

Xavier crashed to the floor behind the bar just as Cubby cut loose with a burst from the Uzi. Exploding bottles showered him with glass and alcohol. Xavier checked Dixon's gun. It was a snub-nosed .44 magnum. Not much on accuracy but hell on flesh. Xavier wished he had his gun, but it was in Trudi's dead hand on the other side of the bar.

"Cubby. You get ready to flush him out," Juju ordered.

Xavier heard a couple of tables crash to the ground as Juju tried to make himself some cover.

Cubby fired another burst from the Uzi as he sidestepped toward the back of the bar. One of the candles ignited the spilled alcohol with a loud whoosh, sending flames spiraling up the wall. In seconds the whole back bar was in flames as more alcohol ignited.

Xavier had to hurry. The way the fire was raging, the restaurant would soon be engulfed in flames. If Min was alive, she would need a hospital quickly. In his heart, he knew she was dead. He'd seen enough wounds in the service to know a lethal one. But still he had to try.

Xavier blocked out the roar of the flames, the chatter from Cubby's Uzi, and the cop's moaning. He looked at the ceiling and saw smoke fanning outward toward the restaurant. When it had no place else to go, it would descend into the room.

He crawled to the wash sink, picked up a stack of glasses and listened for Cubby's footsteps. He thought he heard them above the roar of the flames, but he couldn't be sure. Too bad. No more time. Xavier hurled the glasses in Cubby's general direction. When he heard Juju's pistol fire, he went over the top of the bar.

Juju, jacked up on the action, saw the glasses come over the top of the bar, turned, and fired. He almost hit Cubby, who ducked inside the kitchen, cursing. A blur came over the bar, landing on the floor. Juju stood up to get a better shot and Xavier's .44 roared, catching him square in the chest, slamming him against the wall. Juju tried to lift his pistol but Xavier emptied the magnum into him, splattering him against the paneling.

Cubby, seeing Juju go down from the kitchen, screamed in rage and charged Xavier, spraying the area with his Uzi. Xavier scrabbled on his back toward Trudi, desperately trying to reach his pistol. Bullets shredded chairs and tables, spattering Xavier with splinters of wood. Cubby's Uzi clicked empty. Both men froze and looked at each other.

Cubby reacted first reaching for a new magazine. Xavier frantically rolled to Trudi, yanking the pistol out of his hand just as he heard Cubby slap the fresh clip into the Uzi. Cubby yanked the charging handle as Xavier, rolling onto his back, fired blindly. His first two shots were high, but Xavier pulled down and sent the next five into Cubby's body.

Cubby's momentum kept him moving forward even as he died on his feet. His finger spasmed and tightened on the trigger, emptying the clip into the floor. His body smashed to the ground and skidded into Xavier, splashing him with blood from his pumping wounds. Xavier kicked the body away and rushed to Min, tripping over furniture as he went.

He knelt beside her and felt her pulse. It was nonexistent. Her eyes stared unseeing into space. Xavier's head drooped for a moment. Resigning himself to the awful truth, he raised his head and closed her eyes gently with his fingers.

The heat from the fire was becoming unbearable. Xavier turned to see Dixon struggling with the knife. He felt his body go ice cold in spite of the flames.

Dixon felt the knife twist in his wrist and screamed. A hand grabbed the back of his collar and yanked his head back. What he saw filled him with fear.

Xavier stood over him covered in blood and soot. His eyes sparked rage. His lips parted to reveal gritted teeth, jaws twitching. Xavier's head was wreathed in a halo of fire as the flames engulfed the ceiling over his head. Dixon imagined the devil couldn't look much worse.

"Who sent you, asshole," Xavier demanded.

"I don't know..." he screamed, as Xavier yanked the stiletto back and forth. "I swear I don't know." Xavier gave the knife another violent twist and Dixon vomited.

When he was done retching, Xavier knelt down beside him. "Then tell me what you do know."

Dixon looked at Xavier's face with pleading eyes. "All I know is that someone important wants to ruin your life. A South African named Kruger set up this whole fucking thing."

"A South African?" Xavier asked mystified, as the building started to come apart under the assault from the fire.

"Yeah. Some military type from the way he talks and acts. Ahhh, fuck, my wrist," he cried. Xavier relaxed his hold on the knife. "Kruger fixed everything. The surveillance, the fake coke buy with the New Rebels, everything. I swear that's all I know," he whimpered, as tears streamed down his face.

A beam from the ceiling came crashing into the restaurant, startling Dixon. "You gotta get me out of here," he pleaded. "I'll tell the police everything I know. I'll help you. Just get me the hell out of here, goddamnit," he screamed.

"Tibby, or whatever the fuck your name is. I just want you to understand one thing. It's business, not personal," Xavier said, yanking the stiletto out of his arm.

"Noooo!" Dixon cried.

Xavier rammed the blade into the side of the cop's neck and pulled outward, ripping through the carotid artery and severing his windpipe. Dixon collapsed on the floor, spasms tearing through his body as he died.

Xavier gathered up the corpse of his wife and kicked open the front door of the restaurant. He walked across the street and sat on the curb, cradling his wife's lifeless body in his arms. Xavier rocked her back and forth as the blaze built to a crescendo. He was still rocking her when the first fire engine pulled up a few minutes later.

Kruger had watched the disaster from the surveillance truck. His employer would be enraged when he found out. It couldn't be helped. Kruger would have to call him tonight with the bad news.

Kruger turned off the monitor and ejected the tape. He placed it in his jacket for later disposal. The mercenary then wiped down the entire van, gave it a final inspection, and climbed out, careful to not leave any prints.

Kruger looked at the inferno up the street and saw the man rocking the corpse back and forth, back and forth. Daniels was good. He'd give him that. Crazy but good.

Bloody fucking marines, Kruger thought. It must be something they do to them in training.

Kruger walked down the street away from the carnage. He was passed by two police cars and an ambulance before he disappeared from sight around the corner.

Busambra Brownstone, Manhattan, New York, April 9, 1988

Don Bennedetto Busambra was awakened from a pleasant dream by a gentle shaking of his shoulder. He rolled over slowly, sat up and paused for a moment as he came fully awake.

"All right. You can turn on the light," he said.

The small bedside lamp came on revealing his *consigliere*, Jerry Rizzi.

"I'm sorry to wake you, Don Busambra, but I have some important news," Rizzi said, holding out a glass of water.

"*Sí, Sí,*" Busambra said taking the glass. As he took a sip he waved his hand for Rizzi to continue.

"Your godson, Xavier, has just been arrested for murder. He is being held in the Dallas County jail."

"Zavi? In jail for murder? Preposterous," Busambra shouted, shaking his head. "When?"

"It happened a little over two hours ago..."

"Did Zavi call for help?" Busambra interrupted hopefully.

"No, sir. I'm afraid not. One of our men in the department phoned me as soon as he found out." Rizzi hesitated to continue. Busambra looked dejected.

"How did it happen, Jerry?"

"Details are very sketchy. Our man could only tell us five people are dead. He said it looked like a drug deal gone bad."

"Drugs and Zavi? You and I both know that's impossible. I don't like the way this sounds," Busambra said concerned.

"Neither do I, Don Busambra," Rizzi agreed, sitting on the edge of the bed. "And it gets worse."

"How could it be worse?" Busambra asked warily, not really wanting to know the answer.

"One of the victims was Xavier's wife, Min. And they are saying he killed a policeman."

Busambra was silent. His godson's wife was dead. The boy was in obvious trouble but still refused to call him for help.

Why do you lock me out, Busambra thought. I would do anything for you.

"Jerry. I want you to take the jet to Dallas. Take our best people. I want my godson out of jail as soon as possible," Busambra ordered.

"Sí, Don Busambra," Rizzi agreed, having already anticipated the don's orders. "I will do as you say. But you realize Xavier will refuse your help."

"This time he doesn't have a choice," Busambra stated. "That stupid pride of his will get him killed someday. You and I both know this is not what it seems."

"In our business it never is, Don Busambra."

"Sí. I must get up and call Jacob," Busambra sighed, sliding his legs from under the covers. "Zavi's damn pride will also keep him from calling his uncle."

Rizzi retrieved Busambra's robe from the closet and handed it to the old man. Busambra stood and slid into it with Rizzi's help.

"Who's on duty tonight?"

"Luca Baracca, sir," Rizzi answered. In truth there were seven men guarding the residence. Baracca happened to be the captain of the guard. He would be the only one to deal directly with the don unless specified differently.

"Good. Have him make me a cappuccino."

"After you call Dr. Rabinowitz, you should go back to bed," Rizzi answered.

"Thank you, my friend," Busambra said, laying a hand on Rizzi's shoulder, "but you know I won't sleep until I know what Zavi's up against."

"All right, Don Bennedetto. I will do my best to find out and bring Xavier to you as soon as possible."

Busambra patted him on the back and waved him out of the room. He went to his desk and sat down, staring at the phone. He did not wish to call Jacob. The man was older than he and loved Zavi just as much; the news wouldn't do his heart any good. Busambra reached for the phone and paused, his hand resting on the receiver.

He thought about the dream he was having when Rizzi woke him. It was a wonderful dream. He was with Victor Danielson in Sicily during the war in the hills his father used to rule. So much laughter in those days.

Funny, I should think about you now, my old friend, he thought. *Your son is in trouble. Please protect him until I can.*

Busambra picked up the receiver and dialed Jacob's number.

Greenville Avenue, Dallas Texas, April 9, 1988

Detective Alvin "Red" Macksey got his nickname from his shocking red hair as well as his fiery temper. As he stood across the street from the burned-out cafe, clothes and hair sticking to his skin, thanks to another cloudburst, his temper began to boil. Silently cursing, he huddled in a doorway seeking shelter from the rain.

Damn the rain. Damn the mayor. Damn the police department, and damn my shitty, fucking luck, he thought.

He'd been home asleep when the call from the police department woke him. He was supposed to have the night off, but the mayor's office had requested his presence on the case. Xavier Daniels was involved and Macksey was considered the expert on the family since he had busted the man's father, Victor Danielson. Macksey had never felt comfortable with that case and he was already having similar misgivings about this one even though it was only a few hours old.

The detective fished a cigarette out of his pocket and leaned farther into the doorway to keep it dry as he lit it. The lighter he'd dragged out of his soaked trousers refused to ignite. He looked down at his new tennis shoes covered in ashes turned to mud and let misery engulf him.

"Need a light, Red?" his partner, Detective Larry Garcia, asked.

"Murphy's Law says if your lighter works it blows up in my face," he said, accepting the light.

"Come on, Red. It's not that bad," Garcia consoled.

"The hell it isn't, Larry. I got five corpses, four of which are charred. One of them is an off-duty cop, Tibby Dixon. At least that's what we think. That's his van down there and they recovered his badge, but they're going to have to check his dental records to see what we got," he paused, taking a drag from his cigarette. "Never did like that guy," he added as an afterthought.

"Neither did I," Larry agreed.

"The only corpse that isn't crispy," Macksey continued, "is one Min Daniels, wife of Xavier Daniels, whose godfather happens to be the most powerful mafioso in America, if not the world. And she's got two bullets in her. And then we get an anonymous tip from one of our stellar citizens that a drug bust just went down here involving the New Rebels Posse, concluding with the little gem that Daniels shot everybody."

"Thought it was a foreigner, Red," Garcia interjected. "Guy I talked to at the station said the recording of the caller indicated a male with a heavy accent, definitely European, probably German."

"Great. The guy's probably on a Lufthansa flight back to the fatherland sipping champagne and laughing his ass off," Red lamented. "Where's Daniels?"

47

"At County being processed. He was pretty well done in, from what I understand."

"Well, his day's not done, yet." Macksey dropped his cigarette to the ground and stubbed it out with his foot. "Let's get down to the station and see what Mr. Daniels has to say. He's the only fucking witness to whatever happened here."

"What about the crime scene?" Garcia asked.

"What crime scene. Between the fire and the rain, it's pretty well wiped out. We'll let the arson boys and the forensic techs do their job. Besides I've already ruined my brand new Nikes."

Garcia's beeper went off. "It's the wife checking on me," he explained, after glancing at the number.

"You're a lucky man, Larry. Only woman who's going to be calling me today is that ice queen bitch of a mayor some dumb fucking people elected. And the only thing she's going to want is to see how much farther up my ass she can crawl."

2

Los Angeles, California, April 9, 1988

The senator sighed in his sleep. He was on a barren mountain-top clothed in white robes. Below him countless people knelt in silence. He raised his arm and the people stood waiting to hear the word. He lowered his arm and paused, relishing the moment.

The soft burr of the telephone brought him out of his slumber. He was instantly depressed when he realized he was at home instead of in his dream. Depression quickly led to anger. He snatched the receiver off the cradle and barked into the phone.

"Yes!"

"Sorry to wake you, Senator," a voice apologized.

The senator became cautious as he recognized the voice.

"You know this line is not secure."

His caller ignored the comment. "Your problem did not resolve itself as planned."

"What the fuck do you mean by that?" he growled into the phone so as not to awaken his wife.

"The problem still exists. And with added complications. These complications could have unseemly consequences for you."

The senator gripped the phone so tightly his knuckles shone white. He felt as though he was losing control.

"Yes, Senator. But I have only one option left. Do you understand?"

"Yes. I understand." A promise he'd made to his dying father would go unfulfilled. "Use it." He hung up the phone.

I'm sorry, Father. So sorry.

His wife stirred in her sleep.

"What is it, Honey?" she asked.

"Nothing important, Dear. Just the office." He leaned over and patted her arm. "Now go back to sleep. It's early."

She turned back over and was soon asleep. The senator listened to her rhythmic breathing and tried to relax. The presidential election loomed ahead and with it a vicious rise in the incessant struggle for power. Today was going to be a real bitch and he needed all the rest he could get before flying back to Washington.

Outside the sun rose on a new day.

Caesars Palace Hotel, Atlantic City, New Jersey, April 9, 1988

Anthony Busambra walked through the doors of the casino with his best friend Alfredo "Tiny" Magliocco, heir to the Magliocco crime family. They were followed by two bodyguards, part of the team permanently assigned to Anthony's protection. The bodyguards were handpicked by Don Busambra's *consigliere*, Jerry Rizzi.

In addition to Anthony's protectors, they were shadowed by several of Don Magliocco's soldiers. Anthony Busambra, son of Bennedetto Busambra, was visiting Magliocco territory. The New Jersey don, son of one of Antoni Busambra's Sicilian bandits, took his duty seriously; everything he possessed was a direct result of his loyalty to Don Bennedetto.

Tiny stretched in the early morning air as they waited for the car. "Anthony. You hungry?" he asked.

Anthony ignored the question. "Where's the fucking car, Sal?" he asked one of his bodyguards. He was tired and wanted to go to the hotel.

"I don't know," he answered, glancing at his watch. "Maybe you should go inside until he gets here." The statement had the tone of an order.

"Relax, Sal," Tiny said, slapping Anthony on the back. An evening of gambling and drinking had left him punchy. "Anthony's in Magliocco territory. Anybody'd have to be fucking crazy to try anything here."

"You tell him, Tiny," Anthony smiled, placing an arm around Tiny's shoulders. "Who would dare fuck with you?"

"No shit, brother," Tiny Magliocco answered, hugging him back.

"Mr. Busambra, I think we should go wait inside."

"Relax, Sal. Didn't you hear what Tiny said? His dad owns New Jersey."

"No disrespect meant to Mr. Magliocco, but I think it would be safer to wait in the lobby," Sal suggested strongly.

"Sal."

"Yes, Anthony."

"Fuck off," Anthony snapped. Tiny laughed and they turned to walk to the street. Sal exchanged a look with the other body-guard and they moved to flank their charges. It was the best they could do under the circumstances.

"You remember what you said to me at my twenty-fifth birthday party last year?" Anthony asked his rather drunk friend.

"How the fuck could I remember anything. I was drunker then than I am now."

"You told me I was on the downhill slide to thirty and there was nothing I could do about it. Really pissed me off."

"Ain't life a bitch?" Tiny laughed. His laugh turned into a leer as he leaned on Anthony. Anthony was looking at his friend when the top of Tiny's head disappeared in a spray of pink and gray. The leer lengthened as his jaw sagged open.

Anthony froze, looking at what had once been his friend's face. He was vaguely aware of the sounds of gunfire, but couldn't seem to take his eyes off the gaping mouth until Sal hit him full in the back knocking him into Tiny and taking them both to the ground.

Sal spun around on top of his boss, protecting him as best he could. They were in the open. On the street opposite them, a dry cleaner's van had screeched to a halt, gunfire erupting from the open panel door. Sal's partner screamed and fell to the ground.

"Motherfuckers!" Sal yelled. He raised his pistol and fired into the van.

Anthony heard Sal grunt and then felt him go limp. He was now pinned between two dead men.

With both his bodyguards dead, Anthony pushed Sal's body off of himself and crouched, looking for some of Tiny's men. One of the Magliocco soldiers was shooting at the van, distracting the gunmen. Anthony saw his chance and stood to make his dash to safety inside the casino. Before he could turn, a hammer slammed him in the chest and he flew backwards as limp as a rag doll. He never felt the ground as his body crashed into it.

As quickly as it had begun, the ambush ended. The van sped away, leaving behind seven bodies on the pavement. There was so much blood on the ground the first paramedic to reach the scene slipped in the grisly pool and cracked his tail bone.

When the police arrived, they found what they usually did in mafia murders. No witnesses.

Lew Sterrett County Jail, Dallas, Texas, April 9, 1988

Xavier dreamed of his father. It was a particularly unpleasant dream. Xavier was trapped in a house, hiding in a closet. His father was searching for him. Frightened out of his mind, a little boy hunted by a monster, he held his breath and wrapped his arms tightly around his knees so he wouldn't scream.

Xavier's father was tearing the house apart, getting closer every second. And the horrifying thing was, he knew. His father knew where he was hiding. He could read Xavier's mind.

"So you want to be a Jew, huh, boy?" his father yelled. "No way. I'm not going to let it happen. It's no good for you. Just like it was no good for me."

And for a moment the voice sounded pained. But, when his father spoke again, the fear returned.

"And believe me when I say I can stop you because I know where you are, boy," the voice inside his head whispered. "And when I find you, oh, when I find you, we are going to have some fun." His father laughed. "It's going to hurt you a lot more than it's going to hurt me, boy. In fact, it's not going to hurt me at all," the voice cackled. The door flew open and Xavier jerked awake to find a policeman in his cell.

"Here," he said, tossing Xavier some white coveralls and dropping a sack on the floor. "Get cleaned up. You got ten minutes before Detective Macksey sees you." The cop slammed the cell door, leaving Xavier alone in his wide-awake nightmare.

He put the prison issue coveralls down on the bunk. The sack on the floor held a few generic toiletries. He peeled off his bloody, burned, ripped clothes and examined his surroundings.

An eight-by-eight cell crammed full of toilet, sink, shower, and bed. Not so much a bed as a raised concrete and tile slab with a mattress on it. A scratchy piece of stainless steel served as a mirror. The air had a stale odor of sweat, urine, and disinfectant.

So this is solitary confinement, he thought, staring at the narrow slot in the steel door. He wondered how a tray of food could fit through the slot and hoped he wouldn't find out.

As he showered, he ran his hands over various cuts and abrasions on his skin, trying to sort out what had happened the night before. He'd been arraigned for murder...when? He could have slept a whole day. There was no way to find out what time it was. Solitary, no windows, no clocks.

Sometime after the first fire engines had arrived, they separated him from Min's corpse. He felt an ache rise up in his heart. He leaned into the shower wall and fought for control.

Not now, he cried. Not now. I've got to find a way out of this mess. I'm sorry, Min, but I've got to be able to think. He had to lock her death away until he felt safe enough to deal with it. Obviously, this wasn't the place.

Xavier pressed his face into the tiles and clenched his fists until the knot inside his chest relaxed. He raised his head to the nozzle and turned the water to cold. When he started to shiver, he added some warm water and finished his shower.

He toweled off and sat on the bed to put on his clothes. Coveralls, socks, underwear, and sandals. He stood to zip his coveralls and stared at his face in the mirror. Bloodshot eyes, four-day-old itchy beard. Disheveled hair. He looked in the sack. No comb. He would have to make do with his fingers. Xavier fished out a toothbrush and a small tube of toothpaste and brushed his teeth.

The cell door opened. Right on time. He spit the toothpaste into the sink and turned.

"Let's go," the cop ordered.

Jacob returned from the morgue shortly after noon. Upon receiving Bennedetto's phone call, he'd spent the early morning trying to find out the details behind Xavier's arrest. His efforts were not fruitful. Xavier had been arraigned on five counts of murder, including those of his wife, Min, and a police officer. His bond had been set at one million dollars.

His efforts did earn him a call from a Detective Macksey. The morgue needed someone to identify Min's body. A car had been sent for him. How ridiculous, he thought. One officer said Min was dead. Another wanted a positive identification. Such is the way of bureaucracy.

Dr. Gib Stern, the county coroner, met him at the entrance to Parkland Hospital and escorted him to the basement. Jacob knew the doctor. He and Dr. Stern had both practiced in Dallas for decades. Stern treated Jacob with kindness and dignity hoping to ease the burden. It didn't help much, although he appreciated the support.

They descended into the bowels of the complex. Reaching the forensic and pathology department, Jacob felt as though he'd entered another world. The main corridor was lined with gurneys, many holding corpses. The whisper of sheets and the occasional squeak of a tennis shoe were the only sounds as they passed the bodies. Jacob saw an arm with a large tattoo hanging limply beside a stretcher. The sheet was soaked in blood.

I have crossed the River Styx and am in the land of the dead, Jacob thought.

They entered the main autopsy chamber, the coroner unobtrusively supporting the old man under his arm. The smell assaulted Jacob's nose as soon as the doors opened. It took him back to that horrible day in Vorzel: gunshots, flames, and the sick, bittersweet choking stench of burning bodies. Jacob faltered and leaned on his friend's arm.

"Are you all right?" Stern asked.

Jacob swallowed, the acid rising in this throat, and stood up straight. He patted the coroner's arm letting him know he was okay.

There were eight tables in the elongated room. One wall was lined floor to ceiling with stainless steel refrigerated vaults.

The other side housed workbenches and cabinets containing the tools needed for the various postmortem procedures.

Five of the tables were occupied. At one station the sheet had been pulled back to reveal a horribly charred body. Technicians hovered over the corpse taking photographs. Several scalpels and a saw, bloodied from use, lay on a stainless tray next to the body.

"Not a pleasant odor is it, Mr. Rabinowitz," Larry Garcia said, coming through the door.

"It's *Dr.* Rabinowitz, Detective," the coroner corrected. Jacob turned to see a nicely dressed man of Mexican descent offering his hand.

"Sorry, Doc," he apologized. "I'm Detective Garcia." They shook hands. "The body they're working on is not Mrs. Daniels. So don't worry," Garcia explained. "We appreciate your coming down. It's been a Class A Cluster Fuck since the call came in."

Garcia's comment was greeted with silence. The detective noticed Dr. Rabinowitz' dignified bearing and apologized for his language.

"Are you ready?" the coroner asked. Jacob nodded.

They moved to the third table. The coroner held the edges of the sheet and looked at Jacob. He gave a short nod and the coroner pulled back the sheet.

"Is this Min Daniels?" Garcia asked.

"Yes," Jacob answered. It was the first word he'd spoken since entering the chamber.

The coroner began to put the sheet back in place but Jacob raised his hand. "A minute, please." The coroner reluctantly laid the sheet down.

Jacob looked at the girl's face one last time. It was pale and gray. Her once thick, shiny hair lay dull and limp across her forehead. Other than that, she appeared to be sleeping peacefully. A solitary tear slid down Jacob's face.

Who did this to you? The police say it was Xavier—only you and I know better. If only you were alive to tell us what you saw, what actually happened. Oh, my poor child. What have they done to you?

Jacob bowed his head and muttered the verses of Kaddish, the Hebrew prayer for the dead. When he was done, he lifted his head to Dr. Stern.

"All right," he croaked, and the coroner covered the young woman again.

"Min Daniels. She's from Hong Kong. What brought her to the States?" Garcia asked, looking at his note pad.

Questions. Min's legacy. With the police it's always business, he thought. "She came here to study. She liked it so much she stayed. Then she met Xavier and..." Jacob paused before becoming emotional. "Her parents are in Thailand at the moment. They have a summer home there."

"Yeah. I know," he said, flipping to another page in his note pad. "Bangkok. I found the address and phone number when we searched the Daniels' house this morning. Now that the ID is made, I'll call and give them the news."

Jacob had a flash memory of meeting Min's parents at the wedding. A thoroughly happy couple if a bit mysterious; proud parents of their bride-to-be. Good people. Parents worthy of a daughter like Min and a son-in-law like Xavier.

"Please, Detective. Let me call them."

"I don't know..." Garcia hesitated. "I gotta call them sooner or later. Regulations," he added, hoping to end the conversation.

"They would want to hear from somebody they know. Wouldn't you?" Jacob asked, looking at the policeman.

Garcia looked at the man's wet eyes. "I'll call my partner and see what he says."

"Garcia. I'll square it with Macksey," Stern cut in. "Believe me when I say that redheaded SOB owes me more than a few favors."

In the police business, Garcia understood the sacred cow law. Judges, DAs, and coroners were your best friends or your worst enemies. It definitely wouldn't do him any good to piss off the chief coroner for Dallas County. The old man was obviously more than a respected acquaintance.

"All right, Dr. Rabinowitz. You can inform them as long as you don't discuss the case with them."

"I don't know that much, Detective. I was hoping you could tell me about what is happening to Xavier," Jacob asked, seeing an opening.

"He's being held right now. That's about all I can tell you. You two related?" he asked as an afterthought.

"He is my godson," Jacob answered.

"He certainly has an interesting set of godfathers," Garcia intoned making a note on his pad. Jacob turned and left the room.

At his home in North Dallas, Jacob sat in his darkened study staring at the phone. He had reported the deaths of many patients to anxious families during his medical career. As a flight surgeon during World War II, he'd written too many letters to families of young fliers who had died on his operating table. The letter he'd written to Emil, detailing the mission Victor didn't return from, was as difficult a notification as the one he was about to make. He prayed to God for the right words, as he had done so many times before.

When he was ready, he lifted the phone and dialed.

"Hello," a voice answered, distant and unaware that this phone call would turn his life upside down.

"I am sorry to disturb you. It is Jacob Rabinowitz. I have some bad news."

When the call was done, Jacob leaned back in his chair exhausted. Min's mother had collapsed. Min's father was stunned. All he could think to ask was, "Why?" Over and over again, "Why? Why? Why?" Jacob had no answer for him.

Jacob felt soothing hands on his shoulders as Ms. Perkins, his housekeeper, attempted to knead away his tension.

"This is a horrible thing, Dr. Jack," she said.

"Yes, Ms. Perkins. Horrible."

Jacob felt reassured by the presence of his old friend. She knew just how to approach him. He thanked God for bringing her into his life, she would help him recover. As she had before.

Annie Lee Perkins had begun her relationship with Jacob in 1968. Jacob's wife had passed away the previous year and he had hired Annie Lee to keep house and cook. She was a black woman from the deep South, granddaughter of Virginia slaves. She was the most kindhearted person Jacob had ever met. As they grew older, she moved into a room in his house. Jacob, seventy-six, wouldn't know what to do without her. They were good companions.

Many of Jacob's associates speculated about the depth of their relationship. The women at the synagogue still gossiped about it after all these years. Even Xavier had kidded him about it in a good-natured way, but Jacob never explained. It was not anybody's business.

It was a strange relationship. They came from completely different races, religions, educational backgrounds, and cultures. Yet, they were as emotionally bonded as any married couple of two decades. There was never a physical attraction. They were two lonely people who had filled a void in each other's lives.

Jacob relaxed under her caring hands. "What would I do without you, Ms. Perkins?" he asked.

"Your own laundry for a start," she answered.

He laughed out loud but cut himself off short. His godson was in jail. Min was dead. Jacob felt lost and in need of guidance.

"Would you like to go to the synagogue?" Ms. Perkins asked, reading his mind.

"Yes. Yes, I would," Jacob said, scooting his chair back and standing up from the table.

"You get your things, Dr. Jack."

Jacob went to his bedroom and retrieved his prayer shawl and his prayer book. He took a moment to look around his bedroom at the comfortable clutter. Jacob had never surrounded himself with luxury. He lived simply, choosing instead to give his money and time to medicine and the Jewish community. After the suffering of his youth he consciously sought out a quiet, peaceful existence.

Jacob could hear Annie Lee scurrying about as she looked for the keys, humming a gospel as she searched. When they arrived at the synagogue, she would wait quietly in the back of the hall while he went about his prayers. Then she would drive him back home and patiently try to get him to eat and sleep.

Jacob bowed his head and uttered a prayer for God to watch over his caring friend.

"Come on now. I'm gonna start the car," she called.

Jacob left his bedroom and followed her out the back door to the carport. Just then the phone rang. Jacob hesitated.

"Whoever it is will call back. Right now you needs to go pray," she said, standing at the car door. She was right. But—

"It might be Benjamin calling about Xavier," he said, turning back to the house. Jacob went back up the walk and climbed the steps to the back door. He unlocked the back door and started to the phone on the kitchen table.

A huge roar knocked Jacob to the floor. He was stunned. He heard the sounds of breaking glass and raining debris. His ears rang. When the noise subsided, Jacob slowly made it to his feet. He turned to the back door.

It had been blown off its hinges. All the windows along the back were shattered. And then Jacob smelled the smoke. His body ached from the fall, but Jacob hurried to the back door. He stood on the steps and gazed in horror at the carnage before him.

The carport was gone. The roof and walls had been blown out. He saw a piece of the garage door on a neighbor's roof. The car was shredded. The front half was completely disintegrated and the rest was a blazing inferno.

"Annie Lee?" he gasped. There was no hope. He looked at the ground as ashes from the fire began to float down.

Vorzel, he thought. Fire, smoke, and death. I've come home.

Jacob sat on the steps and began to sob.

3

Lew Sterrett County Jail, Dallas, Texas, April 9, 1988

Xavier had been alone in the interrogation room for about half an hour when the door opened and two detectives entered. A stocky man with red hair and red-rimmed eyes sat across from him. He opened a bulky file and scratched the stubble on his face. His clothes were rumpled, dirty, and smelled of smoke. Xavier could guess where he'd spent his morning.

The other detective was Latin by the looks of him. He was well dressed and appeared a lot fresher than his partner. He sat on a window sill swinging his leg. Occasionally, he looked at Xavier with a snarl.

After a while, the stocky cop looked up from the file and glared at him.

"I'm Detective Macksey and this is my partner, Detective Larry Garcia," Macksey said, never taking his eyes off Xavier. For his part, Xavier stared back without flinching. Finally, Macksey had enough.

"I shot a whole night's sleep, ruined a brand-new pair of shoes, and got the mayor as my constant fucking companion after what happened last night," Macksey lashed out.

"I lost my wife and my business, Detective. Sorry if I don't seem more sympathetic," Xavier shot back.

"While you were in here getting your beauty sleep, we were talking to a dead cop's wife, lowlife. Got any sympathy for her?" Garcia asked, as he stood and leaned against the wall.

"What's his problem?" Xavier asked Macksey without looking at Garcia.

"He takes it personally when one of our fine citizens murders a fellow police officer," he answered. "We all do."

"That's right, *bendejo*," Garcia said.

"*Besa mi verga, joto*," Xavier muttered.

Garcia shot off the wall and grabbed Xavier's hair and yanked his head back. "What did you say, motherfucker?"

"You know exactly what I said, Detective. *Es verdad?*"

"For the sake of the ignorant Irish cop, why don't you translate, Mr. Daniels?" Macksey asked.

"I told him to suck my cock. You got a problem with that?"

"Larry, let him go," Macksey ordered. "We don't have time for this shit. He's just pulling your strings."

Garcia let go of Xavier's hair and went back to the window sill. Xavier slowly brought his head forward and stared back at Macksey.

"I'm not impressed, Mr. Daniels. Punk's flip attitude. I thought I could expect more from you."

Macksey bent back over the file. "Says here you got thrown out of the Marine Corps. ATF busted your ass smuggling arms back from Grenada. Is that when you became a hard case, Mr. Daniels? Or did it happen earlier, when you spent your summers in Sicily with your godfather," Macksey asked, a slight smile on his lips.

"I spent most of the time with my nanny."

"Maria Escalante. Your family's Mexican maid?"

"Nicaraguan."

"Same difference," Macksey shrugged.

"Not to a Nicaraguan," Xavier said. Macksey looked up from the file and nodded, acknowledging Xavier's point.

"Did you learn to speak Spanish from her?"

"Yeah, and I learned Italian from my godfather. So what," Xavier explained. "I also went to school for twelve years with John Davis Jr., whose father has already declared his candidacy for president of the United States in '92. Are they suspects also?

Listen, I'm real impressed with your knowledge of my family history, Detective. But what does that have to do with anything that happened last night?"

"A lot, Mr. Daniels," Macksey said looking up from the file. "Helps me to establish a history of unlawful activity and association with known criminals. It will add fuel to the fire when the DA's office tries you for last night's murders."

Xavier shot forward, slamming his hand on the table. "I didn't commit any murders last night, you dumb son of a bitch. I tried to save my wife's life. Instead of busting my ass and wasting time, you could get on the street and find out who killed Min."

"I got an informant says different. According to him, you were buying a large quantity of drugs from the New Rebels Posse and the deal went sour. Your wife informed on you and when the police busted in, you shot everyone. I got four automatic pistols and an Uzi. I got five dead bodies in the morgue, four with multiple gunshot wounds, and the fifth looks like someone cut his throat inside out. Like something maybe an ex-marine would do. Of course, with the condition of the corpses the autopsy results won't be available for a couple of days. Any questions so far, Mr. Daniels?"

"Did your informant have a South African accent?" Xavier asked. The cops exchanged a quick look before Macksey continued.

"You set the fire to cover up the murders. The motive was revenge. I got your ass on five counts of murder, one count of arson, and a whole bunch of lesser charges I don't care to list at the moment. I suggest you start talking before I get too pissed off to listen."

"If I set the fire to cover up the murders then why did I drag one of my victims out of the blaze? Why would I kill the people I was buying the drugs from? Wouldn't we be business partners?"

"That shit happens all the time in your kind of business," Garcia broke in. "You guys whack each other just for the hell of it."

"I'll tell you what I really think, Detective. You guys don't have shit. The fire wiped out most of the evidence. You've got no witnesses except some South African guy who vanished into thin air and who you have a very sick feeling you're not going to be able to find. So that leaves you with me as your only witness. And, I sure as hell am not going to tell you anything you want to hear! So you might as well take me back to my cell because this isn't going to get us anywhere." Xavier stood, pushing his chair back.

Garcia jumped up from his perch and shoved Xavier back into the chair almost knocking him over. Xavier stood again defiantly and moved toward Garcia.

"Enough," Macksey yelled. Both men stopped and glared at one another.

"You look as good in prison whites as your father did, asshole," Garcia said, baiting Xavier. "We brought him down and now we're going to bring you down."

"I said enough, Larry. Now sit down! We've got a long way to go. Mr. Daniels, please?" he said, motioning to the chair. Xavier slowly sat down.

"Mr. Daniels, you and I both know you don't have to tell us a thing without the presence of an attorney. But I for one would appreciate hearing your side of the story."

"No way," Xavier said, shaking his head.

"And why not?" Macksey asked.

"Because that cop had a hand in getting my wife murdered and I have no reason to believe you're not mixed up in this as well."

Garcia came off his perch again, slamming his hands down on the desk.

"I'll tell you what, you little fuck. You iced Tibby while he was making a righteous bust and for that you're gonna burn," he hissed.

"Larry, sit down and shut up," Macksey ordered.

"Red, this asshole accused a dead cop of being dirty. You gonna take that shit?"

"Larry, you're real tired right now. Why don't you go down the hall and get us some coffee?" When Garcia hesitated, Macksey added, "Like now, Larry." Garcia cursed under his breath and left, slamming the door.

Macksey's expression softened a bit before he continued. "Don't mind Detective Garcia," Macksey apologized.

"Mexican cop named Larry?" Xavier asked. "I'm sure you guys don't give him any shit about that. No wonder he's bitter."

"His father's Irish," Macksey explained. "No, he's just exhausted."

"Yeah. Right. Exhausted, huh? No, he's the hard guy and you're the soft guy and now's the part where we become buddies. Am I close, Detective?"

"Actually, it's usually the other way around, Mr. Daniels. I just wanted to get him out of the way so we could talk in private."

"Yeah. You, me, and the recorder," Xavier said cynically.

"Listen. There isn't any recorder. Just you and me. There's some stuff that's bugging me about this case, which is why I want to talk to you alone. You can tell me to fuck off and go back to your cell or you can talk to me now. Sooner or later you're going to have to tell somebody what happened. I'm as good a place to start as any."

Xavier chewed on that for a moment.

"You can start by telling me how you knew our informant was a South African."

Xavier shrugged his shoulders and thought, what the hell.

"The cop told me. He said the South African planned the whole deal," Xavier offered.

"And why would he tell you that?"

Oh, well. Here goes.

"Because I was torturing him before I killed him," Xavier confessed, waiting for the expected explosion. Xavier was surprised when Macksey just said, "Go on."

So Xavier told him the whole bizarre, nightmarish tale. While Xavier talked, Macksey listened. No notes. No questions. He just listened. For Xavier, reliving his wife's murder while holding his grief behind an iron curtain exhausted him. He slumped in his chair.

"Why do you expect me to believe your story?" Macksey asked after a moment.

Xavier thought for a minute and then sat up in his chair and looked at Macksey.

"If the cop I killed was making a major bust, where was the backup? Where were the rest of your guys? Did he even leave any information about this bust behind?" Xavier asked.

Macksey didn't answer. It was one of the many things that troubled him about this case. That was the reason he wanted Garcia out of the room. If Dixon was dirty then others in the department might be dirty, too. Not that he didn't trust his partner, but if he started looking into this kind of thing it could affect them both. If Macksey was wrong then Garcia might suffer and he wanted to make sure that didn't happen.

Macksey also wanted to protect himself. Cops watch other cops' backs. As soon as he got Internal Affairs involved, some cops might stop watching his.

The detective needed more evidence before he took action. An off-duty cop had been killed. The main suspect was a man heavily connected to the mafia. The mayor's office wanted Xavier Daniels to pay for the crime. The public would scream for justice and the district attorney's office would move heaven and earth to get a conviction.

Macksey's fellow officers would not look kindly on him if he derailed the proceedings. But if Daniels was innocent, that's what he had to do. His job was to find out who was responsible, not to railroad the prime suspect. It was a hell of a juggernaut to stand in the way of, but Macksey was one of the few cops who would try. Besides, he felt he had something to atone for.

In 1978, Macksey had arrested Victor Danielson for money laundering on what seemed like solid evidence. Then the Feds charged him under the RICO statute and the IRS added tax evasion and Macksey lost control of the case. When Macksey attempted to point out new discrepancies in the charges and the evidence, he was told to back off. He did and Xavier's father got thrown to the wolves. In the end, Victor was sentenced to a long term in prison.

And now before me sits his son, Macksey thought. Fate has a funny way of doing things.

"If you're lying to me I'll personally escort you to the electric chair, Daniels," Macksey said, sitting up.

"Detective. I don't care whether you believe me or not. The only thing I'm certain of is someone had my wife killed and I'm going to find out who it is! With or without your help."

Looking into the young man's eyes, Macksey sensed that somewhere down the line there really would be hell to pay.

"Larry!" Macksey shouted. Garcia, who'd been cooling his heels in the hall, opened the door and stuck his head in.

"Yeah, Red."

"Get this guy back to his cell."

Garcia grabbed Xavier under his arm and yanked him out of the chair. "Let's go, Daniels."

He pulled him into the hall and turned him over to two guards.

"OK. Back to your cell," one of the guards said as they led him away.

"No. Wait," Garcia said. "Throw him in the holding tank instead. We're gonna need to talk to him again pretty soon."

"Whatever you say, Detective," the guard answered. "Looks like you get to make some new friends." Both guards laughed as they escorted him down the hall.

"Go home and get some sleep, Larry," Macksey said when Garcia returned.

"OK. But what about you?" he asked.

"Me? I got a few calls to make, then I'm gonna do the same," Macksey answered, stretching. One large yawn later he said dejectedly, "This shit's gonna kill me someday."

"You and me both, pal. What did Daniels have to say?"

"What else? He's innocent."

"Yeah," Garcia said opening the door. "Aren't they all."

Garcia shut the door leaving Macksey alone with the file and his troubled thoughts.

Rodeway Inn, April 9, 1988

Kruger wasn't on a Lufthansa jet headed out of the country. He had decided to stay in Dallas. The only men who knew of his involvement in the plot were dead. The police might have a name, if they were lucky. And since Kruger didn't use a passport with that name he was anonymous. That's why he was still in Dallas. Anonymity was invisibility. Anonymity was a weapon. Anonymity was power.

Kruger went to the bathroom and pulled another beer from the six pack he'd iced down in the sink. He twisted off the top and settled back on the bed to watch TV. He was waiting for word from Lew Sterrett Justice Center. Kruger's informant, on duty at "Hotel Lew," would contact him with news of Xavier's death. He hoped it would be soon as he was tired of the whole bloody mess.

Other plans had been shunted aside for what Kruger considered a profitless mission that had wasted valuable assets. Kruger was, at heart, a mercenary. Profit and power were his sole motivations. Lives had been lost to satisfy the pride of the man he worked for. And money, which could have been better spent elsewhere, had been squandered for no apparent gain.

Useless, he thought. Absolutely useless.

But Kruger would do as he was told—as long as his boss kept paying. Any decent mercenary would.

Kruger's phone buzzed and he snapped it open.

"Yes." Kruger listened intently. "I did not ask to know when the asset was in place," Kruger interrupted angrily. "I only want to know when the job is done." He snapped the phone closed on the man's apologies.

Can't anybody do what they're told in this bleeding city? Kruger fumed. They make a simple murder as complicated as a presidential assassination.

Kruger rubbed the scar on his cheek and pondered the situation. He preferred commanding professional troops in the field. Fewer fuckups and better results. This type of assignment was too open to chance. But what could he do; orders were orders.

The TV screen showed a reporter in front of the Kennedy Memorial. The sound was off, but Kruger could guess that it was another program detailing a conspiracy theory behind the assassination of President Kennedy.

If that stupid reporter knew what really happened he'd shit in his pants, Kruger thought, chuckling.

Kruger began to laugh. He laughed so hard he spilled his beer. Nobody figured on Ruby, the fat guy, he thought. The fucking fat guy.

The laughter was good. He needed the release.

Lew Sterrett County Jail, April 9, 1988

Xavier sat on a metal bench in a large tile cell. The only amenities were the partitioned toilets in the back. Other than that there were no bunks, water fountains, or TVs.

About forty unfortunates were crammed into the cell. Most sat on the benches along either wall or milled around by the bars at the front of the cage. A few exhausted men lay stretched out on the floor trying to sleep. Xavier was amazed that anybody could sleep with all the noise. Some of the men would occasionally get stepped on, but continue to sleep without taking notice.

I guess you can get used to anything, Xavier thought.

Some prisoners were on their way to trial. Others, like Xavier, were between interrogations. Most were waiting for their cell assignments. He had spent time in the holding tank when he first arrived. It seemed like days instead of hours. Hours since Min had been murdered.

The cell contained mostly Blacks and Hispanics with a few Asians. He was one of a handful of Caucasians. Several times in the past hour he'd been harassed by other prisoners. A white guy sitting alone made an easy target but, so far, he had avoided a fight. He didn't want any trouble, but he kept his eye out for any black guys with dreadlocks.

New Rebels, he thought. That's what they had called themselves.

Xavier hoped to meet a member of the drug posse. He relished the thought of the confrontation. Maybe he would learn something before he killed the man.

"Whatcha smilin' about?" Xavier looked up to see a short squat man with a bulging chest and shoulders standing over him. He wore street clothes, a blue jean jacket with cut-off sleeves and blue jeans over black motorcycle boots. The jacket hung open to reveal a black T-shirt that read "Peace sells—but who's buying?" Several tattoos peeked out from under his rolled-up sleeves.

"Nothing much," Xavier answered neutrally.

"Mind if I pull up a seat?" Xavier examined the man's face. His nose had been broken several times. One ear looked like it'd been bitten in half and sewn back together. It was the face of an outlaw. When the biker had entered the cell earlier, the other prisoners had taken pains to leave him alone. Xavier thought he would follow their example.

"Sure," Xavier said, scooting down the bench to make room for the man. The outlaw sat down and leaned over, elbows on knees. He cocked his head at Xavier.

"Looks like you had a rough night."

"Rough enough," Xavier answered. The outlaw leaned in.

"Your godfather sent me to look after you," he said, his voice almost inaudible in the din. "Name's Eli Thomas. Friends call me Batty."

Xavier hid his surprise. He could smell beer on the man's breath. He took the offered hand and shook it; it was calloused and powerful. It felt like a brick.

"Now, listen to me real careful, boy. The niggers are going to start a fight with the spics any minute now. They gonna ice you in the commotion..."

"Who's going to ice me?" Xavier asked, interrupting.

"New Rebels, boy. Now don't go interrupting. I'm trying to save your life." His thick hand grabbed Xavier by the upper arm and pulled him closer. "When the rumble goes down, we head to the back. Me and John Boy over there," he said, jerking his head toward a fellow biker, "are going to cover you while the niggers and spics kill each other. If they don't get you in the first minute, they ain't gonna get you at all."

Batty let go and sat back. Xavier was upset. A minute ago he was enjoying the thought of hunting down one of the New Rebels. Now the hunter was the hunted again.

Will I ever get to turn the tables? he thought. And then he realized, if Benny knew then Uncle Jacob also knew. He shook his head at that.

Shouts brought him out of his reverie. Several blacks were pushing on one of the Hispanics. Some of his buddies came to his aid. Shoving quickly degenerated into punching and the melee was on. A loud siren went off and Xavier heard the shriek of whistles as guards converged on the trouble spot.

Batty grabbed Xavier by the arm and jerked him off the bench. The other biker, John Boy, rushed from the other wall and grabbed Xavier's other arm. They hurried him to the back of the cell and pushed him behind the toilet partition. Xavier turned around and Batty grabbed him by the hair and slammed his head against the wall.

He slumped against the wall trying to keep on his feet. Looking up through blurred vision he saw John Boy hand Batty a knife.

Xavier pushed off the wall and tried to get farther back into the stall as Batty came at him. Dizzy and sick, he had no equilibrium. His face was wet.

Batty grabbed Xavier by his hair and raised the knife. Xavier didn't grab at the knife arm. Instead he mustered his strength and struck Batty in the throat with the extended fingers of his right hand.

Batty let go of Xavier and clutched his throat. Normally, that kind of blow would kill an opponent by rupturing his windpipe. Unfortunately, Xavier was weak and off balance from the blow to his head. The punch only stunned Batty. Already the biker was readying himself for another rush.

Xavier slipped in something slick on the floor and fell between the wall and the toilet. He was stuck. Batty screamed as he lunged for him. The outlaw landed on Xavier, crushing him with his weight. Batty raised the knife for the mortal strike, a wicked smile on his face. Before he could bring the knife down, an arm snaked around Batty's neck and another came across his face. With one quick jerk Batty's neck snapped. His face didn't have time to register surprise.

Batty's body fell on Xavier, pinning him beneath its bulk. The biker's face was inches from his, the smell of beer on his lips. Xavier gagged then retreated into unconsciousness.

Xavier felt a stinging blow across his face and reluctantly opened his eyes. A young Asian knelt over him.

"How long have I been out?" Xavier asked.

"A few seconds," he answered, helping Xavier up. Looking at the ground, Xavier realized that he'd slipped in blood. He and Batty were covered with it.

"Come on, man. We got to get away from here," his rescuer said, leading him out of the stall. Xavier tripped over John Boy's prostrate body. The man's throat had been slit. "The bulls are fixing to bust in and we don't want to be anywhere near those dudes back there."

He led Xavier to the bench and sat him down. "You're bleeding bad, man," he said, ripping off one of his sleeves. He wrapped it tightly around Xavier's head. The noise of the riot faded. He looked into the almond eyes of his savior and thought, what's your name, before he passed out.

Infirmary, Lew Sterrett County Jail, Dallas, Texas, April 9, 1988

As Xavier came to, his head throbbed badly enough to nauseate him. His mouth had a bitter metallic taste. Smacking his lips, he tried to focus his eyes. In blurred double vision, he saw the outline of a figure sitting next to his bed. Xavier made the mistake of trying to sit up. The room swam out of focus and he collapsed.

"Easy, Xavier. You've had a nasty blow to the head," a voice echoed in the distance.

Xavier recognized the voice, but couldn't place it. Memory loss, auditory hallucinations. Xavier was only too familiar with the symptoms of a serious concussion.

He had suffered two before. One during a marital arts contest in college; the other when his helicopter had lost power and crashed during training maneuvers in the Marine Corps. Xavier laid back and allowed the nausea to subside before he opened his eyes.

When he tried to sit up in bed again, he was more successful. His vision cleared somewhat and he looked at his visitor. He didn't have to concentrate this time to place a name to the face.

"I must be dead," Xavier croaked through a dry throat. "It's Charon come to ferry me across the river Acheron."

"What's that?" came a voice from the other side of the bed. Xavier turned his head too quickly and had to shut his eyes to avoid becoming sick. When he opened them again, he saw Detective Macksey standing next to the bed.

"It's a little joke, Detective," Rizzi replied, handing a glass of water to Xavier. "Charon was the Greek god who guarded the gates of hell. Anyone wanting entrance had to pay a small fee to be allowed on his ferry."

"What does that have to do with anything?" Macksey asked.

"Mr. Rizzi is my godfather's keeper of the gate," Xavier answered, his tone of voice indicating he didn't have a lot of respect for Rizzi's position. He finished the cup of water and handed it back to Rizzi. "Do you know how much money he's made off of people wanting an audience with Bennedetto Busambra?"

Macksey didn't respond. He was interested in the relationship between them. His observation of their first exchange told him one thing: Xavier Daniels' barbed humor concealed obvious contempt for Busambra's *consigliere*.

"Xavier does not approve of most of his godfather's employees," Rizzi explained. "I fall into that category."

No doubt, Macksey thought.

"Whether you happen to approve of the counselor or not," Macksey said, "you might appreciate the fact that he has arranged for your release. You can leave as soon as you get your clothes."

Xavier scrutinized Rizzi. Rizzi said nothing. The *consigliere* nonchalantly lit a cigarette and leaned back in his chair. Macksey said nothing to Rizzi as the man violated several city and state ordinances by smoking in a medical facility. Instead, he marveled at the man's gall. Rizzi radiated power. Macksey had dealt with the type before.

"I thought my godfather forbade his people to partake of any tobacco products," Xavier commented. "Or did he start smoking again?"

"No. His lungs aren't what they used to be since he was shot," Rizzi answered, exhaling smoke. He reached down and flicked a speck of dust off his trousers. "No one smokes in his presence out of respect."

"That's one way to look at it," Xavier said.

"I didn't think anyone had ever gotten close enough to attempt a hit on Busambra," Macksey said.

"Please, Detective. Mobsters get hit. *Signor* Busambra is one of the most respected businessmen in the country. Why would anyone want to shoot him?" Rizzi asked, annoyed.

Macksey ignored the question. "You said he took a bullet in the lungs. If nobody tried to hit him, then how did he get shot? Hunting accident, I suppose?"

"Really," Rizzi said disgustedly. "*Signor* Busambra is a war hero, or didn't you know, Detective," Rizzi explained, raising his eyebrows as though the fact was common knowledge. "He served as a gunner on a bomber in World War II. Some shrapnel from a 20mm cannon shell wounded him. Xavier's father saved his life. It's really quite a remarkable story. Maybe someday I'll tell it to you," Rizzi offered without sincerity.

"I can't wait to hear it," Macksey lied.

"How much bond did my godfather post to get me out of here, Detective?" Xavier asked, breaking into the exchange.

"Not a dime," Macksey answered. He didn't seem too happy about it.

"Yesterday, Macksey, you said I was being held for murder. Multiple homicide. If that's so, then how in the hell am I getting out of here so soon? Did Jerry buy you off?"

Macksey's face turned red. He got in Xavier's face. "Listen, you little shit. Nobody bought me off. The truth is I don't have crap. Not one goddamn piece of evidence to hold you on. The mayor wants your ass; the press is screaming for justice; and my fellow cops are demanding retribution, i.e., your butt in the gas chamber.

"I did not win the Queen of the May contest when I would not recommend your case to the DA's office for a grand jury indictment. And I will not send this case to trial until I have completed my investigation and I'm damn sure I've got the correct suspect.

"Now hear this well, asshole. Because of what I've just done, Internal Affairs is gonna be climbing up my butt to find out how much your people paid me to get me to do this. They won't even consider that I was doing my job. They're convinced I'm guilty and are just waiting to see to what degree that guilt extends. Save for my partner, who thinks I'm certifiable, there ain't a soul in the department who's gonna have shit to do with me! I put my career on the line for you, but your attitude makes it real hard for me to want to do the right thing." His outburst spent, Macksey straightened up, breathing heavily. Rizzi looked at him and smiled.

"You forgot to tell Xavier about Jacob Rabinowitz," Rizzi commented, tapping ashes onto the floor.

"What about Uncle Jake?" Xavier asked, concerned.

"Car bomb," Macksey said. "While I was interrogating you, someone tried to kill your other godfather with a couple of pounds of plastic explosive."

THE ARMAGEDDON CHRONICLES

"What?" Xavier asked incredulously.

"While Detective Macksey was holding you for the murder of your wife, amongst others, it seems the real killer was after Jacob," Rizzi said with a reproachful look. "Kind of embarrassing for the department, wouldn't you say, Detective?"

"You better watch out, Rizzi. You or your boss could be next."

"Thankfully, we don't live in Dallas, where innocents are held behind bars and killers are allowed to roam free to choose their next victims. The law enforcement in New York seems much more efficient."

"Fuck you, Rizzi," Macksey fumed. "You guys really make it fucking hard for a cop to do the right thing," he reiterated. Macksey turned to Xavier. "I don't know how mixed up you are in this thing. I have a feeling you're a good guy caught in a bad situation. Take my advice. Grab your Uncle Jake and go on a long vacation until this thing blows over."

"We appreciate your advice. But coming from a policeman who allowed Jacob's friend and companion of twenty years to be blown to bits, we'll take it with a grain of salt," Rizzi said. Macksey, face as red as a beet, looked from one to the other. "You fucking wise guys disgust me," Macksey spat. "Now get the hell out of my jail." He turned and stomped out the door.

"Was he telling the truth?" Xavier asked.

"Essentially, yes, Xavier," Rizzi said, dropping the cigarette on the floor. He crushed it under his shoe before he continued. "There is not enough evidence to hold you. That detective did put his career on the line for you. My presence did speed up the process, however. Bennedetto wants you home immediately."

Rizzi stood and went to the bed adjacent to Xavier's. On it there was a leather bag. Rizzi unzipped it and began to pull out some clothes.

"I'm sure these will fit. I got the sizes from Jacob," he said, laying out the clothes on the bed. "The jet is standing by at the airport."

"You are forgetting something, Jerry," Xavier said softly. "My wife. Her funeral."

Rizzi turned slowly and sat on Xavier's bed. His expression was at once caring and urgent. Xavier marveled at the way this man could change so quickly from arrogant attorney to concerned friend.

"Your life is in danger, Xavier. I am sorry about Min, but my concern is for the living. Min's body was flown to Hong Kong to be buried by her parents. You will…"

"Then I will go to Hong Kong to be with them," Xavier interrupted.

"You will go to New York with Jerry, Zavi."

Xavier turned to see his Uncle Jacob standing at the foot of the bed. The man's face was drawn and his eyes glassy. He looked exhausted. Xavier's heart went out to him. The old man had treated Min like his own daughter.

"Uncle Jake…" Xavier began.

Jacob held up his hand. "Please, Zavi. Do as I ask. I have already lost one child this week. I could not stand losing another."

"But…"

"Zavi, it is not easy for me either. Remember…" the words caught in his throat. "I will be missing Annie Lee's funeral as well."

Xavier's heart cracked at the sight of Jacob's pain.

"As soon as possible you and I will sit *shivah* for Min and Annie Lee," Jacob said pulling himself together, "But now you must come with us."

Rizzi rested a hand on Xavier's thigh. "You might not agree with what your godfather represents. I can understand that. But he loves you with all his heart, Xavier. And right now you are in extreme peril. Bennedetto has sent me to protect you. Despite your feelings for me I will do so with my life if necessary, as will all the men at his command. You have no choice in the matter. If I have to, I will sedate you and bind you to get you to New York."

Xavier looked into Rizzi's eyes. They were deadly serious. They were the eyes of a man who would kill. Xavier looked at Jacob. His godfather nodded his head slowly.

"The forces that consumed your father and Min, which almost succeeded in killing Jacob, are the same forces that destroyed your military career," Rizzi spoke forcefully. "They have been present in your life longer than you know. Those forces are now after you. Escape, Xavier, and I promise you someday we will find the people responsible for this."

"Connected? All these things are connected?" asked Xavier. "But, how?"

Jacob and Rizzi looked at one another. Rizzi turned to Xavier.

"Time enough for that later," Rizzi said. He stood and retrieved a pair of pants from the bed. "Here. Let's get you dressed now." Xavier surrendered and let the two older men help him get dressed. When finished, Jacob went to inform the driver they were ready.

In the elevator Xavier asked Rizzi something that had been bothering him.

"Jerry. Do you change your personality all the time?"

"You mean with Macksey?"

"Yeah."

"He expected an arrogant wop mouthpiece, so I gave him one."

"But why?"

"Adaptability, Xavier. A lesson from Antoni Busambra. Hide your true self and you'd be surprised what you can learn."

The door opened and they exited the elevator. In the limousine Xavier wondered which of the men he knew as Rizzi was the real one: the cocky, self-assured gangster; the concerned friend; the lethal bodyguard; or the fanatical follower. What worried Xavier more was the man who could inspire such behavior from his disciples. A man Xavier was on his way to see. His godfather, Don Bennedetto Antonio Busambra, *il capo di tuti capi*.

The window between the passenger compartment and the front seat slid down. A face appeared in the opening.

"How's your head, Mr. Daniels," the face asked smiling. It was the Asian from the holding tank.

"Jesus," Xavier muttered staring at Rizzi. Rizzi's only response was the ghost of a smile.

4

Busambra Brownstone, Manhattan, New York, April 11, 1988

Xavier sat in his godfather's study alone, staring into the dark empty recess of the fireplace. The sun was descending, spilling rays of dusty light through the half-closed shutters into the room. The only sound was the occasional chirping of a bird in the garden.

Xavier's head still throbbed and he had a slight fever. The specialist waiting for him on the plane had examined him under Jacob's watchful eye. If the specialist was annoyed, he hadn't showed it.

After checking the stitches in Xavier's scalp and cleaning the wound, the doctor pronounced his diagnosis: severe concussion with a possible hairline skull fracture. Xavier could expect headaches, nausea, vertigo, and fever. The doctor recommended x-rays and a complete neurological examination when they arrived in New York, and plenty of bed rest. Instead of alleviating his condition, the pronouncement only added to Xavier's misery. The last thing he wanted was rest.

Jacob was asleep in another part of the house. The old man was exhausted after the ordeal. The loss of Min and Ms. Perkins, his longtime companion, had sapped his will and dulled his normally sparkling eyes. The unavoidable decision to forego Ms. Perkins' funeral only added to his burden.

Xavier knew how Jacob felt but he found it difficult to sleep. The memory of Min's death and his desire for revenge fueled a restless energy.

Min's funeral had been this morning. Xavier had finally gotten through to her parents around noon. Their son-in-law, the husband of their only daughter, was unable to attend the last rites, yet, they showed no anger or disappointment. They seemed genuinely concerned about him. It only made Xavier feel worse.

Xavier had still not seen his godfather. Rizzi had informed him that Bennedetto was away on business and would return later that evening. Jacob had gone to sleep, leaving Xavier alone in the house. Not even Anthony, his godbrother, was to be found. Xavier felt lost wandering around the mansion. He finally sought refuge in his godfather's study.

Some of Xavier's fondest childhood memories were of summers spent with his godfather in Sicily. The vacations always began in this house. He would fly up from Dallas to be met by Bennedetto. Until they left for Sicily they spent all their time together, most of it in this room. Bennedetto would open the doors to the garden, and Xavier would play on the floor with his toys or answer the phone. Sometimes his godfather let him light the votive candle in memory of Antoni Busambra. He loved the smell of the study. Polished wood and leather and scented candles.

The memories brought him comfort. At some point the memories became dreams and Xavier slept. He woke to find his godfather seated across from him in the other high-backed leather chair.

"You are awake," Busambra said.

Xavier sat up in the chair. His neck was stiff and his head ached but he managed a smile for his godfather.

"Hello, Papa," he said, using the name he had called Bennedetto as a child. "How long have you been here?"

"About an hour."

"An hour? Why didn't you wake me?"

"You were sleeping," he answered. "I used to love to watch you sleep when you were a little boy. Seeing you now took me back to that time. You were so innocent. The vision always brought me peace. Even in the toughest times."

It was times such as these that he warmed to the man. He was constantly amazed at the contradiction that was Bennedetto Busambra. A dedicated family man and loyal patriarch, Busambra supported a number of charities. He was also the leader of the most powerful crime syndicate in the world.

"Where have you been all day, Papa?" Xavier asked, realizing he had been looking forward to seeing his godfather.

"I have been at Anthony's bedside most of the day. When I wasn't there I was arranging for your safe passage out of the country."

"What happened to Anthony?" Xavier asked, sensing the answer.

"Someone tried to kill him last night. Anthony was leaving a casino…" Busambra paused with a heavy sigh. "He was leaving a casino and some men with machine guns tried to murder my son. They only succeeded in wounding him. Unfortunately, they killed his two bodyguards and his best friend, Tiny Magliocco."

Xavier knew Tiny. The Maglioccos were part of the Busambra organization, powerful mafiosi who owed complete allegiance to his godfather.

"My God, Zavi," Busambra lamented. "The Maglioccos came to America with my father from Sicily. I've known that boy all his life. I was at his christening. Of course, his family is screaming for revenge."

"As are we all, Papa," Xavier said, clenching his fist. "We have to get revenge for Min and for what they did to Uncle Jake. We have to protect ourselves," he finished, pounding on the arm of his chair.

"No, Zavi. That is impossible now. You must leave the country. It is all arranged."

"That's bullshit, Papa," Xavier snapped. He leaned forward in his chair as his anger took over. "Some son of a bitch had my wife killed and tried to kill Uncle Jacob. I'm going to find out who did it. And you're going to help me, goddamnit."

"That is quite impossible, Zavi," Busambra repeated.

"Which? That I'm going to find her killer, or that you're going to help me?"

"Both, I'm afraid," he answered softly.

"But, Papa. Your power. Your influence. We can use them to find out who did this. For Christ's sake, Papa, they tried to kill Anthony and Jacob. You could be next. Please, Papa. I beg you."

Busambra looked at the floor. He would move heaven and earth to please his godson. In this case, however, it was impossible. The forces arrayed against them were too powerful and too well protected. The safety of his godson was now his utmost concern. Revenge would have to wait. Maybe for years.

Xavier was crushed. On the flight to New York, Rizzi had asked an intriguing question. Could Min's killers also be responsible for his father's imprisonment and the trumped-up charges that led to his dismissal from the Marine Corps? The only man who could answer these questions and find the killers was his godfather. And now the man who had never denied him anything was turning his back. Xavier fell out of the chair onto his knees. He clasped his hands and pleaded with his godfather.

"Please, Papa. I'm begging you. You have to help me," he pleaded, tears streaming down his face. Busambra got up from his chair and sat in Xavier's. Busambra held his godson's head and gently lowered it to his lap. And finally Xavier's body shook with great racking sobs as the grief engulfed him.

"They killed my Min, Papa. They killed my Min," he wept uncontrollably. "Oh, Papa. They killed my Min."

Tears fell down Busambra's face as he stroked Xavier's hair.

"I know, my son," he consoled. "I know."

They stayed like that as time slowly passed. Finally, exhausted, Xavier was helped by two of Busambra's bodyguards to his room. He collapsed on the bed and fell instantly asleep. Busambra watched him from the door. For the first time in his life, the sight did not bring him peace. Bennedetto Busambra, son of Antoni Busambra, knew he would not be at ease until his son and godson were safe and the people responsible for Xavier's pain were punished.

"How is he doing?" Rizzi asked, staring through the door at Xavier.

"His dreams are crushed and his heart is broken," Busambra replied. "And I am powerless to help mend his spirit, Jerry. How is he doing? How would any of us be doing after what he's been through? How is my son?"

"He is resting. The doctors say there are no complications. Our people are on him like glue. No one will harm him again," Rizzi assured the don.

"I wish I could believe that."

"I know. It will take time, *Signor*. But I swear to you we will destroy whoever has brought this grief to your family and your house."

"I know, Jerry," Busambra acknowledged. He turned and put a hand on his *consigliere*'s shoulder. "In the meantime, I want Zavi protected day and night. I also want Jacob to have a constant escort. They might try for him again. Somehow we are all involved. We just need to find out how."

"I'll have Luca handle all the security arrangements," Rizzi said. "And I will personally see to your godson's safety."

Bennedetto nodded his head and patted Jerry on the shoulder. He said a small prayer and crossed himself leaving Xavier to his nightmares. With Rizzi in tow, Busambra walked to his study. Even at this hour of the night there was work to be done.

The following morning Jacob sat in the kitchen with Bennedetto Busambra. Both men wore haggard looks from worry and restless sleep. They picked at their food and let their coffee grow cold. Finally Jacob lifted his head slowly as though its weight was unbearable and spoke.

"Who is doing this to us, Benjamin?" Jacob asked.

"I don't know, Jacob," Busambra answered truthfully.

"But you have an idea."

Busambra slowly stirred his coffee. "Maybe. I don't know."

Jacob turned to Busambra, eyes narrowing. "Maybe? I find that hard to believe with your connections."

"Jacob. Believe me, I am as baffled as you are," he said. "All inquiries are turned away. Men who have always accepted bribes become pious. Informants are, at best, misleading. Disinformation is spread like so much fertilizer. It is very frustrating. Smoke or granite. That is all we find."

Busambra picked up his coffee cup and swirled the contents trying to determine whether or not he should take Jacob into his confidence. At length, he set down the cup and looked at Jacob. "It's happened like this twice before, you know?"

Jacob kept silent, waiting patiently for Busambra to continue. He knew the don was breaking tradition by imparting family secrets to an outsider.

"Remember Victor's troubles with the IRS?"

Jacob nodded. "How could I forget. It was the beginning of the end for him. He should have been more careful. Victor was always showing off," he lamented.

"Yes, Jacob. Victor was very flashy. He enjoyed spending the money he earned working for the Busambra family. But it shouldn't have been a problem. I swear to you the accounts he managed for us in the Caymans were inviolable. Victor was clean and the money was clean. That's why I picked him A respected physician and war hero should have been above suspicion. No investigator, no matter how hard he looked at the offshore corporation, could have seen it as anything other than a legitimate holding company."

"Victor was smart, loyal and careful. He kept flawless books. But someone leaked information, planted false evidence in safe-deposit boxes Victor never knew existed and framed him for crimes he never committed."

"That's what Victor claimed, at least," Jacob stated.

"What he claimed was true. My people got that far in the investigation. Even some of the police were beginning to suspect a frame-up but unfortunately, for Victor, the press had already tried him and no one could get any closer to the truth. No one would talk. So they convicted our friend and wiped him out. Only his deteriorating health and a lot of legal maneuvering from Rizzi kept him from dying in prison."

Jacob looked up surprised. "I never knew," Jacob commented, guiltily. "I never believed him."

"Because you suspected that what he did for us was illegal, Jacob. That's the sad thing. The money in those accounts came from my legitimate businesses. The money might have started out dirty, but by the time it came to Victor it was clean and untraceable to anything tainted by my other interests."

"And you never found out who was responsible?"

"Never," Busambra stated flatly. "I was impotent. My power and influence meant nothing. Someone destroyed my innocent friend and I could not retaliate on his behalf. To this day I still owe Victor a debt."

"And the second time?" Jacob inquired.

Busambra sighed, "When they arrested Xavier for smuggling weapons I sent Rizzi to take care of matters. We did everything we could to find out what happened and ran into the same brick wall I encountered with Victor. The result, Xavier was court-martialed and kicked out of the Corps. Once again I was thwarted in my efforts to protect a person I loved."

"Those charges were trumped up, Benjamin," Jacob snapped, angrily.

"Of course they were. Xavier personified the marine officer. He lived for the Corps. His courage and devotion to duty were represented by the medals on his chest. His fitness reports were flawless. The marines under his command worshiped him. So why does a man of impeccable character jeopardize his career to smuggle a couple of AK 47s into the country as war trophies? The idea is ludicrous, my friend. The only logical answer is that he was framed. But why?"

"To get at you," Jacob answered angrily, without thinking. He felt edgy due to the lack of sleep. "I've always blamed you for what happened to them, Benjamin."

"Why, Jacob?"

Jacob took a deep breath. "Everybody suspects your connection to the mafia but the government has never been able to indict you so they go after those close to you. To bring you down. Even before the IRS and the court-martial, your presence harmed them. Zavi was a pariah in school because of his connection to you. John Davis and his wife weren't the only parents who wouldn't allow their children to play with little Zavi."

Both men paused at the mention of the powerful Texas billionaire with presidential ambitions. Davis' son had been Xavier's best friend and, after he'd forbidden Xavier to play with him, other parents had followed suit. The effect on Xavier had been awful.

"If it weren't for you," Jacob continued, "Victor, Min and Annie Lee might still be alive and your son wouldn't be fighting for his life in the hospital."

Busambra smiled, trying not to take offense at his friend's words. "No, Jacob, think. Would our government incarcerate a law-abiding physician and court-martial a decorated marine officer to get to me? My businesses, legal or illegal, never suffered a bit. None of my people went to jail. What purpose could these persecutions have served? I don't think they would have helped the attorney general at all."

"I would like to believe you, but I find it very hard. Your family has at times helped us. I respect you for that. But your darker nature will always haunt you and those you love, Benjamin. Our government, right or wrong, might destroy innocents to eradicate you for the greater good of society. Your power frightens them, Benjamin. Your power frightens everybody. It would not surprise me to discover that your business associates might be helping them just like they helped the Allies to overthrow Mussolini. Have you thought about that? What other idea could you possibly have that makes more sense than that?" Jacob snapped, rising out of his chair.

"If you calm down, I'll tell you," Busambra, said calmly. "I need your brilliant, analytical mind not your anger and suspicions, Jacob. You're tired. We're tired. If we are to save Xavier and Anthony then we must not waste time misplacing blame. It only puts the ones we love in further peril."

Jacob glared angrily at Busambra for another minute then slowly took his seat. His anger subsiding, he suddenly felt more exhausted than before. He slumped in his chair and stared at the table.

Both men were silent for a moment. Busambra picked up a piece of toast and eyed it, trying to convince himself he was hungry.

"So, you said you have an idea?" Jacob asked, raising his head.

"Possibly. What happened to you and your maid planted the seed. But if it had been plausible, then I'm sure Rizzi would have discovered something by now."

"Did you ever think Rizzi might not want to find out what is happening?" Jacob asked softly. "Every time these troubles happen, you send Rizzi to sort them out, and every time he comes up with nothing."

Busambra started to speak but stopped himself. He pushed some jam onto his toast and looked at it warily. Finally he dropped the toast on his plate and wiped the crumbs from his hands.

"I have thought about Rizzi a lot. But it cannot be so."

"May I ask how you arrived at that conclusion?"

"You have always been on the outside, Jacob. You know very little about my business. Let's say I know things that lead to this conclusion."

"If we are to save our children I think it is best you tell me everything."

"I have been thinking the same thing, my friend," he lied. Jacob, although a dear and loyal friend, wasn't Sicilian and therefore was an outsider. He would never know everything about Busambra's business—only what he allowed the old man to know. "But you are asking me to put you into things you might find distasteful, to say the least. There are risks that go with knowledge, Jacob."

"I realize that. For Zavi's sake, I am willing to take them," Jacob stated, without hesitation.

Busambra nodded his head slightly, acknowledging the doctor's love for his godson.

"Then let us begin," he said, as he paused to collect his thoughts. "Even before Victor ran into his problems in the late seventies, things were beginning to happen. Disturbing things."

"Such as?" Jacob asked.

"Deals went sour at the last minute," Busambra explained. "Loyal members of my family ended up dead. Or worse, vanished without a trace. New markets, both legitimate and illegitimate, were denied to my organization. Taken individually, some might say the incidents were the price paid by a man in my position. I tried to convince myself of that for a long time. The other was too farfetched."

"What other?" Jacob asked.

"That a new organization, intent only on my destruction, was flexing its muscles. An organization connected both to the underworld and the government."

"Not unlike yours, I presume."

"I wish, Jacob. I would know how to deal with it if that were the case. Unfortunately, it is more frightening than that. Let's not kid ourselves. My business was born in the stinking back alleys of Palermo and the treacherous mountains of Sicily. No matter how legitimate I seem, or how well protected I am by my attorneys, I am still, in some ways, a criminal. It has its effects on my power. You see, I am always hunted by the law.

"Our opponent's organization has its origins in the highest echelons of government. It is run by people who can order an innocent man jailed and have a hero court-martialed. The laws which could destroy me can't touch this organization because it is the power behind the law. Yet it reaches into the underworld and can strike at me at will and retreat unscathed."

"But you just said that our government wouldn't do these things, and now you tell me the government's responsible," Jacob responded, exasperated.

"Our principled government wouldn't do such things, Jacob. But one faction or person in the government might."

"What kind of person would do such a thing?" Jacob asked.

"A man with a grudge, Jacob," Busambra explained, looking at Jacob with cold eyes. "Someone with a score to settle."

Jacob and Busambra sat in silence as the cook cleared their dishes and poured them fresh cups of coffee. When she had gone Busambra sipped his coffee while Jacob stared at the table.

"Do you know why my family came to America?" Busambra asked Jacob, changing the subject for a moment.

"Not exactly. I assume you came to America to find a better life, as we all did."

"No, Jacob. My father's family was very powerful in Sicily. His bandits ruled the mountains surrounding Palermo. But there was a war and my father was betrayed. A man named Panzeca, a trusted lieutenant, disclosed the location of their camp to the rival faction. If my father hadn't acted quickly, the Judas goat would have been responsible for the slaughter of dozens. As it was, Panzeca vanished and my father and his people escaped to America."

"Why are you telling me this?"

Busambra ignored Jacob. "Decades later during World War II, a well-liked baker named Litorno lived with his family in Siracusa, a town on the east coast of Sicily. One night they were dragged screaming from their homes by men in black hoods. In the flickering torchlight, the men strapped Litorno to a chair. For hours he watched as the men raped his wife and daughters. Next they dragged his children and grandchildren to where he sat and gutted them like pigs. Then his house and bakery were put to the torch. Finally, the leader burned out his eyes with a hot poker. The last sight Litorno ever saw was the torture and murder of his family."

Jacob had broken into a cold sweat listening to this tale of horror so similar to his own. "Who would do such a horrible thing?"

Busambra looked at Jacob with cold, lifeless eyes. "My father swore an oath that someday Panzeca would suffer for his betrayal. He never forgot it. Not a day went past that he didn't renew his oath. When I came of age he passed on the vendetta to me. And it was I who fulfilled my father's oath that night in Siracusa.

"When I found Panzeca he was living a quiet life in Siracusa as a baker. He should have run farther. Because he didn't, his family suffered the same fate as would have befallen my father's clan but for my father's skill and daring. Most damning of all, Panzeca was left with the knowledge that he had no family left to seek revenge for him and no sight for him to be able to do it himself.

"The circle was completed, the betrayal revenged, and the legend born. Never betray a Busambra lest you suffer the same fate as Panzeca and his family."

"What is the purpose of this story, Benjamin?" Jacob asked, trying to get long-forgotten images out of his mind.

"My Sicilian instincts speak to me. They tell me that our hunter is honoring a vendetta of the same magnitude."

"How can you be so sure?"

"I can't, Jacob. It is what I've felt for a while. But when he went after you, the feeling solidified."

"Why?' Jacob asked.

"Because none of my enemies would go after you. Maybe Victor or Xavier, but never you. None of my competitors would gain financially from your demise and no one in law enforcement could gain any legal leverage over me with a retired doctor. So the answer for our troubles lies elsewhere, Jacob. We must find out why our enemy is after all of us and the answer, I feel, will have nothing to do with *La Cosa Nostra* or the Marine Corps or the IRS."

"Where do we start?"

"To begin, we must hide Xavier. He must disappear from the face of the earth"

Busambra looked at the pained expression on Jacob's face. "Why?"

"Two reasons, Jacob," Busambra answered, finding it hard to believe the words he was about to utter. "Eventually someone would get to him. I'm afraid, after what has transpired, one of my men could be bought or compromised. His disappearance will also force our enemy to expend time and resources hunting him down. Time we will use well.

"You must stay here in New York with me. Rizzi will hunt down the obvious possible enemies to make sure we leave nothing to chance while you and I will chase my ghost."

"How can we do that?" Jacob asked.

Busambra smiled. "We will do what old men do best."

"What can we do better than younger men?" Jacob asked, fearing the answer.

"Think. Daydream. Analyze the life that has passed before. The link is something that happened in our past. We will relive our lives together and you will help me fill in the blanks in Victor's life. It is in the past that we will find our truth and our enemy."

Jacob shivered. Not the past, he thought. Dear God, not there.

Busambra saw the fear on Jacob's face and laid a hand on his arm.

"Trust me, Jacob. It is the only way."

Ritz-Carlton Hotel, Washington, D.C., April 15, 1988

Kruger got out of a taxi on S Street in front of the Textile Museum. He headed west, past Woodrow Wilson House, and turned South on 24th Street, one block from Massachusetts Avenue. The heart of the embassy district. Four square blocks of Massachusetts Avenue were home to twenty-two embassies and legations.

Though the pedestrian traffic had thinned since lunchtime, the sidewalks were still active with people. Just the way Kruger liked: enough people to hide in, not enough to conceal anyone following him.

Instead of continuing to his destination, Kruger cut down Decatur Place past the Egyptian Embassy. For the next thirty minutes, he circled blocks and retraced his footsteps as he searched for a tail. He ducked in doorways and watched the crowd reflected in store windows. He searched the throng of Americans, Koreans, Sudanese and other foreign nationals for any signs of surveillance. Convinced that he hadn't been followed, he crossed Massachusetts Avenue to the Anderson House Museum. He paused once more to be sure before continuing to the famous Ritz-Carlton Hotel.

He entered the suite on the fifth floor using the key he'd picked up in a blind exchange at lunch. The room was dark. The only light came from a small table lamp. Standing by the window, peeking through the drawn curtains was his employer.

"You're an hour late," he snapped, with a disapproving look.

"Sorry, sir. Just making sure I was not followed," he answered in his heavy English.

"I expect the people in my employ to make appointments on time," he chastised. "I've been sitting here with my thumb up my ass when I could have been doing important things. Third party candidate for the presidency, my ass!" the senator snapped, shaking his head. "That bastard Davis out of Texas declared three years ahead of time. People love him. His numbers are already registering in the polls and I have to decide whether or not to join his cause to further mine. Missed lunch with his son Davis Jr., the man who's running the campaign. That does not make me happy. Understood?"

"Yes, senator," Kruger sighed. He took the rebuke in stride. The gentleman from Washington paid him, but didn't control him. Kruger would still take his precautions even if it meant he would be late in the future. The senator needed Kruger worse than Kruger needed him.

The senator clasped his hands behind his back. "Well? Did you find him?"

Kruger ignored the question for the moment. "Do you mind?" he asked, motioning to a chair.

"Of course not," his boss said, impatiently nodding his head. "Just get on with it."

Kruger sat and pulled out a silver cigarette case. His fingers passed over the cigarette containing the cyanide capsule and pulled out another. Snapping the lid shut, he tapped the cigarette on the case until the tobacco was packed. He lit it and inhaled deeply. The senator gazed at Kruger with a look of distaste, but said nothing.

"He's gone," Kruger stated as he exhaled.

"What do you mean gone? Gone where?"

"I do not know. It's really quite frustrating. Xavier Daniels has vanished into thin air."

"That's not possible. He has to be somewhere."

"Well, of course he does, Senator. But where that somewhere is…your guess is as good as mine."

"Guess? I don't pay you to guess. What about our source inside the Busambra organization?"

"Nothing, Sir. Sorry. The Sicilian told me that Don Busambra handled Xavier's disappearance personally. He trusted no one with the information."

"What about the Jew, Rabinowitz? Can we get to the Jew?"

"Not likely. For the moment Dr. Rabinowitz is holed up in the Busambra compound. That place is guarded like a fortress. Unfortunately, we will have to wait for another window of opportunity."

"And how long before that happens?"

"Days, months, years. Who knows? Busambra has covered his tracks well. To try anything now would be extremely rash. We could risk exposure. I know how badly you want this, Senator. But I would recommend caution at this point."

"Kruger. You have no idea how badly I want this. My father lay on his deathbed muttering their names. I'll never forget it." The powerful man hung his head at the memory.

"This obsession could destroy all the work you've done so far."

His head snapped up. "Obsession? No, Kruger, not obsession. Obligation. An obligation writ in stone. Never forget it. And never forget that my father is responsible for all the work I've done, all the work they could have destroyed. Believe me when I say his memory demands revenge."

Kruger stared at the maniacal look on the face of the senator. He was fairly raging. Kruger was glad Xavier had dropped out of sight. This whole business unhinged the senator whenever it came up. Now, maybe, they could focus on more important things.

"I will continue the search, of course, Senator," Kruger said, lightly massaging the scar on his face with his forefinger.

"Of course, you will, Kruger. You'll find him, goddamnit. You'll find him if it's the last thing you do."

Kruger began to speak, but the senator abruptly raised his hand ending the conversation. Turning his back on the mercenary, he peeled back the curtain and gazed at the street below. Consumed with anger, Kruger's mercurial boss had retreated into his own world.

Kruger watched the senator, his right hand clenching and unclenching slowly while he muttered something repeatedly under his breath. When Kruger was finished with his cigarette, he left the senator to his quiet ravings.

PART II
Exile

5

Nicaragua, April 21, 1988

Xavier's car raced toward the fishing village of Tuapi on Nicaragua's eastern coast. Having left his deceased wife, incinerated business, hopes, and dreams behind him, all that remained was a question: who was responsible for it all?

His escape had begun five days earlier. From Baltimore, he caught a flight to Mexico City. The next morning, he hopped a Mexicana Airways flight to Managua, Nicaragua, and hopefully safety.

Landing at Sabena Grande, outside of Managua, he'd stepped off the plane into an alien world. As the door of the jet opened, the heat hit him like a blast furnace. It was worse than anything he had experienced in Panama, Sicily, or even the California desert. The heat was good for one thing: it took his mind off customs.

His godfather had supplied him with a new identity before leaving New York. Xavier worried it wouldn't stand up under scrutiny. When he presented his passport to the agent, the man barely paused. All he saw was a fellow Nicaraguan who had spent too much time in a cooler climate. His papers passed with a cursory inspection. Luis Castillo, citizen of Nicaragua, had returned home.

By the time he had collected his bag and found the appropriate bus, he was dripping wet. He sat in the un-air-conditioned bus for an hour before the packed vehicle lurched into traffic and onto Highway One. The bus headed north, skirting the Lago de Managua until it reached Tipitapa, where it turned northwest into the jungle.

His fellow passengers tolerated the heat stoically. The mixture of farmers, laborers, and Sandinista soldiers spent the trip talking and napping. The children laughed at the monkeys playing in the trees and pointed at colorful birds overhead. A few passengers wrote poetry and exchanged their verse with others. Xavier remembered his nanny Maria writing poetry. She said every Nicaraguan was a poet. Poetry was the national obsession.

El pais de las poetas, he thought. The land of the poets.

Arriving at Matagalpa late, they stopped for the night. Xavier found himself calmed by the *"bien fresco,"* the cool air Matagalpa was known for. He found a small room for the evening and collapsed on the bed for a few hours of restless sleep.

In the morning, the overloaded bus had barely reached the edge of town when it broke down. Due to the U.S. embargo, parts were in short supply and the bus could not be fixed until the following day. Frustrated, Xavier found another room. After lunch, despite his concussion, he purchased a couple of *refrescos* from a street vendor and spent the rest of the day exploring.

Outside the ancient temple, Xavier noticed a large contingent of *compas,* a slang term for anyone wearing Sandinista militia or police uniforms. Matagalpa had been the political base of Jorge Salazar, the charismatic leader of the coffee growers' cooperative. Hard-line Sandinistas, aware of his popularity among the populace, had him assassinated in November of 1980. The Matagalpans, still refused to come completely under the Sandinista banner, thus the armed presence. The citizens ignored them and put up posters of Salazar as fast as the militia could tear them down. Children wrote poems about the martyr.

Xavier was amazed at the fervor with which the Nicaraguans worshiped their heroes: Sandino, Dario, Chamorro; freedom fighter, poet, martyred journalist. The names were uttered with reverence and passion. Maria had filled him with stories of the men and women of Nicaragua when he was a child. Now he was witnessing it. The stories matched the reality.

For the most part, Xavier kept to himself, ate sparingly of the native cuisine, and spoke even less. He was wary of his physical health and his unpracticed Spanish. To tamper with either was dangerous until he reached his destination.

In the morning, his headache from the concussion had diminished noticeably, although he still felt weak and dizzy. To his relief, the bus was repaired and his journey continued.

They drove through the mountains on Highway Five. The bus carried the latest arrivals on the roof with the baggage and caged livestock. Top-heavy, it pitched precariously on its overloaded suspension. Xavier's gorge rose in his throat several times as the bus narrowly missed careening off the highway and over a cliff. The driver always managed to veer away in time and the other passengers took no notice.

At midday they passed through El Tuma, and Xavier noticed a subtle change in the passengers. They became quiet and introspective. The bus entered the huge, unpopulated area that separated eastern and western Nicaragua.

Some said the wilderness was haunted. Others claimed it was inhabited by huge beasts, half-man and half-animal. Dark and forbidding, the interior brought out a sense of dread in the passengers. Xavier understood how it had given rise to such fantastic legends.

The day seemed darker and the jungle more imposing. Not even the playful monkeys were to be seen. He sensed a sinister presence lurking behind the wall of the jungle. Xavier felt he was being watched and he was reminded of the unseen forces that had hounded him to this corner of the world. He shivered involuntarily several times and silently urged the bus driver onward.

Toward evening Xavier was startled awake; heart pounding, he realized he'd dozed off. As he caught his bearings the sound of a high-pitched whistle floated from the jungle. The sound changed to a wailing and then a scream that could have come from a woman. Several passengers crossed themselves. A woman sitting across the aisle gazed into Xavier's eyes with a haunted expression. *"La Segua,"* she explained, crossing herself and praying. *La Segua.* Maria had spoken of the evil spirit, some said descended of a bitter, scorned woman, who hypnotized her prey and ate their flesh.

Xavier felt a sense of relief when they approached the City of La Luz, the light. It was an appropriate name for the city at the end of a long, dark tunnel of primitive jungle.

They passed through Tunki and rolled into La Rosita at nightfall. Exhausted, Xavier paid for his room and went to sleep without eating. For the first time since Min's death, he had a dreamless sleep.

Starving when he woke, he ate a hearty meal of *gallo pinto* (red beans and rice), chicken, and corn tortillas at an outdoor cafe. Feeling healthy for the first time in two weeks, he boarded a new bus, anxious to get to his destination.

Xavier noticed there weren't many passengers on this bus. Their destination was Puerto Cabezas on the Caribbean Sea. The port was seventy miles from the Honduran border. Even though a temporary cease-fire had been brokered with the Contras, most people stayed away from the border region. The Sandinistas were unpredictable and the Contras were untrustworthy.

Most of the passengers on this leg of the trip were Indians rather than *mestizos*. They were nearing the Atlantic Coast, home of the Miskito, Rama, and Sumo Indians. They were proud and independent people who hated both the Contras and the Sandinistas. In personality, they were as open as the *mestizos* from the west. One friendly Miskito insisted on sharing his midday meal with Xavier. Late in the afternoon, they crossed the Wawa River and arrived in Puerto Cabezas. Xavier welcomed the pleasant ocean breeze. When he stepped off the bus, he stood at the side of the road trying to look inconspicuous. Passengers greeted relatives, unloaded baggage, and went about their business. In a matter of minutes, the only people left standing next to the empty bus were Xavier and a skinny Miskito.

Xavier instinctively avoided the man's stare, thinking he might be a beggar or vendor. He had little money to spend either way, but the Indian stood his ground. When Xavier picked up his bag to leave, the man quickly blocked his way.

"*Señor* Castillo?" he asked.

Xavier stared at the man for a minute before reading the sign he was holding in front of him. It had the name Luis Castillo printed on it.

"*Señor* Castillo?" the little man asked again, winking his eye and smiling.

It hit Xavier all at once.

"*Con permiso, Señor. Yo soy* Luis Castillo," he answered. Xavier's face flushed in embarrassment.

The man leaned close to Xavier. "I'd stick to English, *Señor* Castillo," he said in perfect English tinged with a Texas accent. "Your Spanish accent leaves a lot to be desired." He lowered his voice as the bus driver passed by. "And your grammar sucks."

"Thanks, my friend. You're doing my confidence a world of good," Xavier muttered under his breath, watching the bus driver climb on the bus.

"No problem," he said, smiling ear to ear. He offered his hand to Xavier. "Huberto Royo. At your service."

"You already know who I am," Xavier said, returning the shake. "What's next?"

"Your limousine, *Señor*." Huberto picked up Xavier's bag and led him up the street to an old Chevrolet. The sedan was beat to hell. The paint might have been green, but Xavier couldn't tell through the grime and the rust. The windshield was cracked into a large spider web, inhibiting visibility. But the most remarkable characteristic of the vehicle was its lack of doors. They got in and sped off in a cloud of dust, Madonna blaring from the stereo. As they raced out of town, Xavier frantically searched for a seat belt.

"What are your looking for, Luis?"

"A seat belt. Don't you have any seat belts in here?" Xavier shouted to be heard above the deafening music and the wind roaring in through the doorless sedan.

"Who needs seat belts," Huberto laughed as he sped around a corner, almost tossing Xavier out of the car.

"We should be in Tuapi in no time, *Señor*."

"No doubt," Xavier answered remorsefully as he hung on for dear life. This was worse than the bus ride in the mountains. Huberto laughed at Xavier's predicament.

"Relax, *Señor*," Huberto yelled as he stuck his head out of the car to see where they were going. "I haven't lost anybody yet." He pulled his head back in the car satisfied that for the moment he wasn't going to crash into anything.

True to his word, they arrived in the sleepy fishing village shortly thereafter. Huberto stopped the car in front of a small but clean cottage on the beach. Xavier hesitated before getting out of the car.

"Where did you learn to speak English so well?"

Huberto smiled at the compliment, realizing at the same time that Xavier was stalling, trying to make conversation. "At school here in the village and after that at the university."

"In Managua?" Xavier asked.

"No, *Señor*. Lubbock. Texas Tech."

"Amazing."

"Not really, Luis. You have a lot to learn. But now is not the time," he said. "It's been a long time since you've seen her?"

"Yes, Huberto. A very long time." He turned to Huberto, whose head was bobbing knowingly. Xavier found himself hesitant to complete the last few steps of his journey.

"She is in good health, Luis. And she is waiting for you," he said, offering his hand.

Xavier shook it and got out of the car. "Thanks for the ride, Huberto. *Muchas gracias.*"

"Remember to work on that accent. And any time you need a ride, let me know."

"How about getting some seat belts?"

"Who needs them?" Huberto answered, roaring off. Madonna's voice faded in the dust leaving Xavier alone and apprehensive.

Xavier turned and looked at the house. The woman inside the house had raised him from the time he was only a couple of years old. Her love had softened his real mother's total indifference to him. His nanny had been the saving grace of his childhood, praising when his mother insulted, healing when his father abused him. After a moment, he picked up his bag and walked up the steps to the porch. Instead of knocking, he opened the door. After all, with her here, this was his home.

Xavier found her on the back veranda which overlooked the ocean. She was standing by the rail watching the fishing boats bring in the evening's catch. She looked so small.

"Maria?" he asked softly, not wanting to startle her.

She turned to him. Her face had more lines and her hair more gray, but she was the same. As she opened her arms, Xavier dropped his bag and bent to her embrace.

"Javier. *Mi niño*, Javier," she cried as she hugged him. "You've come to your Maria. How I've missed you."

Xavier returned her hug then held her at arm's length. There were tears streaming down her face. "Don't cry, Maria."

"If an old woman wants to cry, then let an old woman cry."

"You're not so old, Maria," he said smiling.

"You're not so young anymore, Javier," she laughed through her tears.

Xavier paused, taking in the moment. "It's good to see you."

She smiled and hugged him again. After a time she turned him toward the ocean. The setting sun turned the clouds into a fiery explosion of purple, pink, and orange. The breeze blew gently across the porch, carrying the smell of the sea. Crashing surf, bird cries, the calls of the fishermen all blended into a symphony that perfectly scored the amazing view.

"Your new home, Javier," Maria Escalante said quietly. "*Nuestra casa*."

Our house indeed, Xavier thought.

They stood that way until the sun went down.

6

"You're doing marginally better, Mr. Busambra," the doctor commented. He scribbled a note in Anthony's chart.

"Then how come I still feel like shit, Doc," Anthony remarked, twisting in his hospital bed as he tried to get comfortable. "You said I'd be ready to get out of here soon."

"You are resilient. You survived the gunshot, the perforated artery, and the blood loss even though it put you into a coma for two weeks. You came out of the coma without any detectable brain damage and beat the pneumonia you contracted while unconscious. Very good."

"Still, you have some symptoms from a secondary infection. You pick at your food with the full knowledge that I want you at a certain weight before I feel comfortable ordering your release. And rest would also assist your recovery, but you refuse to take the pain medication as prescribed."

The doctor snapped Anthony's chart shut and eyed the stricken mafioso. "I can only get you so far. If you'd help me with the rest, then I'd be able to get you out of here much quicker. But we've been over all this, haven't we, Mr. Busambra?"

Anthony stared at the doctor and narrowed his eyes. "I know where your family lives," he replied in his most sinister voice.

The doctor shook his head as if he'd heard it all before. "You should. It's not very far from your father's house. So what's it going to be young man?"

"You're a real bastard, Doc. All right. I'll eat my fucking vegetables and get some fucking sleep. You happy?" Anthony asked, sarcastically.

"How could anyone be pleased after being addressed in such a manner?" Don Bennedetto Busambra asked, as he came through the door. A bodyguard seated at the foot of Anthony's bed jumped to his feet.

"Sorry, Papa," Anthony said, seeing his father. A slight smile crossed his lips. "What kept you so long?"

"Business, Anthony," Busambra responded, returning the smile. "I am sorry to interrupt, Doctor, please continue."

"I'm finished, Don Bennedetto. He's all yours."

"The prognosis?" Busambra asked.

"The same as before, Don Bennedetto. With a little nutrition and rest I could release him in a few days."

Busambra's smile vanished. "You'll do as the doctor says, Anthony," Busambra ordered, sternly.

Anthony stared angrily at the foot of the bed.

"I'll see you on my evening rounds," the doctor said to Anthony. He nodded at Busambra and left the room.

The bodyguard pulled his chair to the side of the bed for the don and followed the doctor.

Busambra sat, shaking his head.

"Why do you not listen to the doctor?" he asked exasperated. "It is simple to eat and sleep."

"Papa. Every time I try to eat, my stomach turns at the thought of what those bastards did to Tiny and Min," he replied, through gritted teeth. He turned and grabbed his father's arm. "And I can't sleep because I worry about your safety."

Busambra patted Anthony's hand, reassuringly. "You must not worry about me, Son. Luca shadows me day and night and I am surrounded by dozens of our best soldiers. As for our enemies, Rizzi is hunting them down.

Anthony turned away, a disgusted look on his face. "Rizzi. Always Rizzi. I should be protecting you, Papa. I should be hunting down our enemies."

"Rizzi is *consigliere* to this family, Anthony. These are the things a *consigliere* does."

"And I am your heir, Papa. It is time we show these pigs that the son is as strong as the father. Give me the power to protect you. Let everyone know that I am to succeed you."

"It is not time yet, Anthony. You are a target as it is," Bennedetto acknowledged, sorrowfully. "If I were to confirm you as the successor then they, whoever they are, would come after you even harder."

"No, Papa. Confirming me would strengthen our position. Right now, if I was to be killed it would weaken your position. With no heir, the bosses on the commission would begin to jockey for position to take over after you died. A war would be inevitable. War weakens us. The FBI and those fucks in the attorney general's office would feast on us.

"And if you die without naming me as your heir, then who is to say the bosses on the commission would follow me? Again a war would come as the greedy bastards fought each other and me for control of your empire. Who is to say I would survive?"

Busambra slumped in his chair. Anthony saw confusion on his face, maybe even fear. Not now, Anthony thought. We are too vulnerable.

Anthony grasped the railing on the side of the bed. He grimaced in pain as he sat up and turned to his father. "Don Bennedetto Busambra, you are one of the most powerful men in history. You are *il capo di tuti capi. La Cosa Nostra* exists because of you. Name me as your successor and give me the power to help save the family before it is too late."

Anthony collapsed back on his bed with a grunt. Busambra stood over him and held his hand.

"You are too weak to take on the duty at this time," Busambra replied. "When you are better we will talk again about the succession. Right now, I fear you have lost too much to think clearly about what has happened."

Anthony looked at his father through eyes heavy with exhaustion. "I have lost? It is true Tiny is gone and I was almost killed. But what of Xavier? He lost a wife, his father, his business, his career. If I know Xavier, then he is hellbent on trying to avenge Min. Do you counsel him to wait until his thinking clears?"

"I have sent Xavier away for his own protection."

"Where?" Anthony asked, surprised.

"Where no one can find him," Busambra answered quietly.

"And you don't trust me with this knowledge?" Anthony asked, amazed. "Xavier and I grew up as brothers. You can trust me with his life. I know I could trust him with mine. Together we would be unstoppable."

Busambra's silence was his answer.

"So this is what we have come to, Papa. The two people in the world who would give their lives trying to protect you, the two who have more reason than anyone to seek revenge are forced to hide like women."

Busambra turned away too disturbed to look at his wounded son.

Anthony shut his eyes, exhausted. He gripped the sheet and twisted it with all his might trying to tear it apart. All he succeeded in doing was pulling it off of his feet. Frustrated at his weakness he dropped the sheet.

They are right about one thing, he thought. I am too weak to function. If I am to prevent a disaster then I have to get out of here.

He buzzed the nurse.

"Yes, Mr. Busambra?"

"Bring me some fucking food and something to help me sleep when I'm done. *Now*," he shouted. I'll do what they say for now, he thought. And then we'll see.

Anthony turned to look at his father, but Busambra wouldn't meet his gaze. Unable to get any answers to his many questions, he closed his eyes and waited for the nurse.

Thoughts flooded his mind. His father's age, the family's weaknesses, his own brush with death, and the enemy that was hunting them. And he thought of Xavier.

I'd like to find you, Xavier, he thought. But for now I have to stay close to Papa.

Anthony wondered if Xavier was obeying his father's orders.

Or are you plotting like me, Xavier, preparing for the storm that must surely come?

Tuapi, Nicaragua, May 12, 1988

Xavier stared at the sand-filled duffel bag hanging from the palm tree. He gasped as he tried to recover his breath. Standing in the sun, drenched in sweat, he thought of Min. Anger boiling over, he approached the bag and swung at it with all his might. The bag barely moved. Enraged, he hammered it with a vicious combination of blows. The bag hung from the tree motionless.

Xavier snapped. He bellowed and launched himself at the bag with a reverse spin kick. His foot connected but his center of gravity was too high. Xavier completely misjudged his landing and plowed into the sand face first.

Gentle laughter and clapping. Xavier spit sand from his mouth and raised his head.

"Maria, *por favor.*"

She continued to chuckle.

"Please have some respect," Xavier pleaded.

"If Min were here she'd be laughing, too," Maria remarked.

"Have some respect for the dead, Maria," he barked.

"I do," she answered, sternly. "Maybe it's time you should have some respect for yourself."

Xavier rolled over and stood up. He raised his finger, ready to tell her off, but stopped. The pleasant smile on Maria's face had settled into a disapproving frown.

Been there, done that, he thought. Not a good thing to upset Maria Escalante.

Xavier dropped his head and sat on the beach. "You're not happy with me?"

"I'm not happy with what you are doing to yourself, Javier," she explained. "There was a time when you could move the bag at will. Even when you were young, Master Kim was impressed with your ability."

Xavier looked up at the mention of his former martial arts instructor. "You liked Master Kim."

"Yes I did. He taught you well."

"And now I am trying to put those teachings to good use, yet you disapprove?" Xavier asked narrowing his eyes.

"*Sí*. I disapprove. You flail about. Your hands bleed. You exhaust yourself. How does this help you, *niño?*"

"I was injured, Maria. I am just trying to get back in shape. It takes my mind off of Min," Xavier explained.

Maria paused, leaning forward. She cocked her head and raised an eyebrow.

"*No creo*," she spoke disbelieving.

"You don't believe what?" he asked.

"I can't believe you lied to me, *hijo*," Maria responded, shaking her head.

"I didn't lie," Xavier snapped back defensively.

"*Un otro!*" she exclaimed. "You lie to me again. I raised you better than that, Javier."

"I just don't want to hurt you, Maria."

"So, there is a worse hurt than lying?" she asked disgusted.

Xavier glared at her and then turned and stared out to sea. "As soon as I have my strength back, I am leaving."

"And where will you go?" Maria asked quietly. "Where will you go against the wishes of your godfathers? Where will you go against my wishes?

"To find Min's killer," he spoke, anger mixed with guilt.

"And after you have defied those who love you, where will you find this *hombre malo?*" she asked, voice rising.

"Anywhere he fucking is, goddamnit!" Xavier shouted coming to his feet. "Why do you try to stop me? What do you know of my loss?"

"More than you will ever know!" Maria raged back. "My country has been torn apart by civil war. I have lost dozens of friends and suffered things you know nothing about!"

"Maybe you can sit by and watch these things happen, but I cannot. I will not!"

"*Bastante!*" Maria shouted. "*Enough*, Javier. Lower your voice and sit down."

Xavier slowly sat on the sand shaking from his rage.

"I will forgive you your lies and your rudeness because you are grieving the loss of your wife. But, so help me, *Madre de Dios*, I will never forgive you if you leave here and get yourself killed," she said with iron in her voice.

"You ask me to forget Min's death, Maria. You ask me to dishonor her memory by letting her murderer go unpunished."

"I ask you to be patient, Javier. That is all."

"If I wait, Maria, then the murderer will escape."

Maria spoke the brutal truth. "Min's murderer has already escaped, *pobrecito*. He has vanished and you know it as well as I."

Xavier sighed, his shoulders slumping, as he accepted the awful truth. Both sat in silence as their anger subsided.

"Remember Master Kim's trick with the ball and the string?" Maria asked after a moment.

Xavier responded without looking up. "Sure. He was mad because I wasn't listening during class."

"He wasn't mad, Xavier. You wanted to know everything at once and in your impatience you weren't learning anything."

"I wanted to impress him."

Maria nodded her head. "Your desire got in your way, though. So Master Kim gave you a simple lesson to master. Remember? He tied a string to the little rubber ball and twirled it over his head."

"Yeah," Xavier remembered. "He looked like a cowboy with a lasso."

"*Un caballero, sí.* And what was the lesson?"

"He told me he wouldn't teach me any more until I could catch the ball."

The whole experience was coming back to him. The frustration as he chased the ball round and round. The scrapes and bruises every time he lunged for it, missed and fell to the floor, Master Kim and Maria laughing at his frustration.

"And what finally happened?" Maria asked.

Xavier smiled. "One day I stopped, turned, and caught the ball when it came around."

"Yes, Javier. And after that day you progressed faster than any pupil he'd had before. Remember?"

Xavier did remember. He remembered the smell of the *dojo*; bamboo, sweat, and burning incense. He remembered the stern, disciplined instruction of his *sensei* Master Kim, tempered always with patience and, in time, love. Most of all, he remembered Maria clapping at his achievements and encouraging him after his failures.

"You were always there, Maria," he offered.

"I am still here, Javier."

"What you ask is difficult," he intoned, taking a deep breath.

"I only ask that you trust me."

She's never let me down, he thought. Never.

Xavier stood and crossed the sand to Maria. He bent over and hugged her gently. Backing away he placed his hands on her shoulders and looked into her eyes.

"So now what do I do?" he asked.

"Get a job," she said, standing. "My friend Oscar owns a boat. You will be a fisherman," she said with finality.

"What do I know about fishing?" Xavier asked exasperated.

Maria waved her arm toward the village. "You see any helicopters to fly? Hard, simple work will help to heal your mind as well as your body. In time, you will practice what Master Kim taught you as well. These things will prepare you."

"For what, Maria?"

Maria looked at him with all the love and strength she could muster.

"For when the ball comes around, Javier."

7

Miskito Coast, Eastern Nicaragua, November 15, 1988

The boat listed to port as Xavier and Pedro Muller hauled in the bulging net. Oscar Reyes, the captain of the small vessel, cursed them good-naturedly as they dragged the day's catch on board. Once the net was in the boat, Xavier drew his knife and cut it open. A mass of live fish spilled into the boat, leaping and squirming everywhere.

Xavier and Pedro quickly culled the desired fish from the net and threw back the rest. The gulls and terns surrounding the boat began to feed on the throwbacks with noisy vigor.

They packed the fish in ice and prepared for the return trip to Tuapi. Pedro set the sails and Oscar manned the rudder for the journey home. Xavier's total lack of sailing aptitude was a constant source of amusement to his mates. Under the usual barrage of insults, he finished stowing the nets and settled into the bow for the ride home. He pulled a bottle of water from his stash in the ice. Rubbing the icy glass over his forehead, he relished the relief from the heat. The wind blew through his hair, adding to his comfort. But even with cool breezes, ice cold water, and frequent rain showers, Xavier couldn't escape the heat.

Eastern Nicaragua had no seasons. It was always hot and wet. After several weeks of acclimating he could endure the heat without trouble, but he could never accept it as the natives did.

Despite the heat, Xavier enjoyed his life in Tuapi. The work was enjoyably physical, rhythmic in its simplicity; the people he'd met welcomed him as family; and the food was delightful. And there was Maria. Without her he could not have made it through the first months without Min.

Maria knew his moods; she accepted his long silences and tolerated his outbursts. She allowed him to grieve and heal in his own time. But she was ever present, full of love and strength.

After Oscar beached the boat, Xavier and Pedro dragged it up on shore. When it was tied down for the night, they unloaded heavy tubs of fish and ice and carried them to the road where trucks from the local fish combine waited to take them to market. Oscar dismissed his crew and stayed to haggle with the combine manager about prices.

Xavier traversed the beach, splashing in the surf as he exchanged greetings with his neighbors. This was the time of day he enjoyed the most. When he got home he would sit on the patio and watch night fall while the ocean breeze dried his skin from his evening shower. Maria would bring him a *refresco* and they would share the dying day in silence. After sunset they would enjoy dinner together before Xavier met his friends at the local *cantina*.

When he arrived at the house, he stripped and stepped into the shower stall at the side of the house. He bathed energetically in the tepid water and emerged dripping wet. Xavier grabbed for the towel Maria always left out for him, but it was not in its usual place. He searched the ground and couldn't find it.

It's only a towel, he thought. She just forgot to put it out.

Xavier couldn't calm down. Maria had created a consistent environment for him, a routine. The predictability helped him repair his shattered spirit. Moreover, Maria loved routine; it was so out of character for her to leave a thing undone that he couldn't help but panic.

Xavier wrapped his shirt around his waist and took the steps to the veranda two at a time. He leapt over the final three and stood under the awning, staring at a stranger sitting in Maria's chair. She stood and smiled.

"I'm Dr. Elena Figueres," she said in English.

"*Dónde está Maria?*" he interrupted in Spanish. He took a step toward the woman. "Where is Maria?" he asked again.

"She has stepped out for a moment," the lady replied, smiling, trying to set him at ease.

"Where? She never 'steps out' at this time of day." Xavier left the doctor standing on the patio and raced through the house searching for Maria. She was nowhere to be found.

Have they discovered where I am, he thought. Have they taken Maria? His mounting anger was so thick it almost choked him. Maria could be shot like Min, blown up like Annie Lee. Not this time, he thought as he returned to the veranda. I won't let you.

He walked to where she stood and grabbed her by the throat, lifting her off her feet.

"Where is Maria?" When she didn't answer he slammed her into one of the supports holding up the awning. Dust fell off the cross beams onto their shoulders.

"Where is she, you bitch?" he snarled. "What have you done with Maria?"

The doctor was too terrified to answer. She felt her face turning red, her head spinning from the blow and from lack of air.

"I'll kill you," he stated, pushing her head back. "Tell me what you've done to her or I'll break your fucking neck."

The woman's arms flailed at him helplessly. Her eyes were glazing over when Xavier heard a soft voice behind him.

"Javier. Put her down!" Maria Escalante ordered. "She is a friend, Javier. Put her down now!"

Xavier slowly relaxed his grip and lowered the woman to her feet. Maria grabbed his wrists and pulled him away from her. Unsupported, the doctor collapsed on the floor coughing and gasping for breath. Maria knelt by her side and brushed the hair out of her face.

Xavier took several steps back. The rage evaporated as quickly as it had come. His face relaxed and the snarl disappeared. He looked at his hands. They were trembling. He stared at the two women with a questioning look on his face.

"Javier. Get some water and put on some clothes," Maria admonished.

Xavier glanced down and realized he was completely naked. His shirt was gone. He shook his head and blushed violently. Turning, he walked into the house.

They sat on the patio in silence. Night had fallen. Maria lit candles and made tea. The peaceful sound of the surf contrasted with the earlier violence.

Elena Figueres was the first to speak. She leaned forward in her chair and set her cup on the table. Smoothing her skirt, she looked at Xavier.

"I am sorry about what happened earlier," she began. "Considering what you've been through, I should have been more careful. I shouldn't have surprised you."

Xavier's only response was to look at Maria before he turned his gaze back at the ocean.

"Maybe I should go and come back tomorrow," Elena said. She got up to leave. Xavier rose also. Their eyes met.

"Please, sit down, Dr. Figueres."

She hesitated and then nodded her head before retaking her seat.

"I came close to killing you," Xavier said. He swallowed heavily before continuing. "I don't know what came over me. I just…" he paused, unable to find the correct words. "I just didn't want it to happen again," he finished.

"It was my fault, Javier," Maria offered. Xavier held up his hand and smiled at her.

"No, Maria. The only fault is mine. I've been trained to control my rage. I have no excuse," he said simply, looking at his feet.

They were silent again. Maria refilled their cups. This time it was Xavier who broke the silence.

"Doctor. You referred to what happened to me. That leads me to believe Maria has spoken to you about how I came to be in Tuapi."

"Javier. I wanted to tell you," Maria sputtered, guiltily. She had placed her trust in God when she violated the trust of Xavier's godfathers. She prayed for forgiveness.

"It's all right, Maria. It's O.K.," he spoke in a reassuring voice. Turning to Elena he said, "Maria knows I am in danger. If she trusts you, then I have no reason not to."

"Elena is here to ask our help, Javier," Maria explained, confidence returning. "To ask your help. I told her you were a good man, a strong man, but that you had suffered a great deal, and are still in danger. She has traveled all the way from Managua to speak to you. Please hear her out."

Xavier looked at Maria a minute before turning to Elena. "What do you want from me, Doctor?"

"To do what you do best, *Señor*," she answered.

"And what would that be?"

"To fly a helicopter," she responded with a look of intrigue.

The candlelight flashed in her eyes, eyes Xavier found himself looking into for the first time. They were a beautiful dark blue, extremely intelligent and very, very serious.

The dishes from the evening meal were done. Xavier had picked at his pan-fried fish and coconut bread. Elena waited anxiously for his reply.

Xavier thought about Elena's proposal. He reviewed the brief Nicaraguan history lesson she had given him during dinner. The thought of flying again pleased him immensely, but his personal mission precluded any involvement in Elena's plan. Deciding, he gave her his answer.

"I can't help you."

There it is, she thought. A plain and simple answer.

Xavier watched her back stiffen. She was a proud woman, and a desperate one. Xavier truly regretted not being able to help her.

"Surely you see the situation we are in," Elena responded. "We have to have your help."

"There have to be a hundred other men who could do the job," he shot back. "You need to look for someone else."

"We don't have time to look for someone else, *Señor*. There are not a hundred other helicopter pilots with your training who are not known to the government. You are our only hope. Please. We need your help," she pleaded.

"If I'm your only hope then you're shit out of luck, lady. You saw what happened to me. What almost happened to you. You don't need my help. You need a man who has control of his emotions. Someone who won't go off half-cocked. I appreciate your position, but I can't help you," he stated again, emphasizing the last four words.

"I don't see how you can appreciate our position," she snapped and immediately fought to gain control of herself. "I'm sorry. It's just that I...we want so badly to make a difference. Have you heard nothing I've said?"

"I've heard everything you said. You want to make a difference? How? Tell me that," he said, sitting up in his chair. He waved his arms around the room. "Look around you, Lady. You've got Cubans and East Germans crawling all over Puerto Cabezas in control of the air base and the port. The Sandinistas walked into a Moravian Church in Prinzapolka and shot four Miskitos at worship, for Christ's sake! The Contras don't fight the Sandinistas. They much prefer shooting up buses of innocent peasants and burning crops.

"Hell, the east coast hates the west coast. The Sandinistas hate the Contras. The Miskitos hate the Cubans. And the Church, the one constant the people turn to for guidance, is having a theological civil war between the politicized liberationists and old-line conservatives. Pulling the strings in this merry little hell you call Nicaragua are the two big brothers, Uncle Sam and the big, bad Russian bear," he said, leaning back in his chair and dropping his hands in his lap. "I listened to everything you said. And, believe me, I'd like to help, but this thing is too big for the both of us. My suggestion is to forget the whole thing, Lady, and go back to your practice in Managua."

"Unfortunately, Mr. Daniels, I can't put aside my whole country for my personal satisfaction. I have a conscience. I only hoped you had one, too." Elena stood abruptly. "Tell me, *Señor*. Do you really believe our cause is hopeless, or do you think that it would stand in the way of your personal plans for revenge?"

Xavier's face colored in anger. "That is none of your damn business. Now get the hell out of our house!"

Elena turned to Maria. "I am sorry for disturbing your evening, *tia* Maria. I only hoped that the son of the great Dr. Danielson would care about us as much as his father."

Xavier looked at Maria suspiciously. "What does she mean about Dad?"

"Elena, please," Maria pleaded. Elena ignored her.

"You don't know, do you?" she asked.

"Know what?"

"Your father built this house for Maria. The clinic in town was a gift from him. Dozens of people from Tuapi received college educations because of his generosity. I myself went into medicine to honor him. He paid for my education. And you didn't know," she said, shaking her head. "The revered son. I am glad he didn't live to see this day. A Danielson turning down a plea for help. No wonder you became a soldier instead of a healer. No wonder you changed your name from his. Your heart is only big enough for your selfish interests, Mr. Daniels," she spat.

She hugged Maria and left without another word. As soon as she was out of the house, Maria went to Xavier.

"I'm sorry, Javier. Please forgive me," she asked, clasping his hands.

"There is nothing to forgive, Maria," he replied gently. He looked around the patio. "So, Dad built you this house?"

"Yes, Javier."

"And the clinic in town?"

"Yes," Maria answered.

"I don't understand. He beat me when he discovered Uncle Jake taking me to synagogue, yet he built you a house and a clinic for the village and sent people to college I never met."

Maria sighed. "You are not the only one confused by your father's actions. I can never forgive him for the things he did to you, Javier. But I love him for what he did for my village and its people."

Xavier shook his head, disbelieving. "Even here, I can't escape his memory."

"Then maybe it is time you try to understand your father," Maria offered.

"Why?" Xavier snapped.

"To find your peace with him."

"There will never be peace between my father and me," Xavier stated flatly. "I find it hard to fathom how you and Jacob can live so easily with what he did."

"Prayer has been my salvation, Javier. I cannot answer for Jacob, but soon you can put the question to him."

"What do you mean?"

"I've had a letter from him. He's coming to see you in a few days. He said he'd promised to sit with you, to help you grieve in the Jewish way for Min. He was sorry he couldn't come sooner, but Don Bennedetto has insisted on every precaution to ensure your safety."

Xavier felt overrun with emotions. His rage and defensive anger after Elena's attack, shame for not agreeing to help her combined with deep sorrow at the thought of sitting *shivah* for Min. Relief that it would be with Jacob.

"After Jacob's visit we will talk again, Javier. We will talk of your father and Min. We will also talk about Elena Figueres and her request."

Xavier looked at Maria and was reminded of the strength that resided in the petite woman.

"It's not just her request, is it, Maria?"

"No, Javier. Nicaragua is my country, too."

Tuapi, November 23, 1988

Xavier sat out on the porch in front of the house, watching the morning sky. Every day for a week he'd come out to watch the sun rise. Jacob's efforts to help him grieve made him yearn even harder for revenge against Min's killers. Xavier found little peace in the traditions of his people.

He was still anxious to speak to Jacob alone about his father. There had been too many people around since Jacob had arrived to have a long talk. Now that everyone had gone he had his chance, but he didn't know how to bring it up. He wasn't sure he wanted to hear anything good about his father. He'd hated him so long that he felt forgiveness was impossible.

Maria had known about his feelings for years. She'd suggested that he might come to understand his father better, even if he couldn't forgive him. But there were too many mysteries.

How could his father love the Nicaraguans so much and still hate his own son? Why had Xavier's Jewish studies always set his father off?

He resented his father for so many things. Even though he adored his godfather, Uncle Benny, he hated his father for tying his family to the Mafia. For all the protection Uncle Benny had provided him, he also cast a dark cloud over Xavier's life.

"I'll never understand," he said to no one.

"Perhaps not, but it is better to try."

Xavier whirled around to see Jacob standing behind him.

"Uncle Jake, I didn't..."

"It is a beautiful sunrise. I am sorry to interrupt your time alone, but I thought we could have that talk. Maria says the father you've always hated is a mystery to you now, one you might not want to solve."

"I don't know. I've been so hurt by him, I was shocked to hear how he's loved and respected here. They have to know he was convicted and sentenced to prison. I can't seem to put the two men together in my mind. My father did...so many things." Now that he was face to face with Jacob he couldn't say his father had beaten him. "He just didn't...couldn't...he..."

Jacob reached over and put his arm around his godson, wanting to protect him from the pain of remembering.

"It's okay, Zavi. I know," he spoke so quietly it was a whisper. Xavier felt himself start with surprise and shame.

"Did you always know?"

"No. I suspected, but I did not want to believe Victor could do such a thing. I wanted to believe in the man you've discovered here. He was my friend. I tried to protect you, so did Maria and Benjamin. Everyone wanted the best for you."

"Not my mother. She barely acknowledged my existence. And Dad? He beat me because of his hatred for me?"

"He didn't hate you, Zavi. He was trying to protect you."

"Protect me from what," Xavier jumped up in a rage. "I needed protection from *him*. His yelling and his hatred, always calling me a filthy Jew. How could he say that when he was Jewish?"

Jacob wondered how much about the past he could reveal to his godson; there were promises he'd made that must be kept.

He hoped knowing some of the past would help Xavier to understand. His recent discovery had alleviated some of his misgivings concerning Victor only to add to his guilt for the way he'd felt about his friend.

"I, too, have judged your father harshly on other matters," Jacob confessed. "Only recently I discovered his innocence. Zavi, your father should never have spent a day in jail."

"That's impossible. You saw the evidence, Uncle Jake. Dad was guilty as sin."

"Now I know the real truth and I view Victor's transgressions in a much different light. Maybe, Zavi, after the story I tell, you will be able to view your father with a gentler heart."

"I doubt it," Xavier retorted, bitterly.

"So do I. You've been through so much, the pain in your family, problems in your career, the fire, losing Min. So much pain. Just like your father, and myself. We too survived a horrible fire."

"I don't believe that my father ever endured what I have." Xavier was defiant, a little self-pitying. It is time, Jacob thought. It is time that he knows the truth about how his father suffered.

"You may be right, Xavier," Jacob acquiesced. "Anyway, it was all such a long time ago."

"What?"

Jacob didn't answer.

"What was a long time ago, Uncle Jake?"

"Vorzel."

Yes, it's time to remember, Jacob thought. Time to tell the stories I've tried for so long to forget. Not just my memories, but those entrusted to me by Xavier's grandfather and Benjamin's father.

Over the past few months he and Benjamin had researched their history looking for clues to the danger facing them. They had relived many things, but nothing as far back as Vorzel.

Jacob looked at Xavier. No more time to hide, he thought. If I'm to salvage my soul and save Xavier's life...

Jacob sat across from Xavier and gazed at the rising sun. He crossed his legs getting comfortable.

"It was bitterly cold that winter, Zavi. But that didn't bother your father and me," he began. "We were too young to know any better."

PART III
Three Blind Mice

8

Moskva/Kiev Rail Line, Ukraine, Russia, March 17, 1917

Captain Doctor Emil Danelsberg stared out the window of the moving train hoping to replace the images of death in his head with those of the countryside passing by. Usually a day's journey, the train had headed due south for two days and only now turned east to Kiev. More evidence of the war, the doctor thought. The crowds of traveling refugees and soldiers, coupled with an unsure fuel supply, had obliterated the schedule. Danelsberg had waited two days in Petrograd before the authorities even released the train, but the wait was worth it. He was almost home, his first visit in almost two years.

Pulling his greatcoat tightly around him, he watched the landscape flow past. Winter had just begun to release its grip on the steppes of the Ukraine and the brisk air penetrated the inadequately warmed passenger car, reminding him of that first horrible winter of the war. It was as if the cold had penetrated so deep, it had set up permanent residence in his body.

Danelsberg's tall frame had shrunk from life at the front. His brown hair was graying and crow's feet surrounded his eyes from three years of squinting into the glare of sun and snow. He looked like a man in his mid-forties. He was thirty-one.

Tired of the cold, the war, and Russia, all he wanted was to get home to his family in Vorzel, a tiny Jewish settlement near

Kiev. He had grown up on the Volga River where his German ancestors had settled centuries before. As the czars solidified their grip on the Russian empire, the Jews were herded into the Pale of Settlement, a giant land ghetto in the Ukraine. When the restrictions were finally loosened a century ago, his family chose to remain close to Kiev. They believed there was safety in numbers. Life outside the village was unknown and therefore feared.

Emil faced the fear. He was the first Danelsberg to break away from the familial line of rabbinical scholars. Emil believed he could help his people a lot more as a doctor than as a dispenser of mysticism. That decision nearly destroyed his father.

The elder Danelsberg believed that the Russian Jews were God's chosen of the chosen and for this reason the rabbinical profession was the highest calling. For a Danelsberg to turn away from the teaching of the Torah was to turn from God. But, Emil had reasons.

His experiences at the University in Kiev showed him how despised Russian Jews were, not only in Russia, but in Europe as a whole. They were the poor Jews. The uneducated Jews. The second-class citizens of a second-class race. Emil hoped to prove that a Jew could get an education like anyone else, and that an educated Jew could live as an equal among his countrymen.

His search for knowledge began with his struggle against a strict quota system applied to students of Jewish descent. Those brave enough or foolish enough to strive for an education found themselves competing against a centuries-old system of patronage and privilege. Many a bright young man was denied admission though his scores were higher than almost all who applied.

Once admitted, Emil endured prejudice from his professors, as well as fellow students. He could not even enjoy the fellowship of other Jews knowing they were constantly competing for the few spaces allowed them. All the years of frustration paid off with his acceptance to the Surgical School of Medicine in St. Petersburg upon the completion of his degree in Kiev.

He traveled to St. Petersburg, home of Czar Nicholas and his German-born wife, Alexandra. Emil brought with him his new wife, Sona, his childhood sweetheart from Vorzel, rented a small flat and began his studies again. He had hoped he would find St. Petersburg, Russia's most cosmopolitan city, more tolerant and enlightened in their treatment of Jews. Once again his hopes were dashed.

The Danelsbergs found St. Petersburg in many ways more prejudiced than the Ukraine. The city adopted its attitude from its most powerful resident, Czar Nicholas II, a fervent anti-Semite. Racism was never overt, never violent as it was in the Ukraine. The bigotry, dispensed in small humiliating doses every day, ground a man down a bit at a time. No way existed to fight it, to defend against it. Emil, working hard to complete his studies, had to find a way to tolerate it. His salvation came in the birth of his son.

The last year of his residency, Sona became pregnant. His child, Viktor, was a perfect being, their only joy. His joy was short-lived. When Viktor was a year old, the war came.

All physicians, even Jews, were commissioned to fight for Mother Russia. Danelsberg bundled his family onto a train to Vorzel for the duration of the war. He reported for duty and was assigned to a cavalry regiment having never been on a horse in his life.

Though racism was rampant in the military, Emil found army life tolerable. He was an excellent surgeon and the men in his regiment made him feel welcome. Emil had a feeling this courteous behavior had more to do with the fact he might be called upon to save their lives one day than his rank as an officer. Nonetheless, he appreciated the respite from bigotry.

As a physician, Emil witnessed firsthand the carnage wrought upon the Russian army. Badly led and ill equipped, the Russian soldier was led by inexperienced, narrow-minded commanders who knew nothing of modern tactics and strategy. They threw away the lives of their men in suicidal frontal assaults and blamed each other for the continuing series of defeats.

Fortunately, Emil's regiment had one of the few bright commanders in the Russian military. Colonel Pavel Krikalev was a brilliant tactician, ferocious warrior and an officer willing to share the privations of the front with his men. Because of this, Danelsberg saw action in almost every major campaign. He also saw more broken and battered bodies than a human mind could fathom.

His regiment participated in the first advance into Prussia in the heady days of August 1914 when victory seemed possible before Christmas. After the disaster at Tannenberg and General Samsonov's suicide, the Russian army fell back in disarray; yet Emil's regiment refused to surrender or retreat. Instead, they fought a courageous rear guard action, screening the remnants of the army as they fled back to Russia. The retreat continued for a full year until the winter of 1915.

Danelsberg was surprised that anyone survived the long retreat. The Russian army, ill-prepared to fight the war, soon exhausted its meager supplies of ammunition. Two million men trained and ready to go to the front to bolster the faltering armies waited for rifles that didn't exist. Russian factories were producing 45,000 artillery shells a month. The army was firing 35,000 shells a day. Each regiment had to do with what they had or could capture. They lived off the countryside, traded space for time, and prayed for winter to end the German offensive.

When the snows finally came, the regiment collapsed in their tattered uniforms, too shell-shocked to realize that less than a third of them were still alive. Endless cases of frostbite, trench foot, and pneumonia drained Emil. With no supplies, it was impossible to treat his patients effectively, but he never quit trying. Eventually, he worked himself into exhaustion and was sent home to recuperate. The time with his wife and child replenished his spirit in ways he hadn't thought possible. When he returned to his regiment in March of 1916, he found a renewed sense of hope among his fellow cavalrymen.

General Aleksey Brusilov had taken command of the southwestern front after a shakeup at *Stavka,* the Russian supreme command. He was one of the few capable generals in the Russian army and the soldiers under his command felt lucky despite his merciless training. He equipped them from the huge supplies of arms newly flowing from their allies in the west and the revitalized Russian war industry. The general was preparing for an offensive that would knock the Hapsburg empire out of the war.

The French were screaming for help from their ally to draw German reserves off to the eastern front before they could be used to finish them off. It was up to Brusilov to attack in the south, thereby keeping the French and British in the war.

In early June, Brusilov attacked the Austro-Hungarian armies on a wide front against the wishes of *Stavka*. This time, the Russians—well led by Brusilov and well supplied by their Western allies—succeeded against strong odds. Danelsberg found himself in the vanguard of the Russian attack, and in a haunting repeat of 1914, a successful offensive was turned into a disastrous retreat because of a lack of support from the generals at *Stavka*.

Brusilov begged *Stavka* to order an attack in the north so that he could sustain his attack in the south; he was on the verge of destroying the Austro-Hungarian army. *Stavka* refused and Brusilov's army faced the German reinforcements alone. The last chance for victory slipped through the czar's fingers.

Unlike the previous year, there would be no more offensives for the Russian commanders. As soldiers realized how their generals had sold them out, they began refusing orders to advance. Strikes broke out all over Russia to force the abdication of the czar. Officers at the front were murdered by their men. It was in this atmosphere that Danelsberg was wounded in an artillery barrage and sent to a hospital in St. Petersburg, officially renamed Petrograd, to recuperate. Upon his recovery, Danelsberg went to work for a former professor, Dr Vorshilov, in his old hospital caring for the wounded.

Throughout the winter of 1916-17, he witnessed the disintegration of the Romanov dynasty. The Russian people, exhausted, hungry, and demoralized by the two million dead in the war, went on strike. Riots over food shortages sprung up everywhere. A passive mutiny in the army materialized over the length and breadth of Russia as replacement units refused to march to the front. The nobility and most politicians believed they could pull the country back together if only the czar would return from the front and take control of the situation in Petrograd. But Nicholas remained in Mogilev at his military headquarters, unwilling to believe what was transpiring in the capital.

Danelsberg received his second leave of the war and left Petrograd, a vat of rage and hunger that was dangerously close to boiling over. He was relieved to be leaving the center of the turmoil and hoped he would get home before revolution broke out.

He knew only too well the danger his people faced during times of political unrest. The pogroms of 1905, for example, had followed an aborted attempt at revolution. Now he worried that similar carnage could be the fate of his people once again.

The train slowed and stopped for no apparent reason; Danelsberg opened his window and leaned out to see what was happening. A blast of cold wind blew through the open window chilling the car, earning him dirty looks and comments from the chilled passengers around him.

A few yards ahead he could just make out a barrier illuminated by a small bonfire across the tracks. Running toward him down the side of the tracks was a soldier carrying a lantern.

"Private," he yelled, "why have we stopped?"

The soldier skidded to a stop, held up his lantern and, seeing the officer's uniform, came to attention and saluted.

"Revolution has broken out, Captain—the czar has abdicated the throne. Revolutionaries and forces loyal to the czar are fighting in Kiev. We stopped the train to warn you," he panted, steam pouring from his mouth.

"How long before we move?"

"I'm not sure, Captain. Nobody knows anything. Some say we will put the rebels down before tomorrow, but I hear the fighting is fierce. We heard that the czarina was conspiring with the Germans and the Jews to help Russia lose the war. My unit is leaving for Petrograd to assist the czar," he answered.

"Thank you, carry on," Danelsberg ordered. He touched his cap in salute to the loyal soldier and wondered how many more would fight for the Romanovs. If there were enough, his country would be torn apart in a bloody civil war. He closed the window to the grumbling of the other passengers.

My God, he thought. It has finally happened. And here I wait, miles away in the empty night while my beautiful Sona and Viktor sit helpless in our village. God, please watch over them until I can return to protect them. His belly full of ice, Emil lowered his head and began mumbling a Hebrew prayer; he spoke, humbly, gently to his God in the way he'd been taught as a child. It was something he hadn't done in fifteen years.

Vorzel, Ukraine, March 17, 1917

At sunset Vorzel was deserted. The chilling late afternoon wind had driven the inhabitants from the streets, reminding them that winter was still lingering in this part of Russia.

Yet, it was not the falling temperature alone that kept the citizens in their homes. It was something more sinister: a dread of events to come that lingered below the surface. No one could say for sure. But the uncertain news from Petrograd, the horrible winter, and the continuing war combined to deeply frighten Vorzel's citizens. Jews suffered even in the best of times and these were far from the best.

The townspeople didn't speak of their fears—as though acknowledging them would bring them to life—but they acted differently. Conversations were short, tempers flared, and attendance at the synagogue increased. They went about their business furtively and Jews who usually only worshiped on high holy days found themselves whispering prayers almost constantly. Even children, noticing a difference in their parents' moods, played more quietly, sensing more than understanding their elders' fears.

Two young boys ran quietly through the streets looking around them as they went. Darkness had crept over the streets, almost overpowering the dim light from the few unshuttered windows in the village. They nimbly avoided stumbling in the long frozen wagon ruts that had caused many a twisted ankle for those less careful. Huffing like locomotives, jets of steam shot from their mouths as they ran through the darkness. Parents had become overly protective in the last few weeks and the boys wanted to avoid distressing them.

Sona Danelsberg was cooking in her kitchen when she heard the boys tumble onto the porch. The door flew open and Viktor came in first, rubbing the *mezuzah* before entering. On his last leave, Emil had lowered the holy marker so his son could reach it. It was the last thing he'd done on the day he returned to the front. She sighed and began to help Viktor take off his coat.

Yakov Rabinowitz came in the door after Viktor so quietly she almost didn't notice him. He was shorter than her son and not as agile—more thoughtful than athletic. Sona was keeping him for her cousin Mika, who was recovering from an almost fatal bout of pneumonia. Yakov's father had died in the war, the news of which had come during Mika's illness, weakening her further. Sona was happy to have him, to help someone who had lost so much.

"How is your mother, Yakov. Is she getting better?"

"Yes, ma'am," he replied in a whisper.

"She smells, *Mutter.* And that horrible Rabbi Vizinsky with his bad breath was there. He made us pray with him. Why do we have to go over there?" Viktor asked.

Sona muttered a small prayer to God asking for patience with her son.

"Viktor! Watch what you say. Your auntie is very sick and she doesn't smell. That is only the medicine. And I send you over there so that your best friend, Yakov, can visit with her."

"But the rabbi. He is always there. If Papa were here, he wouldn't make me pray."

"The rabbi is there to help Yakov's mother keep her spirits up while her body mends. He is a good man, a holy man, and you should respect your elders more. Now go wash up. Dinner is almost ready."

Viktor mumbled something and dragged Yakov to the water pump to wash.

Sona returned to preparing their small evening meal. She was spending more and more of her time looking for food. In the cities she heard people were starving to death. She was thankful it hadn't gotten that bad on the steppes.

Watching her son set the table, she wondered what she would do about him and his education. Her husband's growing distance from Judaism was having its effect on young Viktor. Sona was having a hard time getting her son to attend *cheder*, the Hebrew school for children. Her own family was quite devout, and—while she understood her husband's feelings—she couldn't allow her son to turn from God at such a young age. How she wished for her husband in these times; she needed the help so badly. Viktor needed a strong guiding hand and the more time Sona spent looking for food, the less time she spent with her son. Gunfire echoed in the distance.

"What was that, *Mutter*?" Viktor asked. Yakov looked frightened.

"Nothing Viktor. Sounds from the city...far away. *Kinder*, come to the table and let's say the blessing," she answered calmly, trying to reassure. The children bowed their heads and Sona began to pray.

The villagers had heard bursts of gunfire throughout the day; they only spoke of it in whispers. Some feared it was German guerrillas, others said it was a mutiny in the army. One person had the audacity to suggest the czar had been overthrown, but no one listened to him. The Romanov dynasty was a constant in Russian life and the thought of it being deposed was too much for the imagination.

Sona's prayers were interrupted by the sounds of horses galloping through the streets. Before she could stop them, the children jumped up from the table and dashed to the window pulling back the curtains. As she pulled them away she saw a horse slip in an icy wagon rut. The snap of its leg breaking sounded like a pistol shot as the rider was catapulted over its head. None of the other riders stopped to assist the fallen man who lay still on his back. As quickly as they had come, the riders vanished.

Slowly a group of villagers emerged from the surrounding houses and gathered in a knot around the injured man. The horse stood whinnying in the street, limping on three legs.

"Children, stay in the house. I am going to see what is happening," Sona ordered as she left, latching the door behind her.

No one moved to assist the man. They were held in morbid fascination by the figure whom fate had dumped in their tiny village. He moaned but did not stir.

"Let me through," a voice called out from the back of the crowd. The villagers parted and Rabbi Danelsberg appeared. He was the senior rabbi in the village and carried great authority with his fellow citizens. He knelt over the body, calling for a lantern, and felt the man's neck with tender fingers.

"He's still alive, but I think his neck is broken," the rabbi said to no one in particular. "There is nothing I can do to save him." A villager approached with a lantern and passed to the center of the circle, lighting up the ground.

"My God..." someone whispered.

"...a soldier..."

"What do we do now?"

"The army will blame this on us!"

The villagers melted into the night leaving the rabbi and Sona standing over the dying soldier. The rabbi noticed Sona, stood up and went to her.

"Hello, Sona."

"Hello, Father."

They stood in silence for a minute staring at one another. They had not spoken in some time, and though they should have fled like the others, they could not.

Sona had been one of the rabbi's favorite pupils. Growing up, she looked to him as a second father, but since her marriage to his son, they rarely spoke. Emil still loved his father, but the rabbi felt betrayed by his child's decision to turn his back on their faith.

"Your son is not doing well at *cheder*," Rabbi Danelsberg remarked.

"I know, Father. He is not as bright as Yakov, but I love him just the same," she replied, licking her lower lip.

"I think that he is a lot brighter than he lets on, Sona. He is so much like my...so much like his father. Stubborn and individualistic. Dangerous character traits for a Jew. I've tried to guide him, but..." he raised his arms in a gesture of helplessness.

She nodded. The soldier moaned again.

"I do wish your husband were here, now; he would know what to do. If this man dies...as I think he will...a dead soldier in a Jewish village.... What, I wonder, did we do to suffer this?" he asked, shrugging his shoulders.

They stood for a moment looking at the uniformed figure, steaming breath pouring from their mouths. It was getting colder and she wanted to return to the children and her warm house, but there was something keeping her here.

Finally she said, "He still loves you, Father."

When he didn't respond she added, "I just wanted you to know. His letters always ask me to look after you...I must be going now."

132

"Sona...thank you," he said. There was moisture in his eyes. "Please tell him—tell him that I don't know what to say," he stumbled. His shoulders sagged and he looked at the ground.

"It is awful to talk about this now," Sona commented sadly. "With this poor man dying before us. Did he have the chance to tell his father he loved him the last time he saw him? Now he lies here, neck broken, never to see his father again," she said softly, staring at the soldier. They looked up at the sound of horses approaching the village. The rabbi turned to Sona and spoke quickly.

"Inside with you now, child. I don't know what will happen here, but tell my son that I love him when next you see him." She threw her arms about him, kissing his cheek.

"Come inside, Father. Please. Perhaps they will take the soldier away and leave us alone," she pleaded, holding onto him.

"No, Sona. You know better than that. I am the village rabbi and they will seek me out for their questions. Best to meet them out here so they do not disturb the village looking for me. Now go inside, Child. Hurry, before they arrive," he insisted, pulling her arms from about him. She kissed him again and left him in the middle of the road. He turned to face the oncoming horsemen, their torches casting crazy shadows as they galloped into the outskirts of the village.

Sona hurried into the house and slammed the door behind her, latching it. She turned to see a strange man standing in her house. Her hand flew to her mouth as she gasped in fright. Her eyes hurriedly searched the room for the boys. They stood in a corner, frightened, huddling against one another.

"Mrs. Danelsberg," the stranger stammered, "please do not be frightened. I am here to help."

The peasant's large, powerful body was wrapped in warm clothing. His round face was weathered, but his eyes were kind. He could have been twenty-five or forty-five. Life on the steppes was demanding and men aged before their time. He clasped his hat nervously in front of him, fidgeting under her gaze.

"Your husband, the good Dr. Danelsberg, saved my daughter's life a few years ago..." he stopped as Sona reached out for the children. They rushed to her and hid in her skirts as the horsemen pulled up in the street. She clasped them to her.

"Please," he begged, "we haven't got much time."

"Why are you here?" she croaked. Outside she could hear loud voices interrogating her father-in-law.

"It would take too long to explain," he said, shaking his head as he searched for the words that would make this woman listen. "Your husband saved my daughter's life and I am here to save yours. I hope," he said simply. "I know the doctor is in Petrograd and that you are alone. I am here to help."

A pistol shot cracked on the street and the whinnying horse was cut down, put out of its misery.

"What is happening?" Sona asked, voice shaking.

"The czar has abdicated and the revolution in Petrograd has begun. Army units in Kiev have mutinied causing much fighting. Many are already dead," he said sadly, looking at the ground. "Soldiers loyal to the czar have chased some of the revolutionaries out of Kiev. Those men have come here, to your village. Do you understand?"

Sona didn't answer, but the fear of the peasant lessened as the fear for her village grew greater.

"A whole mob has followed the soldiers here—a deadly mob who are saying the czar was in league with the Germans—and the Jews. We must leave here now."

"I must get my father-in-law," Sona said, turning to the door. The peasant moved quickly and slammed the door before she could open it fully. He then spun her around and gripped her arms with his powerful hands bringing her close to his face.

"Those soldiers mean to burn this village to the ground and kill everyone in it. If you don't believe me, look."

He reached over to the table and extinguished the lamp then dragged her to the window. Drawing the curtain aside, he pressed her face to the cold glass. Out on the street, the rabbi stood in a semicircle of cavalry soldiers pleading with them.

"I keep telling you there are no revolutionaries here," the rabbi shouted, pleading, begging.

"Shut up, Jew. I'm tired of your lying. Solkov, take care of him and the revolutionary," a voice ordered.

A man spurred his horse out of the semicircle and up to the rabbi. He pulled his pistol and shot the rabbi in the head and then shot the soldier twice in the chest. He ceased moaning.

The peasant slapped a hand over Sona's face stifling her scream. He bodily picked her up and carried her to the back door of the house. Opening the door slowly, he peered out into the street and, seeing no one, hurried out the door.

"Follow me children, and stay close," he ordered.

As they hurried down the street, gunfire, screams, and the sounds of shattering glass and splintering wood echoed across the village. He herded his party to the corner of the last building and peered around the edge.

"Damn," he muttered. A squad of cavalry had the main road blocked off. He thought quickly, trying to find a way out. Mind blank, on the edge of panic, he turned to Sona.

"Do you know of a place near here where we can hide for the next few hours 'til they leave? Are you listening to me?" he growled, shaking the lady roughly. She was still in shock from seeing her rabbi and father-in-law murdered. For a second he thought about abandoning them to the mob and saving himself, but decided against it. He had a mission to complete. The peasant felt a tugging at his pants, looked down and saw the two boys motioning him to follow them.

Oh, well, he thought. We've got nothing to lose, and grabbing Sona led her after the children.

They made their way to the front of the village where most of the soldiers and the mob had gathered. He almost pulled them up, but the boys were too far ahead. To shout after them would draw attention to themselves so he followed on, having no other choice. They led him to a huge pile of wood on the edge of the village in view of the synagogue. It was the winter fuel supply for the entire village.

When he arrived at the woodpile, the boys began to remove some of the logs and then amazingly disappeared into the small mountain of wood. He bent down and saw a tunnel leading into the pile. Hearing footsteps approach, he shoved Mrs. Danelsberg in and dove in after her. Before crawling down the tunnel, he did his best to conceal the entrance.

The peasant banged his head several times before emerging into a small cavern. As his eyes adjusted to the darkness, he could just make out the small figures of the two boys at the far wall of the hiding place. The woman was lying on the ground in front of them curled up in a ball, comatose. He moved to the boys slowly.

"Are you all right?" he whispered.

The two boys nodded without answering. The taller boy pulled his arm and pointed toward the wood wall. Moving closer, the peasant could just see through the logs onto the square in front of the synagogue.

The soldiers, backed by a cheering crowd, were herding the Jews into the synagogue at bayonet point, beating stragglers with their rifle butts. Gunshots echoed throughout the village and the peasant could smell burning wood in the air blowing through the cracks in the logs.

"How'd you find this place?"

He looked at the children as they hesitated before answering him. Finally, the larger of the boys explained.

"The older boys in the village built it for a secret fort. We followed them and when they weren't playing in it, we snuck in. It's our fort, too," he said eyes flashing, standing in front of his mother protectively.

The peasant thought the child a lot more defiant than any Jewish child, much less any adult Jew he'd ever met. Fortunately for them all, the boy had kept his head and brought them to safety, else they'd be out among the damned.

A huge roar went up from the crowd and the peasant peered out in time to see the synagogue burst into flames. The smell of burning kerosene wafted across the square as a horrible wail went up from the Jews trapped inside the building. A man burst from a window with the Torah cradled in his arms. His effort to save the holy book ended in a hail of gunfire that threw his body back against the burning wall. A soldier ran up and threw the scrolls back into the inferno. A sickening stench of burning flesh began to permeate their hiding place.

The peasant turned from the hideous sight and knelt over the woman. As she came to, he gently brought her to a sitting position. In the flickering light of the fire, he could see her eyes were clear.

"We are safe for now," he said softly.

"What is happening?"

He paused before answering.

"They are burning the village and..." he faltered unable to finish.

With a quick intake of breath Sona realized what was taking place and recoiled in horror. She bent over and began to retch as the peasant held her head. Hearing the sound of feet close by, he left the woman to her grief and went to peer out.

"Check the wood pile for hidden Jews," a soldier ordered. A squad of men began poking the mound with their rifles. The peasant grabbed the boys close to him to keep them quiet in case they started to panic. Embers from the blazing synagogue floated across the square and settled on the makeshift shelter.

One large ember floated through the cracks and settled on the hand of the smaller boy just as a soldier began poking the wood directly in front of them with his rifle. The peasant held himself and the boys rock still.

The boy's eyes grew wide as the ember burned into his hand; sweat broke out on his forehead. He kept quiet in spite of the pain.

When the soldiers started probing the wood with lit torches, it began to smoke. The soldiers backed off to better see anyone scrambling out of the burning pile to escape the flames. They waited, rifles at the ready.

As soon as the soldiers moved away, the peasant pulled the two boys down to the ground with him to stay under the suffocating smoke. He looked down the tunnel and considered their options: to stay in the burning wood much longer would mean death—the burning cavern would collapse on them—to leave would mean facing the rifles of the soldiers, an equally grim prospect. They had to wait it out.

They all began coughing as the smoke sucked the oxygen out of the air. The peasant heard a high-pitched keening sound and looked down the tunnel at what appeared to be a wave of water rushing toward them. The wave undulated and moved closer until he could see it wasn't water, but a living, moving mass of scampering bodies.

"My God," he thought. "Rats."

He rolled the boys under him and dragged the woman close as she shrieked at the sight of the rats pouring into the cavern. They came out of the wood by the hundreds falling on their bodies and running over them seeking safety. He heard the soldiers yell, abandoning their posts as the wave of rats erupted into the area around the now-raging bonfire.

"Rats! Holy Mother! Look at all the rats!"

"Jews and rats. Vermin and vermin. Living together."

"Shut up about the rats. All I'm concerned about is any Jews hiding in the woodpile."

"Nobody could survive that fire."

"Right. Let's get to the village before the peasants cart off everything worth having."

The peasant half-carried and half-shoved the family down the tunnel and into the night air. The tunnel collapsed behind them. Coughing and half-blind, they stumbled and staggered to the relative safety of the nearby forest where they fell in a heap on the ground.

"Wait here," he coughed, his throat raw from smoke.

He left them in the woods and made his way to the village well. All around him soldiers and peasants ran amuck, burning, looting, and shooting hidden Jews when they were discovered cowering in hiding places. He filled a bucket of water and made his way back to the woods. No one paid any attention to him.

They drank the water greedily, cooling their parched throats. Sona used a kerchief to wipe the smoke and grit from the eyes and faces of the two boys. Noticing Yakov's blistered hand, she gently dabbed it with cool water. It was all she could do. When the water was gone, they sat in a circle—too exhausted to move.

Finally, Sona touched the man's arm. "What do we do now?"

"We wait until the village is deserted. I will go find any valuables that are left. You will need money for your journey. You cannot stay here. The new government might take these massacres differently than the Romanovs did and the pogromists won't want any witnesses left. Do you understand?" The woman seemed lost in another world.

"But my husband? Where will he find us?"

"He won't. You must go to Petrograd and find him. That is your only chance."

"But my village, family, friends. We must stay and help— search for them. They may be hurt," she pleaded.

The woman was so fragile, so helpless. How could he explain?

"Please listen, Mrs. Danelsberg. I have just returned from your village—there is nothing left—no one except for you and the boys. There is nothing left for you to salvage. Your only chance is to go to Petrograd and find your husband. If you stay here, you will be killed."

"But who will say Kaddish? I must at least do that."

The peasant had heard of the Hebrew prayer for the dead, as important to Jews as Last Rites. Still, he could not allow them to linger. Tomorrow, or sooner, the soldiers would return to finish the survivors off.

"Forget the dead, Mrs. Danelsberg. They are with God now. You must think of the boys."

At the mention of the children, Sona looked down at them and back at the peasant. He was relieved to see some strength return to her face. He had to act while she was alert.

"Keep the boys here. I will go to the village and look for food and anything else you might need. When I return, we will make our way to Kiev and I will get you on a train. After that, you will be in God's hands." He grasped her arm and said, "It will be all right. I will do my best to keep you safe."

"Thank you. Mister...I'm sorry. I don't even know your name," she apologized.

"Zenon. Zenon Koniev," he answered.

"Thank you, Zenon. You are a good and brave man." She leaned over to tend to the children as he went cautiously into the village.

9

Kiev, Ukraine, March 18, 1917

Kiev writhed in turmoil. Grenade explosions and small arms fire erupted intermittently throughout the city. Soldiers loyal to the czar battled Kerensky's Mensheviks as well as mutinous army units. The Bolsheviks fought everybody and looters took advantage of the chaos to break into food warehouses and cart off everything in sight. Fires set off during the night raged out of control as the firemen, out of fear for their safety, stayed in their quarters.

Emil Danelsberg had arrived in the city in the early morning hours. When the train stopped and disgorged its passengers, a firefight broke out as two army units fought a pitched battle for control of the railway station. Scores of passengers were caught in the crossfire and cut down before reaching safety. Danelsberg barely escaped.

Emil spent the next few hours dodging bullets and attempting to find some kind of transport to his village. He eventually joined a column of refugees heading north out of the city, hitching a ride with a clockmaker and his family on their wagon. Once out of the city, the doctor surveyed the motley caravan through red-rimmed eyes.

Emil was worn out; twenty-four hours without sleep had numbed his mind. He kept thinking of his family, trying to picture them. Rumors of massacres and pogroms were rampant in Kiev, but nothing could be confirmed. His exhaustion fueled his imagination and fear for the safety of his family brought images of horror to his thoughts.

The clockmaker's daughter reached out to touch the captain's moustache. She received a slap on the hand from her mother.

"Tasha, can't you see the good captain is sleeping? Now leave him alone," the mother scolded quietly.

The little girl sat back silently and listened to the captain's snores. He cried out once in his sleep and then was quiet.

On the road from Vorzel to Kiev, March 18, 1917

Zenon drove his *panje* full of hay south toward Kiev. The high-slung peasant cart was good for driving over mud during the spring thaw and the *Rasputzitza*, the season of mud during the fall rains. Hidden inside the hay were the three Jews from Vorzel.

He had retrieved enough clothing and gold and silver trinkets from the charred wreckage of the village to provide for them on their journey to Petrograd. After they had cleaned up and changed, he had hidden them in the back of his cart and began the trip to Kiev. The Jews huddled quietly trying to rest.

They were passing a group of refugees escaping the fighting in the city when he noticed an officer, a captain, in the back of a wagon. He had his greatcoat pulled tightly about him and his scarf obscured his face. The man appeared to be sleeping.

So even the officers are deserting, Zenon thought. I guess the empire has truly come to an end.

He contemplated this as he drove on. In the distance, he heard gunfire.

Kiev Railway Station, March 18, 1917

Sona Danelsberg had been waiting in the *panje* for most of the afternoon. Shortly after arriving in Kiev, Zenon had pulled into a small warehouse. He left them there, in relative safety, while he went to search for a way to get them on a train to Petrograd.

The boys slept on and off for most of the day. It was just as well; when Yakov was awake, he moaned in pain from the burn on his hand. Fortunately, he was so tired that he soon drifted back into sleep.

Throughout the day, men and woman came in and out of the warehouse, usually carrying weapons or bleeding from wounds suffered in the fighting. They treated Sona kindly and she felt safe in their presence. One man even bandaged Yakov's hand.

Just before nightfall, Zenon returned and told her to wake the boys and gather their belongings; he had found them space on a train bound for Petrograd. They left the building and went outside to a waiting truck. Zenon helped them into the back and then joined the driver in front. The truck started and they headed toward the station. The trip took hours and Sona began to fear missing the train.

Along the way, they were stopped at several newly constructed roadblocks; Zenon talked their way through. At one, she saw him draw a pistol from under the seat. Apparently he would kill to see them safely to the train.

When they arrived at the train station, they found the remnants of a battle fought earlier that day. Dead men lay scattered in the rubble of destroyed buildings, but people just stepped over them. The soldiers appeared nervous, taking orders from civilians. Zenon ordered the driver to stop and came around to help them out of the back of the truck.

"We are here, Mrs. Danelsberg. Hurry. The train leaves shortly," he said, picking up one of the boys. The driver grabbed the remainder of their belongings and followed Zenon to the train.

On the platform, they had to fight their way through hundreds of passengers to get to the train. Everyone was screaming, pushing, and kicking as the throng tried to fight its way on board. A thin line of soldiers tried to hold the mob at bay with bayonets, but even the occasional rifle shot couldn't quiet the mob.

Several times Sona thought she would be dragged under and trampled, but Zenon pulled them to safety. When they arrived at the line of soldiers, he shouted for the officer in charge.

The man came over and, recognizing Zenon, ordered the soldiers to let them in the cordon. As the guards parted, the mob pushed forward to follow the small group and were beaten back with truncheons.

One man grabbed hold of Sona's arm and wouldn't let go. The pain from his grip was excruciating and she thought her arm would be torn from her body. She cried out to an official by her side; he turned and shot the man in the face. The corpse let go of her arm and was trampled by the mob as they struggled to get away from the man with the gun. Sona turned away from the dead man and saw Zenon throw the two boys to a man standing in the door of a cattle car and then turn to lift her up.

"The man there is Ivan. He will watch after you on your journey to Petrograd. Please trust him and you will be all right," he said, as he grabbed her around the waist to lift her up. She placed her hands on his shoulders.

"Zenon, please. What can I do to repay you? I owe you my life and my child's," she cried.

"When you get to Petrograd, tell them what happened to your village and your people. Tell them that the Mensheviks destroyed Vorzel and massacred its inhabitants."

"Tell *who*, Zenon? Who will listen to me?"

"The Americans. Tell a newspaper man from America. He will listen. Please do this, it is all I ask. Maybe somebody, somewhere, will stop this madness and we can live in peace," he pleaded.

"I will do it, Zenon. I swear." Tears came to her eyes as she hugged the stranger, her savior. He lifted her up to Ivan and waved goodby as the train started moving out of the station. She saw him amid the chaos and, wondering who he was, waved at him a final time.

Nikita Sergeyevich Khrushchev watched the train pull out of the station. He thought about the last words he spoke to the lady. Lies. The last thing he wanted was peace. Right now anarchy better served his aims and the aims of the Communist party. The Bolsheviks were not strong enough to seize power, but the more chaos they caused Kerensky and his moderates, the sooner their chance would come.

Kerensky wanted to keep Russia in the war and American armaments and money would enable him to do just that, unless he lost their support. Many of America's influential, powerful, and wealthy industrialists were Jews. If they heard of the pogroms, the slaughter, they would demand that America give no assistance to his enemies. It was all part of a greater plan to destabilize Kerensky's government.

Khrushchev wondered what the Danelsberg Jewess would have done had she known he had planned the pogrom that destroyed her village, that she was a pawn in a political game that would change history. He didn't care. The future secretary of the Communist party and dictator of Russia couldn't afford to care if he wanted to be a part of it all. But it was interesting to think about.

The burly peasant turned and disappeared into the mob.

Vorzel, Ukraine, March 18, 1917

Danelsberg was dreaming of his father when a hand shaking his shoulder woke him. He was groggy, cold, and disoriented.

Kiev, the train, the battle. I must be getting close to home, he thought.

"Doctor, we are here," the clockmaker said.

Danelsberg sat up and rubbed his eyes. He noticed the family staring at him strangely.

"What is it?" he asked.

"Your village, Doctor. Your village..." the clockmaker muttered.

Danelsberg climbed out of the wagon and stood before the burned-out shell of the synagogue. The pungent odor of burned flesh hung heavily in the air. He took a tentative step forward and collapsed.

Great sobs racked his body as he remembered his dream. His father had been saying Kaddish in the middle of the street as Vorzel burned all around him.

The clockmaker and his family watched in silence.

10

The Front, September 24, 1917

A place of death and dying, disease, and lost hope. An asylum with barbed wire replacing padded walls, and rat-infested trenches serving as exercise grounds. A purgatory trapped between revolution and starvation behind them and the Kaiser's inferno on the horizon.

Martyrs went unnoticed and heros were shunned. Fresh untrained recruits marched into the meat grinder of German heavy artillery. They died sometimes within hours of taking over positions abandoned by veterans who had deserted the trenches sick of the slaughter. Officers giving unpopular orders were shot on the spot by soldiers unwilling to die for a government led by men whom none of them had ever heard of. No one, with any sanity remaining, advanced into the maelstrom that awaited them in that no man's land.

The only men left to fight were naive patriots, homicidal sociopaths, or men with nothing left to live for. These pathetically few soldiers were the final thin line, the sole obstacle that kept the Germans and their allies from marching straight to Moscow.

Newly promoted Major Emil Danelsberg rested his back against the wall of the shallow trench. Standing in foot-deep murky water, he surveyed the men crouched before him. They looked at him with resigned, flat expressions, the fear of death having long since been burned out of them.

"Major Danelsberg, everyone is present and accounted for," Lt. Federov, his second in command reported.

Major, Emil thought. Not Major Doctor or Doctor; just plain Major.

His past had been kept secret, a condition Emil had made upon volunteering for combat duty. The colonel commanding his regiment had agreed, realizing it would be hard for anyone to lead men if that man might later be expected to save their lives. Besides, the colonel had reasoned, he didn't give a damn about a man's past as long as he was willing to fight, a rarity these days.

"It's a raid," Emil stated simply. "Headquarters says a new Hungarian division has moved into the line opposite us and they want to confirm the intelligence."

"Bullshit!"

Emil looked to his left and saw Corporal Benezarin staring straight at him.

They don't even try to hide their insubordination any more, Emil thought. We can't say a damned thing to them or we're liable to get shot, he reminded himself, but if I back down I'll lose what little control I have left. Emil stared back at the corporal until Benezarin's head dropped.

"That's better, Corporal," Lt. Federov remarked forcefully, glaring at the corporal. The other soldiers began to grumble.

"Federov!" Emil barked. "Follow me."

They splashed through the muck to a shelter dug into the side of the trench. Emil pushed Federov in ahead of him.

"Major, I..."

"Shut up, Lieutenant!" Emil barked, glaring at Federov.

The youthful officer had just arrived at the battalion from one of the elite cadet schools in Kiev. He came from a line of czarist officers and landed gentry. Federov still believed in God and czar and arrogantly expressed his right-wing views to hide his growing suspicion that something was horribly wrong. He used his words as a cloak to protect himself from the reality of the front and the revolution that was destroying his class and the only way of life he had ever known.

146

"Are you crazy, Federov?" Emil began.

"That arrogant bastard Benezarin should be placed before a firing squad," Federov shouted. "Make an example out of him and a few of his comrades and then maybe we'll restore some discipline to the battalion, Major."

"If you don't watch your mouth then you'll end up being the example, Federov," Emil stated, trying to reason with the young officer. Although he disliked the lieutenant, he needed him. Federov was the only other officer surviving in the battalion. "Take off your blinders, Lieutenant. Rank means nothing to these men now. They'd just as soon kill us as the Germans."

Federov ignored his commander and closed the distance between them. "Maybe you don't have the stomach for it, eh, Major? I heard a rumor you were a doctor before you volunteered for combat. Maybe you should stick to healing instead of killing," Federov sneered. "Before the czar was overthrown, I could have had you brought up on charges for *not* shooting Benezarin. But now," Federov said, as he flicked the St. George medal on Emil's tunic, "men like you get the highest decoration in the land while loyal officers such as myself have to watch as you turn our army into a cowardly mob. At the officers' academy in Kiev we learned about command and discipline, loyalty and sacrifice. We also learned that killing the enemy is easy. Shooting your own men takes courage. Courage that you obviously don't have. And by letting Benezarin live, you abdicate command of this battalion to him and his rabble."

Emil grabbed the lieutenant by the front of his tunic and shoved him against the wall. "Listen to me, you ignorant bastard, while I try to save your life. We need Benezarin. The men respect him and the man is a born killer. As long as he is willing to fight, then so are the rest. The minute we lose him we are dead men. Don't you understand that what they taught you at the academy doesn't apply anymore?" Emil asked, shaking him viciously. "Your way of life is gone forever and it is never coming back!"

"Wrong, Major," he spoke as fear began to show through the anger. "General Kornilov, the last true Russian hero, is in Petrograd. He will destroy the Bolsheviks, subjugate Kerensky, and restore the monarchy. Kornilov is our savior, Russia's savior, and soon you and the rabble you lead will vanish in his wrath," he finished, trying to convince himself as much as Emil by the words he spoke.

He tries to believe what he says, Emil thought, but the frightened look in his eyes betrays his true feelings.

"You stupid naive young man. Haven't you heard?" Emil asked, slamming Federov against the wall for emphasis. "General Kornilov's coup failed! Kerensky had him locked up. Your savior is in prison with the rest of the Romanovs, and with his failure, the right wing's influence on the government has been shattered forever."

Federov's two weeks at the front had obliterated his sense of order in the world. He'd held onto his views to bolster his hope that things would get better. But the words seemed hollow now.

Emil released him and lowered his voice. "The czar is gone forever, Federov. Now what's left is being divided between Kerensky and Lenin. No more czar. No more nobility. No more officers or rich people or respect for authority or officers' academies. It is all history. You need to adjust to the new reality, Federov, or you won't survive."

The lieutenant slumped to the ground. "It's so hard to believe," he said, looking into space. But the tone of his voice made a lie of his words.

"Why would I lie to you, Federov? Open your eyes and look around you. The truth is staring you in the face right here in the trenches. It's over, Federov. Gone. Gone forever."

"All gone...all gone," Federov muttered, as the horror of what he had denied for so long overcame him.

Emil knelt before him. "Not all, Federov. We can save something. We need to hold the Germans. Whether it is Mensheviks or Bolsheviks that end up in charge, it will still be Russians ruling Russians. But if the Germans get to Moscow or Petrograd, then we lose even that."

"Is that why you still fight?" Federov asked, looking at his commander.

"No, lieutenant," Emil spoke, truthfully. "I fight because everything I ever loved and cherished is gone. I fight because I can no longer heal men to send them back to the horror of the trenches. I fight mostly because my death, which I long for, will be a release from my pain and hopefully that death will serve my country."

Federov reached a hand out and Emil helped him to his feet. "I am sorry, Major," Federov said respectfully.

"Don't be sorry," Emil replied, straightening the young man's tunic. "Now go and join the others. We push off in a few minutes."

Federov saluted. Emil was so surprised he returned the salute, something he hadn't done in months because no one practiced even the most remote form of military courtesy out of fear for their lives.

Amazing, Emil thought. I came here to die, Sona, and I actually care what happens to some of these men.

He walked out of the dugout and was blown backwards by the force of an exploding grenade. Several more grenades exploded in the trenches as Emil regained his senses. He snatched his pistol from his holster and rushed toward the battle.

The Hungarians had attacked before Emil was able to organize his raiding party. Caught by surprise, his men reeled backwards. And just when all appeared to be lost, he heard Benezarin.

"Kill the bastards," the corporal shouted. No patriotic slogans. No sacrifice for Mother Russia and the flag. Just kill and survive. And the men responded.

Emil emptied his pistol into several Hungarians, toppling them into the fetid water. Then he picked up a trenching tool and began slashing at the enemy who was pouring into the trenches. He buried the blade in a man's skull and snapped the handle when he tried to pull it out. Searching madly for a weapon, he picked up an empty rifle and used it as a club as the instinct for survival overrode his desire for death.

Emil lunged forward smashing a Hungarian officer's face to pulp with the butt of the rifle. Swinging the weapon back for another blow, he tripped over a corpse and landed on his rifle. As he struggled to retrieve the club, a Hungarian sergeant straddled him and prepared to drive his bayonet into Emil's chest.

Two bullets tore into the sergeant's back and ripped open his stomach, showering Emil with blood and intestines. And there was Benezarin standing over him.

"Come on, Major. Off your ass and back into the fight." He jerked Emil back to his feet and shoved a submachine gun into his hands. They fought together, back to back, working their way down the trench, rallying the men as they went.

Minutes or hours, Emil wondered as the noise of battle subsided. Time seemed to warp during combat.

"We've kicked them back to their lines, Major," Benezarin reported. "You still want to send out the raiding party?" he asked sarcastically, as his boot prodded a dead Hungarian. "Maybe they're just Germans in disguise."

Emil ignored him. "Casualties?" he asked the corporal.

"You count them, Major," Benezarin replied. The man who had saved his life and fought beside him like a brother walked off without another word.

Emil understood Federov and his class. Their entire world had been ripped away overnight, but their confusion and anger would remain for a long time as they tried to grasp what had transpired.

But Benezarin, Emil thought. I'll never understand him and his comrades. They fight like lions for people they hate. He saved my life today, and tonight he could kill me without a second thought.

Emil brushed off his bloody tunic as he observed the carnage that lay around him. He made his way back to the site of the initial enemy penetration, counting survivors. It was easier than counting the dead.

Prayer.

Emil stopped in his tracks. He heard a weak voice muttering a rosary. It was strange. No one prayed. Not in the trenches. Those who believed in God were either dead or deserted. Who could believe in God when they existed in hell on earth?

Emil followed the sound of the voice and found Federov lying on his side bleeding from several wounds. This man who had lost everything still had his God.

And where is my God, Emil asked.

"Major," Federov whispered. "Help me, Major."

"I'll get a medic," Emil responded.

Federov grabbed his arm and pulled him close. "You're a doctor, Major," he said, coughing blood. "I know your secret. The colonel is my uncle and..."

Federov fell back too weak to continue.

He knows, Emil thought. This man knows. And now this young officer wants my help.

Major Daneslberg unbuttoned Federov's tunic automatically and began the process of evaluating the man's wounds. As Emil went to work, tears began to stream down his face. Federov smiled at him gratefully and began to mutter another prayer.

And Emil began to pray with him, in Hebrew, a language he hadn't spoken in years.

If death is not the answer, Sona, then what is? Emil asked, realizing with some base instinct that his killing days were over.

"Thank you," Federov said.

Emil fastened a bandage out of Federov's dirty scarf. He grabbed the lieutenant's wrist and felt for a pulse. Weak. Next, he knelt over his chest and listened for a heartbeat. Almost nothing. Emil sat back and looked at Federov.

This man is dying, yet I feel...good, he thought. Confident, like I have a purpose. I haven't felt this way since Vorzel.

The answer. This dying man had given him the answer. Time to get back to healing.

Forgive me, Sona. Forgive me, Father. Forgive me for dishonoring your memory.

Federov coughed his last breath into Emil's face. Doctor Danelsberg gently closed Federov's eyes and began to recite Kaddish.

11

Petrograd, Russia, October 2, 1917

The first snows of fall had already come and gone and winter was well underway. Food shortages had become commonplace, turning the residents of the city into scavengers, constantly seeking relief from the gnawing pains of hunger and cold. The revolution had not gone as planned—Prime Minister Kerensky was trying to hold together the fourth provisional government since March.

Kerensky had recently crushed an army uprising led by the right-wing General L. G. Kornilov, but he'd had to enlist the help of the Bolsheviks to do it—an unpopular move. Their leader, V. I. Lenin, had been forced to abort his July coup and leave the country when his alliance with the Germans was discovered. Bolsheviks were feared and distrusted by the majority of Russians, but Kerensky's brief alliance gave them a foot in the door.

Evidence of the overwhelming political and social turmoil was prolific. Demonstrations were held all over the city as Social Revolutionaries, Mensheviks, and Bolsheviks marshaled support for their parties. The loyalty of the army was questionable considering the shortages that even they endured, not to mention the horrible mismanagement of the war. Anarchists reveled in the breakdown of the city, pushing it further whenever they could, while thugs and black marketeers made life for the average citizen a walk through the unknown. The country was one spark away from descending into a bloody civil war.

Sona Danelsberg walked home, feet aching from an eighteen-hour shift at the Petrograd Army Hospital—jokingly called the "spa" by those who worked there. Crammed with casualties from the front, it was anything but a resort. In addition to soldiers, the overworked doctors were trying to treat those wounded in street skirmishes and victims of a recent typhus outbreak.

Still, Sona considered herself lucky to have a job in a city with more than a million unemployed workers. At least she could provide, however meagerly, for the two boys.

A man hurrying the opposite direction bumped into her and almost knocked her to the ground. Steadying herself, she watched as more people rushed past her. Then she saw why they were running.

A large group of Social Revolutionaries waving banners and singing the *"Marseillaise"*—the international hymn of the Socialists—was marching toward her. Cursing silently, she ducked into a doorway. If she hadn't been so tired, she would have found another way around; as it was, she prayed they would pass by before trouble started. She had been caught in several dangerous and terrifying riots during the last few months.

The first rows passed her as she pulled herself into the shadows. Factory workers and soldiers with a sprinkling of professionals and priests carried banners that read "Freedom and Bread" and "Land for All the Workers." She wondered how many would live to see the new year.

She watched as they passed without incident and, breathing a sigh of relief, she continued down the street. Several late arrivals rushed to catch up with their comrades. One boy stopped in front of her and asked her to join them. Her response was to hunch down farther into her coat and try to move around him. He grabbed her arm.

"Join us, Sister. We are marching for a free and democratic Russia. We arc all brothers and sisters in the struggle against the capitalists. We will sing and some will make fine speeches when we get to the Winter Palace. Come on, Sister. Join us," he shouted with boyish enthusiasm.

As she pulled her arm away, a friend of his shouted, "Leave her alone, Alex. She's only a Jewess." The marcher left her and joined his companion running down the street.

Some things never change, she thought. Brotherhood and sisterhood. Pooh! They still hate the Jews.

She arrived at her building and entered the foyer.

The house once belonged to one family. Now it housed ten. The foyer, which used to be the domain of the doorman, now housed a family of six.

"Shut the door. You're letting in the cold," an old woman snapped.

Sona closed the door and made her way up the stairs. The smell of mildew, sweat, and open cooking fires permeated the building. She often thought of what had become of the former occupants and how they would have reacted to the treatment of their home.

Some said they had been relatives of the czar himself. If so, they were either dead or in prison and if not, there was nothing left for them here. Everything of value had been carted off; even the banisters had been chopped up for firewood. The thought depressed her.

Sona reached her room and opened the door. There was no lock or knob; the pieces had long since been removed and sold for scrap. She wondered where the boys were. They were always here to greet her.

"Any luck at the market today, Sona?" one of the mothers asked.

"Nothing," she answered, moving to her curtained-off section. "Not a thing. I could only grab a few scraps from the hospital kitchen. If it wasn't for that I don't know how I would feed the boys."

"I know what you mean," the woman replied. "We also rely on what little food Kirsky can bring home from work."

The lady's husband worked in an armaments factory. Kerensky might be unable to feed his people, but he would make damn sure the munitions workers had decent rations. Without the laborers and the munitions they produced, his army would cease to exist.

She drew the curtain aside and blinked in the small light from the single candle in the room. As her vision adjusted, she noticed a man in uniform sitting at the desk that served as their table. The two boys sat in his lap. At first she was afraid, but then she recognized the eyes behind the thickly bearded face and her heart fluttered.

"Emil?" she asked, tentatively not wanting the apparition to vanish.

"Yes, Sona. I'm home," he said.

As he spoke, her relief and shock overcame her, pulling her to the floor.

Sona came to in bed. Her husband was sitting in a chair beside her, watching her with concern.

"Emil?"

"It's all right. I'm here," he answered.

She sat bolt upright in bed and gasped, "The boys?"

"I fixed them some dinner from what you brought back from the hospital," he answered, quietly holding a finger to his lips. "After eating, they went right to sleep."

They stared at one another for a long time enjoying each other's presence after the long separation. Emil leaned over and grabbed her hand, holding it gently between his palms. She noticed they were rough and calloused. Not like the smooth hands of the doctor she married. Finally when they were satisfied the other was real, the questions began.

Sona told her story first. She began with that horrible night in Vorzel and their rescue from death by the mysterious peasant "Zenon."

"I can't ever remember having a patient like that. I treated very few people outside the village, almost none that weren't Jewish. I should remember him. But I can't," Emil said worriedly.

"It doesn't matter, dear. He was a gift from God. His friend Ivan made sure we arrived safely here in Petrograd and helped us find this flat. I've never heard from him since. You should be grateful, Emil," she admonished.

"I am, Sona. I guess my memory is not what it used to be. But that's not important. What is important is that you and our son are alive." He smiled at her, overcome with relief and gratitude.

"Thanks to your old professor Dr. Vorshilov. I am very grateful to him for giving me a job at the hospital. He thinks very highly of you. He said you were the most promising surgeon he has ever seen. Your hands were the fine tools of a master craftsman."

"Not anymore," he sighed holding up his arms.

"Tell me what happened, Emil. It must have been horrible thinking us dead. At least, we had hope that you were alive. Dr. Vorshilov kept reassuring me. He said you would return one day because you had nowhere else to go. And here you are. But you. What was life like without hope?"

"Horrible. You must understand that I had no idea you were still alive." He looked her straight in the eyes. "I thought about suicide. I couldn't imagine life without you and Viktor. Vorzel. Father. But I couldn't bring myself to do it. I guess father's teachings were so deeply embedded in my mind that I chose another route. What I'm about to tell you, Sona, I am not proud of. But it is what I did. You deserve to know what kind of man your husband has become."

"Whatever happened is not important, Emil. We are together now."

"It is important to me, Sona. These things I did...I must tell you. I must tell someone," he pleaded. The look on her husband's face was one Sona had never seen before. He was tortured, lost, and afraid, all at the same time. She was afraid for him.

"I love you, Emil. If it will help relieve you from whatever you are suffering, then I will listen for as long as it takes. And know that no matter what you say, it can never change the way I feel about you."

"Thank you, Sona. We shall see."

He paused for a moment and gathered his thoughts.

"I wanted to die," he began, stroking his beard. "As a Jew, I soon concluded that I would not commit suicide. I did, however, make a conscious decision to seek out death."

As the candle burned low, Emil recounted the horrors he had witnessed, the things he could not forgive himself for doing.

In the dark, he imagined his wife's eyes were hardening against him, but he forced himself to continue.

"Once I realized how I had betrayed my faith and my gifts as a doctor, I requested a transfer back to Petrograd to the army hospital. At first they refused. But I was adamant and, as it turned out, the local commanders considered my insane actions on the battlefield quite heroic. In the end, they gave me another medal and grudgingly granted my request.

"So I returned to Petrograd. My plan was to get passage on the first steamer out of the country. But everybody wants out. My attempts were cut short. They wanted passports, money and, as I am a Russian citizen, a letter of emigration from an embassy official. How could I get those things? I got so frustrated I went to see Dr. Vorshilov. I thought he might have some ideas. I was literally at my wit's end.

"Can you imagine if I had been successful in getting out of Russia? I would have never gone to the hospital and seen Vorshilov. I would have never seen you again. I thought about that on the long walk here. I thought about a lot of things. And here is what I concluded.

"I am a cold-blooded killer. I am attempting to desert the army and leave my country in the middle of a war. I am willing to leave everything I know behind for the dismal chance of finding a new life abroad. I shunned my father's teachings and forsook his religion. I betrayed my Hippocratic oath at the time I was needed most. All I can offer you now is the fervent hope for a new life. Where that life will be and what form it will take I haven't the slightest idea. I must, therefore, conclude that I am also half mad. Or maybe more than half mad. That is the man you see before you now, Sona Danelsberg. That is the father of your child," he finished, looking at his feet.

"The man I see before me now is the same man I married," Sona said proudly. "He is still full of love for his family and filled with concern for their future. Emil, please look up at me."

Emil slowly raised his head until his eyes met hers. She grabbed his hands and pulled him forward until his face was inches from hers.

"What you did at the front was understandable. It was the reaction of a sane man to an insane situation. Without hint or warning you lost everything you knew and loved.

"You are not a lesser man for having done what you did. I can see that, my love. Instead of suicide you chose an honorable death fighting the blood-sworn enemy of your country. When you could no longer save lives with your healing, you chose to save your country by killing its enemies. And in the end, when you regained a sense of yourself, you made a rational decision to leave the country that never wanted you, the country you served so well that repaid you by slaughtering your family and destroying your village and your heritage.

"The husband that sits before me now is a strong and courageous man who is willing to sacrifice everything to give his family a well-deserved fresh start in life. That is the man I see. And I love him more now than the day I married him."

"Oh, God, Sona." He cried. He fell to his knees and, laying his head in her lap, sobbed like a child. Sona stroked his head and rocked him gently back and forth. When his tears had subsided, she took off his clothes and pulled him into her bed. After a while, they made quiet love. When he dozed off, Sona got up to check the two boys. They were still sound asleep.

She got back into bed beside her husband, careful not to disturb his slumber, and thought about the days ahead. She couldn't figure out which frightened her more. The thought of leaving Russia...or the thought of staying in Russia. Eventually, before the dawn, she drifted to sleep and into the nightmare of Vorzel burning before her eyes.

Petrograd Docks, Petrograd, Russia, October 6, 1917

The morning air was crisp with the arrival of snow flurries. Sadly, there wasn't enough snow to cover the dirt and soot of Russia's largest industrial city. It only added to the depressing atmosphere that pervaded the city by washing out the color to a dull gray.

Emil Danelsberg walked quickly through the silent streets. His hands were shoved deeply into his greatcoat pockets and his scarf was wrapped tightly around his face as he tried to keep warm. The uniform was new, courtesy of Dr. Vorshilov. His face was freshly shaven leaving a waxed, military moustache. He looked the part of the professional officer, save his shoes. His boots, new a few months before, had become worn from his service at the front and he hoped to acquire a new pair before they came apart. Unfortunately, shoes of any kind were in extremely short supply, but that was the least of his worries.

Emil had been coming to the docks for the past three days in hopes of finding passage on any of the outbound ships. His success had been nil. A black market for tickets, passports, and the other necessary documents needed to leave Russia had been flourishing since the overthrow of the czar in March. His Russian rubles were worthless as the economy unraveled under the strain of the protracted war. Gold, jewels, and foreign currency were the only things the black marketeers would trade. Emil had none of those, but he was persistent and patient.

After talking to Dr. Vorshilov, he adopted a new approach. Armed with forged documents supplied by the ever-resourceful doctor, Emil could board any ship in the harbor as a health inspector checking incoming cargoes for rats and other infestations. When the opportunity presented itself, he would try to barter his services as a ship's physician for passage for him and his family.

Some captains were extremely sympathetic, others were incensed at his deception and threatened to turn him into the harbor authorities. It was a risky game he was playing. So far no ship's captain had accepted his offer. At the same time, he hadn't been turned in. He couldn't expect his luck to hold.

Today, he was paying a call on an Italian freighter, *Il Santa Milano*. The ship had docked the previous night and he had set up the inspection with the first officer before returning home. He hoped this would be the one.

Emil was having a hard time looking at Sona's expectant face when he walked in the door only to dash her hopes with a slight shake of the head. They hadn't told the boys of their plans in case one of them might inadvertently say something to one of their neighbors. The Danelsbergs couldn't afford to be exposed. The punishment was death.

Emil noticed the crowds at the docks were especially large and surly this day. With the first snows of winter, a fresh panic descended on the city and, with it, renewed attempts to escape the civil war and resultant starvation that everyone anticipated. The soldiers on duty at the port were having a tough time controlling the crowd. Emil pressed his way into the mob and made his way to the manned barricade.

"Major Doctor Emil Danelsberg here to inspect the freighter *Il Santa Milano*," he announced, handing over the envelope containing Vorshilov's forged papers. The sergeant on duty took the proffered documents and pretended to read them. He was an ignorant peasant whose only attributes were his hard-nosed nature and his bulky frame that had earned him his stripes.

"Where are you from?" he shouted loud enough to be heard above the noise of the crowd.

"The Army Health Inspectorate. It's all there in the papers," he shouted back.

The sergeant pretended to look over the documents again, unaware that he was looking at them upside down and, seemingly satisfied, put them back into the envelope.

"These seem to be in order, Major," he said, handing the documents back. He never offered Emil a salute. Very few soldiers did these days. Emil took the documents and passed through the barricade. He let go a small sigh of relief as he passed through the first check.

He made his way through the soldiers, longshoremen, and passengers lucky enough to get a ticket. Even here there was a sense of urgency as the passengers hurried to board before the port authority closed the harbor until further notice. It was a tactic the bureaucrats used to accrue more bribes from the passengers and ship captains. Corruption was rampant. When the authorities were satisfied, they would reopen the port.

Emil approached the Italian freighter and stood at a distance to observe the activity around the ship. He was looking for any sign that would tell him his story had been uncovered and he was about to be arrested. What would alert him to that fact, he had no idea. As he waited and watched, his stomach began to churn as his fear grew. Noticing nothing out of the ordinary, he walked to the two slovenly soldiers guarding the gangway.

"Major Doctor Danelsberg, reporting for an inspection of this ship's cargo. It has been arranged with the first officer." Emil handed his documents to the larger of the two soldiers. Neither came to attention and neither offered a salute. The soldier looked at the documents and showed them to the other guard; they looked up and rapidly came to attention. Danelsberg thought this odd until he heard a voice behind him.

"Let's have a look at the good doctor's papers, shall we?" Emil turned around and found himself staring at a small, bespectacled man in uniform with the rank and insignia of a colonel in the Interior Ministry. He was backed up by four well-armed and smartly dressed soldiers. Danelsberg's blood turned to ice as he realized this man represented Kerensky's internal security forces, the inheritors of the *OKHRANA*, the czar's dreaded secret police. His shoulders sagged under the gaze of the colonel as his fear of discovery and capture materialized.

"Now, now, Major. What are you so upset about?" The colonel smiled warmly. "You have been doing the new government a great service protecting our country from foreign pestilence. Trouble is, no one seems to have a record of your existence or assignment." The fake smile vanished from his face as he grabbed the documents out of the soldier's trembling hands.

The colonel snapped his fingers. "Bring him," he ordered. The four Interior Ministry soldiers surrounded Danelsberg and marched him after the colonel. The crowd quieted and parted before them as the secret police escorted him away from the docks. These weren't ordinary soldiers. They could make people vanish into thin air, never to be heard from again.

"Poor man."

"I wonder what he did."

"Probably a deserter or black marketeer."

"Maybe he's a Romanov trying to escape."

"Impossible. They are either dead, in jail, or out of the country."

Emil listened to the whispered conjectures of the crowd as he passed. They were the only eulogy he was likely to receive. Once outside the port, the soldiers blindfolded him and shoved him roughly into the back of a waiting truck. Before they shut the doors, he heard the din of the crowd as it came back to life and continued its struggle for survival, a struggle he'd just lost.

Dr. Vasily Vorshilov awakened to the sound of loud knocking at his door. The administrator and chief surgeon of the Russian army's largest hospital was used to being awakened at odd hours. He wondered if new street fighting had broken out as he struggled into his robe and made his way across the darkened flat to the door.

When he opened the door, he was shocked to find a near-hysterical Sona Danelsberg. Vorshilov ushered her into the apartment and down the hall before he shut the door.

Vorshilov helped her out of her winter coat and turned up the oil lamp on the kitchen table. Her face was streaked with tears and her eyes swollen from crying. He made his way to the stove, stirred the coals and began heating the tea kettle. She was too upset to speak so he left her in the kitchen and went to his bathroom where he retrieved a small bottle of medicinal brandy. Vorshilov splashed cold water on his face and looked in the mirror. The thinning gray hair was disheveled and his eyes were red rimmed from lack of sleep.

When he returned to the kitchen, the kettle was whistling as the water boiled. He made two cups of tea and poured a healthy amount of brandy into Sona's cup.

"Here you go, my dear," he said, handing her the cup. "Drink this. It will warm you up and calm you down." He took the seat opposite her and waited as she blew into the cup to cool it off. Her hands shook slightly as she raised the cup to her lips. After several swallows, she set the cup down and looked at the doctor.

"I'm so sorry, Doctor. I panicked when I could not find Emil and knew of no one I could turn to for help. Please help," she cried, as her tears began again. "I have nowhere else to go."

Vorshilov reached across the table and gently patted her hand. When she had calmed down, he asked her to start again.

"What exactly happened to Emil, Sona?"

"He went to the docks again this morning. As you know, he has been trying to find us passage out of the country. He always tells me when he will be home so I won't worry. He has never been late, but tonight he never came home." She paused to collect herself.

"After waiting for a couple of hours, I left the boys with a neighbor and went to the hospital. No one had seen him and you were in surgery. So I went to the docks."

"It must be freezing out there. I know it has been snowing most of the day," Vorshilov admonished Sona.

"It is, Doctor, but I had to find Emil. So I went to the docks. It is a madhouse down there. Nobody would listen to me. After several more hours, I found a soldier who told me he had seen an army major placed under arrest by the secret police. He didn't know if it was a doctor, but he described Emil. What will they do with him, Dr. Vorshilov? I have just gotten my husband back. I couldn't stand to lose him again," she wailed.

"Shhh. Shhh. It will be all right, my dear. I will go find out what they have done with your husband."

"Will you, Dr. Vorshilov?" she asked, grabbing his hands in hers and looking at him with pleading eyes.

"Of course. Now you must go home and get your boys. Bring them back here to my flat. I will give you a key. If the secret police did arrest your husband, then you and your family could be in danger."

The doctor helped her back into her coat and saw her out the door. He then put on his clothes and grabbed his heavy coat. When he opened his apartment door, he looked back and wondered whether he would see his home again.

If the secret police had Emil, then they might find out where he had gotten the forged papers. If so, he was in danger. Maybe his flat wasn't safe for Emil's family, but it was too late to think about that now. He closed his door and began the long climb down the stairs to the icy street below.

Fortress of Peter and Paul, Petrograd, Russia, October 28, 1917

The Fortress of Peter and Paul, built by Peter the Great in 1704, stood on Hare Island overlooking the Neva River. It was one of many original edifices of the imperial city erected on the corpses of 325,000 peasants. Its great bastions were named after Peter and his greatest commander. In the past, it had housed elite units of the Russian army. Recently it had become better known as a political prison for enemies of the revolution.

Many a man and woman had disappeared into its bowels never to be seen again. It was home to several Romanovs, including Grand Duke Nikolai Nikolaievich, uncle of the czar and former commander of the Imperial Russian Army, now awaiting trial and execution as the irresponsible architect of the slaughter of two million Russian fighting men in the war with Germany.

Emil Danelsberg, one of the Fortress's newest prisoners, sat in a small cell with four other men. They received one meal a day consisting of a moldy piece of bread and a tepid gruel. The cell was filthy and infested with vermin and rats. Emil was unaware of time deep in the fortress dungeon.

So far he'd avoided execution, but he knew that wouldn't last much longer. Down the corridor, several times a day, men were dragged from their cells and taken into a small room where they were executed by a firing squad. During one of his interrogations by the diminutive Colonel Prosky, he had been dragged past the killing room while the door was open. Soldiers were tossing out a fresh corpse and Emil saw the interior of the cell, walls pockmarked with bullets, floors stained with blood. A solitary stool sat in the middle of the room. This cell was greatly feared in the prison, more so than the interrogation and torture rooms. No prisoner ever walked out of it alive.

Prosky had interrogated him once a day since his arrival. Although the sessions were relatively non-violent, they left him emotionally drained and physically exhausted. The small man was frightening. His job was to break the human spirit and he went at it with technical expertise. The colonel was only beginning to ply his trade on Danelsberg.

The key rattled in the lock and the door swung open. Two soldiers came in and dragged Danelsberg out of the dark cell into the dim light of the corridor. They threw him to the floor while they locked the cell. Picking him up, they dragged him down the hall. Instead of taking him to the interrogation cell, they stopped in front of the execution chamber. Emil's heart began to hammer in his chest as he broke out in a cold sweat. One soldier opened the door to the killing room and the other shoved him into the small, dank room.

"Sit on the stool. Hands on your knees and stare directly at the back wall. Do not look toward the door. Do not move. If you disobey these orders, I will put a bullet in the back of your head. Now move, prisoner!" the guard shouted.

Emil tried to stand, but his legs were too weak to support him. He crawled to the stool and climbed on it facing the bullet-riddled and bloodstained wall. The stones were flecked with tiny pieces of matter that could only be from the brain and the skull. The room stank of decayed flesh. Emil dragged his hands to his knees and tried not to think of what was coming. Behind, the door slammed shut and he was left alone in the abattoir.

An eternity later, the door opened and a man walked in. The door slammed shut leaving the stranger in the room with him. It was unnerving. The stranger neither spoke or moved, but Emil could hear him breathing. Emil's heart was beating so hard he thought it would burst from his chest.

He heard a shuffling and footsteps as the stranger moved behind him. The person stopped, unbuckled a holster and withdrew a pistol. Emil heard the pistol cock and then felt it placed against the back of his neck. He began to mutter the "*Shmae, O Israel.*"

Before he was finished, the person pulled the trigger. He felt the dull thud of the hammer striking home in the back of his skull, but after a moment, he realized there had been no report, that he was still sitting on the stool and his heart was still beating. He gradually let out his breath in a slow hiss as his body went numb from shock.

"Well, Jew. It seems the military wants you immediately," Prosky spoke. "They will get the privilege of executing you for desertion in the face of the enemy. It was a privilege I was looking forward to.

"I was also looking forward to spending more time with you. I know sooner or later you would have implicated our good friend, Dr. Vorshilov, in the matter of these forged documents. But the good doctor cannot escape me forever. The revolution waits for no man," Prosky said, mockingly.

Emil felt a foot in the middle of his back shoving him off the stool. From his knees, he turned to see his tormentor. The colonel clasped his hands behind his back and smiled his false smile.

"Sorry I won't be seeing you again, Doctor. Of course, no one will be seeing you again." The colonel laughed a small laugh and walked to the door. He rapped on it and the door immediately opened.

"One more thing," he said, turning to Danelsberg. "I want this cell spotless before you leave us. Understood, Jew?"

Emil nodded weakly.

"See to it," he ordered the guards before he left. They brought him a bucket of water, a scrub brush, and some dirty rags and Emil set about his task.

Out of the frying pan and into the fire, Emil thought. At least the army won't torture me. Or so he hoped.

The Admiralty, Petrograd, Russia, October 29, 1917

Emil sat in a small room in the basement of a large building. He'd been transported in another truck, blindfolded and shackled. The trip to his present location had not taken long, so he didn't think he was too far from the Fortress of Peter and Paul. He assumed the building he was in was large because of the huge stone supports he saw in the basement.

He'd arrived in his present room blindfolded and was not allowed to remove it until he had taken off all his clothes. The guards left him with a small blanket, his only protection against the damp cold. He was tired, hungry, and numb.

Emil hoped the execution would be soon. He'd resigned himself to death and now each moment he stayed alive separated him from the peace he hoped death would bring. He sneezed and brought his hand across his nose. In his present condition, he would soon contract pneumonia and he much preferred a bullet in the back of the head to that long and agonizing death.

Deep in his thoughts, he hadn't heard the guards come into his room. Before him they set a clean uniform, razor, bucket of cold water, small bar of soap, and a towel.

"Shave and get cleaned up. You have fifteen minutes," a guard ordered. They turned and left the room.

For a moment Emil considered using the razor on his wrists instead of waiting the fifteen minutes for his court-martial, death verdict, and execution. Instead, remembering his father's teachings, he put the thought from his mind and cleaned up as best he could. When he was done, he felt immeasurably better. He found the uniform fit perfectly.

Just like the army, he thought. Wake you up, clean you up, and then shoot you. Now if only I had some food I could depart this world a new man.

The guards returned and escorted him out of the room.

When they arrived at the first floor, Emil looked outside at a snow-covered courtyard. Men were drilling in formation under the barking cadence of an NCO. The sentries stood sharply at attention and the men appeared to be well fed and clothed. It was entirely unusual for a unit of the Russian army to act in a military manner since the revolution. Most units elected their officers democratically and spent more time pursuing women and food than obeying orders.

"Eyes front!" snapped one of his guards.

Emil locked his head forward as they headed up a grand staircase. At the top, the group turned right and marched down several doors to a large double door guarded by two soldiers. They came to attention and opened the doors.

"Enter," a voice commanded.

The party marched into a large, ornately appointed office and stopped in the middle of the room. They came to attention and the NCO saluted and led the soldiers back out, leaving Emil alone in the company of a large, bald officer staring out of a window at the drilling soldiers below. After a moment, he turned and came toward Emil, hand outstretched.

"Well, Major Doctor Danelsberg. I see we have both moved up in the world."

Emil shook the offered hand. "My God. Colonel…I mean *General* Krikalev. Is it really you?" he asked, staring at his former commanding officer.

"In the flesh, Doctor."

"But what of the regiment?"

"Here with me in St. Petersburg… Petrograd. I can't get used to saying Petrograd. Even after three years. I guess those of us who knew the city the way she was will always think of her as St. Petersburg."

Emil felt light-headed. Here resided his commanding officer from the regiment he had served with since the beginning of the war, moved a thousand miles north, in an ornate office in the middle of Petrograd. He felt cold and clammy and began to sway on his feet. The general grabbed him firmly under his arm and helped him to a chair in front of the desk.

"Kubatov!"

The door opened and a guard came in, coming to attention.

"Bring the doctor some hot tea, bread, cheese and anything else you can find. Make it quick."

"Yes, General." The guard saluted and left the room.

"I don't understand, sir. They said I was going to be executed by the army for desertion. What is to become of me?"

Krikalev laughed. "Don't worry. I did not have you brought here to kill you. As for your other questions— the rest can wait until you have had something to eat."

The door opened and Kubatov appeared with a silver tray loaded with a tea urn and food. He set it on the desk, saluted and left.

"Eat!" Krikalev ordered the doctor.

Emil needed no further encouragement. He dug into the bread and cheese. There was smoked sturgeon and a hot bowl of beef borscht. He hadn't seen this kind of food since the beginning of the war. Sated, he sat back in the chair and felt guilty. Sona and the boys hadn't seen food like this in months.

"Don't feel bad, Doctor. You Jews feel guilty about everything. I have never understood that about your kind." Krikalev laid a hand on Emil's shoulder. "You can relax. Your family is here under my protection. They are being well taken care of."

"My family!" Emil gasped, sitting straight up in his chair.

"Yes, your family. When the men found out that they were the family of the great Dr. Danelsberg, nothing became good enough for your wife, your son, and his little friend. You see, they remember you quite well. You saved many a man's life in this regiment. Some more than once. You even saved mine. That is why you are here."

"Dr. Vorshilov?" Emil guessed.

"Correct. When your wife couldn't find you, she enlisted the aid of Dr. Vorshilov. Being in charge of the army hospital, he knew of our regiment's arrival in the city before the revolution.

He treated some of my men. He came to see me and told me of your disappearance.

"It took a while to track you down, but in the end we found you under the care of our new internal security forces. You are extremely lucky to be alive, Doctor. Prosky, that little bastard, is playing Robespierre to Kerensky's Danton. He considers everybody to be an enemy of the revolution, while Kerensky still fights to defeat Germany. Between them the country is falling apart."

"When I left the regiment last year you were still at the front. What happened?" Emil asked. "How did you get all the way to Petrograd?"

"The war was lost during Brusilov's offensive, Emil. You know that. You were there. We had a chance to destroy the Hapsburg empire. Because of the fools at *Stavka*, we lost the opportunity. After that, every order to attack was senseless. I realized that to save the army, and with it Russia, the Romanovs and their lackeys must be deposed. I took my regiment out of the line and marched on Petrograd with others in March.

"My men know I saved them from annihilation at the front. That is why they still maintain discipline and a sense of integrity. I make sure they are well fed and clothed and in return they follow me wherever I lead them. The Provisional Government recognized a disciplined unit and kept us here to protect them. In turn, they made me a general and stationed us here at the Admiralty."

"But the Provisional Government is still fighting. The army is still being destroyed. How can you follow them, if that is why you went over in the first place? To stop the senseless slaughter at the front?" Emil tried to make sense of Krikalev's position.

"I know. I had hope for the government at first, but they are too weak, Russia too divided," Krikalev explained. "They will not survive the year. So we wait, my men and I, to see what will happen next. We will serve any man who stops the war and begins to rebuild the country."

"Any man? Even Lenin or Trotsky? Surely you would not follow the Bolsheviks."

"Any man, Doctor. Any man who will save Russia. But that is not your concern. You won't be here to see the new Russia. Whatever it may be."

"I don't understand," Emil looked up suspiciously. "I thought you had saved me to serve in the regiment."

"I considered it, Doctor. You are a damn good surgeon and they are hard to come by these days. But you are a Jew. And Russia has never been a place for Jews.

"I have spoken to your wife. She told me what happened at Vorzel. I am sorry, but it only goes to prove my point. You are not wanted here and never have been. You are too good a man to lose in something as senseless as a pogrom. I don't know what the future holds for Russia, but it could not be good for the Jews. So I am sending you out of the country."

Emil sat up surprised. "How are you going to do that?"

"The how is not important, Doctor. The why is. You served a country that despises you. You saved men's lives that, during other times, would spit on you. You served the regiment in an exemplary fashion. Your reward will be forced exile and…life for you and your family."

Emil stood and shook the General's hand gratefully.

"It is done. Now come to the window with me, Doctor. I want to show you something," said Krikalev.

They made their way to the window and gazed on the courtyard below. Two companies of soldiers drilled with precision on the snow-covered ground. The captain leading the troops noticed the general in the window and snapped off a smart salute. Their boots echoed in unison off the bricks.

"That is the future, Major Doctor Danelsberg. The Russian army. Someday soon, the sound of its marching boots will make the world fear and respect us. It is what I will bequeath to my family and my country. Strength, power, and the will to use it."

They continued to stare at the courtyard as fresh snow fell on the ground.

12

The Savoy Hotel, London, England, October 30, 1917

Assistant Chief Inspector Dowling Brunswick, Scotland Yard, entered the hotel lobby in a foul mood. He had been at home in his warm bed when the summons came from Chief Inspector Pagly. Brunswick was off duty this evening and couldn't understand why the on-duty inspector couldn't field the call. The chief inspector's messenger was rather vague as to the nature of the summons saying only that it was a matter of the utmost importance and delicacy.

Brunswick took off his slicker and shook the cold October drizzle from it before handing it to Pagly's aide, a man named Lewiston. "Right, Lewiston. Now show me, if you would be so kind, where this matter of utmost importance and delicacy took place."

"Yes, Inspector. Right this way," Lewiston answered, holding out his arm in the direction of the elevators.

They made their way across the lobby of the luxurious hotel toward the waiting elevator, the operator standing by. Brunswick looked around the lobby not surprised to see it this empty, save for a few officers out for a nightcap before bedding down with their whore of the evening.

Who could blame them, Brunswick thought. Home on leave before returning to the bloody horror of the front. If I were them,

I'd get sodding drunk and find the most expensive whore in London, too. Bugger the bleeding politicians who got us into this mess.

He entered the elevator with Lewiston, followed by the operator.

"Which floor, Gentlemen?"

"Four, please," answered Lewiston.

As if he didn't already know, Brunswick thought.

The elevator began its ascent and Brunswick went over what precious little he'd been able to get out of Lewiston. A dead body, probably. Most likely someone important, considering his midnight summons and obviously a murder since the Yard had been called in. Whatever else he would learn awaited him on the fourth floor. The door opened and the inspector, with Lewiston in tow, exited into the hall.

Brunswick moved off in the direction of the uniformed London police standing guard on either side of the double doors of a suite. One of the bobbies opened the door and Brunswick and Lewiston entered the plushly decorated living room. Several men were standing in a group speaking in hushed tones. On seeing Brunswick, a small, rotund man with a balding head and waxed moustache separated himself from the group and approached him.

"Ah, Brunswick. Good to see you," Pagly said, as he shook the inspector's hand. "Sorry to get you out of bed so early, but we've got a rather dicey situation on our hands."

"It's perfectly all right, Chief Inspector," Brunswick lied. "What can I do to help?"

"That's it." He grabbed Brunswick by the arm and ushered him to the group he'd been talking to. He recognized most of the men. They were Yard specialists. Technicians, the coroner, a photographer. Two men he'd never seen before. They were tailored in Saville Row and had the distinct air of Whitehall about them. He wasn't far off.

"Inspector Brunswick, this is Sir Nigel Mansfield from No. 10 Downing Street and Lord Harry Barton, a personal representative from Buckingham Palace. You know the rest."

"Sir Nigel, Your Lordship," Brunswick said, nodding his head in the direction of the two men.

Buckingham Palace and No. 10 Downing Street, eh, Brunswick thought. That means the King and the Prime Minister are involved in whatever happened here.

Sir Nigel nodded back. Lord Barton continued to smoke a cigarette quite nervously. Although Lord Barton outranked Sir Nigel, it was the latter to whom everyone seemed to defer.

"Inspector, there has been a suicide."

"Begging the Lordship's pardon. But suicides are usually handled by the local constabulary," Brunswick snapped. Of all things to be gotten out of bed for—a suicide—even if it was someone important. Sleep was precious to a Yard man, especially during a war.

Sir Nigel raised an eyebrow in the direction of the chief inspector as if asking if this was the right man for the job. The chief inspector nodded his head slightly and went on.

"I understand your misgivings, Dow. But the situation is rather more complicated than simple suicide."

"I'll say," interjected Lord Barton.

"Have you ever heard of Lord Hammersmythe, Inspector?" Sir Nigel asked.

"Well...yes, sir. Lord Hammersmythe is a member of the war cabinet. Assistant to the Secretary of Heavy Industry, I think. He is one of those responsible for hounding Churchill out of the First Sea Lord's office after the Gallipoli disaster. He was right, too. That bastard Churchill got a lot of good lads killed. Maybe Hammersmythe should be the First Sea Lord."

"Well he'll never have a chance, Inspector. It was he who committed suicide a short while ago," Sir Nigel said, looking straight at Brunswick.

"We have reason to believe he was being blackmailed by the Germans," the chief inspector added.

"Stupid, bloody idiot," Lord Barton added, spitting a piece of tobacco from between his lips.

"I see." Brunswick kept silent waiting for someone to continue.

"It is even more complicated than that. It seems as though he was helped in his attempt," Sir Nigel explained.

"So murder has not been ruled out as a possibility?" Brunswick asked.

"Not unless you count talking someone into committing suicide murder, Inspector," answered a voice from behind Brunswick. He turned to see a young man standing in the open bedroom door. The man, immaculately dressed, appeared fresh even this late at night. He was handsome with a confident face.

"You see, Inspector. I talked him into it, loaded my captured German Luger, and handed it to him."

"And who in the hell are you?" Brunswick asked.

"Percy Chadwick Hammersmythe, Lord of Tankenshire. I assumed the title upon my father's untimely death," he answered, smiling.

The room was silent save for Lord Barton, who spit another piece of tobacco and muttered, "Goddamned bloody fool."

Brunswick sat in a comfortable chair facing Sir Nigel, who stood by the side of the fireplace warming his hands. Lord Barton and Chief Inspector Pagly sat on his right and left respectively. The other Yard people were busy in the bedroom investigating, photographing, and cataloging the suicide scene. Lord Hammersmythe had been escorted down the hall to another room where he remained under guard.

"You see now, Dow, the sense of urgency facing us," began the Chief Inspector.

"Yes, sir. But I don't see what it has to do with me," Brunswick said, trying to hide his irritation. "Certainly Intelligence should handle this one considering the possibility of the late lord's collusion with Germany. I am a homicide specialist. Surely counter espionage is way out of my brief."

"Correct, Inspector. But Intelligence is closely monitored by Parliament and we can't afford to have this one leak out," Sir Nigel explained.

"Damn well right we can't," added Lord Barton angrily. "Lord Hammersmythe was a close cousin of His Majesty's. If the press grabbed ahold of this, it could pull down the monarchy.

"A member of the royal household passing state secrets to the Germans. The same Germans, I might add, who mowed down 600,000 British men at the Battle of the Somme. The populace would scream for blood. The Prime Minister would be forced to resign and King George would be pressed to abdicate by the House of Commons. The House of Hanover cannot be destroyed," Barton stated emphatically.

While talking, Lord Barton fished a gold cigarette case out of his jacket. Opening it, he pulled out a Dunhill and snapped the case shut. He tapped the cigarette on the case and paused to light it before carrying on with his speech.

"The resulting German propaganda victory would destroy morale at the front. How would you feel if you were a Tommy in the trenches? You're dying in wholesale lots at the front for king and country and the king's own are selling you out at home behind your back. The potential catastrophe boggles the mind," he said, waving the cigarette case at Brunswick.

"You see, Inspector, the Germans are planning an offensive in the spring," Sir Nigel spoke, picking up where Lord Barton had left off. "A giant push with everything they've got to win the war. America is now in the war, but her troops won't be ready for battle until the summer of next year. We have to hold until then. This...this news could destroy our resolve. We simply cannot allow that to happen."

So they're afraid of losing the war over this, Brunswick thought. I wonder what they're not telling me.

"How can I help?" Brunswick asked.

"Dow, you are my best, most tight-lipped Inspector. We need you to conduct this investigation, tying up all the loose ends as soon as possible. Present your findings to the King and the PM. We also need you to bury it...come up with a plausible story explaining Lord Hammersmythe's death that the press will buy and fabricate a reason for young Lord Percy's sudden departure from the country."

"Lord Percy is leaving the country?" Brunswick asked, raising an eyebrow. "I'd have thought you'd want to keep him here where you can keep an eye on him."

"Lord Percy is an embarrassment to the crown. It is the express wish of His Majesty that he leave the country. As soon as possible," Sir Nigel said. He stood fully erect staring down his nose at Inspector Brunswick.

Brunswick looked at Sir Nigel. The imperious bastard wanted a miracle. He also wanted Brunswick to break several laws. But do laws apply to kings, he thought. And if I act for kings, then can I, too, break laws? Sod all! It's a bloody mess any way I slice it.

Brunswick shoved his anger aside and concentrated on the suicide. "Lord Percy's actions can be explained. He found out his father was a traitor and supplied him with the decent way out. If I remember correctly, he made quite a splash in the press with his heroics in France."

"Your memory serves, Inspector. What didn't make the press was his sadistic treatment of both his men and his prisoners. He was sent home at the request of his commanding officer." Sir Nigel hesitated to continue, his eyes glancing nervously at Lord Barton and Chief Inspector Pagly. It looked as though he wanted one or the other to carry on. Neither of the two men would look him in the eye, so Sir Nigel sighed and picked up a manila folder from the coffee table.

"It is rather distasteful…I mean…Well, you'd better have a look for yourself," he stammered, handing the envelope to Brunswick.

So here it comes, Brunswick thought.

He opened the envelope and pulled out a set of grainy photographs depicting a homosexual orgy. Brunswick wasn't shocked. As a detective, and later an inspector for Scotland Yard, he had witnessed the most depraved acts imaginable. This was quite tame compared to some of the stuff he had seen.

The pictures showed two men and two boys participating in different acts of homosexuality and bondage. Brunswick recognized the late Lord Hammersmythe. The younger man had on a mask but Brunswick made a guess.

"Lord Percy?"

"Unfortunately," replied Sir Nigel, grimacing.

"How do we know for sure?"

"He admitted it to us. And with a smile on his face," said an exasperated Lord Barton. "The whole family's gone lunatic."

"So this is what the Germans used to get to Lord Hammersmythe?"

"Yes, Dow," answered Pagly. "And now you see why we must sweep this whole sordid mess under the carpet and get Lord Percy out of the country as quickly as possible."

"Yes, sir," Brunswick sighed, preparing himself for the hours ahead.

"Good. Then we'll let you get to your job." Pagly and Barton rose from their chairs and made their way for the door followed by Sir Nigel. Sir Nigel paused by Brunswick.

"I have spoken with both the PM and His Majesty. I can assure you what you do here will not go unrewarded."

"Thank you, Sir Nigel," Brunswick answered neutrally.

When the men had left, Brunswick looked at the photos one more time.

So these are the kind of men we are fighting the war for, he thought disgustedly. Centuries of inbreeding, that's what did it. And these bastards will reward me for this cover-up with a promotion to chief inspector.

"Inspector, we're about finished up in here." Brunswick looked up to see the crime scene detective standing in the bedroom door.

"Phillips. Good. Let me see what you've got."

Brunswick discarded his personal emotions and went about his business.

"Bloody powerful thing, the Luger. We just dug the bullet out of the ceiling. Seems the victim placed the barrel just..." Phillips began to explain as Brunswick joined the team in the bedroom.

"Are you sure he can be trusted?" Nigel asked.

"Yes, Sir Nigel. I'd bet my career on it," Pagly answered.

"Well, that is exactly what you have done, Chief Inspector. Bet your career on it."

They exited the elevator. Lord Barton, done with his cigarette, looked for a place to discard the butt. Not finding one, he pressed it into the gloved hand of the elevator operator with a distasteful look on his face. The elevator operator maintained his composure and didn't utter a word. After all, everyone knew the royals were eccentric.

Buckingham Palace, London, England, November 2, 1917

George V, King of Great Britain and Ireland and Emperor of India sat in his study beside a roaring fire, drinking brandy. He was not a happy man. His reign had been anything but fruitful.

His father, Edward VII, had given him little formal education or direction in ruling the British empire. Edward, himself, had received precious little from his mother, Queen Victoria, who chose to exclude the Prince of Wales from state affairs. Edward, whose main accomplishment was restoring pageantry to the monarchy, knew little of diplomacy and cared even less. George was left to learn how to rule on his own.

God blast you, Albert, he thought. Why did you have to die? See what a fine mess you've left me in.

His older brother Albert, Duke of Clarence, died in 1892 leaving George first in the line of succession. George assumed the crown on his father's death in 1910. In just a few short years, Europe was embroiled in war and George watched as house after house of European nobility was pulled down. Even worse, he was having to sacrifice his favorite cousin, Nicholas II of Russia, to preserve the House of Hanover.

The prime minister was attempting to secure the Romanov family's release from Kerensky. George was doing everything in his power to prevent it. His cousin was extremely unpopular. The working classes called him Bloody Nicholas because of the Winter Palace massacre of innocent men, women, and children. His presence in England could touch off a wave of resentment leading to riots and bloodshed.

Poor Nicholas, George thought. You once had the power to help prevent all this. Alexandra, Rasputin…how could you allow such incompetents to destroy the House of Romanov? And now I must leave you to the fates to preserve my country and my family. Please forgive me.

George was fairly sure his monarchy would be the only one to survive the war intact. That is, if his cousin the Kaiser didn't lead Germany to victory.

Cousins…Nicholas and Wilhelm. When nations go to war, they send anonymous men to battle one another. Monarchists fight cousins, nephews, nieces, aunts, and uncles. We fight our own blood. War, to us, is an extremely personal matter, he thought.

"Is my cousin here?" the King asked.

"Yes, Your Majesty," Brunswick answered.

The King fell silent and stared into the fire. Brunswick felt extremely uncomfortable in the presence of the monarch. He stood stiffly in the middle of the study. He was tired and yearned to pull up a chair next to the fire, but that was impossible in the presence of the King.

Brunswick had spent the last two days with little sleep. His investigation completed, he waited to present his findings to the King. Everything was set, needing only the approval of the monarch. He waited in anticipation of the order.

"Everything is taken care of?"

"Yes, Your Majesty. The German contact was arrested earlier this evening. He is being held incommunicado at the Tower. He will be tried in secret, convicted of espionage, and executed in the morning. I have determined that the spy had yet to contact any other agents in his network. He was in possession of the negatives. Luckily, he was a freelancer working out of the Spanish embassy. Anything else and the information would already have been passed to contacts inside the German embassy in Spain.

"And Lord Hammersmythe?"

"A story will appear in the *London Times* tomorrow reporting the accidental death of the late Assistant Minister of Heavy Industry. It seems he was cleaning a Luger, a war trophy from his son's service at the front, when it went off. It will be a short and boring story, Your Highness."

"And young Lord Percy?"

"I have set up a position for him at our consulate in California. It is far away from Washington, D.C., and any political mischief he might otherwise find himself getting into."

"Are you sure I have to deal with him?" King George asked, obviously ill-disposed to the thought.

"Yes, Your Majesty. Lord Percy is a member of the royal household. Only you have the power to banish him and remove his title. Sir Nigel, Lord Barton, and myself have done all that we can. The rest is up to you."

"I see," George V sighed. The King hesitated for a minute, readying himself for the encounter that lay ahead. "All right. Show him in, Inspector."

"Right away, Your Majesty." Brunswick turned and walked to the door. King George V set down his glass of brandy and rose from his chair. Clasping his hands behind his back, he waited for the young nobleman.

"Your Majesty, Percy Hammersmythe, Lord of Tankenshire," Brunswick announced. He held the door open as Lord Percy walked into the room. "I'll be outside when you need me."

Lord Percy bowed from the waist. "Your Majesty."

King George did not reply.

"'When you need me'? I take it you're not done with the good Inspector Brunswick then."

"No. But I'm just about done with you, Lord Percy."

"My dear cousin, what do you mean?"

"This damn mess you've got us into could cost us the war, you bloody fool," the King snapped.

"I have spent a good deal of time with the inspector, Your Majesty. He assures me no information was passed. And with the death of father, the whole uncomfortable episode is behind us. I rather saw to that," said Lord Percy, smiling.

"'Uncomfortable episode' is a bit mild, wouldn't you say, Percy? Sordid affair, depraved situation would come a lot closer to describing the insanity you and your father were involved in."

"Your Majesty, I dare say your father was involved in quite a few peccadilloes that made the press. And he was the King. He was an embarrassment for quite a number of years," Percy shot back.

"What my father was—or did—is none of your damn business. Kings can do as they damn well please. Right or wrong. It is the privilege and burden of the crown. However, snot-nosed spoiled lords haven't that privilege. And never will as long as I rule. You bastard, to pretend to your station and rank with behavior like this! To toy with the reputation of the crown! I should have you shot!"

"I doubt that will happen, Your Majesty. Parliament removed that power a couple of centuries ago. Which makes this whole meeting rather absurd. Don't you think?"

The King walked over to the young lord, raised himself to his full height and stared into his eyes.

"You are so right, my young lord. But I still have the power to disenfranchise you. Take your lands, your title, and banish you from this country, and that is exactly what I intend to do."

The smile disappeared from Percy's lips. "You can't do that. You couldn't afford my going to the press. You are bluffing."

"And what would you say to the press? All the evidence is destroyed thanks to Inspector Brunswick. The blackmailer? He'll be dead before the next sun has set and the trial records destroyed. Your catamites have been moved out of the city and given to foster parents to be raised. You could never discover their whereabouts, even if you tried. And the pimp who accrued your boy lovers has returned to Italy rather than stand trial here for his crimes. Lord Percy, you have absolutely nothing to say to the press or anyone else for that matter. Do you think me a fool? Do you think I would let a mere lord destroy my family? You disgust me," the King spat.

Lord Percy wilted under the king's withering glare. The full force of Imperial England had been brought to bear on him and he began to understand for the first time the danger he faced. The King took a step back and added with a tone of menace, "The crown no longer has the legal power of execution, but I have the money and the means to make you disappear. Do you understand?"

"You would have me killed?"

The king's only answer was to smile coldly.

Percy hung his head in defeat. "What is to become of me?"

The King let his breath out and walked back to the fireplace. He leaned on the mantle and rubbed his temples for a moment. Turning back to Percy he spoke.

"You will leave England as soon as it can be arranged. You will be allowed to leave with whatever property you wish. Except for the Tankenshire jewels. Those you will turn over to Inspector Brunswick. Your lands will be put in trust and sold after the war. Your assets in the Bank of England can be transferred to the

United States to your personal account when the war is over. You will be allowed to keep your title for appearances only.

"When you've arrived in the United States, you will report to our consulate in Los Angeles, California, where you will assume unimportant duties for the duration. When the war is over, you will retire from public duty and, at the earliest possible moment, Americanize your name and assume American citizenship. You are never to return to England or any part of the Commonwealth. You are forbidden to communicate with me or anybody in the House of Hanover. I am allowing you to keep your family fortune so you will not be tempted to use your knowledge for financial gain. Any questions may be directed to Inspector Brunswick. Is that understood?"

Lord Percy did not answer. He continued to stare at the floor.

"I said, is that understood?" King George barked.

Lord Percy looked up with a pained expression on his face. "Yes, Your Majesty. I understand."

"Fine, you worm. Get out of my presence. You are a commoner and, as such, are not allowed in my presence unattended. Inspector!"

The door opened and Brunswick walked in. "Yes, Your Majesty?"

The King turned his back to Percy. "Get this piece of filth out of my sight," he ordered.

"Yes, Your Majesty." Brunswick took Percy by the arm and escorted him out of the study, shutting the door quietly behind him. The King turned slowly and sat heavily in his chair.

Why in the hell did you have to die, Albert, he thought. One can only know how hard it is to be the King by being the King. Sometimes I think you are better off where you are. This war is destroying our family. All the royal houses of Europe are suffering. I fear our way of life has come to an end. The people have no more need for us and are discarding us like scrap to the scrap heap. Better you died than to live and see Armageddon.

The King pulled a Monte Cristo from his humidor. He removed the band from the smoke and examined the royal crest stamped in gold on the paper. Crumpling it in his fist, he tossed the band in the fire and watched it burn.

13

Palermo, Sicily, October 2, 1917

A land as violent and harsh as its birth, forged from a volcanic firestorm when the world was young. A sun blasted island of rock whose distinct geographic misfortune placed it at a strategic crossroad between Southern Europe and Northern Africa. Beginning with the Greek invasion of 413 B.C., Sicily's three native peoples, the Siculi, Sicani, and Elmyi were overrun and scattered by successive armies of Roman legions, Carthaginian hordes, Norman knights, and Bourbon kings.

By 1860, when guerrilla leader General Garibaldi liberated Sicily, the native Sicilians had become a mongrelized race reflecting centuries of foreign occupation. Their freedom was short-lived as King Emmanuel united Italy and brought Sicily under the protection of the Crown and the Papal State in 1879. The peasants' lands were delivered to the nobility, their souls to the care of the merciless Catholic Church, and their fates to the mafia, the bandits, the unpredictable harvest, and the brooding presence of three active volcanoes: Mt. Etna, Vulcano, and Stromboli.

By 1905, most of the population, fed up with mafia intimidation, government taxation, and church indifference, began a mass exodus to the United States. Those who could, secured seaward passage for the journey to the promised land. By 1910, only the wealthy and the poor remained. Sicily's middle class had vanished. As opportunistic as ever, the mafia moved in to fill the vacuum, sealing the fate of those left behind.

Sicily's poor, faced with a future of despair and agony, toiled on in the roiling, choking clouds of dust kicked up by the ocean winds. The men, mostly farmers, fishermen, and laborers, worked without every parents' hope of providing their children with a better life. The women, baptized in the Catholic Church, went secretly into the hills to worship at hidden pagan shrines, sacrificing animals in front of statues with grotesquely engorged genitalia, in hopes of bearing male offspring. The children, brought up without benefit of education or health care, were left to continue the cycle of poverty into the next generation.

Even in their wretched condition, the Sicilians were a proud and hardy people. They loved their beautiful if inhospitable island and dreamed of independence and prosperity. The islanders had a strong sense of family and supported and protected one another. Foreigners, even their Italian cousins from the mainland, were distrusted and treated as intruders. To be Sicilian was to belong. To be anything else was to be a stranger, detested and unwanted.

The small streets of the Punti di Valezzo stank from the accumulation of a week's worth of garbage. Palermo's northern slum failed to meet its tribute to the mafia chieftain and the punishment was the cessation of sanitation services to the district. The Punti di Valezzo's lesser crime lords scrambled to meet the increased payment as their illicit businesses suffered. No decent man would brave the stench to visit the slum's infamous brothels and gambling houses. The money dried up as the street traffic disappeared.

On this night, a lone man traveled the back streets of the crime-ridden neighborhood. Those who heard his footsteps, through shutters drawn tight against the evil smell, whispered he was either a fool or a drunk. No one walked these streets alone. A lone man would be an easy mark for the local gangsters.

Antoni Tocelli walked steadily up the Calle di Conzi. He was neither a fool nor a drunk. He was, in fact, one of Northern Sicily's most feared bandits. He wasn't using the slums for the various pleasures they offered, but rather as a cloak to conceal him from the gaze of his numerous enemies, enemies he hoped to confront before the night was over.

A seaman's cap was pulled low over his brow and his hands rested inside his worn coat. His face was hidden by the raised collar, but his eyes, darting about his surroundings, missed nothing. He readjusted the shotgun strapped to his back as his boots splashed in the open sewage running down the street.

Two men, braving the stench, stared out of an open doorway at the passing stranger. Tocelli ignored them and kept walking. The criminals, noticing the powerful build of the man and the shotgun strapped to his back, chose to keep to themselves. They cursed Don Chinnici for Punti di Valezzo's predicament. It made it hard for an honest thief to make a living when there was nobody to rob.

The smell of rotting garbage didn't faze Tocelli. The stench reminded him of the caves his bandit gang occupied in the hills outside Palermo. They had been living like animals for a month hiding from executioners sent by Palermo's mafia chieftain, Fillipo Chinnici.

Chinnici was acting on the behalf of Prince Riina, an absentee landholder, who had become fed up with the bandit raids on his lands and businesses. The prince, aware of the ineptness of the local militia, had been forced to hire the mafia to protect his interests on the island. The mafia was virtually the only organization Sicily's absentee land owners could turn to for protection. They were, in fact, the only men, save for the mainland Italian army, powerful enough to deal with Sicily's bandit hordes.

Tocelli silently cursed the prince, who had to buy Chinnici's help because Italy's local government was too weak to challenge Tocelli's mastery of the hills. The mafia was always available to act as a middleman in sensitive situations for the correct price. It was the Sicilian way.

Unfortunately, Riina's contract with the mafia terminated Tocelli's business arrangement and ended an easy life of raiding the fertile plains of the Val di Mazara. It was the mafia that purchased the spoils of Tocelli's raids, those spoils that weren't distributed to the local peasants, that is. Chinnici's men then resold them on the open market.

It was also the mafia who protected him and his men from the police and kept the militia from searching for their hideout on Rocca Busambra. Now it was the mafia who would end his life with a bullet in the brain and exterminate his men and their families like a pack of wild dogs. This was also the Sicilian way.

Tocelli was attending a meeting with Chinnici and his underboss Giacomo Nicotera in hopes of arriving at a new business arrangement. Chinnici had sent word into the hills that he was willing to grant amnesty to Tocelli's men provided certain conditions were met. Tonight, Tocelli was going to find out what those conditions were, or, if in fact, as he suspected, the whole thing was a ruse to trap him and his men.

His situation was desperate. With little notice, his hideout on Rocca Busambra had been invaded by Chinnici's assassins. They had been saved by a timely warning from a local peasant. His *cosche* had been on the run ever since.

Tocelli didn't know how much longer his men and their families could hold out. They were subsisting on meager rations and the constant threat of discovery was particularly hard on the women and children. Tocelli would discover the sincerity of Chinnici's proposal and if he didn't feel that it was honest, he would kill the mafia don and his underboss and escape to warn his men.

To do this and live, he would have to be especially cautious. That was why he came without armed escort through the deserted Punti di Valezzo. He was looking for an advantage over Nicotera's soldiers, who would be watching all the approaches to the chapel. He learned, as a bandit, that stealth and surprise were more valuable than a large force in achieving victory. Chinnici wouldn't be expecting his approach, or so he hoped. Either way, Tocelli would know by sunrise.

The meeting was to take place at the chapel of a Palermo undertaker, one of Chinnici's fronts. Chinnici wanted to give Tocelli the feeling of sanctuary that he hoped a church would provide. Antoni was no fool. He realized Chinnici would as soon as kill him in sight of an altar as anywhere, if that was his wish. Tocelli's mission was to survive, to determine the real reason for the meeting. He had to survive if he was going to save his family.

Tocelli spat on the ground and thought about the danger in which Don Chinnici had placed him. The fat Calabrese pig enjoyed the killing, the power, and the pleasure of seeing more worthy men stoop to kiss his ring. Tocelli had yet to find a mafioso who commanded enough respect to have his ring kissed. If he ever found such a man, Tocelli would do it once out of respect. He didn't think he could do it twice. The mere thought of subjugating himself before another man raised his blood pressure. No, once would be enough but he doubted it would ever happen.

Crossing the Plaza di Cutera, fronting the Palermo Opera House, he made his way into a wealthier section of Palermo. The dwellings of the Monte delle Pisa were built one next to the other like their counterparts in the slums, but there the similarities ended. The streets were wide and clean. The buildings were freshly painted and well kept. A difficult area in which to stay anonymous, especially in his tattered clothing.

Tocelli knew if the meeting was a trap, Nicotera's guards would lay a net for him far away from the chapel. He would fall into that net if he continued on the streets. But for this, he had a plan, as he had a plan for everything.

Tocelli scaled a drainpipe on the side of a three-story dwelling and began carefully crossing the rooftops. When he reached the end of the row of buildings, he made his way back to the street by either a trellis or drainpipe. Crossing the street with the stealth of a mountain lion, he repeated the process.

It was exhausting, time consuming, and dangerous. One slip would see his body smashed and bleeding on the cobblestones below. Exposed nails, jagged masonry, and rough beams tore at his skin and clothing. The risk was worth the reward as Tocelli invaded the bowels of the Monte di Pisa unnoticed and unchallenged. He would make his meeting with the mafia don, but as an unwelcome guest instead of a fearful, defeated prisoner.

The hair on the back of Tocelli's neck stood on end as he got closer to the undertaker's chapel. He had yet to see any of Chinnici's soldiers, but his instincts told him they were there just below him. Those instincts, finely developed after a lifetime of survival in the hills, had saved his life and those of his men numerous times. He listened to them now. To doubt them was to doubt Chinnici's true nature.

Reaching the last row of buildings before the chapel, he risked a look below. What he saw confirmed his suspicions. Two men smoking in the shadows of an alcove cradled shotguns. Across the street a lookout peered from a second story window, his rifle resting on the sill, and at the top of the street, in front of the undertaker's, sat two men astride horses, shotguns laid across their saddles, guarding the entrance to the walled compound.

The bastard had set a trap for him. It meant Chinnici feared him, and what Chinnici feared, he destroyed. Now he knew the game. Tocelli's pulse began to race as the confrontation came closer.

Moving quietly over the rooftops, Tocelli made his way to the last house across the street from the chapel. Peering cautiously over the side, he examined the street for other guards. He saw no others besides the two on horseback, but he knew they would be there.

Moving to the center of the roof, he found a door built into the roof. He opened it carefully and looked down onto a darkened staircase. The servants used this passageway to bring the laundry to the roof to hang and dry. He left the door open and moved back to the edge of the roof and looked below. The two horsemen were still at their station. He knelt down and thought for a moment. A cool breeze blew over his sweat-soaked clothes giving him a momentary chill.

Making up his mind, Tocelli began searching the roof for the right object. He found it shortly—a piece of tile lay broken in half by the door. He picked up the pieces and moved to the edge of the roof. Setting them down, he unstrapped his shotgun and cracked it open to check the loads. Satisfied, he strapped it tightly to his back and pulled out his two pistols. Cocking them, he replaced them in his jacket and picked up the tiles. Tocelli said a small prayer to the Virgin Mother and gathered his strength.

Tocelli took a deep breath and stood up, throwing one of the tiles as hard as he could down the length of the street. Ducking down, he heard the tile shatter and shouts from the two guards as they spurred their mounts to the source of the noise. He counted to five and then repeated the motion with the other tile only down the opposite direction of the street.

After the tile smashed on the ground, he stole a quick look onto the street and saw three men, two from out of a doorway and the third from behind a tree next to the chapel wall, race off down the street in search of the sound made by the second object. Without a second look, he stole down the stairs with the grace of a cat and out onto the street. He quickly crossed it and leaped into the tree that the one guard had hidden behind. Climbing it, he swung over onto the wall and waited, crouched on top.

Peering into the darkness below, he saw a small path that wound around either side of the chapel. Tocelli prepared to jump, but hesitated as he listened to what he thought were footsteps. He was glad that he had waited as two guards rounded the chapel on the path below. They walked to the spot just below where he was crouched and stopped.

Tocelli considered going back down the tree to the street when he heard the three guards return from their diversion. He was trapped. If any one of the five men looked up for any reason, he would be exposed. His heart stood still as he listened to the men talking below.

On the street:

"Hey, Tupo. What do you think the old man is doing in there?"

"Drinking wine. What else?"

"Oh, to be don for a day."

In the chapel grounds:

"Pino. Why is it you never have any matches?"

"Why should I bother, when you always do."

"You're an asshole, Pino," the guard said as he gave him a light.

Tocelli watched the two separate vignettes as he crouched in the air feeling like a spectator at two plays running at the same time. He couldn't afford to miss a line, a nuance, the smallest move. To do so could spell disaster. His legs started to tingle from the lack of circulation and his arms began to tremble as he fought to keep his balance on the narrow wall.

On the street:

"Shit, it's Gullo." The men in the street straightened and shuffled around. A rough voice from behind.

"What are you assholes doing hanging around here? Why aren't you at your posts?" the voice asked angrily.

"We heard a noise, Gullo."

"Up the street," one guard pointed.

"What did you find?"

"A broken piece of tile on the street. It probably fell off a building." Gullo grabbed the nearest guard and hit him in the face, knocking him to the ground.

"Did anyone think to check the roof? These bandits are like mountain goats." Gullo's question was greeted with silence.

"It figures. Tupo, take this idiot Molinelli," he gestured to the bleeding man on the ground, "and go check out the rooftop. Rimi, you get back across the street. A bullet in the brain for the person who lets Tocelli get by him."

The guards picked up their comrade and hurried off leaving Gullo standing under the tree. Tocelli felt a drop of sweat run down his forehead and inch down his nose. It stopped at the tip of his nose and hung there. Tocelli had an incredible urge to itch his nose, but knew if he moved, he would lose his balance and fall. Instead, he concentrated on the man named Gullo.

The burly guard had a thick moustache. The ends moved up and down as Gullo sniffed the air. His head jerked up suddenly and he stared straight at Tocelli crouching on the wall amongst the tree branches. Tocelli almost came out of his skin, but held his position as Gullo spoke.

On the street:

"I'd better not come behind this wall and find the Parrino brothers sharing a smoke when they should be walking guard duty. Because if I do, *Signora* Parrino will be wearing black tomorrow."

In the chapel grounds:

The two guards froze. Tocelli watched as the guards dropped their cigarettes and ground them into the dirt with their heels.

"If he could see, as well as he could smell, he might not bump into so many walls," one brother muttered to the other.

On the street:

"What was that, Pippo?"

In the chapel grounds:

"Gullo is that you?" Pippo asked, feigning ignorance.

His brother hit him on the arm. "You forgot about his hearing, you fool!" he hissed.

On the street:

"You know goddamn well who it is, you worthless peasant trash. I'm coming in and you'd better be on patrol," Gullo said, menacingly.

Tocelli watched as Gullo stormed off and the Parrino brothers went off in separate directions to continue their guard duties. Tocelli grabbed a branch for support and stood up slowly on the wall allowing the blood to rush back into his legs. When he had stopped shaking, he crouched back down and waited, hardly believing his good fortune. Maybe the Virgin Mother was answering his prayers.

Soon a guard walked by, shotgun cradled in his arms. It was Pippo's brother. Tocelli dropped on top of the guard knocking him to the ground and quickly broke his neck. He dragged the body noiselessly into the bushes by the chapel, unstrapped the shotgun, and waited.

Shortly, he heard the sounds of boots scuffing the dirt as another guard rounded the building. Pippo, not seeing his brother, called out quietly and came forward. Tocelli could see him through the bushes. He was a large man, larger than Tocelli. He carried a shotgun and had a bandolier draped across his shoulder. A large hunting knife hung at his side. Seeing it, Tocelli smiled.

When the guard had taken two steps past Tocelli's hiding place, the bandit emerged silently from the shrubbery and slipped up behind the unsuspecting guard. He quickly took the guard's knife from its sheath. The guard turned around, a look of surprise on his face, and attempted to raise his shotgun. Tocelli slashed the sharp blade across his throat and caught the guard as he fell, head almost completely severed from his neck.

Before Tocelli could drag the man behind the bushes to join his dead brother, he was covered in blood. Little matter. He took off his clothes and replaced them with those of the first guard. Now he was ready to meet Don Chinnici. Before leaving the bushes, Tocelli looked at the two brothers. Gullo was right. To-morrow *Signora* Parrino would most assuredly be wearing black.

Don Chinnici sat in the undertaker's office with his deputy Giacomo Nicotera. He had polished off a full bottle of wine and was well into his second as they waited for news of the capture of Antoni Tocelli. The meeting was a setup to draw Tocelli out into the open. The offer of amnesty was as fake as the toupee on Chinnici's balding head. He wanted only to separate the crafty bandit from his gang. Once this was accomplished, Tocelli's men, leaderless and paralyzed, would succumb quickly to his assassins.

Nicotera looked at his boss slurping nervously at his wine. The don was fat with bad teeth. He sat sweating and wheezing under the slowly rotating ceiling fan. He had a nervous rash on his chin that he continually rubbed. The sweat, seeping into the raw flesh, did nothing to improve the don's already foul mood. Nicotera pondered what penance God was making him serve. The underboss hated working for Don Chinnici.

Nicotera was amazed the don could drink in this place. In Sicily's heat, the dead ripened quickly. The odor of chemical preservatives from the basement mortuary, mixed with the smell of decaying flesh, permeated the air. The scent of the perfumed candles, intended to mask the smell, only added to the bilious odor. Don Chinnici seemed to be unaffected. Nicotera remembered the man's only expression of human feelings came in the form of cruelty, hatred, and homicidal rage.

Nicotera's boss was a vicious man whose only attribute was a sadistic streak that had served him well in his early years in the *'Ndrangheta*, Sicily's other major crime organization. Chinnici had murdered his way into the mafia and become one of its most feared chieftains. But getting power was easier than holding it. And to hold the power, Chinnici needed the other dons' complete trust. It was here Chinnici faltered.

Being feared couldn't bring complete respect or trust in the mafia. The skills of diplomacy and organization, valued highly by the other dons, evaded Don Chinnici. He leaned heavily on Nicotera for his talents in those areas, taking Nicotera's successes as his. Still, acceptance eluded him through an act of ancestry. Chinnici was only a first generation Sicilian, his family having come from Calabria in the south of Italy just before he was born.

Nicotera hated the Calabrese, as did most Sicilians, and dreamed of the day he would take over Chinnici's family. Unfortunately, one could not kill a don and become a don or Nicotera would have sent Chinnici to his death long ago. All Nicotera could do was bide his time. Sooner or later he hoped the fat slob would keel over from a heart attack. Until then, he had to follow Chinnici's orders no matter how bad they were for business. He considered the present situation a prime example of Chinnici's complete inability to comprehend the effects on business when he allowed his blood lust to control his emotions.

Prince Riina had given Chinnici a portion of the profits from his landholdings in payment for stopping the Tocelli bandits' raids. In normal circumstances, Nicotera would be ordered to execute a few bandits as a message to Tocelli and a demonstration to the prince. The raids would not stop. After a brief respite, they would move on to the property of unprotected land owners and the bandits would continue to bring the stolen property to Chinnici's fencers for money. Strictly business. The way Sicilians had been conducting it for decades. Everyone understood their roles—the bandits, the mafia, the police, and the landowners. But now Chinnici was about to change the way the game was played.

By ordering the termination of the entire gang, Chinnici had overstepped his authority. The trade in stolen merchandise would dry up as the island's other bandits took their loot elsewhere for distribution lest the same fate befall them. But most important, the fundamental bond of trust between bandit and mafioso would be broken. The alliance that bound the mafia and the bandits together in a symbiotic relationship would be sundered. They would become enemies instead of partners, and a devastating war would take place. The government, who tolerated the mafia and allowed and encouraged it to flourish because of its ability to keep the peace, would be called in to restore order. The army would come and put an end to the criminal civil war. After that, the future was undeniably bleak for the mafia. The bureaucrats in Rome would search for a new organization to keep the peace once the soldiers had been withdrawn.

The mafia, in disgrace, would be shunted aside for the *'Ndrangheta*. Their way of life would cease to exist. Nicotera was powerless to stop it all. He was prevented by the mafia code of allegiance to take the one action that could preserve their order.

The one class of men the mafia tolerated less than bad businessmen were traitors. In the strict mafia code, a man owed his complete allegiance to his don no matter the circumstances. It held the organization together and kept men from changing families for profit and promotion. The code also helped to keep the peace between the families.

If Nicotera chose to inform the other dons of Chinnici's plans, no matter the fact he would be trying to save them all, his action would be looked upon as an act of treason. It was an underboss's duty to help his don find the correct decision in business matters. If he couldn't do that, then he was of no use to anybody. Nicotera was in a hopeless situation. He prayed to his patron saint for deliverance from the madman he worked for.

"Hey, Giacomo. It doesn't look like that peasant pig Tocelli is going to show. What should we do now?" Chinnici asked, tongue thick from wine as he poured another glass.

Another thing I detest about you, you Calabrese pig, Nicotera thought before answering. A real don would stay sober before a business meeting. You Calabreses can't even hold your wine.

"He'll show, *padronè*. I guarantee it. He will be here."

"How do you know that?" Chinnici asked, looking up at him through squinty eyes.

"You have never met the man. I have had many dealings with him over the years. He is brave, intelligent, and a tough negotiator. I always had to give him top price for his goods. The crafty bastard seemed to know how high I would go. In his way, he is a very shrewd businessman."

"So what does that have to do with the meeting tonight? Certainly he must have an idea this could be a trap?"

"Yes, Don Chinnici. He would definitely consider that. But he is a businessman and you are interrupting his business, besides threatening the lives of his men and his family. If he has any hope of saving them at all, it is through negotiations with you. And if he can't negotiate, then he will try to kill you to save his people."

"Impossible!" Chinnici growled. "The bastard couldn't get close enough to do it. You said we have fifty men out watching the approaches to the chapel. If he does come, they will catch him, bring him to me, and that will be that. But I don't think he will come. I think this plan of yours is a waste of time. If we had followed my plan, then he would already be dead. These bandits are cowards. They hit and run and hide in their caves, afraid of the daylight. They are not true Sicilians like you and I, Giacomo. Next time, listen to me. Trust in my wisdom. That is why I am your don."

Nicotera bristled at Chinnici's last comment.

Trust in me? My wisdom? Sicilians like you and me? Pigshit, Nicotera thought. The only reason we have a business is because of my wisdom, you fucking Calabrese goat herder. Without it, we'd be the ones living in caves.

"What are you thinking about, Giacomo? Are you listening to me?" Chinnici asked with anger in his voice. Nicotera, recognizing Chinnici's quickness to anger, spoke to placate his boss.

"Sí, Don Chinnici. I have heard every word you said. Maybe you are right. Making a deal with the bandit Panzeca to discover Tocelli's hideout was prudent. I believe it is also prudent to behead the beast before attempting to destroy it. Tocelli has eyes in the hills. The peasants worship him and warn him of our every move. That is why we have yet to run him to ground. And his men will fight more ferociously in his presence, possibly defeating us. It is a risk I tried to avoid," Nicotera explained.

"Preposterous. He could never defeat us in battle and you know it. I think you have been stalling for time, hoping the other dons would find out my plans and attempt to dissuade me. I think you are a coward, Nicotera, unworthy of the position I have given you. After this Tocelli business, we will have to consider other options.

"I think Gullo would be more than capable of taking your place. Of course, I would compensate you generously for your years of service. Think about retiring, Giacomo. It has its advantages," Chinnici said slyly. He took another drink from his glass and smiled at Nicotera.

Nicotera stood up and leaned over the desk, pressing his palms into the surface. His face was red with anger as he tried to contain himself.

"Gullo's a fool. A sadistic fool. He would do a great deal of damage in my position. He hasn't the brains of a mule."

"But he is loyal, Giacomo. He follows orders without question," Chinnici bellowed, slamming his fist on the table. He wasn't used to being challenged and he didn't like it. "He honors his don while you make excuses for your mistakes. Retirement, Nicotera. Take it while I am still in the mood to offer it," Chinnici added menacingly as his bug eyes bored into Nicotera's face.

Nicotera took a deep breath and sat back in his chair. The old man was baiting him and if he didn't watch out, he would end up with a bullet in the brain.

Diplomacy, Giacomo, he thought. Save yourself while there is still time.

"I am sorry, *padronè*. I sometimes let my concern for you get in the way of my judgment. I only want your life to be a long and fruitful one. Please forgive me. I am yours to command." After a moment, a smile came across Chinnici's lips and he offered his hand to Nicotera.

"Your apology is accepted, Giacomo. I appreciate your concern. But let me worry about the consequences of my decisions. That is why I am the don."

Nicotera stood, grabbed Chinnici's hand, and stooped to kiss the ring. The ruby showed blood red in the gold setting. It was the symbol of a Sicilian mafioso's power, a simple, elegant statement. Chinnici's palm was slimy and his fingers smelled of sausage. Nicotera had to fight to keep from gagging.

"Thank you, Don Chinnici," he said, as he kissed the ring. There was a knock at the door as he released Chinnici's hand.

"Maybe that is Gullo with some news," he said to Nicotera. Turning to the door he shouted, "Gullo, come in here. And you'd better have news of the bandit."

The door opened slowly and Gullo walked in followed by a guard.

"What of the bandit, Gullo? Have you caught the bastard, yet?" Chinnici asked.

"No, *padronè*" Gullo answered, hesitating.

"No? Is that all? Come here to me, Gullo. And tell me what you do know," Chinnici ordered.

Gullo hesitated, then moved to the undertaker's desk slowly, the guard right behind him.

As Gullo moved into the light of the desk lamp, Nicotera could sense something was wrong. Gullo's face was pale. His lips twitched. Cursing to himself, Nicotera reached for his pistol, but froze when he heard the unmistakable sound of a shotgun being cocked.

"That's right, *Signor* Nicotera. Please stay seated and place your hands on the arms of the chair. As for you, Don Chinnici, if you enjoy life, you should hold onto your wine glass with both hands," ordered Antoni Tocelli.

"You peasant bastard! How dare you come into my presence armed. You are a dead man!" Chinnici roared, but he held his wine glass with both hands as directed.

"I think the only dead man here tonight will be you, Don Chinnici. You broke your bargain with me. You offered me safe conduct to this meeting, yet you placed men in my path to kill me. You offered my men and me amnesty, but your assassins scour the hills under orders to exterminate us even as we speak."

"It was Nicotera who gave those orders. Against my wishes, I might add. I was going to have him killed for his insolence. You may do so now if you wish. I give him to you as a symbol of our continued friendship and business relationship." Chinnici took one hand from his wine glass and motioned to Nicotera across the desk. "There is your enemy, my friend. There he is."

"Put your hand back on the wine glass, Don Chinnici."

"As you wish, my friend," he said casually, and slowly placed his hand back on the glass. Tocelli forced Gullo to his knees and rested the barrel of the shotgun against the back of his neck. His flinty eyes fell upon Nicotera.

"What do you have to say to Don Chinnici's accusations, *Signor* Nicotera? What you say will determine whether you live or die. I would take my time if I were you. It might be the only time you have left."

Returning Tocelli's stone-cold stare with a look of defiance, Nicotera said, "I will not beg for my life. If I am to die then so be it. My fate rests in God's hands. He will guide your heart if you are a wise man. If not..." Nicotera added falling silent.

Tocelli turned back to Chinnici. "A man of honor would not sacrifice his chief lieutenant to save his own neck. Of course, a Calabrese goat herder has never even heard of the word, you fat pig."

"You bastard!" Chinnici roared, coming out of his chair spilling his wine all over his shirt. Tocelli raised the shotgun to his shoulder and pointed it directly at Chinnici's head. "Sit down," Tocelli barked. "Sit down. Now, before I blow your ugly head off."

Slowly Chinnici sat back in his chair breathing heavily. "You will not get out of here alive. If you shoot me, the sound will bring my men running. They will cut you down before you can leave the chapel."

Tocelli's answer was to bring the butt of the shotgun crashing down on Gullo's head. His skull split with a dull crack and his body fell heavily to the floor. Tocelli then raised his boot and stomped on Gullo's throat, crushing his windpipe. Gullo twitched twice and then was still.

Seeing his chief henchman killed wiped the mask of rage from Chinnici's face and replaced it with a look of fear.

"I have money," Chinnici stammered.

"Not enough, goat herder. Not near enough after you destroyed our home on Rocca Busambra," Tocelli said, pulling Pippo's hunting knife from his belt. With a smooth motion, he hurled it at Chinnici, burying it in his chest. Chinnici grabbed at the handle as blood erupted from his mouth. His hands covered in blood from the pumping wound kept slipping off the knife. With a groan, he fell back in his chair and died.

Tocelli trained the shotgun on Nicotera and paused.

"Why don't you pull the trigger?" Nicotera asked, conversationally.

"You never tried to cheat me, *Signor* Nicotera. Not in all the years we've done business. You are a good businessman. You take care of your own. I don't think you wanted this any more than I did. I think you always wanted to run this family. Everyone knows you would do a better job than that scum, Chinnici. And I have just removed the only two obstacles in your path. Am I not correct?"

"You are correct, Tocelli. But now that I am don, you know it will be my duty to kill you to avenge Don Chinnici. The other dons will expect it."

"Yes, I know. So where does that leave us, Don Nicotera?"

Nicotera held up his hands. "If I may?"

Tocelli gestured with the shotgun and nodded his head. Nicotera stood up and slowly reached behind his back. Tocelli raised the shotgun to his shoulder and Nicotera froze.

"Easy, *Signore*. I'm just taking off my belt." Tocelli relaxed slightly, but kept the shotgun pointed at Nicotera. Nicotera reached behind him and fumbled with something. When he pulled his hands out, he was holding a bulky money belt that slid out from under his vest. He threw the money belt on the desk.

"There is enough money there for you and your family to escape to America and start a business. In the belt, you will find instructions on how to find a boat in Palermo harbor. There should be some money left for your gang as a going away present. It is best for both of us."

Tocelli looked at the money belt on the desk and smiled. The realization dawning, he looked back at Nicotera who was also smiling.

"You hoped this would happen tonight. Now I know why I was able to get in here so easily. None of the rooftops were covered. Was that your doing?"

"Yes," Nicotera nodded. "I placed the outer guards. But Gullo was responsible for the perimeter guards. Chinnici had longstanding doubts about me and always allowed Gullo to handle his personal security. Frankly, I am surprised you made it. I see you met the Parrino brothers," he said, pointing to Tocelli's clothes and the knife embedded in Chinnici's chest.

"Yes, I did. Unfortunately, we didn't have much time to talk."

"I see. You are an exceptional man, *Signor* Tocelli. The Parrino brothers were the best. And Gullo was an animal. How did you manage that?"

"He didn't see me coming until it was too late."

"Ah, his eyes. The vain fool. He thought glasses would make him look old and weak. Now he'll never get the chance. But I'm glad to be rid of him. He was a sadist like Chinnici. Now for you, *Signor* Tocelli," he said, sitting back in his chair. "I will give you a head start. A day. No more. Then I will be after you. That should give you enough time to warn your men and gather your family.

"You must change your name when you arrive in America. As you know, our arms stretch across the sea. I think you will do well in America. It is a land ripe with opportunity. Make a name for yourself. Start your own family. And when you are ready, contact me. I think we can make each other rich beyond our wildest dreams. A partnership across the ocean. Now you must be off."

"Thank you, Don Nicotera."

"One more gift before you go. Your man Panzeca was captured awhile back. It was he who sold us the location to your hideout on Rocca Busambra. Panzeca is your Judas, Tocelli. He returned to your camp as a paid spy for Chinnici."

Tocelli's face went red with rage. He shouldered his shotgun and went around the desk. He grabbed Chinnici's hand and yanked the gold ring with the ruby stone from the fat finger. Tocelli took the ring to Nicotera and placed it on his hand. Leaning over, he kissed the ring. "Thank you, Don Nicotera. Thank you from the bottom of my soul."

It was the first ring Tocelli had ever kissed. He swore it would be the last.

14

Palermo, Sicily, October 4, 1917

    Giuseppe Alliata was working in the hold of his small ship when he heard someone jump on board. Cursing, he set his tools down and climbed the ladder to the deck. The sun had dropped below the horizon while he was trying to fix the sea locker. In the twilight, he could make out a large man standing by the pilot house. Giuseppe, sensing trouble, made his way forward.

    "What do you want?" he asked.

    "*Signor* Nicotera sends his regards. He said you would be expecting us," answered a large peasant in tattered clothing. The peasant stroked his thick moustache and smiled at the captain.

    "Expecting you for what?" Alliata asked. He felt a twinge of fear as he made out the shotgun strapped to the man's back.

    "Passage to the mainland."

    "That will cost a lot of money," Giuseppe said, peering at the group of people on the dock. They were dressed in rags like the peasant on his boat. The men carried weapons and the women and children looked as though they had suffered recent hardship. "Especially for this many."

    "*Signor* Nicotera said he is happy to consider your debt paid in full and that when you return from this trip to drop by his office so that he may give you the deed to this boat."

Alliata swallowed hard. Nicotera, Chinnici's underboss. If indeed Nicotera was relieving him of his obligation, then these people would be awfully important. With importance sometimes went danger. But he had no other choice. To turn down Chinnici's underboss was asking for a bullet in the brain. Besides, he had heard rumors that Chinnici was dead and Nicotera was the new don. If so, he would be assisting the new godfather. A feather in his cap.

"Bring them on board. I'll send for the rest of the crew and we'll be off. By the way, what is your name? I'll need it for the log," Alliata asked, realizing the name would most likely be false.

"Busambra. Antoni Busambra," Tocelli answered with a nod of his head. He turned and waved his arm to the group on the dock. As the men helped the women and children onto the boat, Tocelli walked to the bow and gazed out over the dark expanse of ocean.

I have saved what I could, he thought. My best men and their families. Sabelli, "Bent Nose" Streva, Coldiretti. The Magliocco orphans will grow up to be strong men.

Tocelli knew he faced an impossible task. The families already in operation in the United States were firmly entrenched. They had men, money, and influence. His people would have to learn a new language, new customs, a new way of life. But they would learn. Tocelli would see to that.

Of the many things Tocelli had learned as a bandit, the most important lesson had been adaptability as the key to survival. It was more important than bravery and fighting skills, more important than business acumen. Adaptability would be his weapon. Tocelli would use it to defeat his enemies and carve out his empire in the new world. He would become so powerful, so feared, his family would never doubt their safety again. But, as with so many things in life, the power would have a price. Nicotera was correct. He would have to change his name, to forget it ever existed.

Antoni Tocelli looked up at the stars in the sky. He felt as though a part of him was dying as he thought of the name his father had passed on to him. Tocelli was a proud name, known in the hills of Sicily for generations. Tocelli had killed men that defied his name. He had treasured the day when he could pass the

Tocelli name to his sons. Now that hope was gone. He was destroying it by forgetting it.

Forgive me, Father, he thought. For their safety, your grandchildren must never learn of you or our history. A man may never kill a don and become a don. But I will remember you in my dreams. I swear it.

Antoni Tocelli swallowed the bitter taste in his mouth and thought of his father one last time.

Antoni Busambra turned and walked to the hold to settle his people for the beginning of their long journey.

15

Liverpool, England, November 10, 1917

The small office door to the huge warehouse opened and a British army major, resplendent in creased khakis and campaign medals, strode to a large platform followed by a sergeant major and two corporals. As the officer entered, silence descended like a wave over the thousands of bodies crammed into the building. A sound like the fluttering of birds' wings was all that was heard as people shuffled for positions to observe the proceedings.

The major climbed the stairs to the podium followed by his subordinates. He faced the crowd and slapped his swagger stick under his left arm. He held out his right hand and the sergeant major placed a clipboard in it. The major glanced down the sheet of paper and gazed at his rapt audience.

"Right. Now listen up. The following ships are departing on the morrow at these times. If your ship is called, form up to the right of doors A and B three hours before departure. Have your tickets ready. Nobody leaves this building and boards a ship without a ticket. The ships leaving the port tomorrow are as follows: HMS *Culloden*. The Greek freighter *Hermes*. SS *New Zealand...*"

As he called out the ships, the corporals mounted stepstools and wrote the ships' names, dock numbers, and departing times in huge block letters on a giant blackboard. There was a sudden surge forward as the crowd strained to see the announcements. The major stopped reading and stared at the crowd until they calmed down. Back in control, he continued his recitation.

"All those who booked passage on the SS *Northern Star* will be rebooked on another ship. The *Northern Star* was sunk yesterday by a German U-boat. That is all." The major handed his clipboard to the sergeant major and left the platform followed by his retinue. When the men had entered the office and shut the door, there was an explosion of activity as the crowd rushed the platform to get a closer look at the blackboard. Those people who couldn't speak or read English mobbed those who could.

The major moved to his desk and took his chair, listening to the roar of the crowd outside the office door. After a moment, he turned to his visitor and apologized for the interruption.

"Sorry about that. Had to get the schedules to the bloody heathens on time or they'd rush the office. Let me see, where were we? Ah, yes. You have a special passenger for me to be placed on the SS *New Zealand* tomorrow. Sergeant Major, let me have the SS *New Zealand* manifest."

The sergeant major took a clipboard from the wall and handed it to the major. The major flipped through the passenger list shaking his head.

"I'm afraid that's impossible. She's fully booked. Your special passenger will just have to wait for another ship on another day, Detective..." the major explained although he knew exactly who the man was who sat before him.

"Inspector. Assistant Chief Inspector Brunswick, Major," Brunswick repeated, trying to hide his irritation. "Scotland Yard would consider it a special favor if you could work this one out for us."

"I'm afraid it's out of my hands, Inspector," the major replied, lacing his fingers and placing them on the desk in front of him.

Of all the gall, the major thought. Scotland Yard trying to manipulate the army. Didn't they know there was a bloody war on and the Yard was mighty small in the pecking order?

The major gave the inspector a classic look of false sympathy that really said he wouldn't help even if he could. Inspector

Brunswick despised arrogant prima donnas like the army major. He smiled to himself, knowing he would enjoy what was to follow. Brunswick pulled an envelope from his pocket and handed it to the major.

"I think you should read this, Major. It isn't just the Yard that wants our passenger on this ship."

The major took the envelope with a small amount of apprehension. He became nonplussed as he read the letter.

"You expect me to believe this? What rubbish. The King of England? I don't know what you people are trying to pull, but I intend to get to the bottom of this. Sergeant Major, show this man out."

"Major, before you make a career-ending decision, I suggest you pick up the phone and dial your superior at Whitehall. If you don't have the number, I could get it for you," Brunswick offered magnanimously.

"I've got the bloody number, Inspector. Sergeant Major, get the Imperial Staff's office at Whitehall. The office of the Chief of Staff," the Major ordered.

"I suggest the right Minister of War would be better able to help you," suggested Brunswick.

The Major hesitated, then said, "All right, Sergeant Major. Get the bloody Minister of War's office on the phone so we can get this charade over with," he barked. Then turning to the Inspector, he added, "What about the Prime Minister at Number 10 Downing. Should we call him next?"

"That won't be necessary, Major. I spoke with him this morning and he is having the Minister of War handle it," he answered, smiling slyly.

The Major felt a hot flush rising in his cheeks as he felt the first creeping doubt.

"Major, I've got the Ministry on the phone. A Colonel O'Donnel, sir."

The Major picked up his phone. "Colonel O'Donnel. I've got an Inspector Brunswick from Scotland Yard with a supposed letter from His Majesty. I know it sounds like rubbish and I'm sorry to disturb you with it, but I...Yes, Sir. I see, Sir. Of course, Sir. I just wasn't..." the major stammered. His face reddened as he sat bolt upright in his chair.

Colonel O'Donnel chewed on the major for several more minutes before hanging up on him. The major slowly set the phone down and eyed the inspector with a new sense of respect and fear. He had come close to the inferno that destroyed men's careers and he didn't want to come any closer. He stood at attention and offered an apology to Inspector Brunswick.

"The colonel has ordered me to apologize for my lack of propriety. He told me to tell you that the Imperial Staff and the Ministry of War apologize to Scotland Yard and specifically His Majesty's emissary, Assistant Chief Inspector Brunswick, for my rude behavior," the major said, voice quavering. He swallowed hard before continuing. "I am also instructed to inform you that most majors are insufferable prigs, which is why they never make it to the rank of colonel. It is for you to decide if I am an insufferable prig, Inspector. The colonel will be calling you later for your opinion. In the meantime, I am at your complete disposal," he finished to the open-mouthed looks of astonishment from his staff.

"Quite right, Major. Now, have a seat and let's get down to business." The major took his seat without a word and listened to the inspector's every word as though Jesus, himself, was giving the *Sermon on the Mount*.

On the Docks, November 10, 1917

Emil Danelsberg worked his way back through the crush of refugees to his family. He couldn't wait to tell his wife they would be leaving for America the following day. Their harrowing journey, that began in a burned-out village so many months before, was nearing its last leg. In his heart, Emil firmly believed safety was waiting for them across the sea.

Emil's ears were assaulted by the dozens of different languages spoken by the horde of refugees. The kaleidoscope of colors from the varied native clothing made his head swim. The smells from the cooking fires of the different foreign cuisines made his eyes water and his stomach growl. Unfortunately, the smells from the cooking pots weren't from native dishes, rather the spices they carried with them to make their potatoes taste more palatable.

Greeks, Montenegrins, Serbians, Hungarians, Bulgarians and dozens of other cultures were forced to live with one another in the giant warehouse. No matter the hardships many of these people faced on their journey, it was better than the fate many of them left behind: starvation, revolution, anarchy, and war. Emil wondered at the size of a conflict that could force so many people from their homes, their countries, and their ways of life.

"Good news," he said in greeting to his wife, as he stepped into the small circle formed by their belongings. This had been their home for the last fortnight. "We leave tomorrow."

"Thank God," Sona answered without looking up. She was busy preparing the evening meal. Emil glanced down with a look of distaste. "I know what you're thinking. Potatoes again. Unfortunately, my dear husband, that's all we have."

"You know I love your cooking. I just think for some crazy reason a chicken will wander into our pot and I am constantly disappointed to find that it doesn't happen."

Sona looked up at him, smiling. "You have always been so practical, Emil. It's not like you to dream like a child."

"A man needs hope, Sona," he answered with mock gravity. And he remembered the long nights in the trenches when the dreams of his wife and child were the only thing to keep him going—one more day, hour, minute.

"Well, my dear Doctor, I can't give you chicken, but the Barazonovs will share their cabbage with us if you go fetch some water."

"Oh, joy. Cabbage," Danelsberg said in despair. But the truth being, he was happy to have anything to alter their steady diet of potatoes. He picked up their pail and was about to set off when the boys stumbled into their small area. "Anyone want to help me get some water?"

The two boys looked at each other before Yakov answered. "I'll go, Uncle Emil," he said simply.

"Good. Viktor, you stay here with your mother. Come along, Yakov."

Viktor plopped down next to his mother and began toying with a potato. His mother gently slapped his hand and placed the potato back on the small pile.

"Hurry back, Emil," she said.

"As fast as my feet will carry me, my lady," he answered and grabbing Yakov's hand set off for the water station.

As they made their way through the crush of bodies, Emil placed the pail in the crook of his elbow, hefted the boy and swung him up onto his shoulders. He's light, Emil thought. Too damn light.

They had all lost weight on the journey from Petrograd. As Emil held the boy's small hands in his, he tried to remember the last time they had eaten a well-rounded meal. Helsinki. That was it. Cooked fish, chicken, and steamed vegetables. The meal was courtesy of the ship's mess cook whose stomach malady Emil had cured.

They had boarded a tramp steamer in Petrograd and traversed the Gulf of Finland to Helsinki. They possessed precious few belongings. The only things of value they carried were a brand-new set of gleaming surgical instruments packed in a medical kit full of medicine and dressings and some precious gems sewn inside the lining of one of their suitcases.

The surgical kit was a gift from Dr. Vorshilov. The gems were given to them by Colonel Krikalev along with a few gold coins. When Emil had asked how the colonel had acquired such things, Krikalev had only smiled and wished them a safe journey. Emil wondered which poor Romanov's palace had been looted of the priceless items.

Emil used a few coins to purchase passage on an empty ore freighter out of Helsinki bound for Stockholm. The remainder of the coins had gone to pay for their passage from Stockholm to Liverpool and the following trip to New York. He was determined to hold onto the gems until they arrived in America. His family would need housing and clothing. They would have to purchase a whole new life and the gems represented the only hope of doing so. Meanwhile, they subsisted on whatever they could scrounge in the way of food.

Emil had known true hunger on the Eastern Front during the war. His men would have killed for the potatoes he was tired of eating. Sona had a strong constitution and would recover quickly when they reached America, but the children would suffer the most. The effects of long-term malnutrition in the young were sometimes irreparable. As a physician, he understood this better than most. And as he carted his light burden across the floor of the warehouse, he said a small prayer for the health of Yakov and his son, Viktor.

Emil hummed a soft tune while he and the boy waited in line for their chance at one of the three water pumps. Yakov, as usual, was silent, his eyes darting about the warehouse as he observed the many goings on from his perch atop Emil's shoulders. Emil let the boy have his peace.

Yakov rarely talked to anyone save for Viktor. Emil could only imagine the effect the boy's terrible loss was having on him. At least, the Danelsbergs had each other. Yakov had no one. Try as Emil did to make him feel a part of their family, the boy remained distant. It was as if he didn't want to chance becoming part of another family only to lose them again. Only time and love would bring the boy back to life again and Emil was determined to give him both

"*Scusi, Dottore. Per favore, vene mia. Per favore.*"

Emil stopped his humming and stared into the eyes of the man who had spoken to him. He was as tall as Emil and powerfully built. He had a thick moustache and weathered face. His skin was of an olive complexion and his eyes were as dark as coal. He wore a frayed peasant blouse and dark trousers tucked into knee-high boots. A sea cap covered his head. The hand he held out to Emil was large and calloused.

"I'm sorry, *Signore.* I don't speak Italian," Emil answered. At the university, he had heard a smattering of most every language in Europe, learning conversational French and perfect English.

"*Parlez-vouz Français?* How about English? Can you speak English?" Emil asked, switching languages. The man only stared at him. "*Deutsche. Sprechen Sie Deutsche?*" Emil asked in the language of his ancestors, as a last resort. No response. He also spoke Yiddish and Hebrew but was doubtful the man knew either of those.

Exasperated, the peasant shook his head in frustration and grabbed Emil's arm with a powerful grip. Emil stood his ground. He'd been through hell and back in the war and was afraid of very little, but something inside him warned him that this man could be dangerous. The peasant relaxed his grip and tugged more gently, looking Emil in the eyes.

"Per favore...Per favore?"

Emil took one step forward and then another. There was something in the man's eyes that was impossible to resist.

"Grazie, Signor Dottore. Grazie," the man said and then turned and led them through the crowd.

The empty water pail banged noisily at his side as they pushed through the throng. In his time spent in the warehouse, Emil had learned where most of the nationalities were grouped. The people of common language and custom banded together for security and comfort. He thought they were headed for the Italian "compound" but passed right by it. Eventually, they entered a small group of people. In the center of the group lying on a makeshift pallet lay a pregnant woman sweating and groaning.

"Per favore, Dottore," the peasant said, motioning to the woman. Emil moved to the woman's side and knelt beside her. A woman cradling the expectant mother's head gave the doctor a cold look and spoke harshly to the peasant. He cut her off in mid-sentence with a one-word reply. Reluctantly the woman stood, crossed herself, and moved away.

Emil felt the woman's forehead and checked her pulse. She smiled at him bravely and gripped his hand and let out a small shriek as she was racked by a fresh wave of pain. Emil felt her belly with deft hands and turned to Yakov.

"Yakov. Go fetch my instruments. Do you understand? Get my bag from your Aunt Sona. You," Emil said, pointing to a short heavyset man standing next to the peasant. "You go with him. Go! *Go!*" he ordered. Yakov ran to the large man and grabbed his hand and dragged him into the crowd.

"You, there," Emil said, pointing to another of the men. He tossed the pail to the man and said, "Water. Bring me some water."

This man looked at the peasant. The peasant gave a slight nod of his head and the man disappeared into the throng. Emil returned his attention to the woman and checked her pulse. It was faint. He stood and walked to the peasant.

"I know you can't understand a word I'm saying, but we need to find someone who can translate for us. You, Italiano. Me, Russki. You understand?" he asked, his frustration mounting.

"English. *Français. Deutsche,* any one of those languages will do. Please..." the woman's scream cut him off.

When Emil looked back at the peasant, he detected the traces of a smile on his lips. The peasant rattled off some Italian to the group and two young men, obviously twins, detached themselves and hurried away. The peasant smiled more fully at Emil as if to put him at ease and motioned back to the woman.

"I sure as hell hope you understood me," he said, kneeling down beside the woman. She shrieked again and he placed his hand on her forehead gently and spoke quietly to her. "Help is on the way, my dear. Just please hold on a little longer."

There was a commotion on the periphery of the group and the circle parted revealing his wife, the two boys, and the heavy-set man carrying his medical kit.

"Sona, quickly, my bag."

She took the black bag from Yakov's escort and knelt beside her husband.

"What is wrong with her, Emil?"

"Possible breech birth, but I can't be for sure until I examine her. Here, help me."

They switched positions just as the man arrived with the water.

"Good. Over here," he ordered.

The man set the water down and Emil rolled up his sleeves and washed as best he could. He opened his bag and began to lay out his instruments and medicines. Positioning himself between her legs, he lifted her skirt and began his examination. Sona took a clean towel from the kit and soaked it in water. She placed the cool towel on the woman's forehead and gently held her hand.

"Now there, my husband is a very good doctor and he will deliver your child without much fuss. You must be brave and do what he says."

Bending over his work, Emil muttered, "She can't understand a damn word you're saying, Sona. And she will kill herself and this baby unless I can make her understand what is happening. The baby is turned the wrong way in the breech. Her natural inclination is to push when her contractions hit, but that only makes things worse. Unless I can get her to stop pushing, she will cause herself to hemorrhage and I will lose them both."

The woman felt another contraction and breathing heavily began to push.

"No! No, damnit! You mustn't do that," he yelled. The woman, lost in her pain didn't even hear him. When the contraction was through, she collapsed, face white, trembling.

"Emil?"

"She's bleeding, Sona. God help me, she's bleeding," he said, voice full of despair. Emil was frantically trying to turn the baby before her next contraction.

"May I be of help?" a voice asked in English.

"Do you speak Italian?" Emil asked without looking up from his patient.

"I should hope so considering I am Italian."

"Then get over here, now," Emil ordered.

"*Mio Dio!*" the stranger exclaimed on seeing Emil's hands and forearms soaked in blood.

"Don't look if it makes you sick. I can't afford to have you pass out on me," Emil snapped, glancing up at the well-dressed translator. The man's answer was to nod his head and gulp a breath of air. He removed his derby from his head and clutched it to his chest.

"Tell her not to push. No matter how bad she wants to. Tell her she can't because the baby is upside down and she is killing the child."

The man translated rapidly. A look of fear appeared in the woman's eyes. When Emil saw it he quickly added, "Tell her if she can give me enough time, the baby will be fine. All it will take is a little time," he pleaded.

After hearing the translation, she looked at the doctor and nodded her head. She spoke to him in a voice made hoarse from screaming.

"She says she will do her best, Doctor, but asks that if it comes between her life and the life of the child to please save the child."

Emil looked into the woman's eyes and after a moment he spoke to her.

"It will be as you ask."

The stranger translated and the ordeal continued. Emil used all his skill to aid the woman. His time spent mending shattered bodies at the front was of no use to him here. He hadn't delivered a baby since medical school. Please, God, he prayed, please let this woman and child live. I've lost too many men to this war. If you have a shred of decency, you'll let this child live.

And with one final manipulation the head came into view.

"I've got it. Tell her to push now," he shouted to the translator. With a shriek, the woman gave one final effort and the shoulders popped out. Now Emil was able to pull the baby out. He turned it over and slapped the rear end. No sound. He quickly removed the mucus from its breathing passages and slapped it again. Still nothing and Emil slipped into despair. What to do now, he cried to himself.

"Emil, quickly. Put the baby into the water," Sona ordered.

"What?" he asked incredulously.

"The baby into the water. It is something I learned from a village midwife."

"I don't understand," he said, confused.

"Emil! The shock from the cold water will wake it up."

The baby was dead anyway, so Emil took the child and plunged it into the pail of cold water. The mother screamed, holding out her arms and the men rushed forward, and Emil pulled the baby out of the water as the men were grabbing him and—the baby screamed. It took another deep breath and screamed again and the men let him go and the crowd looked silently at the miracle of the tiny life as Emil placed him into the mother's arms.

"A boy. Tell her she has given birth to a healthy baby boy," said Emil exhausted and smiling. He caught Sona's eye as she gently held the woman's head and she smiled back at him. He then went to work to stem the flow of blood. After he washed up, he gave her some sulfa tablets to help her fight against infection. His duty done, he washed his instruments and helped his wife to her feet.

"You suppose the Barazonovs have any of that cabbage left?"

"They are still waiting for the pail of water I promised them you would fetch," Sona answered, laughing.

"Then let us not disappoint them, Sona. Take my bag and the boys back and I will fetch the water."

Sona turned to look at the mother and child resting peacefully and smiled. She remembered giving birth to Viktor and thanked God again for the miracle of life.

"Come on, boys. It is way past your dinner time."

The boys ran ahead of her into the crowd and she followed them clutching the medical bag in both hands. Emil turned to his translator taking full measure of the man. He was short and slender with nervous eyes. His moustache was trimmed short, neat. Although he wore an expensive suit, it showed signs of wear. His shoes, however, were highly polished. Seeing Emil's smile, the man bowed slightly from the waist and extended his hand.

"Mario Scelba at your service, Doctor."

Emil shook the extended hand. "I am Dr. Emil Danelsberg. Thank you for your help, *Signore*. Without it, I might have lost them."

"Oh, I doubt it, Doctor. You seem quite competent to me. And being an expert tailor, I know a good stitch when I see one." The peasant had been eyeing this exchange curiously. Emil turned to him and offered his hand. After a short pause, the peasant shook it, his grip amazingly powerful.

"Tell him the woman will be fine," he said to the tailor. "As will the child. I have sutured the tear in the mother and stopped the bleeding. She is not to be moved. Her condition is extremely delicate. Tell him my name. He knows where to find me should the woman experience any difficulties. Otherwise, I will return in three hours to check on her progress."

As the tailor translated, Emil noticed how nervous the little man was, almost fearful. As he listened to the peasant's reply, the tailor turned his hat nervously in his hands and bobbed his head up and down.

"This is *Signor* Antoni Busambra. He says that you have saved the life of his sister and his nephew and for that he is eternally in your debt as is his whole family. He wishes to know how he may repay you, that if there is anything he may do for you, at any time, he will do it."

"Tell *Signor* Busambra that the pleasure of bringing a healthy child into the world is enough payment."

Busambra looked from Emil to the tailor as he waited for the translation. The tailor looked at Emil with fear in his eyes.

"*Scusi, Dottore.* The man has offered you his services. It is something not given lightly by these people. It is a matter of honor with him. To turn him down would offend his sense of honor and decency. Believe me, it is not wise to do so."

Emil watched the tailor glance nervously in the direction of the peasant as he spoke. He wondered what type of man it was who could create such fear in a man.

"All right. Tell the good *Signore* that my sons need a chicken for the dinner pot." Emil said this knowing full well that no such chicken was available. There was a war on and these people were refugees, entitled only to subsistence rations, nothing more. The tailor translated and the peasant nodded his head and spoke.

"He says it will be so, but a mere chicken will never relieve him of his debt to you. He asks that you remember that."

They shook hands all around again and Emil and the tailor departed together. Emil, on his way to retrieve water for his wife, felt someone following him. He turned to find the tailor standing behind him. The man was obviously in fear as he looked over his shoulder and back at Emil.

"*Signor* Scelba. What can I do for you?"

"I must talk to you, Doctor," he answered, clutching his derby close to his chest.

"*Signore*, I am very tired and I need to get water for my family so that we may eat. If you please…"

"*Signor Dottore.* I do not think you know what you have done, saving the life of that woman and child back there. It has placed you in a position of peril. I only feel it is my duty to warn you."

"*Signor* Scelba, I…"

"Please, Doctor. Just a moment of your time," Scelba pleaded.

"All right," Emil relented with a heavy sigh. "Where would you have this talk."

"Outside. Away from prying eyes and ears."

"Lead on," Emil said, motioning with his arm.

Outside the warehouse the sun had set taking with it what little warmth it had offered. The wind whistling off the harbor cut through their clothing like a knife. Emil began to stomp his feet and swing his arms against his chest to keep the circulation going, a lesson he'd learned at the front. After a moment, the tailor followed his example. Their breath poured out in bursts of steam as a few flurries of snow descended from the sky.

"All right, *Signor* Scelba. You have me here, alone. What is it that is so vitally important? And please make it quick before we freeze to death. I didn't survive the war to catch pneumonia in an English harbor."

"The man, the men you are dealing with are Sicilian. They are peasants from the mountains in Sicily. Most assuredly they are bandits, *Signor Dottore*. Very dangerous men."

"I saved the life of a woman and child. Nothing more, nothing less. That man, Busambra, said he is in my debt. What do I have to be worried about? I don't care if he is a bandit. It should have no effect on me whatsoever," Emil said, irritably.

"You are quite mistaken. By saving the lives of his family, you have become a part of his family. He is in your debt forever." Seeing the look of cynicism on the doctor's face, he hurried on. "It is not something that can be easily explained or ignored. The Sicilians have a rigid code of honor. They live by the vendetta. The merest affront can lead to a quick and violent execution. They are extremely clannish, almost tribal. By your gift of mercy, you have been drawn into their world. It is a dangerous and lethal world, *Signor Dottore*. I just wanted to warn you so you may become aware of what you have become a part of."

"How is it that you know so much about these Sicilians?" Emil asked, his voice full of pessimism.

"I was a successful tailor in Rome, like my father and his father before him. It was a family business going back generations. Some of my clients were the most powerful and influential men in Italy. Nobility, politicians, generals, and admirals. Industrialists and musicians. The elite of society. Unfortunately, my expertise also attracted other elements of society. Namely…" and here he paused to look around to reassure himself that they were alone. "Namely the bosses of the mafia."

"The mafia?" Emil asked.

"A secret criminal society born in Sicily and exported to the shores of Italy. The members are sworn to an oath of fealty and secrecy. Only Sicilians are allowed to become members. Their tentacles reach into the pockets of politicians, the coffers of the royal family, the very halls of the Vatican, itself. They have spread like a disease. Nobody can stop them."

In spite of the cold and his fatigue, Emil's interest was piqued. "You still haven't told me how you know of them."

"I was getting to that. It is important for you to know everything, *Signor Dottore*." The tailor breathed into his hands and rubbed them together before continuing. "As I said, I had a successful business. At the start of the war, I almost lost it. Due to the demands of the army, all textile manufacturing was switched to making uniforms, tents, canvas to cover the airplanes, et cetera. Overnight, my supplies of cloth dried up. I was in despair until one of my most frequent customers offered to help secure my needs. I was in a dilemma for the man was Sereni Montanelli, a *mafioso* godfather, the most powerful in Rome.

"You must understand. The Sicilians don't understand fashion or the value of the materials they drape over their bodies. They are ignorant when it comes to style or class. They are merely animals trying to dress the part to impress their constituents and gain acceptance in the upper reaches of a society that abhors and fears them.

"In the end, I accepted his offer. What was I to do? My family had to eat. I paid him a fair market value for his product. Everything was fine until this year. He made it quite apparent that he wished to have my daughter for himself. She is quite beautiful, you see. Fortunately, she was engaged at the time and I explained this to Montanelli. He only smiled and left my store.

"The next day I woke to my daughter's screams. Her fiancé had been murdered the night before by unknown assassins. My whole body grew ice cold. I knew what Montanelli had done. He came to see me later that afternoon and said that now that my daughter's engagement had been terminated, he would like to see my daughter. He gave me a week to allow her to mourn.

"A week, you understand," the small man said, trembling with rage. "A week he would give my daughter to mourn before he would come to take her away. And not even to be his wife but his mistress because she is not Sicilian and he would only marry one of his kind as he put it.

"I went to all my old customers. One was even a cabinet minister in charge of industry. They—none of them offered to help. They were all afraid. Afraid of Montanelli and the mafia. Finally an old retired general offered to help me escape the country… for a fee. I had to leave everything behind and I am still afraid they might find me."

Emil stared at the tailor for a minute. The man had been telling the truth. Emil could sense it. But the story was so outrageous. So unbelievable.

"I am sorry to hear of your predicament, *Signor* Scelba. But you can't tell me all the Sicilians are alike. They are not all criminals and bandits. That is impossible."

"No. You are quite right, Doctor. Not all. But I can assure you these men are not unlike Montanelli."

"How can you be sure of such a thing?"

"The eyes, Doctor. It is in the eyes. Especially the eyes of Busambra. If you trust your instincts, you will know what I mean. He can get anything with that look. The most dangerous of them—their eyes are that way."

And Emil remembered. The eyes. The eyes that said trust me and fear me at the same time. The eyes of a cunning predator. Irresistible and repelling.

"Why did you come to translate? What did they say to you?" Emil asked, not wanting to hear the answer.

"The twins said that if I did not come that they would kill my family and me before the day was done," he answered simply, looking at the ground.

"And you believed them?"

Scelba raised his head and looked into the doctor's eyes.

"Yes."

Emil could see the truth and the fear in the man's face. His stomach knotted involuntarily.

"Then if what you say is true, my family, as well as myself, are in danger."

Scelba's silence was his answer. Emil nodded his head once and hurried inside, followed by the tailor.

Out of the shadows of the warehouse wall, a man stepped into the open. He struck a match and lit a cigarette. When the match was out, the man walked slowly back into the warehouse.

Emil hurried back to his family. The two boys were fast asleep when he arrived. Everything seemed normal.

Sona looked up at him. "Where have you been?" she asked full of worry.

"I'm sorry, Sona. I was detained."

"The mother and the baby?"

"Yes," he lied, not wanting to alarm his wife. He then realized he was carrying the still-empty bucket. Holding it in front of him he sighed. "Sona, I'm sorry…" was all he could say.

"It's all right," she smiled. "Look what Yakov's large friend brought us." She held up a platter containing the better part of a large, cooked chicken.

Emil stared dumbfounded. "Yakov's friend?"

"The short, large man you sent with Yakov. The one with the broken nose. I think Yakov called him Strelba or Streva. Something like that. Anyway, he brought it for you and was surprised you weren't here. As least that is what it looked like. I couldn't understand a word he was saying," she paused, looking at her husband strangely. "Emil, are you all right?"

"Yes," he answered sitting beside her. "I'm fine. Just very tired. I need to get some sleep before checking on my patients again."

"Before you sleep, eat. You will need your strength," she said, setting the platter on his lap.

Emil stared at the chicken for a long time. A chicken. Cooked, he thought in amazement. Where do you get something like that in the middle of all this? And then he thought about the eyes. Those eyes. Emil realized he had suddenly lost his appetite.

16

SS New Zealand, *November 11, 1917*

Antoni Busambra cradled his baby nephew in his arms while the Magliocco twins made his sister comfortable. Guards were posted cordoning off their section of the hold. Mothers kept their children quiet while the men secured their belongings. Streva, ever watchful, directed Busambra's people as they settled in for the journey to America.

"Here you are," Busambra said softly, handing the baby to his sister. "If you need anything tell the twins and they will see to it."

"Thank you, Antoni," she muttered, turning her attention to the newborn infant.

Busambra looked up and caught the eyes of the twins. They acknowledged the stern gaze with a slight nod of their heads.

"We're all settled in," Streva reported.

"What of the good doctor and his family?" Busambra asked.

"They are close by," Streva answered.

Busambra looked at Streva and arched his eyebrows.

"Guarded as one of our own?"

Busambra gave an imperceptible nod.

"I'll have Coldiretti look after them."

Busambra looked at his sister and the baby. He thought for a minute and replied without looking at Streva. "I have plans for Dr. Danelsberg."

"Plans?" Streva asked, curiously.

Streva, Busambra's chief lieutenant, was the only one of the *cosche* allowed to address him in such a manner.

"Are you tired of living in caves, Streva?"

"*Sí, padrone.*"

"So am I," he replied as an idea crystalized in his head. "The doctor is educated. He knows several languages and is respected. He can go anywhere in the world without question. He is free. His respectability is his cloak, his education his weapon. Soon the doctor will show us how to achieve these things, for my children will not be raised in caves, Streva. They will walk free. Free as any prince in Rome."

"I will see to this personally," Streva said, bowing slightly. "And Scelba the tailor?"

"I could have employed him to start teaching our people English today. But..." Busambra said, his voice trailing off.

Streva waited a breath and then turned.

"Not 'til after we arrive in America, Streva," Busambra said, smiling at the baby. "Dr. Danelsberg must never know."

Streva motioned Coldiretti to his side as he left the hold. He never once thought about the fact that Scelba had helped to save the baby. They were hunted men and Scelba suspected their secret. He couldn't be allowed to live.

Busambra watched Streva go. For the time being they were safe. But he knew from experience that safety was only an illusion. It never lasted. The doctor would help him change that.

Busambra knelt beside his sister. "America will be a much better place. Just you wait and see," he promised.

Hammersmythe observed his stateroom with disdain. "It's not quite what we're used to, is it, Alistare?"

"No, my Lord, not quite," his bodyguard answered as he continued to unpack Hammersmythe's belongings. "But I trust it will be better once we arrive in the States."

"You can trust that, my good man. Most assuredly," Hammersmythe emphasized by slapping the arm of the chair.

I'm tired of being herded about like cattle, he thought. God-damn you, Father. Goddamn you for ever getting me into this awful mess.

Hammersmythe got up out of his chair and began to pace.

That bloody Inspector Brunswick. Sod him, Hammersmythe thought, anger burning high in his cheeks. Sod the lot.

Hammersmythe sat back down as quickly as he had risen. Crossing his legs he began to think out loud.

"In America there are no kings to muck up your life?" Hammersmythe asked.

"Last I heard, Sir, not a king in the whole country."

"Titles mean nothing to them there, do they?"

"Seems they fought a whole war just to prove the point, Sir Percy," Alistare replied.

"So what do they worship in America if they have no kings, Alistare, no lords or dukes?"

"Rich people," Alistare answered without much thought. "All they write about in the American papers are the ones with scads of money."

"Exactly, Alistare. And why do they worship the rich?"

Alistare paused to think. "Because they can buy whatever they want?"

"No, Alistare. They worship the rich because the rich are powerful. The rich can do whatever they want. The rich control their destinies and the destinies of all the millions of their fellow citizens who have no money."

"What's your point, my Lord?" Alistare inquired, finishing the last bag.

"Do we have any money, Alistare?"

Alistare turned to his master and smiled wickedly. "Loads, my Lord."

"Exactly."

"I'm not feeling well," Sona remarked as she settled the boys on the bunk. "Maybe it was the chicken."

Emil felt her forehead and checked her pulse. "I'm afraid it's not the chicken, Sona."

"Not seasickness. Not again," she sighed. She had been sick on all three ships since they'd left Russia. She plopped on the bunk beside the boys. "You'll have to tend to the children again."

"I'm sorry, Sona." Emil felt her forehead and observed her color. She was already turning a sickly shade of green. We haven't even left port, he thought. "I'll go look for a bucket."

Sona clutched the children to her. "Don't be long, Emil."

"I'll hurry, my lady."

Emil turned toward the deck and almost ran into the large Sicilian. "Strelba?" Emil asked, not sure.

"Streva," he responded gruffly. The Sicilian peasant looked at Sona and then back to Emil. He smiled slightly and patted the doctor on the shoulder in a stay-here gesture.

Emil smiled back nervously. "She's going to be sick. I've got to get a bucket," he said, gesturing with his hands.

Streva looked at Sona and although he couldn't speak English he understood the doctor's dilemma. He shook his head *no* and patted Emil on the shoulder again. He motioned Emil back toward Sona and set off down the gangway.

Well, I guess if he can find a chicken, Emil thought.

He returned to his family and sat on the bunk beside his sons.

Sons, he thought. I don't think of Yakov as anything other than my son.

The thought made him feel good. He thanked God for allowing him the privilege to love this small child who had lost so much.

I will do my best, God, to honor the trust you have placed in me, he prayed silently. Yakov and Viktor will be raised as brothers and taught Moses' laws as my father would have taught them.

Emil gazed happily at the boys. He'd been given the gift to heal. He'd found his family after he thought them lost. Most of all, Emil had received a second chance from God at a life he'd almost given up needlessly and recklessly.

A miracle, he thought looking at his family. We are in the presence of a great miracle.

A shadow loomed over them. Emil looked up to see Streva. He had two buckets, one empty, one filled with water.

Streva set them down and smiled. Emil felt a twinge of fear, but smiled back. The small giant left after patting him on the shoulder again.

What strange angels are these, God? Emil wondered.

As he dwelled on the Sicilians and what they meant to his family, Sona cried out.

"Emil!"

He barely got the bucket up in time as she vomited last night's supper.

Emil held her head as she retched again. "It will be all right, Sona. I promise. In a few days we'll be in America and you'll never have to get on another boat again."

From across the hold, Streva lit a cigarette and watched the Danelsbergs.

17

North Atlantic Ocean, November 13, 1917

The SS *New Zealand* pitched about in an increasingly rocky sea. On the bridge, the captain heard the reports from his lookouts and watched the changing barometer. His instincts told him the ship was headed into an early winter storm, bringing huge ocean swells and gale force winds. An experienced mariner, Masden's gut feelings had always been correct. This time, unfortunately, would be no different.

The captain ordered the ship rigged for foul weather. His crew strung lines on the deck, checked the lashings on all the cargo and made the ship as watertight as possible without alarming the passengers. Lookouts on the forward bow reported the ominously approaching line of dark clouds and the captain went over last-minute instructions with his officers covering all emergency contingencies.

Across the length and breadth of the convoy, ships exchanged nervous messages by wireless about the approaching weather. On this rare occasion, the sailors worried more about the storm than about the Imperial German Navy's U-boats. Even so, the allied naval escorts prepared for the weather without relaxing their vigilance for the dreaded enemy submarines.

On the SS *New Zealand* the passengers, ignorant of the storm, became subdued as the sky grew gray.

Fate: "Bent Nose" Streva was momentarily distracted from his duty watching over the Danelsbergs by a work party of sailors as they rigged lines in the hold.

Fate: Emil was too busy tending to his wife's seasickness to notice the two boys slip off.

Fate: In his stateroom, Lord Hammersmythe, noticing the change in the weather, decided to take his evening walk early. He ordered his bodyguard to fetch him his long coat and his walking stick.

Hammersmythe, emerging on the deck, shivered in the cold sea breeze. He pulled his scarf tightly around his neck and motioned Alistare to follow him. He was thinking of his father, his banishment, and the time he was forced to endure the company of the boorish Inspector Brunswick. Hammersmythe had rarely thought of anything else since boarding ship.

Brunswick, the consummate professional, kept his feelings to himself during most of the investigation. Hammersmythe was still in name a royal and, therefore, protected by his title, or so he thought. When Brunswick inquired as to the nature of the procurement of and activities with the two young boys, his tone became menacing.

Hammersmythe, still feeling untouchable, answered him quite honestly with a lecherous smile on his face. In an instant, the inspector had crossed the room and thrown him against the wall. After he got up, screaming words of protest, the inspector slapped him full force across the face knocking him back into the wall and splitting his lip. The inspector then calmly retook his seat and stared at Hammersmythe.

When the stars had stopped swimming in front of his eyes, Hammersmythe, full of his old righteous rage and breeding, started to protest again. But he stopped before the words could leave his mouth.

Who can I protest to, he'd thought. Who would listen to me now? No one, that's who.

And then the utter realization came crashing down on him sending him into a deep, dark despair. I am powerless. Completely and utterly powerless and alone. He sagged back against the wall.

After a long time he stood up, a broken and defeated man, and took his seat opposite the inspector. He looked up at Brunswick, waiting calmly with lifeless eyes. The inspector reached in his jacket and drew out a handkerchief which he tossed to him. Hammersmythe did not attempt to retrieve the cloth.

"You're bleeding, my Lord," Brunswick said somewhat flippantly.

Hammersmythe picked up the handkerchief and absentmindedly dabbed at his bleeding lip.

"And now back to the boys, your Lordship. Let's have it again to make sure I've got everything straight."

The boys, he'd thought. The two young boys. And a fire began to burn in his belly.

I had power once, he'd remembered. I didn't know what I had until I lost it. What a thing to lose. And the rage burned higher into his chest.

I had the power to squash you like a bug. To make you live in poverty the rest of your life, he thought, as he stared at the face of his tormentor. And someday, by God, I'll have it back so I can squash little bugs like you whenever I want.

The life came back into his eyes as the rage burned higher and filled his head like a swarm of bees.

But I must be careful now.

"I see you're back with us, my Lord. That's a good lad. Now back to the two young boys. Let's start at the beginning, shall we?"

Oh, you're right, so right, my dear Inspector Brunswick. I am back, you bloody fool. But do you know what you've awakened? I think not.

Hammersmythe picked up his pace as the memory played itself out in his mind. He rapped his walking stick on the deck with each stride. His bodyguard hurried to keep up with him.

He strolled around the bridge structure and noticed two boys playing under a stairwell. And he stopped cold. He didn't even notice Alistare run into him after the sudden halt to their walk. Nor did he hear his bodyguard's apologies. Hammersmythe just stood and stared. And listened to their singsong voices and watched them at their play. Two boys, he thought. Not much younger than the boys father and I...two boys. Two young boys. He unconsciously rubbed his still-puffy lip.

Hammersmythe felt a fire in his lower belly and his skin broke out in a cold sweat. He was excited and enraged at the same time. It was a feeling all too familiar.

Two boys... Two boys...

"Alistare..." he said, turning to his bodyguard.

"Yes, my Lord," Alistare answered, looking into the cold, cruel eyes of his master.

Hammersmythe didn't say anything. He slowly turned to look at the children. Alistare followed his gaze. When Alistare turned back to his master, Hammersmythe said simply, "You know what to do."

Emil gently felt his wife's cheek. This was a lot worse than their previous trips. Finally, she was resting after having been up all night. Many passengers were suffering in a similar manner. All they could do was ride it out.

He looked around the hold of the ship. It was a smaller version of the warehouse with hammocks crisscrossing the compartment. The ship's owners had converted the empty cargo compartments into giant berthing areas to accommodate the refugees. They were cold, stark, and extremely uncomfortable.

Soon we will be in America, he thought. And all this will be a memory.

Emil heard others retching in the compartment. The pitch of the ship had increased with the larger swells. The more pronounced roll of the deck caused many people, heretofore unaffected, to become seasick.

He felt his stomach growl and realized it was dinnertime. Tending to his wife, he'd forgotten to eat lunch. He decided to leave his wife sleeping and take the boys to the galley to get something to eat.

Emil looked around the compartment and didn't see them. He paused to listen for the sounds of their voices at play, but didn't hear them. He searched the whole of the hold and failed to find them. He asked the Barazonovs and others if they'd seen the boys. But no one had seen them in quite some time. Standing at the hatch to the cargo hold, he felt the deck lurch under his feet as the ship slid into a deep trough. He grabbed onto the hatchway to keep himself from falling.

My God, he thought. Don't let the boys be on the deck. But he realized, with a sick feeling, that was where they were. The air in the hold was thick with the smell of vomit as it was throughout the ship. The only fresh air was on the deck. He straightened himself and pushed through the hatch. And came face to face with "Bent Nose" Streva.

"My sons!" he cried. "My sons!"

Yakov and Viktor were playing catch under the stairs with a colored ball Streva had given them. They were happy to be in fresh air even though the wind was freezing. The oppressive air of the hold was more than the boys could bear and they had stolen off as soon as they could.

Viktor threw the ball to Yakov. Yakov, the clumsier of the two, missed the catch and it bounced off him and rolled away. Both boys got up to chase the ball, but stopped when a large, well-dressed man picked it up. They instinctively huddled close together as the stranger bent over to hand them their ball back.

"There now, lads. Is this what you were looking for?" he asked with a smile. One of his front teeth was shiny, like gold. Neither boy understood what he was saying, but Viktor reached out tentatively for the ball. The stranger handed it to him with a flourish.

"There you go, lads. Now what would two skinny boys such as yourselves be craving most? I think Uncle Ali knows."

He held out his left hand. In it a handkerchief lay flat. With a flourish he yanked the handkerchief out of his left hand and a pile of dark chunks of chocolate candy appeared. The boys looked on, transfixed with watering mouths.

"Come on now, lads. Let's have a piece," he said, lowering his hand right in front of their faces. Both boys reached up and grabbed a piece.

"That's it. Eat 'em up, lads."

The boys gobbled them down and looked at the pile with longing in their eyes.

"Oh. I see you'd like some more. Well then, follow me to Uncle Ali's cabin. There's plenty more where this came from," he said as he motioned the boys to follow. Months of deprivation had taken their toll. The boys couldn't resist the temptation and followed the smiling man with the shiny tooth without hesitation.

They forgot all about the ball. Emil and Streva found it an hour later where they had left it, rolling back and forth with the motion of the ship, but the boys had disappeared into thin air.

When the boys disappeared, Emil and Streva had gone to the ship's first officer. A search had been conducted with no luck. The boys had vanished. The first officer did not seem greatly interested in continuing the search. The SS *New Zealand* was heading into a vicious winter storm and the ship needed all hands to secure the ship for foul weather. The boys would have to wait.

Frightened and frustrated, Emil and Streva sought out the tailor Scelba and took him to the Sicilian Busambra. When Emil requested his help, Busambra nodded his head and began issuing orders to his men. For a peasant, unable to speak English on an English ship, the man got rapid results. His inquiries had brought them to a stateroom in an area strictly forbidden to all but first-class passengers and crew. Barely two hours had elapsed since Emil had first discovered the boys were missing.

"Take this," Busambra ordered, holding out a sharp blade to Emil. Emil didn't understand him, but took the offered knife and stuck it in his belt. Over the pounding of the storm Emil thought he could hear whimpering coming from behind the door.

"Hurry up, dammit," Emil hissed at Busambra. Busambra muttered something to Streva and jerked his head down the direction of the empty gangway. The huge man moved off silently.

"Now we go," Busambra said quietly. He produced a set of keys and, selecting one, inserted it into the lock. He slowly turned the handle until it clicked open. With a grunt the Sicilian shoved the door open and burst into the stateroom with Emil following closely behind. Both men stopped, stunned at the nightmarish vision exploding in front of their eyes.

"What?" Emil croaked. Before he could react, Busambra moved in a blur across the floor.

Emil Danelsberg stood at the railing of the SS *New Zealand* with his wife and the two boys and watched the Statue of Liberty come into view as the ship entered New York harbor. He looked at his wife and they smiled at each other. The boys remained silent.

Neither child had spoken about what happened during their short captivity. Yakov spent most of his time crying in Sona's arms. Viktor awoke screaming from horrible nightmares every time he fell asleep, which was rare the last three days. Even now dark circles were forming under his eyes.

Emil wondered about what he could do for the boys. The leather straps and the marks on Viktor's back only told part of the story. If only he had a clearer picture of what had happened during the early part of their captivity, he might be able to do something to alleviate the boy's suffering. Unfortunately, the boys refused to speak about it.

He'd quit inquiring at Sona's insistence. He understood her concern. The boys became extremely upset whenever the subject was broached. Emil only wished he could use his surgical skills to cut away the memories of their horrible ordeal. He was only now beginning to understand that they might not ever know what had transpired. Seeing the boys' further suffering, he regretted not killing the English lord while he had a chance.

Sona left with the boys to get them out of the cold air. Alone with his thoughts, he remembered the incredible suffering of their long journey.

I hope it was worth it, he thought. Please, God, let it be worth it.

He felt a presence next to him and looked up to see Antoni Busambra standing next to him.

God only knows what he has been through on his journey, Emil thought. From the looks of his group, it was as harrowing as ours if not more so.

He smiled at Antoni. Antoni clapped him on the back and pointed to the Statue of Liberty.

"*Ameriga*, Doctor. *Ameriga*."

"Yes, my friend. America."

PART IV
Crucible

18

Tuapi, Nicaragua, December 5, 1988

Jacob took several deep breaths and looked at the sun descending toward the horizon. His story had taken them through lunch and late into the afternoon.

Xavier looked at his godfather with concern. I thought I'd suffered, he thought. Jacob was obviously exhausted after reliving the ordeal of his journey to America. He placed a hand on Jacob's shoulder.

"I had no idea, Uncle Jake," Xavier spoke. "None."

Xavier felt less sorry for himself after hearing about the agonies his family had suffered. His grief and desire for revenge remained undiminished, but he felt remorse for his recent mistreatment of his family and friends.

Jacob regarded his godson. "It is the first time I have told that story to anyone. I won't do it again," he sighed.

Xavier squeezed Jacob's shoulder. "Thank you for confiding in me. You are an amazing man, Uncle Jake."

"I don't feel amazing, Xavier. I just feel tired."

"Then rest. I'll help you to bed."

"I can rest later," Jacob said irritated, as Xavier tried to help him out of the chair. He waved Xavier away. "Now, what I want—is to know."

"Know what?"

"I want to know how you feel about your father?"

Xavier paused, leaning back in his chair. He was more confused about his feelings for his father than ever. Xavier now understood where his father's rage came from, but he couldn't forgive. Jacob had suffered the same torments and had never raised his hand in anger in his entire life.

"How could you and Dad turn out so differently?" he asked.

"I did the only thing I could. I let your grandmother and grandfather love and protect me. Your grandfather shared the joy of his religion with me and I found my life's work through him. It is the essence of being Jewish; despite our sufferings, we worship God and help others. Becoming a doctor seemed natural."

"But didn't my grandparents offer Dad the same love?" Xavier asked.

"Of course! They treated us the same."

"Then why did Dad turn into such an angry man?"

"Because he couldn't forgive himself. Or your parents, or that English lord," Jacob answered.

"And you did?" Xavier asked in disbelief.

"Yes, I did, Xavier," Jacob stated a little too emphatically. "Don't you remember anything the rabbis taught you in synagogue? God demands that we forgive lest our hate destroy us."

"And Dad never forgave."

"No. He couldn't forgive—so he blamed God. And the only God he knew was the one he worshiped in Vorzel, the God of the Jews. That was why he fought against your religious training.

"It's no excuse, Uncle Jake. I still hate the bastard."

"And the child?"

"What child?" Xavier asked.

"The child who your father used to be. The child who was tortured and molested. Do you hate him?"

"Of course not. How could I?"

Jacob smiled. "Then that is where your path shall begin."

"My path to what?"

"Your path to forgiveness," Jacob explained. "Love the child your father was and someday you may be able to forgive the man he became."

Xavier smiled back. "I walked right into that."

"It's easy to trap a blind man," Jacob shrugged, pleased with himself. "Are you ready to see again?"

"Maybe." Xavier looked up and raised his arms unsure what to say. "Where do you suggest I start?"

"Maria tells me a Dr. Figueres has requested your services," Jacob remarked nonchalantly.

"Yes she has. She's putting together a mobile medical team to take health care to the Nicaragua-Honduras border. Some of the villages up there get cut off for months at a time because of the fighting."

"Then I think you should help her."

"I don't know," Xavier said, shaking his head. "I have a feeling there's more to this *humanitarian* mission than she's letting on. Besides their war doesn't involve me. I'm a U.S. citizen and we're not particularly popular down here."

"Emil found himself alone with his family in many strange places during their journey to America," Jacob said, commenting on the story he just told. "He survived the journey and prospered because he helped strangers—people who didn't speak his language or worship his God. He healed their wounds, cured their sicknesses, and brought babies into the world. These services saved his life."

Xavier turned toward the sea and leaned on the veranda rail. His momentary anger at Jacob quickly passed.

"God I miss Min," Xavier confessed. He heard Jacob rise and approach the rail. They gazed at the sea together.

"Be careful, Xavier," Jacob said, squeezing his arm. The old man turned and walked into the house.

Jacob lay in his bed trying to rest before dinner, but he was unable to sleep. A ghost kept him awake, the ghost of an English lord. Busambra had told him the man was long dead, but Busambra was wrong. The bastard was alive in the bedroom of a small house in Nicaragua.

Emil said he never knew your name, Jacob thought. But I do. I know you. You are the devil.

Jacob felt fear, but under that, he felt a rage buried by a lifetime of denial.

I tried, God, Jacob cried. I tried so hard to forgive, but I have failed.

Xavier watched Maria fix dinner.

"You can stare or you can help me, Javier," Maria stated.

"*Lo siento.*" Xavier grabbed a head of lettuce and began to shred it.

"I've been talking to Jacob," Xavier began as he dumped the lettuce into a bowl. "He told me things I never knew. I think he's trying to help me find peace."

"And did he?"

"Between what Dad did to help you and your village, and what I now know he suffered as I child, maybe. I don't know. It is very hard—this forgiveness thing."

Maria browned some meat in a frying pan. "I can't explain why you should forgive your father. He did some horrible things to you, maybe forgiveness is not possible. I know that.

"I also know that when I came to him for help years ago, he gave it. In his heart, I believe there was good. This house, the clinic, the educations he provided Elena, Huberto, and others proves that he had some admirable qualities. I think his charity was a way of making up for his sins. Maybe, no matter how difficult things were for him in Dallas, he could always look to his work here to find comfort and peace of mind. But he was so complicated I can only guess at his motives. I hope his work here in Tuapi helped him to face his God."

"Yeah," Xavier said, part of him hoping his father had a very hard time when he came face to face with God.

They remained quiet as the meat sizzled in the pan. When Maria was satisfied with it, she removed the hot pan from the stove and set it on a cooling stone. She wiped her hands on her apron, looking at Xavier.

"Dr. Figueres called while you were talking to Jacob. She wanted to know if you'd changed your mind."

"I still think about my wife all day, every day, Maria," Xavier confessed. "I still want to find those responsible for her death. Helping these strangers might get in the way of my duty to Min."

"Strangers? We are strangers?" Maria asked, exasperated. "We took you in knowing the danger. This village has been your home and my friends have become your family. Is there no room in your heart for anything other than revenge?"

"Forgive me, Maria. Believe me when I say I love this place and these people. Tuapi has become my home, but I have my duty to Min. I have to see it through," he said, trying to convince her. "I want to help—to honor your wishes. But how can I do both?"

Maria stared at Xavier.

He is safe here, God, even as he plots his revenge, he is safe, she thought. And while he is safe, I can help him see the futility of revenge. But with Elena lies danger, maybe death, and I couldn't stand to lose him. Hasn't he made up his mind? Must I push him? Please show me your will, God, she prayed.

In the end God's will was clear. The soul of Nicaragua demanded it.

"I have one question to ask you, Javi," Maria said. "If Min were here now, what would she have you do?"

Xavier found Elena sitting on the beach, her arms wrapped around smooth, shapely legs. Her dark hair shimmered in the moonlight. He sat next to her, unsure of what to say.

"I've been looking for you, for hours," he said trying to start a conversation. When she didn't respond he looked at her. "You know you're crazy." She shrugged her shoulders.

"Well, we both know I'm crazy. Okay, Doctor. Us crazies need to stick together. When do we leave?" he asked, smiling.

Her response was to reach out and briefly grasp his hand and return his smile. Xavier marveled at the gentleness of her touch.

I hope you are as brave as you are handsome, Elena thought.

They sat together for some time, listening to the surf's never-ending motion.

Managua, Nicaragua, December 7, 1988

The streets of Managua were flowing with people. Fireworks erupted overhead bathing the festivities in kaleidoscopic colors. Children ran from house to house accepting candy from the masked homeowners. The Subtiavan Indians played drums and paraded the giant female puppet *la Gigantona* and her dwarf-ish companion, *Pepe*. In front yards, parents gathered at elaborately decorated homemade altars to drink, socialize, and worship.

All across the city people called to each other, "What brings so much happiness?" and were answered with the refrain, "The Immaculate Conception of Mary."

It was *la griteria*, the shouting, the second night of *Purisima*, the celebration of the Virgin Mary.

Elena led Xavier through the streets of the capital. They had arrived that afternoon on a flight from Puerto Cabezas accompanied by Huberto Royo and Alberto Diaz. Elena was serious despite the festivities, but Huberto was whistling and flirting, ignoring the disapproving looks from the doctor. Xavier was unhappy and trying not to show it.

The mission was shrouded in secrecy and Elena refused to tell him more than she already had. Xavier, true to his marine training, wanted all the intelligence he could get his hands on. Diaz, a former career military officer, looked as unhappy as Xavier.

Xavier had seen the man in Tuapi, but had not met him until yesterday. Diaz, Xavier learned, was a former officer of the National Guard under Somoza. He was exiled to Tuapi after refusing an order to fire on unarmed civilians during a peaceful demonstration. Other than that, the man was an enigma.

Adding to Xavier's discomfort was his feeling of vulnerability. He felt safe in Tuapi. Here in Managua, he felt exposed. Every time the fireworks exploded, Xavier winced. He found himself furtively scanning the crowd, searching for signs of trouble. The celebrants, made grotesque by the eerie light of the fireworks, magnified Xavier's paranoia. He was relieved when they arrived at their rendezvous.

The group walked across a field of overgrown grass, weeds, and rubble. It was one of thousands of buildings destroyed by the 1972 earthquake. The Managuans, too poor to rebuild most of the structures, turned the lots over to grazing livestock.

The inhabitants of this field, four cows, chewed their cud in indifference. Xavier suppressed the urge to moo at the bovines, while Huberto, unable to pass up an opportunity to converse with anyone or anything, mooed to his heart's content. The only response he got was from Elena, who told him to shut up.

The group approached a large warehouse at the far end of the field. Elena tapped out a rhythm on the wall. Xavier couldn't see the point as there was no door. After a minute, the wall itself opened up to give them admittance. Once inside, the door shut automatically leaving them in the dark.

Huberto turned on a flashlight. The beam revealed a rusted structure containing several old automobiles, stripped and on blocks. Elena led the men to the back of the warehouse and up some stairs to a well-lighted, comfortably furnished office.

As Xavier's eyes adjusted to the light, he heard a familiar voice say, "You're looking good, Xavier. I guess the beach agrees with you." Jerry Rizzi stood and shook his hand. "I hope you can tell me what I'm doing here," he said, looking none too comfortable in the heat that pervaded even the air-conditioned office. Despite Xavier's long-standing antipathy toward him, he found himself sympathizing with Rizzi.

"I had no idea you were coming, Jerry," Xavier remarked, perplexed. He was also surprised at how happy he was to see a familiar face, even if it *was* Rizzi's. "Hell, I'm surprised to be here myself. What's going on?"

"If you don't know then maybe our gracious hostess can tell us," he said, motioning to a dignified woman sitting in a wheelchair. "Allow me to introduce, *Señora* Violeta Barrios de Chamorro."

Xavier walked over to her. At his approach, two bodyguards standing behind her visibly stiffened.

"Don't mind them. They think everybody is a potential assassin," she said, motioning him closer. She grabbed his hand in both of hers with a firm grip. He stared into her kind face and felt as though he were in the presence of royalty.

"It is a pleasure to meet the son of our good and generous friend, Dr. Victor Danielson," Chamorro said, shaking his hand. "My friends call me *Doña* Violeta. And you most assuredly are one of my friends. Please sit here next to me," she asked, releasing his hand and patting a chair to her right. "And you here, *Señor* Rizzi," she said, pointing to a seat at her left hand. Both men did as requested. Xavier wondered if Rizzi could sense the concern of the two bodyguards as two complete strangers sat so close to their leader. He was sure he did. Rizzi wasn't the kind of man to miss anything.

Xavier looked at his three companions. They stood respectfully, even Huberto the comic.

Whoever this woman is, she must be pretty important to get Huberto to calm down, he thought.

"What is it that we can do for you?" Rizzi asked, sweating profusely in his three piece suit.

Doña Violeta held their hands as a grandmother would.

"*Señores*. You may help me save my country," she smiled.

The cows grazing in the lot twitched uneasily. A few things could upset the docile beasts: earthquakes, predators, the smell of death. However, their tails swished restlessly and they shifted on their hooves as something stirred in the shadows at the edge of the field.

He approached the side of the warehouse where he had last seen his quarry. Not finding a door, he moved to the rear of the building. Circling the warehouse, he failed to find an entrance besides the huge chained doors in front. Puzzled, he retraced his steps.

He knew they were inside the building—he could feel them. But he couldn't figure out how they got in. He pulled a flashlight from his pocket and turned it on. An amber lens rendered the light almost invisible to passerby.

After a few minutes' search, he found what he was looking for. His fingers traced the narrow outline of the hidden door. He could feel it more than see it, but he knew it was there. He would return later to find a way inside. For now, he was satisfied he'd discovered the building's secret.

The interloper took his knowledge and melted into the night. The cows watched the man until he was out of sight from the far side of the field as his smell lingered.

"Is that all?" Rizzi asked in relief. "I thought Xavier had been discovered. I was afraid he was in danger. The message I received from Maria seemed to indicate the very same."

"Please forgive Maria. We are old friends and I persuaded her to send the message. It was the only way we were sure you would come. We desperately needed to speak with you, *Señor* Rizzi. The future of my country may well depend on your assistance."

"*Doña* Violeta, I don't know how we can help," Rizzi spoke after a brief pause. Both Americans had been taken aback at her request.

"*Señor Rizzi*, we have an opportunity to take a step toward peace. With your financial assistance and Xavier's talent, we can take that step."

"Please forgive me, *Señora*, but I can tell you up front that though we appreciate your situation, we are unable to help in anyway," Rizzi said apologetically, while tugging at his collar. "Xavier is down here hiding. The more he is exposed, the more likely that harm could come to him. As for me, my hands are bound. My duty is to *Signor* Busambra. You are aware of who he is?"

"I am aware of the powerful Don Busambra," she responded.

"Then you can understand that my involvement in a potentially explosive situation could harm him. I am prevented by personal oath from endangering him. You do understand." It was a statement not a question.

"*Yo se, Señor*. I understand. But would you please indulge an old woman?" she asked, smiling.

He nodded his head, "Of course. Please continue." Rizzi pulled out his handkerchief and mopped his forehead.

"Before I begin, Ramon, *dos refrescos, por favor*," she requested from one of her bodyguards. She leaned over and placed a hand on Rizzi's arm. "For the heat, *Señor* Rizzi. A Nicaraguan fruit drink. Quite refreshing."

"*Gracias, Doña* Violeta," Rizzi replied, trying out his Spanish.

The guard returned with two plastic bags. *"Que tipo?"* she asked him as he passed them to Xavier and Rizzi.

"Tamarindo, Doña Violeta," he answered.

"Ah, one of our native fruits, *Señor* Rizzi. You are in for a treat."

Rizzi stared at the brownish liquid dubiously. He looked at Xavier with a raised eyebrow. Xavier smiled and bit a hole in the plastic and began to suck out the liquid.

When in Rome, Rizzi thought, and carefully bit a hole in his bag. He sucked a tiny bit of the *refresco* from the bag and was surprised at the taste. It was sweet and fruity and refreshingly cold. Without further ceremony, he began to drink the rest of the contents gratefully.

"To continue," she said. "The Contras operating out of Honduran territory are causing terrible damage to our people along the border. They are more concerned with depriving innocent citizens of food and transportation than they are of battling the Sandinista army. I am sure a man of your intelligence is aware of the situation in spite of the propaganda that hails the Contras as freedom fighters."

"I am aware of the Contras' tactics, *Señora*," Rizzi acknowledged. "And I am also aware that you left the Sandinista government in 1980. And not due to ill health, as the *Barricada* newspaper reported. You left under protest because you violently disagreed with the direction the Sandinistas were taking."

"Not all of them," she interrupted. "Two of them are my children. My youngest son, Carlos, is the editor of the *Barricada*. He wrote the misleading article about my departure from the council."

"Interesting," Rizzi mused before continuing. "It is still a matter of record that you would prefer the ouster of the regime. Am I correct?"

"You are correct, *Señor*. Daniel Ortega was my friend before he was the leader of the Sandinista party or president of Nicaragua. After leading the people to victory over Somoza, he promised open elections. But Communists often do that. I admit that I was taken in. Daniel is very bright and charismatic, but I realized that his aim was not a free and open democracy but primacy for the Sandinistas. We traded one dictator for another. When I realized this, I quit the revolutionary council and decided to implement other ideas to free the people."

"Then why are you so opposed to the Contras, *Doña* Violeta?" Rizzi asked. "Not only are they enemies of the Sandinistas, their threat to the border has been greatly diminished since the U. S. Congress cut off their aid."

"As long as the Contras continue to fight, the Sandinistas have an excuse to exercise authoritarian control in the name of national security, and Daniel Ortega is seen as a hero," Chamorro explained. "Assassinations, deportations, and censorship proceed unabated. Fully fifty percent of our gross national product is spent on the military. That leaves very little for the people. And, trust me when I tell you that the Contras are still receiving aid from your government."

"*Doña* Violeta. Our Congress enacted the Boland amendments barring the president and our intelligence agencies from assisting the rebels," Rizzi countered. "The administration is reeling under the Iran-Contra investigation. Under such close scrutiny, I find it hard to fathom anyone finding a way to support the Contras."

"Nevertheless, it is happening," she said seriously. The grandmotherly tone had left her voice. "The CIA is still supplying weapons and money to the Contra leaders, who use them to terrorize the population in brutal border raids. These leaders," she grimaced as though she would spit on the ground, "were former right-wing officers in Somoza's national guard. They forcibly recruit young men into their ranks. They murder, rape, and pillage in the name of freedom while claiming to represent Nicaragua's fight against tyranny. It makes me ill."

She paused, regaining her composure. "If we can stop the aid to the Contras, they'll wither on the vine. The Sandinistas will lose the justification for their Draconian measures, including our current rule of censorship. The threat gone, the military could be reduced to provide more money for education, health, and agriculture.

"Only then will the true voice of the people be heard. Free elections in which everybody has a voice and a vote—that is our mission. And it begins with the discovery of the link between your government and the Contras. In short, it begins with you,

Señor Rizzi, and you, *Señor* Daniels," she finished, looking from one to the other.

"Why us?" Rizzi asked.

"To start with, we need a helicopter. That is where you come in. I am sure you could arrange this for us."

"Possibly, but what will you do with it once you have it?" Rizzi asked, intrigued with the woman's boldness.

"We will do exactly what we've told Xavier. We will take medical care to the Honduran border."

"But that's not all is it, *Doña* Violeta?"

"No, that is not all. The medical mission will give them access to areas where the Contras operate. If we are lucky, the medical team will uncover the evidence we seek. Xavier will pilot the helicopter, assisted by Major Diaz who is an intelligence expert."

"Why Xavier?"

Doña Violeta glanced up at Elena, then shifted her gaze toward Xavier. "The Honduran army recently acquired several Stinger missiles from the United States. We believe the Contras have also purchased these missiles, courtesy of the CIA. I believe Xavier has flown in hostile environments before. He has the specific experience we need to make this mission a success. Being American, he makes our mission look less suspect, more international."

"Impossible. I'm sorry," Rizzi said, standing. "Xavier, we must go. I will find a new place to hide you. Your presence in this country is no longer a secret and these people don't give a damn about ensuring your safety." Rizzi could not hide the irritation in his voice. "Well?" he asked, waiting for Xavier.

"Sit down, Jerry."

"What? You're in danger; we need to leave. Now."

"I'm staying, Jerry. And you're going to help."

"Listen to reason, Xavier!" he demanded.

"I have," Xavier said, smiling at Elena. "That's why I'm staying."

"What about Min? Have you forgotten about what happened to your wife?" Rizzi asked to provoke Xavier.

"No, Jerry. I haven't. But I believe if she were here she would support my decision. So would Jacob and so would my father."

"Your father!" Rizzi barked. "What the hell does he have to do with this?"

"More than even I know," Xavier answered. "You will go home to Bennedetto and tell him what we need. When you do, please give him my love."

"And what makes you think your godfather will listen to your demands?" Rizzi asked, pissed.

"He will listen because you will tell him I am rejoining the living. He will understand that, and he will do as I ask."

"The hell he will!" Rizzi yelled.

"The hell he won't, *Consigliere*. Maybe you forget who I am." Xavier stood and declared, "I am Xavier Daniels, godson of Don Bennedetto Busambra, *il capo di tuti capi*." He paused, glaring at Rizzi, daring him to defy his wishes. Xavier's happiness at seeing Rizzi had evaporated as the old contempt returned. "Now do as I tell you."

Rizzi looked at Xavier's face. It was firm and strong. The eyes were determined and in control. It was the look he had left with before the invasion of Grenada. He won the Navy Cross in that short conflict. Rizzi had the brief impulse to kiss Xavier's hand. He truly had the power. Instead, Rizzi stood and took Xavier's right hand in both of his.

"It will be as you command."

"Thank you, Jerry. Now let us sit down and finalize the details before enjoying the rest of the holiday."

Doña Violeta beamed, immensely pleased. She asked Alberto and Huberto to join them. They discussed the operation at length. Rizzi noticed Xavier glancing at Elena furtively throughout the meeting. Occasionally, she would catch his eye and quickly look away blushing.

My God, Rizzi thought. He doesn't even know it, yet, but he's fallen in love with the doctor. What is it about these Nicaraguan women? he asked himself. They have stolen more than one heart.

Rizzi listened to the concussion from the fireworks in the distance. He remembered the sound of the artillery in the hills of Vietnam. The same fear stole over him, and his flesh quivered.

At the conclusion of the briefing, with the facts safely stored in their heads, they left the warehouse. Xavier was all smiles as he clapped Rizzi on the back.

"Join us in *la griteria*. They tell me you'll never forget it."

Presidential Palace, Managua, Nicaragua, December 7, 1988

"Where is Kruger?" Major Ricardo Sanchez asked. He tapped a Marlboro out of its pack and lit it.

"Sifting leads," Kurt Boüldt answered. Sanchez nodded and exhaled slowly. He placed the cigarettes and lighter on the small table beside his chair.

"What leads?" Sanchez inquired with the relaxed tone of a man used to conducting interrogations.

"Things he has discovered," Boüldt replied. He smiled at Sanchez, indicating he knew the game as well.

"And how did he discover these things?"

"Searching for leads." A small laugh escaped his throat.

"*Bastante!*" Daniel Ortega shouted to the men in his salon. The president of Nicaragua had been pacing in front of an open window watching the streets of Managua below. "We employed you to get results. And you've given us nothing."

"You employed us to help you stay in power," Boüldt said to Ortega. "Kruger knows what he's doing. Dragging him back here to give you status reports only impedes his progress. Don't you agree, Major Sanchez?"

Ortega turned to Sanchez. "It is better if he is allowed a free hand, *mi Presidente*," Sanchez agreed.

Ortega puffed on a large cigar and resumed pacing. "Then tell him that with such a free hand he should get results *mas rapido*."

Sanchez turned to Boüldt. "Will you pass along the concerns of *nuestro Presidente?*"

The mercenary nodded his head. "*A sus ordenes, Señor Presidente!*" he intoned with a slight hint of mockery. Ortega snatched the cigar from his mouth and glared at Boüldt.

"You have no manners, *Señor*," Ortega remarked.

Boüldt smiled at the president. "And what a problem it's been for me."

Kurt Boüldt had all the physical tools and instincts to make an excellent soldier, but his unwillingness to obey superior officers, combined with his mockery of their station, caused constant irritation. His combat record saved him from a court-martial, but his superiors failed to find a place for him. His file was bounced around to various departments of the South African Defense Forces before it crossed Kruger's desk.

Kruger liked what he read and recognized what others had missed. Boüldt enjoyed killing and was completely amoral. Kruger transferred the disaffected soldier to his little outfit and, soon, Boüldt had risen to second in command. The mercenaries got along well. Boüldt loved the killing and, working for Kruger, there was always plenty of that.

Ortega pointed his cigar at Boüldt. "You have no idea how tenuous our position is."

"Actually I've got a fairly good idea. As long as there are Contras, the people have a focus for their troubles. If Chamorro gets rid of the Contras, where will the people look next, *Señor Presidente*? Right at you and your corrupt Sandinista party, that's where."

"Watch what you say, Boüldt," Sanchez warned. "The Sandinista party is the soul of Nicaragua. The people have been misled by capitalist propaganda. That is all. In time they will see the way once again. We must stay in power until that day arrives."

"Believe what you will, Major. Personally, I don't give a fuck. We get paid to do a job. We do it. End of story."

Boüldt smiled again. If only you knew who we're really working for, you fucking spics, he thought. His maddening smile widened even farther.

Ortega glared at the mercenary a moment longer, then continued his pacing.

19

Xavier banked the helicopter to port as he approached the Coco River. His maneuver brought him parallel to the natural border between Nicaragua and Honduras. Below him, the lush green canopy of the jungle spread out in an impenetrable weave of branches and vines.

Xavier turned to his co-pilot, Alberto Diaz, and nodded. "Let's see if Huberto's toy is working."

Diaz leaned over and flipped a switch on the console. A loud tone filled his headset and his hands instantly became sweaty. They were being tracked by a missile radar from across the river.

"It's working, Javi," Diaz stated unhappily.

"Yeah, I know," Xavier added.

Huberto had installed the gadget as soon as it had arrived from Rizzi at their base of operations in Puerto Cabezas. The sophisticated package had been stolen from an American air base.

Rizzi waited to send it until the last minute. They were operating out of a Sandinista installation and Rizzi feared discovery. The Vietnam-era helicopter had been subjected to several searches by the Sandinistas during the last few weeks.

Xavier followed the river toward their destination. The village of Bilwaskarma sat in a small bend of the Coco. It was near deserted due to the constant fighting between the Sandinistas and the Contras. Their publicized mission was to render medical assistance to villagers caught in the crossfire. Their actual mission concerned itself with the hidden cache of arms and explosives they carried under the seats in the cargo bay.

"*Madre de Dios!*" Diaz exclaimed. "I wish they would quit tracking us. I feel like pissing in my pants."

"You get used to it after a while," Xavier responded, remembering his experience over Grenada.

"How could you get used to anybody shooting at you?" Diaz asked.

"As long as you're flying, who cares?" Xavier asked, smiling.

"No one could love flying that much," Diaz answered, glancing nervously at the Honduran jungle across the river. "They'd have to be fucking *loco*."

"How right you are, *mi amigo*. I'd have to be crazy to love flying this much."

Xavier laughed out loud. Nothing mattered when he was flying. The mission had put him back in the pilot's seat again. His hatred for Kruger and heartache for Min faded with the smell of jet fuel and the exhilaration of lift-off. The beating blades and engine roar were music to his ears. If it came to a matter of choice, Xavier would rather fight and die in the clouds than on the ground.

Diaz was another story.

The rough-and-tumble soldier was a competent helicopter pilot, but he excelled in jungle fighting. He would rather take on a company of infantry in the sweltering, bug-infested undergrowth than one man with a Stinger anti-aircraft missile from the air. Xavier never understood ground pounders.

Xavier felt someone tapping on his shoulder. "Bilwaskarma up ahead," Huberto shouted into his headset. An engineering wizard, Huberto Royo had been recruited as the mission's crew chief and occasional navigator. Xavier followed his pointing finger to a small clearing below and to their left.

"Thanks, buddy. How are the doctor and her staff doing?" he asked.

"They're fine—quiet for the most part. I think our guests are making them nervous," he said, referring to the three soldiers who had joined them for this specific trip. "Diaz' men are all right, but they can seem pretty rough. Don't worry, I'll keep an eye on the ladies."

"I bet you will," Xavier said. "Especially Nurse Alonso."

"She is a very good nurse."

"Have everybody settle in for the landing, Huberto." He looked at Diaz. "What do you think?"

"No one in sight. No cooking fires. No animals. I don't like it, Javi."

"Me neither. I'm going to circle for a closer look before we land."

Xavier banked the helicopter into a sharp descent and flew around the perimeter of the village. The thatched huts were falling down and refuse was scattered among them. The thunder of the engine didn't flush any livestock. Bilwaskarma was a ghost town.

He brought the Huey to rest just outside the village and cut the engine. The turbine slowed to a stop. The only sounds were the wind rustling the leaves and the faint sound of the river flowing on the far side of the village.

Xavier turned to Diaz and was about to speak when he heard a loud shrieking sound coming from the jungle. The hairs stood on the back of his neck.

He looked into the cargo compartment into Elena's eyes. The confident gaze had been replaced by a look of fear. Griselda Alonso, seated next to Elena, crossed herself and muttered, *"La Segua."*

No one moved.

"All right everybody. Let's snap to it," Diaz shouted, breaking the spell. "Elena, you and your people check out the village for any signs of the inhabitants. Dario, take your men and do a sweep of the area. I want to know what's out there—if anything."

"Sí, jefe," Dario responded. "Can we take heavy weapons?"

"Sorry, poet. Just your side arms. If we stumble into a Sandinista patrol, I don't want to have to explain why a Red Cross medical mission is armed to the teeth."

"Entiendo, jefe," he replied, not sounding pleased. But he issued orders to his two men and they exited the chopper. The patrol, dressed in camouflage fatigues, formed up and disappeared

into the jungle. The men had been handpicked by Diaz. If a hostile force was out there, the patrol would find them.

"Poet?" Xavier asked, eyeing Diaz.

"He writes verse, Javi. Runs in his family."

Xavier shook his head. Odd group. Poets, engineers, doctors, and a lunatic pilot, he mused. Not quite what you'd expect to send on a dangerous mission.

Huberto helped Elena and her two nurses gather their supplies while Xavier and Diaz finished shutting down the helicopter.

"Huberto. I want you to stay here with the chopper in case something comes up and we need to leave in a hurry."

"But, *jefe,* who will look after the women?" Huberto whined.

"Oh, don't worry, Huberto," Diaz smiled. "I'll take good care of them for you."

"But, what if you get into trouble?"

"We'll handle it. We need you here. Monitor the radio, Huberto. Although, I don't think you'll need a call from us to tell you to warm up the chopper. If anything happens, I think we'll all know it."

"But..." he started before Diaz cut him off with a hard look. Huberto frowned and slumped back on the bench. While he didn't relish the thought of staying alone with the helicopter, he accepted his fate. Huberto, despite his sense of humor and carefree ways, was a practical man who could do what had to be done.

Xavier and Diaz followed Elena and the two nurses into the seemingly deserted village. It looked far worse up close than it did from the air. The smell of rotting garbage filled the air and the carcasses of several goats and pigs lay scattered about.

"Some cease-fire, eh, Javi?" Diaz said, surveying the scene. "Those animals were shot within the last week. Obviously, someone hasn't heard about the Sapoa agreement," he remarked, referring to the peace treaty signed the previous March by the Contras and Sandinistas.

"Obviously not," Xavier agreed. "Could be Sandinistas exacting revenge for the assassination of Major Hidalgo in Chontales."

"Hidalgo? He was a bastard all right," Diaz commented. "Killed a lotta people in the battle for Bocay. But this could just as easily be Contra work in retaliation for the June crackdown." Beginning with the brutal repression of an opposition rally in the city of Nadaime, the Sandinista government had arrested opposition leaders, shut down the Catholic radio station, and expelled Richard Melton, the United States ambassador to Nicaragua. *"Quien entiende?* Who knows? It is still *hermano contra hermano."*

"Brother against brother. Makes me sick," Xavier smirked.

"It should, considering your government is behind this," Diaz commented.

Xavier stopped and grabbed Diaz' arm. His face darkened. "Not my government, Alberto."

"If not your government then who, Javi? Who signs the checks and buys the arms? Just because your Congress enacted the Boland amendments after the Sandinistas shot down Hasenfus, doesn't mean your country is not behind this. I've been in your country. They trained me for war. I know exactly what they are capable of," Diaz said, pointing to the destruction. "Take a look around you. Even if it was the Sandinistas, do you think they would be here if they weren't afraid of an invasion?"

Xavier hesitated before answering. "I'm sorry, Alberto. I guess it's the marine in me coming out."

"Remember what your government did to you, my marine friend. Doctor!" Diaz shouted, spotting Elena entering one of the shacks. "Don't touch anything. This place could be booby trapped."

Elena froze in the doorway and turned to her two nurses. *"Tiene cuidado,"* she ordered. They disappeared inside the building.

When the search was complete, they regrouped in the center of the village. Not one inhabitant had been discovered. An eerie silence hung over the town.

"We camp here for the night," Diaz ordered. He pulled a radio from his harness. "Huberto," he said keying the mic. "We're on our way back."

"Sí, jefe. Find anyone?" he asked.

"Not a soul," Diaz replied.

The party made its way back to the helicopter.

"How long will your men take?"

"They won't be back until they're sure we are safe," Diaz replied. He offered nothing else.

Huberto was already preparing the clearing for a campsite. Griselda and her fellow nurse, Rosa Riguero, pitched in to help. Diaz pulled out his canteen and passed it to Xavier who drank and passed it to Elena. As she drank, Xavier looked at her and smiled.

During their weeks of preparation, he had grown quite attached to her. They had become friends. He enjoyed her intellect and her fiery loyalty to Chamorro and Nicaragua. When it came to admiring her beauty, he cut himself short. He could not allow himself to feel attracted to her. He thought of Min and the smile vanished from his face.

Elena handed the canteen back to Diaz. She had seen Xavier smile and seen the smile abruptly disappear from his face. It was not the first time. Xavier would only share himself with her to a point.

It is just as well, she thought. I can't allow my emotions to harm the mission. She sighed and went to help the others with the campsite.

Elena acknowledged her feelings more readily than Xavier could. She knew that she was definitely attracted to him. How deep the attraction went and whether it could be explored depended on the success of their mission and Xavier's feelings.

She hacked at a clump of undergrowth with a machete. Pausing to wipe the sweat from her face with a bandanna, she regarded her companions. They had become a tight unit during the last few weeks. Roaring around Nicaragua, they had brought basic health care to various remote regions of the country. Even the Sandinista press had covered their mission. Had they known the true nature of their business, the coverage would have been a lot less praiseworthy.

Operating out of the Sandinista air base at Puerto Cabezas, they ferried medical supplies to the northern part of the country. Without full Sandinista approval, the whole project would have been doomed from the start. As it was, they operated under the noses of the Internal Security forces. As Xavier had said, if you want to hide something, hide it in plain sight. So far, they had been successful, or so she hoped.

Elena hated the deception involved in their cover story. Their notoriety spread as the citizens of Nicaragua looked to her and her flying hospital with hope. She dreamed one day of having a fleet of helicopters and a staff of nurses and doctors to treat all who needed it. But her dreams would probably never bear fruit. In twenty-four hours the mission would be over.

Diaz' agents had discovered the possible whereabouts of a CIA-funded Contra camp. It was their mission to infiltrate the operation and bring back proof of a CIA connection. Breaking this news to the world would embarrass the new American president's administration into abandoning the Contras. Or so Chamorro hoped.

As she pocketed her bandanna and lifted the machete, she saw Dario walk into camp carrying a child. Elena dropped her machete and ran to him.

She ran her hand over the boy's forehead and realized he had a fever. "Where did you find him?"

"In the jungle. He's scared to death, but too weak to get away," Dario responded.

"Over here, quickly," Elena ordered. "Griselda—my kit."

Dario laid the child on a poncho and knelt beside him, shielding his face from the sun. The boy groaned in pain. Diaz and Xavier hovered as the medical team ministered to the child.

Griselda started an intravenous drip into the dehydrated patient as Elena examined him for wounds. He was bruised, had several infected cuts on his body, and his right ankle was swollen. Fortunately, she found nothing more serious.

"Rosa. Clean and bandage his cuts."

"*Sí*, Doctor."

"How is he?" asked Xavier.

Elena answered as she prepared an injection of vitamins and antibiotics. "Malnutrition, dehydration. The fever could be from malaria, but I don't think so. Skin color isn't right. Probably from his infected cuts. He's injured his right ankle, but it doesn't look broken, more likely a sprain. He'll be okay."

"*Quien esta?*" Diaz asked.

Elena swabbed his arm with an alcohol sponge. "A victim, Major. Any other stupid questions?" she snapped. The boy winced as she inserted the needle. Diaz cringed. Xavier smiled; he loved the passion with which Elena approached her work.

"Dario?" Diaz looked down at his sergeant.

"We'd just started our sweep when we came across him wandering through the jungle," Dario reported. "He tried to run, but we caught him. He was yelling some gibberish."

"What gibberish?"

"He pleaded with us not to take him away with the rest of the men. He must have thought we were with the bastards that raided his village." Dario looked at Diaz, shaking his head. The soldier's eyes filled with hate. "I swear I'll make these *animales* pay for their sins. I swear to God, *jefe*."

"Hopefully we'll get the chance, Dario," Diaz replied. He gazed at the huge soldier. Dario, the grandson of Latin America's most revered poet, was a fierce warrior. At the same time, his heart had a gentle place, especially for children.

Dario had three children. One died in infancy from disease and another, not much older, had been killed in a Contra mortar attack. In despair, Dario had sought solace at an orphanage, giving the love he had for his dead children to living ones who desperately needed it. The plight of this small boy fired Dario's temper into a murderous rage. Diaz was doubtful that he could keep him under control if they went into combat.

"Did he say anything else that might help us?" Diaz asked, placing a reassuring hand on Dario's shoulder.

"Other than that, I couldn't understand him."

Elena pulled the canteen from her belt and poured water over her bandanna. She gently wiped the cool rag across the boy's face, reviving him. His eyes locked on Elena's and he began to speak earnestly. She bent over to better hear his rasping voice.

"What's he saying?" Xavier asked. Elena looked over her shoulder and kicked Xavier in the shin then bent back to the boy. Dario kept his mouth shut. His face had much the same look as Diaz'. The boy's whispers became louder and more desperate as he told Elena his story.

His back arched and he shouted. *"No mas, por favor, no mas!"* He collapsed on the poncho and passed out. Elena checked his pulse and breathing. Satisfied he was out of danger for the moment, she stood up.

"Griselda, Rosa. Stay with him and let me know of any changes in his condition."

"*Sí*, Doctor," they answered in unison. Elena took Xavier's arm and led him to the other side of the Huey. Diaz followed with Dario.

Once they were where they could not be heard, Elena stopped them.

"Okay, Doc. What's up?" Xavier asked.

"The boy was up the river fishing when the soldiers came. He heard gunfire and ran toward home, but hid in the woods when he saw the men with guns. They separated the male villagers from the rest of the people. Some of the soldiers took women into the huts. He heard screams." She looked at Xavier and saw his teeth clench and his jaw twitch. She hurried on. "The men became angry, but the soldiers clubbed them into silence. He saw his father get beaten. They ransacked the village and then herded the men off into the jungle."

"What happened to the women and children?" Diaz asked.

"They were taken to the far side of the village. He heard them screaming and begging for mercy and then he heard gunfire—a lot of it. Then silence. He says they are dead. Could this be true?"

"I'll send Dario to find out," Diaz answered as Dario nodded his head. "Why is he still here? Why didn't he go for help?"

"He was waiting for his father to come home when we arrived. He thought we were the bad men who took his father."

"*No mas, no mas…*" Xavier muttered.

"Did the men head south or did they cross the river?" Diaz asked.

"He said they headed for the river and disappeared like ghosts."

"Damn. Did he say anything about the weapons?" Dario asked. "Were they carrying M-16s, AK-47s?"

"He's just a boy, Alberto," Elena admonished.

Diaz did not hesitate. "Dario take your men and see if you can find the women and children." Just then the wind changed direction bringing with it the smell of decaying flesh. "I think you'll know where to look."

Dario paused and looked up at Diaz. "*Sí, jefe.* May I help get him settled in a hut?"

"Yes. All right, Dario. Just make it quick."

Dario gently picked up the boy and left with the nurses to find shelter.

"Huberto!" Diaz shouted.

The skinny Miskito bounded through the cargo doors of the helicopter and ran to the group.

"*Sí, jefe.*"

"You and Xavier will take the last watch. I want the chopper prepped and ready. I also want a weapons check-in," he looked at his watch, "in two hours. And when you're done, you'd better get some sleep. You are going to need it. We go tonight," he announced.

"Anything else?" Huberto asked sarcastically.

"*Sí, mi amigo.* Since my men and I will be asleep or on watch, boil enough water to fill our canteens."

Huberto started to speak, but thought better of it. He already had too much to do and obviously the major didn't want him spending time with Griselda. The officer was a hard man. Huberto stomped off to check the Huey.

Diaz and Elena shared a long look. They seemed to arrive at the same conclusion and nodded their heads knowing what must be done. The simple exchange was lost on Xavier. Diaz motioned Dario and the other two soldiers over for a last-minute briefing, leaving Elena alone with Xavier. He smiled at her encouragingly.

"It will be all right. I'll drop them off and pick them up a few hours later. Before you know it, we'll be back in Puerto Cabezas." He grabbed her shoulder reassuringly. "Let's go join the others."

She walked with him back to the encampment. She checked on her patient who seemed to be resting peacefully. She watched Xavier and Huberto work on the helicopter in preparation for the mission. She grabbed a rucksack and began to make her own preparations.

If you only knew what we must now do, I don't think you'd have smiled at me, she thought. *I can only hope you will forgive me.* The Contras had raised the stakes with their brutal massacre and now Elena and her little band were prepared to risk war in retaliation.

Xavier sat in the undergrowth, staring across the river. A half-moon glowed in a cloudless sky. He listened to the sounds of the night and occasionally lifted the starlight scope to scan the opposite bank. The jungle burst into view bathed in an eerie glow of green and white. Somewhere in that jungle the enemy waited for them, but they would not have to wait long. Lift-off was less than an hour away.

He wiped the sweat from his hands and hefted his weapon. The DAEWOO USAS-12, an automatic 12-gauge shotgun, was light, durable, and awesome in a firefight. Not that Xavier planned to get in one. But after Diaz had seen Xavier's dismal performance with several other rifles, he decided to find something with which even a blind man could hit a target. With its 28-round drum on full auto, Diaz was reasonably assured that Xavier could protect himself.

Xavier was chagrined at his poor display on the rifle range. Marines prided themselves on their marksmanship, and Xavier's ability to hit a moving tank with a missile while flying full out was legendary. His inability to hit the side of a barn with an M-16 was notorious.

Xavier often wondered what he could have done differently in his effort to save Min. That night, he hit everything he shot at, but if he had to do it again, he didn't think he could. He hoped he wouldn't have to find out.

Xavier heard someone approach, their feet shuffling through the ground cover. He raised the shotgun in the direction of the noise. His heart began to pound. The moonlight offered visibility to about five feet. Beyond that, blackness. He raised the night vision scope to his face with a shaking left hand. His right forefinger rested on the shotgun trigger.

The wall of the jungle appeared before him. The leaves parted as a nightmarish shape pushed through. As his finger tightened on the trigger, the image resolved itself into Elena. He lowered the scope and laid the shotgun in his lap. Elena sat down next to him.

"I hope I did not startle you," she said quietly. "Stumbling about in the dark is tricky."

"No," he hissed. "But be more careful. One of the other men might have shot you."

"I'll be more aware," she said, taken aback.

Xavier realized she sensed anger in his voice. "I didn't mean to snap at you," he apologized. "We just have to be careful. That's all. We're so close to finishing the mission, it would be stupid to lose someone."

Elena wrapped her arms around her legs and rested her chin on her knees. It reminded him of the night they talked on the beach. Despite the fatigues and combat boots that had replaced her skirt and blouse, she was still beautiful.

"I know you sacrificed a lot to be with us, Javi. I want to thank you."

"What sacrifice? For the first time in weeks, I don't smell like fish." She laughed at his remark, but Xavier could tell there was something on her mind.

"I know you enjoy your life in Tuapi. Even if you make fun of it." She pulled the fatigue cap from her head and played with it nervously.

"It is peaceful," Xavier agreed. "I have regained some of my sanity."

"You left something very important to you in Tuapi."

"I think Maria will be fine. It has been a blessing to be with her after all these years."

"It was not only of Maria that I was speaking. I took you away from your..." she paused searching for the correct word. Elena gripped the cap tightly in both hands. Xavier sensed her distress.

"My vendetta?" he asked.

"I know how important it is to you to find the men who killed your wife," she answered quickly, feeling his irritation.

"There is no way on this earth that you could know how important it is to me."

"How can you say that?" she asked. "I can't count the number of friends and loved ones I have lost in this war. I know the pain of loss better than most."

"You say you have lost loved ones. I know that's true. But there are two things you have loved with passion: medicine and Nicaragua. Your heart has never had room for romantic love. The love I had for Min was so passionate it made my heart ache. And now it's gone. Forever. When you have loved someone with all your heart and lost him, you can tell me you know how important it is that I find Min's killers."

They sat in silence and listened to the river rushing by. Elena realized that some of what he said was true. She was unfamiliar with lasting, passionate love. She'd had a few flings in the past, but nothing serious. Romance got in the way of her education and her fight to free her country, and those things meant too much to her. She thought of how it would feel to lose her country, or her ability to heal. She couldn't imagine living and not fighting for her people.

Occasionally, she was lonely for a companion who could share her passions. Someone to confide in and work alongside. She did have longings for romance as well, but these feelings frightened her and she buried them.

Xavier made her question her feelings for the first time in years. She was starting to think she could share herself with him, but touching Xavier was another matter. His vendetta consumed him and she doubted he could allow himself to feel the love of another woman. Still, she wanted to reach him, to strive for a deeper friendship.

"I was born a peasant in Tuapi, Javi. I can't begin to describe to you the poverty that surrounded me when I was a child. You were born to wealth and privilege. Another planet in another galaxy. That distance separates us. I don't begrudge you your circumstances, but I want you to understand where I came from.

"When my mother died, I became determined to give myself and those around me a better life. Since I made that decision, all I have done is fight battle after battle. You see, Javi, peasant girls are supposed to know their place. Those who try to rise above their station become outcasts. Not only did I have to fight my economic situation, but the prejudices of my friends and family. Violeta Chamorro and your father saved me.

"The education your father gave me allows me to heal the people I love. Pedro and Violeta Chamorro showed me how I could fight for my country. I have never looked back, and I couldn't have lived my life any differently. But I know there is something more to life than causes and missions. As strongly as I fight for my country, I don't live entirely for the fight. If I did, my hatred and anger would grow too strong. They would control me. I hope they don't control you."

"I have survived hate before," Xavier responded. "I have hated one thing or another my whole life, Elena. My father—the wonderful man you talk about—used to beat the shit out of me. Mainly because I wanted to be a Jew. He tried to keep that part of my heritage from me. Every time I went to Hebrew school or synagogue and my father found out, he beat me. I was a child, and he made me bleed.

"At some point, I decided to kill my father. I started studying martial arts with a man named Ky Dae Kim in order to learn how. But I never killed my father. Never even fought him, even though I could have made him pay for all the pain he'd caused me.

"You see, Kim not only taught me to defend myself, he taught me to endure pain and use it to make myself stronger. When I was a teenager, my father finally stopped. I had won. I had endured everything and still wouldn't bend to his will. And, unlike my father, I hadn't used violence to survive. He died a few years later, bankrupt financially and spiritually.

"But all the pain in my past hasn't prepared me for this. Kim's teachings in pain endurance, my relationship with my father, my battles in the Marine Corps. Nothing prepared me to endure this kind of pain. The loss I feel constantly is driving me to the only solution that makes sense to me. Death to the people that caused it. Then I will be free again."

Elena listened in silence. There was nothing else she could say. She had tried to break through Xavier's shell. Time would tell if she had been successful.

"I came on this mission for Maria, for that incredible woman, Violeta de Chamorro, and for you. I am glad I did. Diaz, Huberto, and the others have become good friends. I appreciate what you are doing, but it isn't my fight. After tomorrow, we go our separate ways. Tuapi returned me to physical health, Maria restored my emotional balance, and this mission has given me back my faith in myself. I am ready to continue on my quest, and I wish you luck on yours. I hope you will wish me luck on mine."

Xavier flipped up his watch cover. Time to go. He snapped the cover shut and stood. He took one last look across the river with the night scope.

He held out his hand to her and she grabbed it, letting him pull her up. They found themselves standing face to face. Her hair glistened in the moonlight. Xavier reached out to touch her face and hesitated. He dropped his hand and hefted the shotgun.

"We'd better go. The others will be waiting for us."

He disappeared into the jungle and she followed him.

"Glad you could join us, Javi," Huberto said wryly. "We almost left without you."

"Oh? And who was going to fly this bird?" Xavier asked, setting his shotgun in the cockpit.

"I was, Javi," Diaz answered, climbing out of the cockpit. "You're not the only pilot on this mission, if you haven't forgotten."

"Oh yeah, Diaz. I forgot our local helicopter genius. Since you know so much, why don't you tell me what you're standing on."

Diaz looked down at the landing skid he was perched on and thought for a long time. He looked at Xavier and answered, "My feet?"

"Smart ass," Xavier muttered as the others laughed. "It's not enough that I have to contend with Huberto, the comedian. Now you've got to start, too."

"Relax, Javi," Diaz said, smiling. "In a few hours this will all be a memory."

"We can only hope, *mi amigo*." Xavier sighed.

"We're loaded, *commandante*," Dario said. Xavier didn't recognize him. His face and arms were covered in camouflage paint.

"Very good, Dario. Have the men get on board. We'll join you shortly."

"May I say good bye to the boy, *jefe*?" he replied.

"That's fine, Dario. On the double."

"*Sí, jefe*," Dario saluted and bounded off to the hut.

Diaz turned to Xavier and flopped open a plastic-encased map. Xavier illuminated it with his flashlight. It was a detailed map of the border region in which they had camped. Diaz began to explain the mission brief even though Xavier had heard it that afternoon.

"We will have to fly along the river until we get out of Stinger range. Then we'll risk a border crossing," Diaz said as he applied his camouflage paint. "Wearing night vision gear, I'll navigate to our dropoff point. Fly as low as you can."

"No problem," Xavier answered, rubbing his chin.

"No problem until you drop us off. You'll have to find your own way back. I suggest you clip the map to your thigh. It's the only way to read it without taking your hands off the controls."

"I know the drill, Diaz. But, you forget that I'll have Huberto with me."

"Not on the way back. He'll man the M-60 until the LZ. After that he goes with me."

"That's not the plan," Xavier said, eyebrows narrowing.

"Plans change, Javi," Diaz said without looking up from the map. "I need the extra firepower."

"Bullshit. For an infil-exfil operation, you don't need more firepower. You need less noise. Huberto doesn't know the jungle. He's a liability to you."

"You afraid to fly back alone?" Diaz asked, staring into Xavier's eyes.

"Fuck you," he said, standing. "It's your funeral."

"Huberto," Xavier yelled. "Is the pre-flight check finished?"

"*Sí*, Javi," Huberto answered, jumping out of the helicopter.

"Good. Then get your ass back up there on the door gun."

Huberto didn't move. "What is it, Huberto?" Xavier snapped.

"*Con permiso*, Javi. May I say goodbye to Griselda?"

Xavier started to explode, but the sad look on Huberto's face deflated him. "All right. Just hurry up, goddamnit."

Xavier had grown close to Huberto, and the thought of losing his friend made him angry. He watched Huberto approach the women and throw his arms around Griselda. He looked for Elena in the group, but didn't see her. She was probably off setting up the first-aid station in case they needed it when they returned.

It's for the best, Xavier thought. I hate saying goodbye anyway.

Huberto gave one final hug and ran to the helicopter as Griselda started to cry.

"You done, Huberto?"

"Yes. *Gracias*. We may go now."

"Thanks for your permission, *Señor*," Xavier said with mock grandiosity.

"*No problema*," Huberto said, smiling. But his smile was not sincere.

Xavier walked around the helicopter for his last check. He looked in the cargo bay and was stunned to see Elena. She was dressed like the others down to the camouflage paint and carried an AR-15 Colt Commando assault rifle. The men shifted uneasily while Elena stared at him defiantly.

"Diaz. Get your ass out here!" Xavier's anger was back in full force.

Diaz unbuckled his harness and climbed down from the cockpit.

"What the hell is going on?" Xavier hissed.

"Elena is going along as our medic in case someone is wounded."

"No one's supposed to get wounded, and if they do, we have help here. You said so yourself in Puerto Cabezas, you son of a bitch," he said, shoving Diaz against the fuselage. "'Just drop us off, Javi,'" Xavier sneered sarcastically, "'we'll slip in, take a few pictures, steal some documents and slip right back out.' You lied to me, you bastard!"

"What makes you think so?" Diaz asked innocently.

"Why the explosives, the Claymores, the Frags? Everybody's suddenly carrying extra ammo for Dario's M-60. Pretty big machine gun for a quickie mission, huh, Diaz?"

Diaz shrugged his shoulders in response.

"And now you're taking Huberto and Elena. What are you taking a doctor for, Diaz? Planning on getting into a firefight? Tell me I'm stupid."

"They volunteered long before you came into the picture. And, no, you're not stupid. But you are goddamn naive, *maricón*."

268

"*Maricón*, you motherfucker. You're not going on a discovery mission. You're going on a mission of annihilation. You're going to nail that Contra camp, aren't you?"

"Our mission is none of your goddamn business. Not that you'd care."

"I might care if you fanatics would tell me the truth. But you're too busy playing macho-martyr-Nicaraguan-hero to ask for my help honestly. It's called trust, Diaz. Or don't you trust any *gringos*?"

"We trusted your father. Too bad you're not your father's son."

"You motherfucker!" screamed Xavier. He drew back to hit Diaz, but before he could throw the punch, he was flat on his back staring down the barrel of Dario's M-60. When Xavier tried to get up, Dario planted his foot on Xavier's chest and shoved him back to the ground. The look on Dario's face told Xavier the man was ready to kill and wouldn't mind starting here.

"Let him up." It was Elena. She roughly pulled Dario away from Xavier.

"What's going on?" he demanded.

"We don't have time, Javi."

"Time enough, if you want my help."

Elena looked at Diaz. After a minute he sighed and nodded his head. "What the hell. He'll help us or he won't. We go with or without him."

"We are going into that camp to fight," Elena explained, talking quickly. "We didn't lie to you before. The plan to go in, steal a few documents, and take pictures of any American spies we might find was shot to hell when we discovered that pile of bodies outside the village today. We decided together to rescue the people they have conscripted before they, too, end up dead. We should have told you, but it doesn't change your part of the mission."

"Maybe that's what they want you to do. Maybe they want to create an incident as an excuse to invade. Have you thought about that?" Xavier asked.

"Perhaps it is a trap, but we have to risk it. These Contras are exceptionally brutal. They've never killed this indiscriminately before. And they are sponsored by your government, Javi. Your CIA. We must stop it."

"But why do you have to go? Certainly they could have found someone else."

"He's a coward, Elena." Diaz said. "Forget him. He was a mistake from the beginning. *Vamanos!*"

"*Callete*, Alberto!" Elena shouted at Diaz. She turned back to Xavier. "They could have found someone else, Javi. But I want to go. I am here because I want to be here."

"And if you die?" he asked.

"Then she dies, Javi," Diaz said, climbing back into the helicopter. She looked up at Xavier who was watching her intently.

"As he says, I die, Javi. But I'll die trying to help. Trying to save lives. Could you say the same thing?"

Xavier looked at her face and was reminded of Min. For once he didn't shove the thought from his mind. Elena believed in what she was doing. If he was truly her friend, shouldn't he help her?

"All I wanted was the truth. Thank you." He grabbed her shoulders and pulled her close. "Be careful. I'll be back to pick you up."

"I'll count on it," she smiled. Impulsively she hugged his neck. Xavier was so surprised he did not have time to respond. She waved at her nurses and boarded the helicopter.

Xavier stared at Dario, rubbing his chest where the man had planted his foot. "I thought you were a poet."

"That was my great-grandfather, " Dario said, smiling. "He was the most famous poet in Latin America. As for me. I'm just a grunt who writes verse."

Xavier had read the famous Dario. "Well, I'll be damned," Xavier responded, returning Dario's smile. "Time's short, poet. Let's get going."

"*Gracias, primó*," he said before boarding.

Xavier was taken aback by the name. *Primo* meant more than friend; it was a term of endearment. Xavier circled the helicopter and climbed into his seat.

Xavier strapped on his night vision glasses and placed the flight helmet on his head.

"Let's start her up, Diaz."

"*Sí*, Javi." The engine revved up and moments later the rotors began to spin.

"Tell me, if you had known we would be going on this kind of mission, would you have helped us?"

Xavier thought for a moment. He had vacillated on this choice since meeting Elena. "Probably not. But I feel different now. I have come to know all of you, and I'm glad I came. You should have told me of the change of plans, though. I'm a member of this mission and I won't be lied to."

"Then I am glad I did not tell you, Javi."

"Why? Because you got such a great pilot?"

"No, Javi. Because I would have had to kill you."

Xavier couldn't tell whether or not Diaz was lying. In the cargo bay, Huberto listened in on his headset and smiled one of his famous smiles.

Five minutes later, they crossed the Coco River into Honduras. There was no turning back.

The Contra sergeant watched the helicopter take off from his position across the river in Honduras. He turned to the man lying next to him in the bush.

"How long do you want us to wait, *Capitán*?"

"Get the rafts ready now. There's only a couple of nurses over there now. They shouldn't be a problem."

"*Sí, Capitán*. I will tell the others."

Felipe Hurtado, a former major in Somoza's national guard, gathered his men and ordered them to prepare for the river crossing quickly. While serving in the counterintelligence branch of Somoza's army, Hurtado had come to know many sadistic officers and had committed acts of brutality himself in the name of the government. But his *capitán* was the most brutal and cunning officer he had ever served with.

"Ready?"

"*Sí, Capitán*."

"Good, Sergeant Hurtado. Keep your men quiet. If I hear any undue noise, I'll cut open the bastard who makes it and leave him in the river for the snakes. Understood?"

"*Yo entiendo, Capitán*. It will be as you say."

The rafts slid quietly into the water and made their way across the river.

Honduras, January 25, 1989

Xavier flew the helicopter nap-of-the-earth, tracing the contours of the jungle. His adrenaline was pumping as he concentrated on his task. The Huey responded well to his commands in spite of its age.

"Come right sixty degrees," Diaz ordered.

Xavier yanked the stick hard right and goosed the collective to push them over a ridge. As soon as the skids had cleared the treetops, Xavier pushed the helicopter down into the valley. The wild ride was necessary if they were to get to their insertion point undetected.

Xavier could imagine the tension in the cargo bay. Diaz had forbidden the use of night vision gear to conserve the batteries. The passengers were making this roller coaster flight in complete darkness. If Xavier made the tiniest error, the combat team would never suspect it until it was all over.

"At the end of this valley and over that ridge, turn due north. Our LZ will be two clicks from there."

Xavier prepared for his next course adjustment, praying they did not fly over a stray Honduran army patrol.

Griselda mopped the boy's head with a damp cloth. His fever had dropped considerably since the first injection had been administered. The boy still groaned in his sleep and thrashed about from fever-induced nightmares. She checked her watch. It was almost time to wake Rosa for her shift.

The shack that held the aid station was the best of a bad lot. The Contra raids had left the village in decrepit condition. Though the door had been torn off its hinges, the roof was relatively intact. This was the only edifice Elena figured might keep the rain out. Griselda was not too sure about that. As if in answer to her fears, thunder cracked in the distance.

Griselda shivered involuntarily. She did not like being left behind. The deserted village was spooky. She could not wait to wake Rosa so she could have some company.

Griselda had not been able to shake the feeling that some-one had been watching her all night. She had kept her fear to herself so as not to alarm Rosa. The feeling had intensified since Rosa had fallen asleep, so she busied herself with her patient to keep from succumbing to panic.

She slipped a thermometer into the boy's armpit. After the appropriate amount of time, she checked the temperature. It was near normal and the boy was resting more peacefully. She smiled gratefully and began to swab the thermometer.

Griselda froze. She listened for noise and heard nothing. The hair stood on the back of her neck and her arms. No noise. No insects. No birds. Even the wind had died. She spun toward the door and saw a figure standing in the gloom. Lightning flashed, illuminating the man in the doorway. The scar on his face glowed white. The following clap of thunder so unnerved the nurse she promptly wet her pants.

Pedro Urcuyo sat huddled in his cage, pulling his shirt closely around his body at the sound of the thunder. Lightning flashed far off in the mountains. The storm would be coming soon.

Pedro thought of his son, Jose. He hoped the boy had escaped the Contras. At least he had not been brought to this camp. If it were not for the clouds, Pedro knew that, within the hour, the sky would be tinted orange and purple as the sun began its ascent. Tonight, the sky would remain pitch black. The storm would see to that.

Pedro cocked his ears to the wind straining to hear—what? A thunderclap stirred one of the other men in the cage.

"What is that?" he asked.

"Nothing, *viejo*. Just a storm. Go back to sleep."

The fellow prisoner settled back into his slumber as Pedro thought about the sound in the night. For a minute he thought he heard the beating of helicopter blades.

"This damn storm should cover our approach. Pretty lucky, eh, Diaz?"

"Not really. A lightning flash could illuminate us from the ground and the sound on these winds sometimes carries for miles."

"Thanks for the encouragement, pal," Xavier despaired. "Now where's the goddamn LZ?"

"There!" Diaz shouted, pointing at the ground.

"Where?" Xavier asked frantically, looking around.

"We're flying over it right now, dammit!"

A flash of lightning lit up the small open space in the jungle canopy. Xavier overshot the LZ and reeled the helicopter back around for a quick landing. As soon as the skids touched the ground, the combat team dived out of the helicopter. Xavier turned to wish Diaz luck, but the door had already slammed shut. His flight helmet lay rocking in the empty seat. Xavier searched the clearing for his friends and caught a glimpse of one body slipping into the jungle. He could not make out who it was. In the blink of an eye, they had vanished.

Xavier poured on the throttle and the helicopter leaped into the sky. He had been on the ground less than ten seconds.

Xavier landed the helicopter just as the clouds erupted. He was drenched to the bone in the short time it took him to reach the aid station. He ran through the doorway and slid to a stop in the shack. Griselda and Rosa were sitting on the ground beside the boy. They looked at him but did not speak.

"You guys staying dry?" he asked as he stripped off his soaking fatigue shirt.

They did not answer. Xavier paused to look at them. There was fear in their faces. He understood too late.

Xavier began a spin move aimed at the presence behind him. Before he could complete it, he felt a gun jammed in his ear. Xavier's head rocked back and he almost lost his balance. Someone shoved him to his knees while other hands forced his arms behind his back and bound them tightly. His wrists were yanked up forcing his head to the dirt floor.

Xavier heard other people crowding into the room. Griselda began to speak and received a slap across her face for the effort.

For a time, the only sound he heard was the whimpering of the injured nurse.

Some of the men moved out of the way as another person entered the hut. Xavier could sense a change in the atmosphere with the arrival of the newcomer. The whimpering stopped and an uneasy tension filled the air. Without warning, he was dragged roughly to his feet.

"We meet at last, Mr. Daniels." Xavier stared into black, lifeless eyes and felt fear crawl into his gut.

20

Contra Camp, Honduras, January 26, 1989

Under the cover of the storm, Diaz had moved his men into place. He looked at his watch and checked the sky. His plan was to hit the camp just before sunup, when the Contras would be dulled from sleep. It was his experience that surprise assaults worked best at this time.

The storm was breaking up. Already the downpour had dissipated into a mild sprinkle. As the clouds thinned and moved north, the sky began to lighten. Almost time. Diaz readied his weapon. The attack would begin on his signal.

The darkness began to lift, allowing Diaz to see without the aid of his starlight scope. The compound was surrounded by barbed wire. A twenty-meter swath of ground had been cut down around the perimeter. This was the kill zone. Ten-foot-high sandbagged guard towers stood at the corners of the perimeter. Inside the barbed wire stood four buildings.

Two long shacks at the south end held the Contras. A smaller raised building contained the officers' quarters situated close to the shacks along the west wall. An open area for drilling stood between the officers' quarters and the fourth building. The fourth structure was, itself, surrounded by barbed wire and two sandbagged emplacements guarded the lone entrance. This was the prison where the conscripts were kept. At the north end, farthest from the sleeping quarters was a latrine. A corrugated tin roof protected the stalls from the elements.

Dario and Indalecio had cut through the wire, mined two towers, and taken refuge in the latrine. At Diaz' signal, Huberto and Elena would race to the prison under covering fire, eliminate the bunkers, and free the prisoners. It was up to him and Rafael to take out the Contra buildings. If the forty-man contingent was not dealt with quickly, the mission would end in disaster. Diaz had a plan for that task.

Diaz tapped Rafael on the shoulder. *"Ahora,"* he ordered. They raised their rocket launchers simultaneously and zeroed in on pre-selected targets.

"Fuego!" he shouted, and the rockets left the launch tubes and streaked toward the northern guard towers.

Pedro saw the rockets streak out of the jungle. The old man stood up and pointed shouting, *"Mira! Mira!"*

Pedro lunged for the old man and dragged him to the ground just as the rockets exploded.

As far as Vietnam-era castoffs went, the LAW-72 light anti-tank weapon was a good idea on paper. The lightweight, one shot, cardboard launcher was easy to carry and fire. Unfortunately, the 66mm rockets sometimes failed to ignite in the humid jungle and, worse, they were practically useless against armored vehicles. Only foolish soldiers took on tanks with the LAW.

Diaz, however, had discovered that the small rockets were highly effective against bunkers and pillboxes. The LAW could function as a mobile, short-range artillery piece. For this reason, foot soldiers world-wide loved it.

Diaz watched the 66mm rockets strike the towers. The explosions obliterated the sandbagged emplacements, killing their occupants. Seconds later, Dario fired his mines and the two southern structures came crashing to the ground in balls of flame. Diaz heard a long burst from Dario's M-60.

"Vamanos!" he yelled at Rafael, and they ran down the short hill and into the open. The men crossed the kill zone to the barbed wire fence. Rafael dropped to his knees and began to cut

the wire while Diaz covered him. Diaz did not need to tell Rafael to hurry. The young Nicaraguan was a professional and knew what was at stake.

Diaz heard the firing rise on the other end of the compound and hoped his companions weren't being held up. Rafael finished his last cut and the two men scurried through the opening.

Huberto sprinted across the kill zone to the barbed wire fence followed by Elena. Indalecio held the barbed wire open and the doctor and the engineer raced through unimpeded. Dario opened fire with his machine gun spraying the officers' quarters and the enlisted men's building with a hail of bullets. Indalecio fired his AK-47 at the bunkers guarding the prison compound keeping the guards pinned down.

Huberto and Elena skidded into the wall of the nearest bunker. A guard fired his weapon directly over their heads at Dario and Indalecio, unaware of their presence.

Too bad, Huberto thought. Joke's on you.

Huberto pulled a grenade from his belt and yanked out the pin.

"Did you hear the one about the mule and the priest?" he asked Elena.

"I don't believe you," she exclaimed.

"If you can't laugh at work," he said, releasing the arming lever on the grenade, "then you need to find another job."

He smiled and tossed the lethal object over the wall into the bunker and crouched over Elena. Shouts emanated from the bunker as the guards saw the grenade land in their midst. They were attempting to escape when it exploded, hurling a guard's torn body onto Elena and Huberto.

Huberto pushed the bloody corpse off them and looked at Elena. Her eyes were wide with fear and her clothing soaked with the dead man's blood, but otherwise she was unhurt.

"I don't think they liked the punch line."

Huberto's humor calmed her down. They proceeded to the next bunker, taking it out in similar fashion. Once past the bunkers, they raced to the prison building and shot the lock off the main cell. They made it inside just as a burst of gunfire tore up the ground outside.

Elena was lying on top of two men. She rolled off of them and asked if they were all right.

"We're fine, *señora*. Who are you?" the prisoners asked excitedly.

"Friends come to free you," she answered. Huberto fired a sustained burst from his weapon and shouted for her help. She readied her weapon and moved to the door hoping she had told them the truth.

Diaz and Rafael moved cautiously against the back of the barracks. They heard shouts as the Contras, roused from their sleep by the attack, frantically grabbed weapons and ammunition. Diaz wanted to keep them from reinforcing the building Dario was tearing up with his M-60.

Diaz motioned for Rafael to move to the other end of the barracks. When he was ready, Diaz nodded his head and they tossed large blocks of C-4 plastic explosive through open windows. Diaz threw himself to the ground, covered his head, and yelled so the noise wouldn't blow out his eardrums.

The C-4 charges blew and the walls bulged out of the building. Chunks of roof, pieces of equipment, and parts of bodies rained down on them. Diaz waited five seconds for the force of the explosions to dissipate and leaped to his feet. He fired a full magazine from his M-16 into the shattered building. Rafael joined him and they walked their combined fire over the length and breadth of the ruins.

Diaz turned to Rafael. The man was bleeding from a cut on his forehead. Rafael signaled he was fine and they made their way cautiously around the shattered wreck to the other building.

The remaining Contras were panicking. The force of the explosion had paralyzed them and cut off their only means of escape. The soldiers fired wildly from the windows not knowing at what they were shooting. Diaz and Rafael took advantage of the confusion and crept under a window. Diaz grabbed a grenade and pulled the pin. He released the lever, counted to three, and tossed the grenade through the window. It blew immediately.

Two seconds later, Rafael stood on Diaz' back and fired into the building.

Dario, sensing the decrease in fire from the barracks, yelled for Huberto and Elena to cover him. He sprinted across the open compound while Huberto and Elena, joined by Indalecio, poured fire into the officers' quarters. Bullets kicked up dirt around Dario, but he ignored them and kept moving. As he ran, he changed the belt in his gun; an incredible feat in itself, an insane act in the middle of a firefight.

Dario ran up the steps to the remaining barracks and kicked in the door. With a wild battle cry he pulled the trigger and emptied a hundred rounds in long sustained bursts into the Contras. The fight was over in a matter of seconds. Backing out, he tossed in a couple of grenades before shutting the door. Anybody left alive was annihilated in the succeeding explosions.

Diaz motioned his troops to remain in place as he approached the officers' quarters. The building was quiet. He made his way to the steps leading to the front door. His soldiers covered him silently. He crouched beside the steps and rested his back against the wall.

Diaz reached out and pushed open the bullet-scarred door. As the door swung open, fire erupted from inside, splintering the stairs and the railing in front of Diaz. No one returned the fire for fear of hitting Diaz.

Diaz unhooked a grenade and hurled it through the doorway. The blast silenced the gunfire. Diaz rolled onto the steps and cautiously entered the building. Several bodies lay scattered about. The smell of sulfur and blood filled the air.

An officer, bleeding from several wounds, rose from behind an overturned table. He raised his pistol and shouted, *"Viva, Somoza!"* Diaz blasted him in the chest with a burst from his M-16. The man, chest shredded, toppled over in a bloody heap.

The Contra camp was a shattered, burning ruin. Fifty-two officers and enlisted men lay dead. The attack had lasted less than four minutes.

Bilwaskarma, January 26, 1989

Xavier sat on the ground in the middle of the village. The Contras stood or crouched in a circle around him. Their captain stood before Xavier, resting his foot on a radio he had retrieved from the shack.

Xavier concentrated on the number of soldiers and their positions. He held his fear and anger in check as his mind worked on a solution to his dilemma. He tried to ignore his pain, but the screams from the shack distracted him. Xavier fought to keep his concentration.

The captain waited patiently in the morning sun. The village was silent except for the screams of the nurses coming from inside the shack. One exceptionally long shriek caused several of the men to smile. The captain gave the men a hard look and the smiles disappeared.

Xavier memorized every detail on the man. White hair, tan complexion. Scar on the right side of his face. A large man, but extremely well-conditioned. He moved like a professional soldier. Xavier knew the type. And that thick accent. Xavier could not place it, but it definitely sounded German.

The radio crackled to life. "This is the comedian. Mission successful. Request pickup as soon as possible. Relay your ETA." Silence. "This is the comedian. We are ready for pickup. Acknowledge." Silence.

"I wonder how long they will wait before they realize you aren't coming to get them?" the captain asked Xavier. "How long before they realize you turned tail and ran, leaving them at the mercy of the Honduran army and the jungle? It's a good question. Would you like to lay odds on the time, Xavier Daniels, son of Victor Danielson, grandson of Emil Danelsberg?"

"Come in, please." Huberto pleaded on the radio. "We are ready for transport. Transmit wit—." The voice was cut off in a hail of gunfire. Xavier heard frantic yells, explosions, and gunshots. A loud crack followed by a high-pitched feedback was the last sound from the Contra camp. Static filled the air.

"My guess is your comrades will be too busy to worry about what happened to you. That is, until they die. Then they won't be worrying at all, Xavier Daniels, godson of Dr. Jacob Rabinowitz."

Xavier's hold on his emotions finally snapped. "Just who in the fuck are you?" he snarled.

"I'm the angel of death come to settle a long overdue account." He smiled, kicked over the radio, and came at Xavier. "Seventy-one years overdue to be exact."

The cross-hairs centered on Xavier Daniels' left ear. The right index finger, skin filed smooth to allow a more intimate touch with the trigger, rested lightly on the trigger guard. The rifleman knelt behind a fallen tree, three hundred twenty-five yards southwest of Bilwaskarma.

The shooter had been tracking the target for three weeks. Now, at last, conditions were perfect for his assignment. The distance to the target was less than half the effective range of the H&K PSG1. The storm had disappeared leaving a cloudless sky for perfect visibility, and more important, still air. Not the hint of a breeze rustled the leaves of the jungle. The bullet would fly straight and true without the necessity of compensating for windage. The target was a dead man.

The shooter, as well as the gun, were well camouflaged. A person standing next to him would find it difficult to see the prone figure. The special noise and smoke suppressor made it impossible to determine the location of the rifle shot. The shooter was not just well concealed. He was invisible.

The shooter moved his finger from the trigger guard to the trigger. He let out his breath and squeezed gently. At the last second the target jumped out of the scope. The shooter froze.

Xavier's head rocked back from the blow. He fell over on his back and spat blood. Rolling to his side he struggled to sit up, but he had a difficult time. The restraints kept him from using his arms.

Xavier was roughly yanked back to a sitting position by his hair. He sat sweating. No breeze cooled the sweat on his skin. No cloud covered the blazing sun. And no one offered him water to quench his thirst.

The captain pulled out his canteen and took a long drink of water. Xavier tried not to eye the container, but his thirst won out.

"Thirsty, Xavier?" asked the captain. Xavier did not respond. The shrieks from inside the shack had fallen to subdued sobbing. Xavier tried to think.

"I guess not," the captain answered himself. "Oh, well. This is thirsty work. I have a feeling before we are done you will be begging for some water. And then again, you are a strong one, former Captain Daniels, aren't you?"

Xavier had been concentrating on the accent and not the words. "What?" he asked in a daze.

"Oh, come now, Xavier. You marines pride yourselves on your ability to endure the most difficult hardships. Isn't that true?"

"I don't understand," he stated, confused. He was observing the captain's face. The man was perspiring only lightly. The heat did not seem to affect him. Xavier wondered what part of the world such a man might be from. The captain was talking again, and Xavier tried to concentrate.

"Frankly, I don't enjoy torture in the least. But my employer insisted on it." The captain took a combat knife from its sheath and admired the blade in the sunlight. He thumbed the sharp edge once, twice, and looked at Xavier. He seemed upset. "In my opinion, this whole damn thing is a waste of time and effort. Many more important things to be doing than hunting down Jews."

"Mercenary," Xavier croaked through swollen lips.

"What was that?" the captain asked curiously.

Xavier spat blood onto his fatigue top. "Mercenary. Bounty hunter. Paid assassin. Outlaw. You're probably a soldier who couldn't cut it in whatever army you pretended to get your training. Most likely a coward, a sadist, or both. Whatever you are, you're most definitely not a professional."

"Like you marines," he answered, smiling, refusing to rise to the bait. "Met a few of you in my time. Hot heads the lot. And fools. No, where I come from you wouldn't have lasted a week. We are true professionals, Xavier. And I'm definitely not an outlaw. My government encouraged me to take this job...at least a certain faction of my government. I operate on behalf of my present employer with their full approval."

"What employer?" Xavier asked nonchalantly. He blinked sweat from his eyes and waited for the response.

"Cutting to the chase, are we? Too early for that. But we'll get there," he promised.

The captain took another long drink from his canteen, poured the rest on the ground and tossed it to one of the Contras.

"Now, where were we?" he asked. "Oh yes, marines. I saw you in action a while back. Pretty impressed. I think your performance had more to do with your martial arts training than your military skills. Am I right, Xavier? Of course I am. But what I want to know is where you got that training?"

Xavier had a memory flash of a dusty gym and the smell of sweat. The gentle face of his master Ky Dae Kim hovered over him. The memory gave him a warm feeling.

"Don't want to tell me, Xavier? That's all right. I know the answer. I also know why you took the training."

Xavier dropped his head to his chest. Another vision. This memory was not as pleasant. He was a child running for his life. The captain grabbed his hair and yanked his head up painfully.

"You took the training because your father used to beat the shit out of you. Isn't that right, Xavier? He beat the shit out of you because you wanted to be a Jew. Now why the hell would you want to be a Jew? No wonder he beat you. I would have, too. Jews are cowards, cunning and deceitful like your father.

"Of course that's why he beat you. You reminded him that no matter what he did, however much money he made, whatever religion he joined, or what gentile name he adopted, he was still a damn Jew. And the more you tried to be a Jew, the more he hated you and the more he hated himself. So the beatings got worse. And you never fought back. Not even after Kim trained you. You're pathetic," he said and shoved Xavier's head back to his chest.

"Victor changed his name to distance himself from Judaism and you changed your name to distance yourself from your father. But you couldn't escape your true natures. Victor was a coward and you were born a loser for life. Min was a beautiful woman. I wonder what she ever saw in you?"

Xavier slowly raised his head. His eyes cleared. The look of despair and confusion was replaced with one of menace. "Min." He spoke the name softly but the sound hung in the air.

"I told you I saw you perform. That night in the restaurant. You put on a hell of a show."

"Kruger." The name spoken by a fat cop in a blazing inferno. "Kruger." The name repeated over and over in his nightmares.

The captain smiled slyly. "Now you know the game," Kruger said, happily. "I was wondering when you'd figure it out."

Xavier came to his feet in a blaze of speed and launched himself at Kruger. The mercenary kneed the defenseless man in the stomach knocking his breath out. He slammed Xavier back to the ground with a vicious spin kick to the side of his head.

Xavier was not completely unconscious. His head buzzed and the left side of his face felt thick and numb. He fought to stay awake. Min's killer stood just a few feet away. If he was going to kill Kruger he had to act. Soon.

"I'm almost tired of this game. Your companions are dead and it's time you joined them."

Xavier did not hear Kruger. And had he heard him, he wouldn't have cared. The only sensation he felt was the blood roaring through his head and heart. It was a primitive sensation, born of rage and despair. The last time he felt it, five people lay dead in a burned-out building.

21

Contra Camp, Honduras, January 26, 1989

Diaz and his raiders were not dead, but their situation was extremely precarious. Rafael and Huberto were wounded. Ammunition, at the moment, was plentiful and they had a few more of the LAWs, but food and water were scarce. The prison building would not stand up under a sustained barrage; it was not designed for that purpose. The radio had been smashed shortly after the ambush began and Xavier was nowhere to be found. They were trapped with no means of escape.

Diaz observed his soldiers. Indalecio was stringing up claymores around the perimeter as fast as he could. Anybody fool enough to rush the building would die in a hail of shrapnel. Dario was switching the barrel of his machine gun. Ever-prepared, the man always carried spares. Huberto crouched to one side of the door shooting at anything that moved. One of the prisoners had taken Rafael's weapon and crouched opposite Huberto. The man had a bad leg, but appeared eager to help. Diaz was grateful his men had not panicked.

"I've got some bad news, Alberto," Elena said, ducking behind the wall. Bullets hammered the concrete filled cinder blocks making her flinch.

"Don't worry, these walls will keep the bullets out," he said, hoping he sounded convincing. She looked at him doubtfully.

"Rafael won't last much longer unless we can get him out of here and back to the aid station. Even then I don't know if I can save him."

"What's wrong with him?" he asked, shouting to be heard above Dario's M-60 now back in action with a fresh barrel.

"He took a bullet in the stomach. It nicked an artery and tore up his intestines. The main thing is the artery. He's bleeding to death and there's nothing more I can do," Elena replied, exasperated.

"What about Huberto?"

"He took some shrapnel in the back. Not too bad. He also sprained an ankle running over here. Other than that, he's fine and making jokes. Bad ones at that. You know Huberto."

Diaz remembered the mad scramble to the prison building. Huberto was trying to raise Xavier on the radio when all hell broke loose. Rafael and Huberto had gone down and the rest was chaos. Diaz could not understand why the Contras had not finished them while they were in the open. Their mistake. Now they would have to dig them out and Diaz would make the idiots pay in blood for their mistake. Not that Diaz expected to live. He just relished the thought of killing some Contras before he died.

"We got people moving into the compound behind the officers' quarters and the barracks," Dario shouted.

So they're moving in for the kill, Diaz thought. We'll see about that.

"Damn," Elena muttered. Her hands were shaking badly, making it difficult for her to reload her rifle.

"It's all right. Here let me help you." Diaz slid the new clip in for her. She cocked the weapon and smiled gratefully.

"At least there aren't more prisoners to get killed. At least we know that."

Diaz looked around as if seeing the prison for the first time. He counted four prisoners, four old men, not the twenty-five to thirty men who were supposed to be in this building. He left Elena at the back wall and made his way to Dario at the north wall.

Dario was squeezing off carefully aimed bursts at the gutted barracks buildings. Contras moved among the fiery ruins, establishing firing positions. Diaz peered through the barred window and saw the figures moving like ghosts through the smoke. Dario pulled the trigger and two Contras dropped in a spray of blood.

"Good shooting."

"*Gracias, jefe,*" Dario said, squeezing off a few more rounds.

"Does this seem like a set-up to you?" he asked conversationally.

"*Sí, jefe,*" he answered, flinching as bullets smashed into the wall around the window. Dirt and bits of concrete flew through the window. "Most of the prisoners are gone. They only left the ones who couldn't make a long journey on foot. And the ambush was zeroed in…"

"…as if they were waiting for us," Diaz finished his thought for him.

"*Sí,* Major," he said and looked at Diaz with sad eyes. "They allowed their comrades to be slaughtered so that they could trap us. They will show us no mercy."

One of the old men began shouting excitedly to Elena. She crawled to Rafael and hurriedly checked him over. She sagged over the body and crossed herself. Elena looked at Diaz and shook her head. He watched her close the young man's eyes and cover his body with a poncho.

No mercy.

Mark Kinlan watched the attack on the prison compound from his observation post in the jungle. He adjusted his binoculars and the battleground came into view. No movement. An occasional burst of gunfire erupted from one of the windows of the prison building; nothing more.

He gave an order to his radio man in Spanish and watched as an infantry squad took up firing positions in the rubble of the officers' quarters. Satisfied, Kinlan handed his binoculars to one of his three bodyguards. He'd seen enough to know that everything was going like clockwork.

Kinlan tolerated the humid jungle conditions quite well for a man in his fifties. His stoic attitude came from three decades spent in jungles all over the world. It was this experience that brought him to the battle at the Contra camp.

Kinlan was the planner for this operation. He trained the troops and coordinated the logistics with the Honduran government. He was the liaison with the Honduran army and the overall mission commander. Most important, Kinlan was the CIA point man for all black book operations in Honduras and Nicaragua.

Bilwaskarma, Nicaragua, January 26, 1989

Kruger collapsed on the ground holding his groin. Xavier's unexpected attack had come with lightning speed and painful results. The kick had incapacitated him momentarily. He lay on the ground helpless, retching as he waited for the pain to subside. Kruger watched Xavier move toward him through squinted eyes, blurry from the tears of pain.

Xavier felt the Contra come up behind him. He spun quickly onto his back as the rifle butt whistled over his head. Xavier kicked the man's legs out from under him and kicked him viciously in the face. He stood up and crouched warily as the soldiers around him wavered unsure of what to do.

Xavier moved toward Kruger slowly. A few of the soldiers raised their weapons, but none of them fired. Xavier cursed his restraints. He would have loved to have gotten his hands on Kruger. Unfortunately, he wouldn't have time. He would have to finish Kruger off with a well-placed kick.

Xavier knew he would die, but it did not seem to matter. The man who killed Min lay helpless before him. If Kruger died, Min's death would be avenged.

Kruger looked at Xavier and grunted. He tried to stand, but only got as far as his knees before he collapsed. Xavier moved in for the kill.

The guards hesitated, confused. Kruger had ordered them under pain of death to leave the one called Daniels alive. No one wanted to go against the order. They had seen the way the South African dealt with those who failed to obey his commands. No one had the courage to physically subdue the angry prisoner either. They had seen the way he brought down Kruger and their companion. So they hesitated. And watched Xavier kick Kruger onto his back and place his foot on the man's throat.

289

Xavier was smiling as he ground down on Kruger's larynx. He had the skill to finish the job quickly, but much preferred to watch Min's killer suffer. He began to smile as Kruger's face turned purple. Xavier thought the color was beautiful and squeezed harder. Kruger's face was the center of his universe. A scream snapped him out of his trance.

Xavier looked up to see the boy Dario had found in the jungle standing over the corpse of a Contra soldier. The boy held a bloody knife in his hand. One of the soldiers cursed and brought his rifle to his shoulder. The boy stared at the soldier defiantly.

Xavier crossed the short distance to the Contra mercenary and kicked him in the head. He fell to the ground as his finger tightened on the trigger. The burst killed two Contras. One Contra standing next to his fallen comrades turned to Xavier.

"*Es mi hermano, maricón!*" he screamed and pointed his rifle at Xavier.

Alex Corona had watched Xavier's torture from the safety of his hillside sniper's nest. He was running out of options fast. His target was surrounded, the situation tense. He had little hope he could salvage the mission.

Corona was considered the best of his profession in an extremely elite group. His prowess was legendary. But there was only so much one man could do. Although Alex considered himself an exceptional man, even he had his limits, legend or not.

Corona almost wished he had taken the advice of his employer and brought along a full team. But even now, he preferred the odds of being the lone shooter. Corona trusted very few people. A couple of sergeants from his days in the Corps, his mother, that was about it. Other than that, Corona was distrustful of others and completely self-reliant. A loner. The best snipers always were.

He watched the boy approach the group of soldiers unnoticed. The boy raised a bayonet and plunged it into the back of a Contra It was now or never. He whispered, "Mother Mary," and squeezed the trigger.

The Contra's head exploded with a dull thwack spraying Xavier and the boy with blood and bits of flesh. Another Contra flew back through the air as a bloody hole was punched in his chest. Xavier threw himself to the ground and watched two more mercenaries die. This time Xavier thought he heard rifle shots, but only after the bullets had found their targets. The Contras were scrambling for cover, firing in all directions.

Xavier spotted Kruger being dragged to safety by two of his men. He got up to go after him, but was pulled back to the ground. Xavier spun around to defend himself and came face to face with the boy from the jungle. The child turned Xavier onto his stomach and cut his bindings.

Xavier reached for a rifle but could not grab it. The ropes had cut off his circulation, leaving his arms temporarily useless. He threw a heavy arm around the boy and propelled him to the safety of the hut. As they reached the door, he remembered the screams coming from the hut. He tried to turn the boy away, but a burst of gunfire slammed into the wall next to his head and forced him into the dubious sanctuary.

His eyes adjusted to the dimmer light. He blinked a few times and saw three Contras scattered on the floor in bloody heaps. Kneeling in the far corner, Griselda Alonso held an M-16 at the ready. She was gulping air and looking at them through eyes wide with fright. The boy went to her and placed a hand on the rifle, lowering the barrel until it pointed at the ground.

"Where is Rosa?" Xavier asked. Griselda pointed at the wall behind Xavier. He turned and saw the nurse tied spread-eagle on a cot. She was naked, bloody, and quite dead.

Xavier looked back at Griselda, observing her more closely. Her clothes were in shreds, lips swollen and bloody. Pieces of rope hung from her wrists.

Xavier took the bloody knife from the boy and cut the ropes from Rosa's lifeless body. He bent over to close her eyes and a burst of fire tore apart the wall just where he'd been standing.

"Get down!" Xavier yelled. Griselda and the boy did not need the warning as they dove for the floor. Xavier moved to the door and dared a look outside.

Several Contras were scattered about the village. Some were firing in his direction while others fired at the hills overlooking Bilwaskarma. He wished he had his automatic shotgun but realized it was in the helicopter and might as well have been in Dallas for all the good it would do him there. Bullets slammed into the wooden door frame, blowing splinters into his face. Xavier decided he'd seen enough and yanked his head back inside.

"A rifle, *Señor*," Griselda said, shoving an AK-47 into his hands. Her face still showed fear. He looked at her reassuringly and took the weapon. Xavier tried to pull back on the charging handle, but his fingers were still numb.

"*Què pasa?*"

"The ropes," he explained. "They cut off my circulation."

"*Aqui, Señor*. Let me help."

She grabbed his right arm and began rubbing vigorously. He felt the blood rushing back into his arms as painful needles stabbed at his flesh. When he could make a fist, Griselda went to work on the other arm. The work seemed to calm her. Xavier looked over her shoulder at the boy who held her M-16. The rifle was almost as big as him.

"What happened, Griselda?" Xavier asked.

Her hands slowed as she looked at him. She dropped her gaze and returned to massaging his arm.

"After they took you outside, they tied us up. They taunted us telling us how our friends had walked into an ambush and were being killed as we spoke. A while later they began to…began to amuse themselves with us." She paused again before continuing. "I was first. When they were done with me, they started on Rosa. They were so busy with her, they did not notice that the boy had regained consciousness. He took a knife from one of the discarded packs and cut my bindings. Then he snuck out of the door."

Tears sprang into her eyes. "I did not know what to do, *Señor*. I was so afraid. Rosa was fighting them very hard. She bit one of the men and he began to beat her. I did nothing. I watched him beat her to death."

Another memory flashed in Xavier's head. His wife flying through the air as blood poured from her body.

"When I heard the screams and gunfire outside, I finally acted and killed the bastards. But it was too late for Rosa. She was so brave and I was such a coward. Oh, *Señor*. I am so ashamed. She was my friend."

Xavier held her as she sobbed and listened to the sounds of diminishing gunfire outside. When her sobbing subsided, he released her and ventured another look outside. He saw Contra corpses strewn about the compound. Nothing was moving.

"What happened out there?" Griselda asked, wiping tears from her face.

"I honestly don't know, Griselda," he answered. "But I'm going to find out."

Before she could protest, he darted out the door, AK-47 at the ready.

Xavier's eyes glanced about the village. He could sense no movement. He kept to the shadows at the sides of the huts. Examining the corpses, he discovered only one bullet wound in each. A perfect kill shot. Head or chest. Nowhere else. The entry wounds were small, the exit wounds much larger. Spooky.

He eyed the chopper, gauging the distance from the closest hut. He was ready to chance a run for it when he heard a voice behind him. "Ought not to go running about out in the open. Liable to get yourself killed."

Xavier whirled toward the voice and was confronted by a half-man, half-bush. The thing had a rifle pointed directly at his heart. He had been in Xavier's six. Stupid.

"Take it easy," the bush-thing spoke. "I'm a friend."

The thing removed its kill suit revealing a man underneath. The man, face painted black, smiled and said, "Your godfather says hello."

Xavier shook his head and muttered, "Son of a bitch."

Contra Camp, Honduras, January 26, 1989

The heat inside the prison was unbearable. The sun's rays beat down on the tin roof raising the temperature above 120 degrees. There was no breeze to circulate the stifling air. The soldiers and prisoners suffered in silence.

The men had stripped to the waist. Elena had to be content with her undershirt. Sweat ran down her forehead and into her eyes. She blinked it away and tried to sight down the barrel of her rifle.

One of the old men they had come to rescue was dead. His bullet-riddled body lay next to Rafael's. There was nothing with which to cover him. The corpse stared impassively at the ceiling. Elena was too tired to close his eyes.

The battle was lost. They had failed. They knew now there would be no rescue. No one spoke about Xavier. No one said anything.

Dario thought about killing. He wanted his death to be an expensive one for their tormentors. He prayed for targets and caressed his machine gun.

Pedro prayed for the safety of his son and cursed his old body for not being strong enough to help his rescuers.

Huberto dreamed of days that would never be with Griselda.

Diaz, ever the professional, refused to acknowledge defeat. His mind plotted tactics and strategy.

And Elena despaired over Xavier. How could she have been so wrong about the son of Victor Danielson?

Coco River, January 26, 1989

Kruger called his men to a halt. The pain between his legs was excruciating and he needed the rest. He could feel his groin swelling. It felt the size of a cantaloupe. The bastard Xavier had kicked him expertly and now he was paying the price. In anger and frustration, he grabbed his radioman. He could still make the man pay.

"Call Kinlan and have him wipe out the entire force. Forget about capturing them. I want the whole lot dead!" he grunted through teeth clenched in pain.

His radioman didn't move. "What the fuck are you staring at you bloody spic? Don't you understand me?"

"*Sí, jefe,*" he stammered. "But I forgot to bring the radio."

"You bloody idiot!" he yelled, and having nothing better to vent his rage on, he shot his radioman, emptying a full clip from his machine pistol into the man's twitching body.

The others watched impassively. Better him than them.

Bilwaskarma, January 26, 1989

Xavier and Corona turned at the sound of the gunfire. It came from the jungle. They looked back at each other and momentarily locked eyes. Xavier seemed sad and hesitant.

Then man responsible for Min's death was close by and hurt badly. He could find him and avenge her death, or attempt to save his friends. He knew he didn't have time to do both.

What a choice, he thought. But in the end, there was really no choice at all.

Xavier crossed the village, picking up a rifle and ammunition as he went. Corona followed close behind.

"Wait up, Xavier!" Corona shouted. "Wait the fuck up." When Xavier didn't respond, Corona ran after him and spun him around. The look on Xavier's face was one of pure determination. Sensing danger, Corona lowered his voice, but kept hold of Xavier's arm.

"I don't know where the fuck you think you are, but we got no more business here. The bad guys are dead."

"But my friends are still alive."

"Friends?" Corona asked.

"Elena, Diaz, Huberto. I left them in Honduras, and now it's time to go back and get them. I only hope I'm not too late."

"You want to fly a chopper into an enemy country in the daylight? You're fucking crazy!" Corona remarked.

Xavier sighed. "Seems to be the general consensus. I'm okay with that. But a good man accused me of cowardice last night. I'm definitely not okay with that."

"You don't have to prove your manhood to me. I saw what you did here just now, but the rest is not our concern, Xavier. It's not our war," Corona said, trying to sound sympathetic and realistic. "I'm sorry, but your godfather ordered me to bring you back safely if things got out of hand. Judging from what I see," Corona said, looking at the results of the firefight, "I would say things are way beyond out of hand. Now let's go while we still can."

"Go?" Xavier asked, confused.

"Yeah. Go. Like by boat, train, or car. Fast and far before our luck runs out."

Xavier yanked his arm out of Corona's grasp. "The only place I'm going is over to that chopper. And then I'm going to fly that bird into Honduras and get my friends."

"I'm sorry. I can't let you do that," Corona said, raising his rifle.

"What? You gonna kill me? I don't think my godfather would appreciate that."

"I won't kill you, Xavier. But I will put a bullet in you and carry you all the way back to New York if that's the way you want it."

Xavier dropped his rifle and ammunition and grabbed Corona's rifle barrel, holding it to his chest. "You want to shoot me? Do it now or leave me alone whoever the hell you are, because I got no more time to fuck around. Your choice."

The two men stared at one another.

"What's your name?" Xavier asked.

"Corona. Alex Corona. The guy who is supposed to take you back safely when things get out of hand."

"You ever leave any friends to die in the jungle, Corona? You still think about them? Dream about them?" Xavier asked, searching.

Corona's eyes dropped a fraction in acknowledgment.

"Then help me out. Let's not leave my friends in the jungle."

"Don Busambra ordered me to watch out for you."

"Listen, my godfather ordered you to watch out for my safety. You made a covenant with him by choosing to come here. Nobody breaks a covenant with *Il Padrino*. Nobody. You understand exactly what happens if you do that?"

"Yes," Corona swallowed hard.

"Good. Then if you're going to watch over my ass, you go where I go. Correct?"

Corona nodded.

"I'm glad that's settled, because I need your help. I need the pro who did this," Xavier said, waving his arm at the village. "To help me save some very good friends of mine. You in?"

"Sure, I'm in. What's the plan?" Corona, who knew he should be hating this man but found himself respecting him, was amazed at his own response.

Xavier relaxed his grip, the smile returning. "Let me show you what I've got stored on the chopper."

Contra Camp, January 26, 1989

Kinlan was furious. He hadn't heard from Kruger. His men had lost radio contact with the raiding party. He raised his binoculars and surveyed the compound.

The Contra soldiers were in position for the final part of the plan. After forcing the civilian raiding party to exhaust their ammo, they would pump tear gas into the prison and force them into the open. The whole purpose of the mission was to capture the Nicaraguan soldiers and expose them to the world as invaders. The Honduran army with its Contra allies was poised along the border to begin an invasion as soon as the capture was complete and the plot uncovered to a world-wide audience. The United States would be dragged in and Nicaragua would be free of the Sandinista threat forever.

Kinlan had been setting traps like this for months all along the border. This was the first time anyone had taken the bait. This was also the first time Kruger had slaughtered an entire village of innocent women and children.

I'd have come, too, Kinlan thought.

Kinlan had his men try the radio again. All that he waited for was a report from Bilwaskarma detailing the elimination of all possible leaks. He wouldn't proceed until he got the word from Kruger.

Fucking Kruger, he thought. Kinlan spit on the ground. Damn him. His gut told him the South African had his own agenda. He hoped it wouldn't interfere with the mission.

Frustrated, he dropped his binoculars to his chest and glanced at his watch. Kinlan was glad this was his last assignment. The slaughter of innocents for the cloudy ideal of his country's greater good had long since ceased to assuage his guilt. Kinlan loved his country, but hated the men who ran it. He knew from intimate experience that they were the most cold-blooded men on earth.

His personal life, exemplified by two busted marriages and three children who hated him, was the price he had paid to be black ops point man. The longer he worked in Central America, the more he wanted to help those he was supposed to be fighting. Many agents who lived on the edge as he did finally went that way.

Kinlan secretly admired the mavericks, but knew they all ended up one of two ways—dead in a back alley in some forgotten country, murdered by the very government they served, or lobotomized in the anonymous clinic run by the shop, spending their remaining days shuffling along silent corridors in paper slippers.

Kinlan didn't want either one. His only hope was to gut it out until his retirement and disappear. He longed to spend his final days by the seashore nursing his damaged soul. He was a week away from his dream. Only the completion of this damned mission stood in his way.

The gunfire from the battle dissipated until silence hung over the jungle. His men shifted nervously as they prepared for the next phase of the operation. They didn't have to wait long.

Blam! Blam! Blam!

Three explosions to the north. He could see the smoke rising behind the hills. A larger thunderous explosion followed, sending a huge fireball rising into the sky.

Kinlan watched through his binoculars. The staging area. The ammo dump. Damn! Instinct told him Kruger had fucked up and the mission was a hair's breadth from total failure. He grabbed his radioman.

"Order a general attack. Now!" he shouted. "We've got to take the compound. It's our only chance!"

The radioman shouted into the microphone and gunfire erupted all over the compound. Some soldiers began to advance across the open ground when a helicopter roared overhead and dropped a small object over the officers' quarters. All motion ceased as the men watched the object land in the middle of the destroyed building. A second later it exploded, obliterating what was left of the structure and killing the entire squad using it for shelter.

C-4. Plastique. The fuckers were dropping plastic explosive.

"Fuego! Fuego!" Kinlan shouted, as he raced down the hill and into the fray, followed by his three bodyguards. All doubts

about his life were forgotten as he entered the pitched battle. All Kinlan could think of was getting to the prison.

Xavier brought the helicopter around for another pass. He flew with grim purpose. It was the first flying he had done devoid of pleasure. Xavier wanted to get on the ground as fast as possible, and to do this, he had to kill everything in his way.

He flew toward the demolished barracks buildings. The Contras, surprised by his first attack, had recovered and were firing at him as he approached. Xavier depressed the trigger on his stick, and the 20mm Gatling gun, newly mounted on the right side of his aircraft, whirred to life pouring a lethal fire into the rubble.

As they passed overhead, Griselda lobbed a couple of C-4 charges onto the barracks while Corona sprayed the compound with the port side mounted M-60. The pass had taken less than five seconds. The helicopter disappeared leaving carnage in its wake.

Elena had just bandaged the bullet wound in her scalp when the Contras renewed their attack. She was dizzy, but she grabbed her rifle and went into position. She had no choice.

The battle paused as a helicopter flew over the compound and explosions sent everyone ducking for cover. As debris pelted the roof, Elena scrambled back to the window. The Contras redoubled their efforts in bombarding the prison.

They came in waves. As Diaz fired the claymores, shrapnel sliced through the advancing columns of men and equipment. Those who were left continued to advance. Dario switched barrels once again and sprayed rounds waist high, knocking men back like stickpins. Diaz and Huberto fired the LAW rockets straight into the dirt at the attacker's feet. And still they came. It was a bloodbath.

Far from feeling fear, Elena was exhilarated. With death just on the other side of the wall, she found renewed hope, and with it, the strength to continue the fight.

My Xavier has come back, she thought. He has come back for me.

Kinlan was pinned down outside the fence. The last pass had decimated the platoon of soldiers positioned in the wreckage of the barracks. His carefully coordinated assault had come apart under the blistering fire from the gun ship.

Kinlan was prepared for alterations to his assault plan. Few plans stood up once the battle began and men started dying. But this onslaught could have been prevented. Kruger had fucked up and left his command hanging in the breeze.

Kinlan tried the radio one last time and tossed the microphone on the body of the dead radioman. The staging area failed to respond, and none of his men answered. Without leadership, the Contras would continue to attack with suicidal results, or they would disappear into the jungle. The battle was lost. His only hope lay in his personal survival. Kinlan had to get into the compound to insure just that.

"Stop firing," he ordered his bodyguards. "We lay low until the helicopter lands. Then we rush the building. We must capture the Nicaraguans if we are to survive. Otherwise we die here."

Xavier completed two more passes and decided to land. He knew he couldn't eliminate all of the resistance. The longer he waited, the more chance the Contras had to reorganize. Xavier also worried about a reaction force coming from the staging area. It was now or never.

The Huey flared to a landing outside the southern fence. Xavier leaped from the cockpit. He cradled his automatic shotgun and raced to the fence, climbing through the same opening Elena and Huberto had used. Corona's M-60 chattered away as he provided covering fire. Griselda guarded Corona's back to prevent any surprises.

Xavier paused by the latrines and observed the devastated camp. Both the officers' quarters and the barracks were in flames. Ammunition cooked off in the buildings sending explosions skyward and stray rounds whizzing around the compound. Corpses littered the ground. The smell of sulfur, blood, and burning flesh permeated the air. He could see no movement from inside the prison.

Xavier hesitated, unsure what to do, when a body appeared in the prison doorway. The figure staggered toward him through the smoke. He raised his weapon waiting to see who it was when he heard Dario shouting.

"Elena! Elena, get down!"

Xavier's heart froze. Four men jumped up from the fence and raced toward her. The men in the prison couldn't fire for fear of hitting her. It was up to Xavier.

He stood and began to fire at the four men. The shotgun bucked in his arms and sprayed the men blasting them to the ground. Xavier began to move toward Elena as she staggered toward him. Other Contras raced from behind the rubble and charged him. He killed them all. Still more came from the jungle. Xavier fired and reloaded as Dario came screaming from the building firing his machine gun from the hip.

Huberto and Diaz fired the last of the rockets and followed. Three old men emerged from the prison and stayed close to Diaz. Two had rifles and fired where Diaz pointed. The third had his arm under Huberto.

It was in this scene of chaos, death, and destruction that Elena staggered to Xavier. She heard the explosions and smelled the smoke, but saw only him. If she could only get to him, then everything would be all right. He seemed so far away.

Xavier fought his way to Elena. He was enraged at the sight of the blood on her face. He was a few feet away when she began to sway. Xavier ran to her and caught her as she collapsed. He swung her into his arms and pressed his face close to hers.

"You came back," Xavier heard her whisper. He looked at her face and her eyes fluttered open.

"Of course, I did," he answered in a voice choked with emotion. "And I'll never leave you again, Elena. Never."

He kissed her lips tasting the sweat and the blood, then turned and made his way back to the helicopter, Elena hanging limply in his arms.

Kinlan watched the helicopter land and saw the lone figure race toward the fence. When the woman came stumbling from the compound, he ordered his final attack. His small force jumped from the fence and ran for the girl. Before they had made ten paces, they were mowed down.

Kinlan lay bleeding in the dirt. The Nicaraguans fought their way back to the fence. Two old men carried the woman to the helicopter. Another prisoner assisted one of the wounded attackers. Others covered them from the fence.

Kinlan was wounded, but not badly. His bodyguards had taken most of the fire, leaving him with a few pellets in his face and chest. They were bloody wounds, but not fatal. The Contras now coming into the battle were from the staging area. About time.

With a renewed effort, Kinlan staggered to his knees and began to crawl to the fence. All was not lost. With the Nicaraguans' attention occupied by the reinforcements, he just might be able to outflank them before they took off. Small chance, but he was going to try like hell.

"Thought you might need these," Corona said, plopping to the ground alongside Dario.

"*Gracias*," Dario answered, admiring the shiny belts of ammo.

"You're supposed to be with the helicopter, Corona," Xavier snapped, as he fired at the enemy.

"Griselda's got plenty of company, Xavier. Don't sweat it."

"Who's our friend?" asked Diaz.

"No time," Xavier answered. "Take his ass back to the helicopter and get it ready to fly. Dario and I will follow shortly."

"No way, Xavier. I'm still here to protect you. And now that this is finished, I'm going to do my original job. I will stay here with the guy on the '60. You get your ass on the chopper. We'll haul ass when you're gone."

"Bullshit! I want you on that chopper. Your mission is to guard Elena with your life."

They argued as they fought, seconds growing more precious as the attack grew more ferocious.

"*Callete!*" Diaz screamed. "Shut up. Both of you. I'm the ground commander. We do it my way."

Corona glared at Xavier. Xavier glared at Diaz. Dario continued to hammer away at the advancing soldiers.

"You two get back to the Huey," Diaz ordered. "I will stay with Dario until it is time to leave. Now move!"

Xavier left reluctantly, followed by Corona. Diaz moved beside Dario to help feed ammunition to the machine gun.

Dario spoke as he squeezed off three-round bursts from his M-60.

"You know one of us has to stay behind, *amigo*," he said matter-of-factly.

"I know," Diaz answered.

"And you know it is me. I am much better on the M-60 than you are. Wouldn't you agree?"

Diaz thought it was a massive understatement. "*Sí, amigo.*" You are the best I have ever seen."

"And the only thing that can hold them off is this gun."

"It is best suited to that purpose. Yes."

"Then I think it is time for you to return to the helicopter, old friend."

Diaz did not speak. Dario paused and grabbed Diaz' arm.

"Remember me to my family, *amigo*."

"I will, *amigo*. I will."

Diaz left his friend and pushed through the barbed wire. He crouched and ran to the helicopter.

"Diaz!" Dario yelled.

Diaz turned to see Dario crouching, fist raised defiantly in the air. "*Viva Nicaragua! Viva la gente!*"

Diaz raised his clenched fist in reply and turned back toward the helicopter.

Dario fed a new belt into his machine gun and resumed firing. His heart raced. Not from fear, but from pride and anger. The patriot, the blood of Nicaragua's most famous poet coursing through his veins, smiled as he killed his enemies.

Long live Nicaragua. Long live the people.

It was a fitting epitaph.

Xavier watched Diaz run toward the helicopter without Dario. He unbuckled his safety harness and jumped from the helicopter.

"Where the fuck is Dario?" Xavier yelled above the roar of the engine.

"Doing his duty," Diaz yelled back, shielding his face from the prop wash. Before Xavier could move, Diaz grabbed him and said, "Dario knew it and there's nothing we can do for him but live. Now let's go."

"Goddamnit!" Xavier screamed in frustration as he shook himself from Diaz' grasp. "God-fucking-damnit!" Xavier ran to the helicopter with Diaz in tow. A burst of gunfire hit Diaz, knocking him to the ground. Xavier turned in the direction of the shots and saw a bleeding Contra trying to un-jam his rifle. Xavier bent over and retrieved Diaz' weapon. Diaz was bleeding profusely from his right side, his face contorted in pain.

Xavier snarled and brought the rifle to bear on the soldier. As he pulled the trigger, an arm snaked around his neck and grabbed the stock of the rifle yanking it up. A pistol extended in front of him and he heard Corona say, "Mother Mary," as he pulled the trigger.

The soldier was hit in the leg and dropped to the ground. Corona let go of Xavier and ran to the wounded man while Xavier knelt over Diaz. He was breathing and conscious. Xavier lifted him gently and carried him to the helicopter. He heard the chatter of Dario's M-60 fire more sustained bursts. Time was running short.

Xavier left the cargo bay and opened the cockpit door. Corona was carrying the wounded Contra on his back. Before Xavier could complain, the sniper hefted his burden into the cargo bay, adding the body to the bloody tangle Griselda was trying to sort out. Several explosions shook the ground around the helicopter sending fountains of dirt into the air.

"Incoming!" Corona shouted, as he dove into the cargo bay.

"Mortars," Diaz grunted, as he held a bandage to his side. "They've got us bracketed. Fly this thing, Xavier!"

Without further prompting, Xavier leaped into the pilot's seat and raised the helicopter off the ground. Seconds after lift-off, mortar rounds exploded where the Huey had been resting. Xavier gave one quick glance over his shoulder at the camp. Dozens of soldiers were running past Dario's position. Xavier cranked the throttle and pushed the helicopter over a hill and out of sight.

Corona joined Xavier in the cockpit shortly before they crossed the Coco River back into Nicaragua. He had been helping Griselda perform first aid on the wounded. He slapped on Diaz' flight helmet and smiled at Xavier.

"Diaz took a round in the side," he began, anticipating Xavier's first question. "Griselda says he'll be fine. So will Elena and Huberto. They all need a hospital and a doctor, but they will survive if we can find them proper care. Any ideas?"

"The clinic in Tuapi is set up and ready to go," Xavier explained, scanning the missile detector. So far no one was tracking them. With luck, they would make the border. "What about the Contra you kept me from killing? Is he going to be all right?" Xavier asked sarcastically.

"Yeah. He'll be fine. I bandaged his wound personally."

"Well, aren't you a regular Florence Nightingale! May I ask why you didn't let me kill him after he damn near killed Diaz?"

"I had my reasons."

"For saving some Contra mercenary's life? I'd like to hear just one."

"Look at him, Xavier. He might be a lot of things, but he sure ain't no Contra."

Xavier looked over his shoulder. Griselda was washing the blood and grime from the man's face. It was a white face, not a brown one. Beside Griselda, Elena lay, face pale. He looked back at Corona.

"Who the hell is he?" Xavier asked angrily.

"He's the reason ya'll came on this crazy mission in the first place. Your proof of CIA involvement."

"He's a spook?"

"Oh, much more than that, Xavier. Our late-arriving passenger is Mark Kinlan, Central American Operations Chief for the Central Intelligence Agency."

"What?"

"He's the guy who plans and leads all the dirty black book ops in this part of the world. A real son of a bitch."

305

Xavier stared at him with a look of disbelief. "Now just how do you know that?"

"I used to work for him," Corona stated simply.

A moment later, the Huey crossed the Coco River into safety.

22

Tuapi, Nicaragua, February 2, 1989

Xavier forced himself to open his eyes, although his body screamed for more rest. He checked his watch—just after 7:30 in the morning. He wiped the grit from his eyes and tried to stretch out his aches. He'd been asleep less than four hours.

He pulled his body off the narrow cot and stepped to Elena's bedside. Brushing the hair from her forehead, he felt for fever. Her skin was cool. The fever had broken during the night. She stirred slightly at his touch, then was still again. Xavier smiled in relief.

He left her room and walked to the nurses' station for a cup of coffee. The duty nurse greeted him with a smile. Xavier stifled a yawn and stretched his arms while she poured him a cup.

"Her fever broke about five this morning," she commented.

"I know," he said. He sipped at the hot brew and decided to let it cool for a minute. "She's resting more peacefully."

"Yes. And her color's back. I would have woken you, but you have slept so little the past week, I felt guilty disturbing you," she explained.

"It is all right. I needed the sleep." Xavier stuck his finger in the steaming cup and decided it was cool enough to drink. Besides, he needed the caffeine. "Has the doctor been in?"

"Oh yes, *Señor*. I called him as soon as her condition changed. Dr. Palmeiro said she was out of danger, thank God. He will be by to see you later in the morning."

"*Gracias*, Consuela. And the others?"

"*Señor* Diaz complains incessantly. He wants to be well yesterday. But he is still confined to his bed. He is not very pleasant."

"I know, Consuela. I'll speak with him later today." Diaz' injury was more serious than they first thought. After his condition had stabilized, he'd refused to use a bedpan until Xavier intervened. The man's embarrassment had been the main source of amusement in the infirmary the past few days. The more Diaz swore he would get even, the more Xavier laughed.

"And Huberto?"

"He's fine—telling jokes and pinching the nurses. Griselda is beside herself."

"I'll talk to him, too," Xavier added.

"Oh, no, *Señor*," she started then stopped herself as she blushed. "He means no harm."

"I'll bet," Xavier grumbled. He didn't ask her about Kinlan, the CIA man. He was under armed guard in a safe house, being looked after by a specialist from Managua. Corona was handling Kinlan's security arrangements personally. The man's health and safety were of paramount importance.

Xavier took coffee and walked back up the hall.

"*Señor* Daniels," she called after him.

He stopped and looked over his shoulder. "Yes, Consuela?"

"Now that Dr. Figueres is out of danger, you should rest. We are all worried about you."

"*Gracias otra vez*, Consuela," he said, forcing a smile. "I will try and do that."

Xavier knew that he had exhausted his physical and mental resources. His pace since their return had been brutal, but necessary. Of everyone on their mission, Xavier alone was capable of tying up loose ends.

He paused at the entrance to Elena's room and rested his head on the door jamb. He knew he was on the verge of collapse, but he wasn't ready to give in just yet. Putting his best face on for Elena, in case she were awake, he pushed through the door.

"You look like shit," Rizzi rasped, his face showing concern.

"Hello, Jerry," Xavier said. "It's nice to see you, too."

In different circumstances, Rizzi might have been his friend. As it was, Xavier'd learned to tolerate his godfather's assistant despite his repulsion for what Rizzi represented. Seeing him now, Xavier realized his respect for the man had grown as a result of Rizzi's contributions to the mission.

Rizzi genuinely admired Xavier and wanted the best for him. But he saw how the don's love for his godson distracted him and pushed him to make risky decisions. It was bad business, and it made Rizzi uncomfortable.

"How is she?" Rizzi asked.

"Better, thanks," Xavier replied softly, motioning to Rizzi to follow him outside.

They walked to the beach two blocks from the clinic, and strolled in silence along the shore. Rizzi, having learned his lesson from his first trip to Nicaragua, was dressed in thin cotton slacks and shirt. Still, he sweated profusely.

"Are you going to drink your coffee?" Rizzi asked.

Xavier stared at the cup in his hand for a minute. "Forgot all about it," he said, shaking his head. The liquid was cold, but he downed it anyway. "What brings you?"

"Don Busambra sent me to check on you. He wanted to be sure you were still alive and in one piece." He looked at Xavier, eyeing him up and down. "You may still be in one piece, but you look like a walking corpse to me."

"Haven't had much sleep. The Sandinistas were all over us as soon as we landed," Xavier trailed off. He was having a hard time concentrating. "By some miracle, Corona managed to sneak off with Kinlan, the spook. The Sandinistas interrogated me for two days before they let me go on to Managua. I came back here to check on my friends, especially Min—I mean Elena," Xavier smiled weakly shaking his head. "I assisted Chamorro during her negotiations with the U.S. envoy, although I'm not sure what help I was. As the only ambulatory member of the mission, she really wanted me involved in all the media interviews and conferences. I feel like all I've done for the last week is tell the same story over and over. All in all, I think I'm holding up rather well."

"You may be the only healthy survivor of the mission, but you won't be for long if you don't start eating and sleeping again. You're losing weight and I could pack a week's worth of clothes in the bags under your eyes."

"I think Dario would trade places with me if he could," Xavier commented.

"Dario?"

"A friend who wasn't as lucky as I was. He made the last stand so we could get away."

"I see," was Rizzi's only response. They walked in silence for another minute.

"Took a poetry course in college back in my younger days," Rizzi continued. "A man named Dario is this country's most famous poet. Did you know that?"

"It was his great-grandson we left in Honduras, Jerry."

Rizzi thought about combat as they walked. He was a veteran who knew intimately the experience of losing friends in battle. He also knew the feelings were extremely personal. Rizzi would ask no more questions. If Xavier wanted to talk, he would.

"How are Benny and Jacob?" Xavier asked after a moment of silence.

"They are fine, Xavier. They send their love and want to know when you are coming home."

Xavier didn't answer. He stopped walking and watched the fishing boats in the distance. It was easier than thinking.

"I had the bastard, Jerry," he rasped, staring out to sea. "Had the son of a bitch who killed Min right under my boot, but I couldn't finish the job." The exhaustion had fried his emotional control. Tears of frustration streamed from his eyes. "I'll get him someday. God willing, I'll kill him."

"I know. And we'll help you, Xavier. But right now you must forgive yourself and believe you made the right decision. You saved your friends and brought them home. Be proud of that fact."

"I had help. Without Corona, we'd all be dead. Thank you for sending him."

Not knowing how else to answer, Rizzi said, "You're welcome."

Corona was as much of a surprise to Rizzi as he had been to Xavier. Don Busambra had sent him without consulting his *consigliere*. It made Rizzi wonder how much the old man knew. So he kept his peace and shifted the subject.

"What happened to Kinlan?"

"He's being guarded by Chamorro's people around the clock. He seems to be having some kind of breakdown. Says he's fed up with the whole damn mess down here and he wants to change sides. It isn't the first time a spook's changed teams—the unusual part is his willingness to spill his guts on tape."

"That tape rocked the White House to its foundation." Rizzi commented.

"Chamorro's ecstatic."

"I can imagine. The CIA's head of black book operations in Central America confessing on videotape about the executive branch's collusion in the attempted invasion of Nicaragua. The CIA's continued involvement in circumventing the Boland Amendments to provide aid to the Contras. A lot of people in Washington are going down with the ship. What got into this guy?"

"Like a lot of us, Kinlan's had enough meaningless killing to last several lifetimes. He just reached his limit, that's all."

"Could it really be that simple?" asked Rizzi.

"You'd have to talk to the guy, Rizzi. He's quite a man."

"For a spy who planned to kill you and your friends, you seem to respect him."

"He was doing his job, Rizzi. I see that now."

"That sounds idiotic, Xavier. You should hear yourself."

"When you were in 'Nam and you knew the war was lost, and that every death you caused and every soldier killed under your command was senseless, what did you do?" Xavier asked.

"I kept fighting, of course," Rizzi replied, as if the answer was self-explanatory.

"Why?"

"We were there to do a job, Xavier. Even though we knew it was useless, we still had a job to do. It's all that held us together when everything fell apart—the job. It gave us a purpose."

"That's almost word for word what Kinlan said when I asked him the same question," Xavier smiled.

"Different war, Xavier."

"It's still a jungle, Rizzi," Xavier retorted.

Rizzi thought for a moment. "I think I understand." He leaned over and picked up some shells. After examining them, he began to toss them in the ocean.

"When will you go public with the CIA information?" Rizzi asked.

"We won't."

Rizzi quit throwing shells and faced Xavier. "What do you mean?" he asked amazed.

"I'm not happy about it either, Jerry. The president has quashed the whole Contra—CIA involvement for good. He's sending millions of dollars in aid to Nicaragua in exchange for our silence."

"A bribe."

"Exactly. Chamorro tried to explain it to me." If Xavier hadn't been so tired his face would have been full of disgust. Instead, he just looked sad. "The U.S. is out. If the Contras want to continue fighting, they'll do it alone. That was the point of our mission—stopping the aid that made the fight possible. In addition to the aid for Nicaragua, the U.S. will press the Contras and the Sandinistas to come to the peace table. Chamorro hopes the result will be open elections within a year or two. All we have to do is keep it quiet. Make pretend like Bilwaskarma, Kinlan, and the proposed Honduran invasion never happened."

"You think the government can be trusted?"

"We have too much on them for them to screw us now."

"No shit. Sounds good so far. But what about Kinlan and the Sandinistas?"

"*Doña* Violeta seems to feel that, without the threat from the Contras, the people will have no use for the Sandinistas. She could be right. As far as Kinlan goes, the U.S. has offered him a very nice retirement plan."

"I'll bet. In the millions?"

"Five," Xavier came back, shaking his head. "It's amazing how a government espousing frugality can come up with the cash when it needs to save itself."

Rizzi began throwing shells again. "Is Kinlan taking it?"

"I don't know. Once you get righteous, it's hard to go back. If he takes the deal, I have a feeling it won't be the last we hear from him."

"How do *you* feel about it, Xavier?"

"I don't know, Jerry. I honestly don't." Xavier picked up a few shells, but dropped them after a couple of tosses. He was too tired. "We got everything we set out for and more. At the same time, the U. S. government hasn't learned a lesson. They just didn't get exposed that's all. And as long as they don't get caught, they'll continue doing whatever they want until they are held accountable to the people."

Rizzi noticed how Xavier said "we" when referring to the mission, and even to Nicaragua. He wondered if Xavier realized how much he'd changed. "It may never happen, Xavier."

"I know. But it sure was nice to think about," he said, wistfully.

"What about the press you've been getting? Is that going to throw a wrench into the U.S. offer?"

"The Sandinistas don't know about Kinlan, Chamorro, or the negotiations. They might suspect something, but they have no proof. Our story has centered on the raid to rescue some Nicaraguan farmers from a vicious splinter group of Contras. The deaths of the women and children in Bilwaskarma were blamed on rogue mercenaries to keep the peace with Honduras. The Sandinistas are saying the rescue was their plan. No one is saying anything about the CIA, treaty violations with Honduras, or anything that would harm the U.S. position. So far, no sweat. I cooperated with the Sandinistas on the stories, and they turned off the heat."

"You've become a hero to these people, Xavier."

Xavier shrugged his shoulders. "Sandinista propaganda."

"Except that it actually happened, Xavier. You actually saved those people," Rizzi said in admiration.

"My fifteen minutes of fame. They'll forget about me in a week. Then life will return to normal."

I doubt it, Rizzi thought. "What about Kinlan?"

"If the Sandinistas find out about him, it could go either way." Xavier eyed Rizzi. "Let's just hope they don't."

They stood for a while in the cooling ocean breeze. The silence soon became uncomfortable. There was no more small talk to keep them from the subject at hand. Finally Rizzi broke the silence.

"When will you be ready to come home, Xavier?"

Xavier looked at Rizzi and smiled softly. "This is my home, Jerry."

"Your home is with your family. Jacob and Bennedetto."

"I will have family here soon, Jerry."

"Elena?" Rizzi asked although he knew that's exactly what Xavier meant.

"Yes."

"You plan to marry her?"

"If she'll have me."

"Then bring her with you," encouraged Rizzi. "Back to America where we can protect you."

"Elena is Nicaraguan through and through, Jerry. She'll never leave here. And I don't plan on leaving her. So here I stay to make a new life."

"But why here?" Rizzi asked upset.

Xavier paused to think. It was becoming harder. If he didn't rest soon, he would collapse.

"You know what the government did to me and my family. They destroyed my father! They framed me and cashiered me out of the Corps. I get down here and find out Kruger was working with the CIA to destroy Nicaragua. It doesn't take a genius to figure out that the government, or someone high up in it, had my wife killed! Fuck the good ol' U.S. of A! They took my life away once—I won't give them another chance.

"I want to help these people to recover from what has happened to them. I'll do my best to see this country free and prosperous. Not a bad way to spend one's life, eh, Jerry?" Xavier intoned, defying Rizzi to contradict him.

Rizzi didn't respond. He was looking at Xavier swaying on his feet. The last outburst had drained him of what little energy he had left. Without warning, Xavier sat heavily, then laid his head back and passed out.

Rizzi didn't know what to do. In the sun, Xavier would fry. He turned and headed for the hospital to get some help.

By the time he returned with Griselda, a crowd had gathered around Xavier. Rizzi pushed his way through the silent throng, terrified that something had happened to Don Busambra's godson. What he saw left him dumbfounded.

Someone had erected a tarp, placing Xavier's body in the shade, and his body had been placed on a mat and was covered by a light blanket. His head rested in the lap of an old woman who fanned his face.

Some of the villagers were on their knees mumbling quiet prayers. Several jugs of water and plates of fruit and dried fish sat at his feet for when he woke up. And not a word was spoken.

Rizzi took a last look at Xavier and pushed his way back through the crowd. Griselda was waiting for him on the other side.

"He is okay?" she asked, concerned.

"Yes," Rizzi answered.

He felt in his back pocket for a thick envelope and pulled it out. Rizzi hesitated and then placed it in Griselda's hands.

"What is this?"

"It is his father's. Hidden from the IRS and his family, it has been protected for Xavier by his godfather, Don Bennedetto Busambra."

She didn't understand. For that matter, Rizzi didn't understand his own actions. The envelope contained a letter from Don Busambra and a bank book to an account in Switzerland. *Il Padrino* had intended to use it as a bribe to lure Xavier back to New York.

Rizzi now knew that would never work. He hoped that the money would protect Xavier and bring him some peace. Rizzi felt sure the don would understand.

"Give it to him—he'll know how to use it. And tell him if he ever needs us..." Rizzi stopped not knowing what to say.

"Yes?" Griselda questioned the *consigliere*.

"Just tell him good luck. He'll understand."

He took one last look at the crowd and turned toward the village.

Griselda watched him go, not sure of what to make of the *gringo*. She examined the envelope and thought about what Rizzi had told her. She knew this was something important. If it was important to *Señor* Xavier, she would guard it with her life.

For the few hours she possessed the envelope, Griselda was unknowingly the richest woman in Nicaragua. The bank book was the access to an account containing over $225 million dollars.

The crowd kept vigil over Xavier until he woke to begin his new life.

Honduras

Kruger lay on his cot, waiting for the nurse to come with his pain medication. He abhorred the use of chemicals that dulled his senses, but then, he'd never been wounded quite like this. Thinking about his injury soured his mood, and looking around his cramped room didn't help matters.

He was confined to a filthy shack on the outskirts of a Honduran army camp. The building had previously been used to house gardening tools. The smell of humus lingered in the air. The Honduran army command had placed him here to keep him out of sight.

Kruger was kept under armed guard twenty-four hours a day. Access to him had been limited to a couple of nurses and doctors and an army officer or two. He wondered if the outside world had forgotten about him when the door opened and James Halloran, chief of staff to the senator, was admitted by his guards.

"Hello, Kruger. How are you feeling?"

Halloran sounded neither sincere or concerned. He disliked Kruger and couldn't help showing it.

"What the fuck do you care?" Kruger asked sarcastically.

"I really don't give a damn, Kruger. The senator wants to know, not me." The Honduran military wanted Kruger taken out for obvious reasons. Halloran thought it was a great idea, but shelved it. The senator wanted this man alive.

"You tell him I'll be bloody better off when he gets me out of this country."

"We're working on the arrangements. Relax," Halloran said, picking an imaginary piece of lint off his shirt.

"Relax? How the hell am I supposed to relax?"

"Easy, Kruger. Lie there and breathe deeply. We'll clean up your mess."

The assassin glared at Halloran. The man was dressed in safari jacket and pants complete with brimmed hat. Beltway bureaucrats had a costume for every occasion. Kruger thought the man looked ridiculous. Kruger even detected a slight scent of cologne.

"If the senator had let me take him out when I wanted, it would have been over quickly and cleanly. I just followed orders. Against my better instincts," Kruger added.

"You get paid just like the rest of us. Instincts or no. You do as you're told. Don't worry about it. There will be another time, Kruger. The senator always finds a way for his employees to redeem themselves."

"You're damn right there will, Halloran. And when my time comes, it will be handled my way without any putzing about." Kruger writhed in pain and lay back slowly on his pillow. "Now that you've finished your errand, get the fuck out of here," he muttered, eyes closed. "Run back to the senator. I'm sure he'll have another little errand for you."

Halloran bridled at the comment, but kept his mouth shut. Kruger was an extremely dangerous man who had the utmost confidence of the senator. But sooner or later, he would screw up so badly that even the senator would be forced to reevaluate his opinion of the South African. And as always he, Jimmy Halloran, would be there to whisper the best advice.

Kruger lay on his back, sweating. Thoughts of Halloran quickly slipped from his mind as the pain took hold. The son of a bitch Daniels had burst his left testicle. The resulting infection had almost killed him. He would carry the scar for the rest of his life. And someday, Daniels would pay.

Kruger gripped the blanket tightly, grimacing in pain. Where was that goddamned nurse?

Tuapi, February 17, 1989

Elena opened her eyes. Xavier was sitting on the bed watching her. She smiled at him and stretched her arms.

"How you feeling?" Xavier asked.

"Fine. Even better now," she answered, hugging him tightly. In the two weeks since her fever broke, both she and Xavier had made speedy recoveries.

"I told the doc we were lucky it was your head that was hit. You got rocks for brains. You should be bitching at nurses and reprimanding patients in no time."

She pinched him playfully.

"Ouch!" Xavier exclaimed. "You're supposed to be resting."

"I've had enough rest, Javi," she said. "I'm getting crazy sitting in this bed, this house. I want to go out for a while."

"I'm sorry. According to Maria, you're not well enough to be going anywhere yet."

"And where did she get her medical degree?"

Xavier stared at her sternly. She folded her arms and pouted. He loved seeing the playful side of her. It balanced her otherwise cool, professional demeanor.

"Where is Maria, anyway?" Elena asked.

"One of your patients had a baby. Maria has gone to take care of her other children while the mother recuperates."

Elena played with Xavier's hand. "And when will she be back?"

"Not until sometime tomorrow."

Elena looked at him mischievously.

"Oh, no, you don't. Plenty of time for that later. The rest of our lives, as a matter of fact," he smiled.

Unwilling to be put off, she took his hand, slipped it inside her nightgown and pressed it to her breast. Xavier could feel the nipple grow hard under his palm. She smiled at him coyly.

"Elena, please—" he pleaded. She put a finger to his lips silencing his protests.

Xavier's heart was beating hard in his chest. He felt his breath grow short and his resistance dissolve. Elena slid her hand around his neck and pulled her to him. Xavier kissed her softly, trying to be gentle, but she mashed her mouth to his and pushed her tongue between his lips. He sucked at it greedily, wanting to go on, but in the end, he pulled back.

Elena knelt beside him and pulled her nightgown off over her head. Her light brown skin was smooth and glowed like gold in the candlelight. Her breasts were firm and round and her black hair cascaded over her shoulders and down her back and arms. There was fire in her eyes.

She took his hand and brought it to her mouth, kissing his palm and tracing the outline of his fingers with her tongue. She guided his hand to her neck and then moved it down to her chest and then over her breasts. She slid it down over her flat stomach and between her legs, positioning his fingers over her mound. It was wet and inviting.

Xavier watched her seductive play, caressing her as he went. His excitement was fired by the way she looked at him while touching herself. She moaned softly and pulled his hand from between her thighs, pressing it against his face. His hand was wet with her juices. Her smell made him dizzy.

She slipped his fingers between his lips so he could taste her. He rolled his tongue over his fingers and looked into her eyes.

"Please," she whispered. "Now."

Xavier's head was rushing. He knew where he had to be and urgently pulled her to him. He kissed her lips and pulled on her hair to expose her neck. His tongue traced a line up her neck to a point just behind her ear. Elena's head fell to her chest as he gently bit her.

His tongue traveled down her chest between her breasts. Xavier turned his head so his ear was pressed to her chest. He could feel as well as hear the roar of her heart. He stood quickly to remove his clothes.

Elena's eyes hung heavy with sex as she watched Xavier undress. He knelt on the bed and lifted her up to him, kissing her passionately. Her hands ran down his body and reached between his legs. She felt him hard and ready.

Xavier lifted her petite body and she wrapped her legs around him. Elena guided him into her while he supported her body. She felt him groan deep in his throat as their bodies joined together. He rocked her body gently to the sound of the surf breaking on the beach.

Elena looked into Xavier's eyes and reached down between their sweating bodies. She wanted to feel them come together, to know that it was really happening.

"Do you feel us, Javier?"

His head fell back as he answered, "Yes, Yes."

"We are together, my love. Together," she panted.

Her fingers rubbed her most sensitive spot as Xavier began to thrust harder. She could feel her pleasure mounting and her fingers began to move faster with a will of their own.

He brought his mouth to her neck and bit down. This last act of his lust brought her over the edge, and she shuddered as her climax ripped through her. Slowly their passion faded until the only sounds came from their rhythmic breathing and the surf pounding on the sand.

Elena cradled his head to her breast. She smoothed his hair and traced the outline of his ear. His breath was warm on her skin. Elena marveled at the power of her feelings for this man. It was a completely new experience for her.

You are mine now, Xavier, she thought. And no one can take you away from me. Ever.

Eventually they slept.

She woke later to find Xavier gone. Startled, she sat up in bed.

"It's all right, Elena," Xavier spoke softly. "I'm over here."

She saw his outline in the moonlight, his hair floating gently in the wind. He was watching the ocean. She tossed the covers aside and went to him, wrapping her arms around his stomach. He put an arm around her shoulder and pulled her close. The cool sea breeze played delightfully over their naked skin as they watched the reflection of the moon flash on the water.

As Elena's warm body pressed close to his, Xavier thought about the twists of fate that had brought him to this paradise and the woman he loved, this amazing woman. He would have never guessed his life would turn out as it had.

Ten months ago, he was holding his dead wife outside their burned-out business. Wanted by the law and by a nameless assassin, he was forced to flee the country in fear for his life.

Now, he was a trusted member of Chamorro's inner circle. His father's surprising financial legacy could help make Elena's dreams for Nicaragua a reality. And he was in love. He thought it could never happen again. He squeezed Elena's shoulder at the thought.

"What are you thinking about?" Elena asked.

"Possibilities," he answered. "Endless possibilities."

PART V
Abyss

23

Landringham Estate, Northern Virginia, August 23, 1994

The Landringham Estate was a pre-Civil War mansion nestled in the woods of northern Virginia. It was secluded from the world by high fences, thick woods, and alert guards. Landringham was not off the beaten path. Dulles International Airport lay a few miles to the east, and beyond that, the capital itself.

Landringham was leased from one of the senator's largest political contributors. The lease was paid for out of a secret campaign slush fund buried under layers of corporate owners.

The estate had been fully restored and furnished in its original style. The gardens were well-tended horticultural masterpieces. The interior was tastefully laid out with period furniture accompanied with more modern appliances. The kitchen staff served expertly prepared meals that ranged from southern cooking to nouvelle French cuisine.

The second story was surrounded by a large balcony supported by massive colonnades typical of the period. Spaced at intervals on the massive landing were several collections of wrought iron chairs with comfortable cushions. The furniture was arranged for conversation and situated to take advantage of the beautiful panorama of the Landringham grounds.

One man occupied the balcony. He sat sipping a mint julep and watched several gardeners pruning the trees.

The master and his servants, the man thought. In the old days, Father would have sat drinking tea at this time of day watching his trainers work the hounds. Different countries, different estates, diffcrent times.

"Different libations," he said aloud as he raised his glass at the memory of his father. "But some things never change," he said, as he eyed his employees. Those who have power always thirst for more, he thought to himself.

"Senator, your guests are waiting," a servant announced.

"Tell them I will join them shortly," he sighed, as he finished his mint julep. He was in no hurry to remove himself from the comforts of his estate.

It was a pity that his guests were unable to enjoy Landringham's charms as they sat in the recesses of the basement in a secured and monitored chamber.

With another sigh, Senator Marion Hammersmith rose and gazed on his domain one more time before he walked inside. He had business to conduct.

Hammersmith descended to the basement and entered his specially designed conference room. The chamber was decorated in marked contrast to the spirit of Landringham. It was ultimately modern in style and sparing in atmosphere—primarily constructed in chrome, graphite, and stark black and white. The latest in computer and communication technology was available in the recessed areas of the walls, ready to be accessed at the flick of a button. Soft, muted lights reflected off the ceiling.

In the center of the sterile environment stood an oblong conference table, black granite on brushed aluminum supports. The high-backed, black leather chairs were occupied by a group of men intent on the business at hand.

"Then we are all agreed. The operation goes off as scheduled," Hammersmith began without greeting anyone. He sat at the head of the table and looked up to see all heads nodding except one.

"You, who have so much to gain and nothing to lose, are so ready to begin. I, on the other hand, have everything to lose if we fail," Colonel Ricardo Sanchez explained. "So I hesitate as we rush ahead."

"You also have the most to gain, Colonel Sanchez." This was spoken by Per Bota, former defense minister of South Africa. He was a large man with a bald head except for a thin strand of gray hair behind his ears. "Your country, for one thing."

"I want assurances, Bota. Assurances that you will not fail," Sanchez demanded, pointing at the table.

"Assurances, *mi amigo*? Hell, we're all takin' risks, and in this kind of operation, nuthin's for sure."

Sanchez looked at Tucker Barton with distrust. Barton, head of the CIA and an Oklahoma oilman, smiled condescendingly at Sanchez. The Sandinista colonel knew how Barton felt about anyone who wasn't white. His genteel demeanor was a mask that hid his racism. Sanchez disliked Barton even more than the others at the table.

"And what risks are you taking, *Amigo*?" Sanchez asked sarcastically. "Your drug operations in Central America are filling the CIA coffers with millions of dollars. If we fail, you simply switch transshipping operations somewhere out of Nicaragua. And the money keeps flowing in. To pay for your covert operations and your yacht in the Virgin Islands, I might add. Such a valuable piece of equipment is indispensable to the defense of your country, I suppose."

The smile on Barton's face turned into a snarl. "Listen, Sanchez. That money makes up for the cuts in my budget that the president ordered. That Texas hustler doesn't give a damn about the defense of our country, in fact..."

"I understand your position, Director Barton," Sanchez said with a wave of his hand. He'd heard all of Barton's arguments before and didn't care to again. "What I meant was, you gentlemen have a fallback position. Whereas, the Sandinista party and I will be doomed if something goes wrong."

"What can we do to assure you?" Bota asked. "We've all agreed to the plan. You yourself had plenty of input during the development of the mission. What now are your misgivings?"

"Your man Kruger, for one. After the fiasco in Honduras, I'm not sure he's up to this assignment."

"First off, Colonel, he's not my man," Bota explained. "He has been on loan to Senator Hammersmith for several years now in exchange for certain…information. But I'm sure the good senator would be more than happy to vouch for him."

You bastard, Hammersmith thought. You're not going to lay all this in my lap.

Sanchez turned to the senator. "Senator?"

"Kruger is an exceptional man. Capable of accomplishing anything or Mr. Bota would never have recommended him. Isn't that correct, Mr. Bota?" he asked, smiling at the former defense minister.

Bota nodded his head. *Touché.* "His track record with the South African Defense Forces was extraordinary. He is a brave and cunning commander who carries out his assignments with ruthless precision."

"So you both agree, he is the man for the job."

They nodded their heads in unison.

"Then could you explain to me the Honduras affair? If he was so capable, what went wrong?"

Hammersmith and Bota looked at each other. Neither one wanted to answer the question. It was Hammersmith who spoke first.

"We did not anticipate the reaction of Xavier Daniels. And we were completely in the dark about the sniper Corona. It will not happen again."

"You are quite right, Senator. It will not," Sanchez affirmed. "Corona and Daniels are our problem this time and we have taken measures to see that they are liquidated quickly." He narrowed his gaze at Hammersmith. "No fucking around, as you say. But how can I be sure Don Busambra doesn't have any more surprises waiting for us?"

All eyes turned to the Sicilian sitting at the far end of the table. He was the best dressed of the lot, sporting a handmade Italian silk suit. He was an attractive man physically, but he also wore an air of menace that had caused the other men to avoid addressing him.

"My word, Colonel Sanchez, is all that I can give you. No surprises from New York. Is that enough?" the Sicilian asked.

Sanchez wanted more, but hesitated to ask. Doubting this man could have dangerous consequences, so he answered meekly, "No, *Señor*. Your word is more than sufficient."

"Then what are your other doubts? Please tell us. I for one, would like to know."

"Very well, *Señor*. How can you prevent the Americans from reacting to the Sandinista coup? Once we commit our forces, we will be in the open and exposed. If the U.S. military invades, we will be annihilated."

"Mr. Barton, I think, could best answer that question for us," the Sicilian said. Without a contest, he had taken control of the meeting. Senator Hammersmith, the official chairperson, reacted calmly. Inside, he was seething.

"Yes, Ed. Why don't you tell us what you intend on doing," Hammersmith suggested. Barton, who distrusted the Sicilian, had waited for the senator to call on him before answering. He had no fear of the arrogant gangster.

"After Kruger delivers his groceries, the president will be too busy dealing with the Panama disaster to focus on much of anything else for days, maybe weeks. To keep him further off kilter, I will feed him false intelligence estimates and distorted information to further distance him from what is really taking place. He won't be able to tell the crap from the cow. The president will be concentrating on Libya, not Nicaragua. By the time he figures out the only place a new canal can be built is Nicaragua, the Sandinista government, as in you and your friends, *mi amigo*, will be firmly entrenched, backed up by a mutual defense treaty with South Africa."

"We have earmarked an armored brigade for transport to your country as soon as the ink is on the treaty, Colonel," Bota added. "If the United States invades Nicaragua, the problem will be political dynamite. When South African forces are engaged, the U.S. will be fighting two nations, not one. Also, the military equation becomes much more complex." He failed to add he considered the armed forces of his nation to be far superior to those of Nicaragua. Any modern military power would hesitate to fight them.

"Are you sure they will be focusing on Libya and not us?"

"Yes, Colonel," Hammersmith answered. "The only evidence the world will find after the balloon goes up will point directly to Qadhafi and Libya. Kruger has seen to that. And once the momentum of world opinion has focused on Qadahfi, your little coup d' état will be a small footnote in the history books. The American public will be screaming for revenge. And if the president so much as looks at Nicaragua, the Congress of the United States will force him back on track. I have a certain amount of influence there," he smiled self-importantly.

"But what of the rumors of your appointment as the head of this super drug force? If you are given this new job, then we lose your voice in the Senate."

"And gain it in the president's cabinet," Hammersmith added. "The appointment carries with it Secretarial authority."

"Like moving the fox into the hen house," Barton said laughing. "Isn't that right, Senator?"

"In your vernacular, yes, Ed. Something like that."

They all laughed, including Sanchez, though he didn't understand the humor.

"I think you can tell the Ortega brothers not to worry, Colonel. Everything, as you see, is in order. Just concern yourself with taking your country back."

Sanchez stood. "With every last drop of blood in our bodies, we will fight to free Nicaragua," he stated heroically.

The other men at the table smiled uncomfortably at the Colonel's fervor. Though they thought of themselves as patriots, the last thought on their minds was of personal sacrifice. The conspirators had formed the plan with more tangible results in mind.

"Any more questions?" Hammersmith asked.

None were forthcoming. "Good, then let us celebrate."

Hammersmith pressed a button. Instantly the doors to the conference room opened and James Halloran appeared, pushing a serving cart. A large silver champagne bucket held several bottles of Taittinger. The senator's chief of staff popped open a bottle and poured the contents into crystal champagne flutes. When the glasses were distributed, the senator stood and raised his glass.

"To our success!" The others stood and returned the toast. "Success!"

The meeting broke up on a positive note. After handshakes and small talk, the participants returned to their rooms for a more intimate celebration. Halloran had procured several beautiful courtesans to cater to the senator's guests. The women had all been here before and knew what was expected of them. The senator had a reputation as an excellent host. The women were employed to see that he kept it.

In the privacy of his bedroom, the Sicilian watched two women perform on one another. One blonde and fair, the other brunette, they moaned as they sought to satisfy the man watching them. He was happy with the performance.

The women were all fingers, tongues, lips, and smooth flesh. They were animated and vocal and seemed to enjoy each other with a genuine enthusiasm. The Sicilian had witnessed many such shows—this was close to the best. As they thrashed about in the frenzy of their first orgasms, the Sicilian joined them.

As they began to work on him, he thought about hens and foxes. Although the conspirators didn't yet realize it, he was the fox invited into their hen house. Or the wolf in sheep's clothing let into the sheep pen. Whatever metaphor best fit the situation didn't really matter once the killing started. The only thing that mattered was that he was the strongest, and his fellow plotters had no idea of his power.

The Sicilian laughed aloud as the women tried to please him. They paused and looked at one another before continuing their ministrations with redoubled efforts. Before they were done, this man would take them seriously. As they sucked and licked with abandon, the Sicilian fell back on his pillow, all thoughts of hens and foxes and sheep vanishing as he concentrated on his pleasure.

24

Managua, Nicaragua, August 23, 1994

Xavier drove the jeep through the sweltering Managua heat. As he neared the center of the capital city, the traffic grew more dense until it came to a standstill. Xavier whipped the wheel around and drove the vehicle over the curb and down the sidewalk. Pedestrians scattered, cursing the madman. As an afterthought, Xavier tooted the horn.

Xavier cut down an alley and found a relatively empty street. Wheels screeching, he turned onto the avenue and raced through the gears as he sped down the street.

"Jesus, Javi," Huberto whined. "We're not in a helicopter."

"No shit," Corona grumbled from the back seat.

"I don't want to be late," Xavier explained.

"We won't be late," Huberto stated.

"It'll be close, but we'll make it," Corona prognosticated.

"Damn right!" Xavier agreed, swinging the jeep back onto the main thoroughfare just ahead of an oncoming bus.

Huberto grabbed onto the documents in his lap to keep them from flying out of the Jeep. *"Madre de Dios!* I thought I was the only one who drove like this."

Xavier was nervous. He always was when he met with the president. Even more so today because he did not like reporting bad news.

332

As an official in the Ministry of Finance, he had been assigned the task of attracting foreign aid and investment capital for Nicaragua. He also managed the funds to insure they were spent in the proper manner. Xavier did an excellent job with what he solicited, but the well had just about dried up as far as international monetary aid was concerned.

About all that Xavier had to sell was the energy and intelligence of Nicaragua's citizens. In the shaky world financial market, this opened awfully few doors.

Nicaragua, with its nightmarish fiscal debt and tenuous political climate, would have to do with what meager contributions Xavier could scrounge.

"What about Tito? He's fixing to go over budget, Huberto. I told that son of a bitch his financing was fixed," Xavier growled.

Huberto shuffled through some papers and came up with the appropriate file. Quickly he glanced over it. What he saw caused him to smirk.

"He's building by the specs we gave him, Xavier," he said, scanning some figures. "To do that is costing more than the budget you assigned him."

"He accepted the bid. You think he's skimming?"

"Not Tito. He's above graft."

"Nobody's above graft, Huberto. Remember that."

"He is. That's why you hired him. And the way you monitor the funds, you'd know if he was stealing from us."

Xavier grumbled something about the money before he continued. "You're my in-house engineer. Does this guy know what he's doing? I mean is he wasting time and materials having to go back and fix his mistakes?"

"We've both been down there, Javi. You know, as well as I do, he's the best construction engineer in Nicaragua. The project is beautiful, efficient, and safe."

"He's building a goddamn irrigation canal. Not the fucking space shuttle. Tell him to bring it in at cost or I'll get someone who can!" Xavier yelled.

"You're not going to find anyone better, boss," Corona stated. He rarely commented on business, but he respected Tito.

"I...uh...think you should tell him yourself, Javi," Huberto said hesitantly. He hated telling his boss something he didn't want to hear. Xavier's reactions were less than pleasant. Today would be no exception.

"Goddamnit, Huberto! I didn't hire you so that I would have to hold your hand. Just do what I said!"

Maybe it was the heat or the traffic, but something caused Huberto to react in unaccustomed anger.

"No, Javi! You're the one who gave him the job and the budget. You're the one who ordered him to build it to specs so the people wouldn't be poisoned like they were in Matagalpa two years ago. You give us impossible tasks and then chew our asses when we don't come through. I'm tired of this *caca*," he said, slumping in his seat and looking at the street. "You're the big *chingadero*. You tell him."

Xavier drove on in silence, hating himself. These men had saved his life. They were his friends and, as much as he hated to admit it, his bodyguards—men willing to give their lives to save his. And because they chose this fate, their rewards were long hours, little social life, and Xavier's frequent outbursts of temper.

"Why the hell do you guys stay around?" Xavier asked after a moment.

"Your charming personality," Corona said dryly. Xavier took a glance in the rear view mirror. Corona's face was a blank.

"I like the perks of the job, myself," Huberto answered.

Xavier looked at the little engineer. "Such as?"

"Exotic women, great pay, and an understanding, caring boss."

Huberto was kidding, of course. The shadows under his eyes told of his sleepless night preparing the report they were about to deliver. He rarely saw Griselda, his wife, and although his salary was adequate, it was far beneath what the talented engineer could have made in the private sector.

"Okay, Huberto. I'm an asshole. I work you guys like dogs and reward you with more work and less appreciation than any man in Nicaragua. I have no excuses for what I have become. I just appreciate the fact you stay around in spite of what I do."

"*No problema, jefe.* I wouldn't have your job for all the money in Nicaragua," Huberto offered, accepting the apology.

"You forget. There isn't any money in Nicaragua. At least none coming in during the near future. And without it—" he let his thought go unfinished.

All three men knew their country was broke. Xavier did not need to explain that the outlook was bleak. He had worn himself out trying to refinance the debt. As of yesterday, they were cut off by the International Monetary Fund. His deal with a huge European consortium for two factories in Nicaragua had fallen through last week. Xavier was out of answers, money, and time.

His dilemma was further complicated by the fact that he hated failing his adopted country. These people had given him love, respect, and most of all, a purpose to continue living after Min's murder. They had accepted him as one of their own, and their admiration bordered on worship after the heroics he had performed and the sacrifices he'd made on their behalf. Xavier loved this country as passionately as any outsider ever could. Maria and Elena often commented on how Nicaraguan he'd become. Thinking about all this deepened his depression.

"Do you think she'll understand?" Xavier asked, referring to his upcoming meeting with the president.

"Of course she will, Javi," Huberto answered. "That is why she is *Doña* Violeta."

Xavier gripped the steering wheel tightly as he approached the Presidential Palace. He hated giving Violeta Chamorro bad news. She was getting so old.

The guards passed them through the gate after a thorough inspection. Major Alberto Diaz, head of Chamorro's security detail, met them at the door.

"I see your people are as efficient as ever," Xavier commented, shaking his hand.

"Not as efficient as I would like," he said, pointing at Huberto. "Once again, they let the comedian through."

"*Chíngate,* Major," Huberto laughed good naturedly. "This place could do with a little humor."

"You're right there, *amigo.* I trust you've brought us something to smile about."

Huberto looked at the floor.

Xavier sighed and shook his head as the levity of their meeting evaporated.

"I didn't think so," said Diaz. "We'd better go see her. She likes to hear bad news right away."

Diaz led them to her private chambers. Here, upstairs in the back of the Palace, Chamorro conducted most of her business. As in the days of her candidacy when she met with her campaign staff in the kitchen of her home, Chamorro liked to do business in familiar, less official surroundings. She rarely used the presidential office, saving it for meetings with foreign dignitaries.

"Where is Corona?" Diaz asked as they passed through the final checkpoint.

"He stayed with the jeep. Alex figures I'm safe with you."

"A good professional always has appreciation for a competent peer," Diaz noted.

"I think he's more worried about one of your competent guards planting a bomb in the jeep than he is about how well you can protect the boss."

"I trained all my people personally," Diaz said irritated.

"That's what he's worried about," Huberto explained.

"Do you two ever stop?" Xavier sighed.

The banter ceased as they stopped outside her quarters.

"Ready or not, Javi," Diaz whispered, knocking quietly on the door. He opened it and ushered Xavier and Huberto into Chamorro's private study.

"Hello, Javi," Chamorro smiled brightly from behind her desk. "And you, Huberto. Have you been staying out of trouble?"

"*Sí, Señora*," he answered sheepishly. Huberto had never gotten used to the president's familiarity. He was still in awe of her.

Doña Violeta maneuvered her electric wheelchair out from behind her desk and glided toward her guests. The motor hummed softly in the quiet.

"You are looking very tired, Javi," she said with concern. She grabbed his hand and held it between hers. "You are working too hard."

"No one works as hard as you, *Doña* Violeta."

"Ah," she said waving her hand. "A myth. I am a grandmother. It is the easiest job in the world. Now come and sit my friends. Alberto, could you bring us some *refrescos?*"

"Right away." The three arranged themselves in the sitting area while Diaz rummaged in a small refrigerator for the drinks. He handed out the plastic bags and retired, leaving them to confer in private.

"How is Griselda?" Chamorro asked.

"She is fine, *Doña* Violeta. She is pregnant again."

"*Qué magnifico!* And this will be your second?"

"Third, *Señora*."

"I will pray for her health."

"*Gracias, Doña* Violeta. She will be pleased."

"And you, Javi? When are you and Elena going to have children?" she asked, continuing in the role of the grandmother.

"Uh, someday, *Señora*. We are both so busy. We hardly see each other."

"Well, that will have to change. Without children, you cannot have grandchildren. They are one of life's true pleasures. I should know, Javi."

Xavier nodded his head in agreement, although he did not know when, if ever, he and Elena would have time for a family. She ran a department of the Health Ministry. The job was as demanding and time consuming as Xavier's and kept her away from home much of the time. The last year or so they had often felt like strangers when they were together. Xavier hoped the condition was only temporary.

"So tell me what news you have brought me. Was your trip to Europe a success, I hope?"

Well, here it is, Xavier thought. Time to ruin her day. "I'm sorry, *Doña* Violeta. I failed to procure either the refinancing of our debt or the factories for Matagalpa and Leon."

"And where does that leave us?" she asked.

"In a very precarious position, I'm afraid." Xavier paused to look at Huberto's notes. He didn't need to, he knew the information by heart. He just hated having to tell her what she already suspected.

"The immediate results of the loss of the factories will be less dramatic than the long-term effects. A loss of hope here at home will be our main concern. The people were looking to those factories with a great deal of anticipation. As for the future? When EurTel backed out of the deal, they sent a message to the rest of the industrial world that will be hard to overcome. If EurTel won't invest in us, no one will. We are considered too great a risk. We will have to make do with what we have here at home. Create our own industries so to speak."

"Then that is what we shall do. The people are strong. We will survive."

"I'm afraid it is a bit more complicated than that, *señora*." Xavier paused and took a deep breath before continuing. "The IMF refused to refinance our debt. You can argue which was the result of which. Did the IMF refuse to refinance because EurTel backed out and they were afraid, without the consortium's backing, we would be unable to pay the interest? Or did EurTel withdraw because the IMF won't salvage the debt, making our economy a target for rampant inflation? It's like trying to guess which came first, the chicken or the egg. In the end, for us the result is the same. A complete economic disaster."

"But we finally managed to get the inflation under control. What are you so worried about?"

"*Señora*, the only way now to pay off the debt and create financing for industry at home is to print money. The more money we print, the less valuable it is. Prices rise out of sight and the economy collapses. No food. No work. No money. Civil unrest like we have never seen. Hitler and Lenin took advantage of very similar conditions to instill their will over Germany and Russia."

"Pezullo?" she asked worried.

"Pezullo and his party of National Salvation. Yes. Or the Sandinistas. Whoever it is, it won't be you and your democratic party. It is time to think about saving yourself, *Doña* Violeta. This is not your fault, but you will be the scapegoat. Resign gracefully while you still have a chance. You are old and frail. The people love you and will understand. In a few months they might forget."

"I will not resign. I will not let someone step into my shoes and take the blame for my situation. That is the coward's way out. *Qué necesitamos es uno milagro!*"

"What?" Xavier asked.

"You have been speaking Spanish for six years, Javi," she chastised him. "What we need is a miracle. What about your godfather? *Señor* Busambra."

"My godfather is, above all else, a businessman. There is no opportunity for profit in our small country, *Señora*. And as much as he loves me, he will not throw money away on a hopeless cause. I'm sorry."

"Well, the miracle will come from somewhere, Javi. Of that you can be assured."

"I hope you are right, *Doña* Violeta."

"You must have hope, Javi. Hope and faith."

"Hope and faith won't feed our people, *Señora*. I failed, and because of that, I find it very hard to be hopeful."

"Nonsense, Javi. You just haven't examined all the possibilities."

Xavier was amazed at her positive outlook. He'd just told her Nicaragua was broke and heading for disaster, that her very life was in danger, and she managed to brush it off and look to the future. Either she was growing senile or he was getting too damn cynical. Probably a little bit of both, he thought.

"Now enough of this business. You have both been working too hard. It is time for some well-deserved relaxation."

She pressed a button on the side of her wheelchair and the door opened. Diaz walked in, followed by a noticeably pregnant Griselda and her two children. Trailing the noisy bunch, Elena walked in almost unnoticed in the uproar that followed as squealing children leaped into their father's arms.

"Hello, Xavier," Elena said quietly.

"Hi, honey," Xavier replied.

They looked at one another. It was obvious they were uncomfortable.

"What a surprise."

"I'll say," Elena added. She realized they were standing out in sharp contrast to the emotional reunion of the Royo family. Under Chamorro's watchful eye, Elena leaned over and gave her husband a perfunctory kiss.

"You have been working too hard," Chamorro observed. "I think it is about time you two got reacquainted. All of you are to be my guests this weekend. A reunion of sorts."

Xavier and Elena complained at once, insisting they had too much work waiting for them. Chamorro held up her hand silencing them in mid-sentence.

"I am the president and I am ordering you to rest for the entire weekend. Now, since that is settled, let us enjoy ourselves. Come here, *niños*," Chamorro said, opening her arms.

The children disengaged themselves from Huberto's grasp and ran to Chamorro. She magically produced some sweets and passed them out to the delight of the youngsters.

"You spoil them, *Doña* Violeta," Grisleda observed.

"You are correct, my dear. It is one of the few pleasures I have left in life. Now, you and your husband go get settled in. Alberto will show you to your rooms. That includes you, Xavier and Elena. Maybe you'll find the time to make me more grandchildren."

Elena blushed while Xavier shuffled his feet. "Really, *Doña* Violeta."

"Yes, really, Xavier. That is what married people do. They make babies. Or have you forgotten how?"

Xavier opened his mouth and shut it quickly. He was at a loss for an answer to the president's question.

"I'd quit while you are ahead, *jefe*," Huberto offered, amused at Xavier's embarrassment. "Now come on, children. Let's go to our room."

"Don't worry about the children, Huberto. They are going to stay and play some games with *Tia* Violeta."

"Yeah!" the children yelled.

"You're sure, *Doña* Violeta," Huberto hesitated. This was the president of Nicaragua after all.

"They won't be too much of a problem, *Señora Presidente?*" Griselda asked as concerned as her husband.

"Rest easy, *mi amigos*. If I have any problems, Alberto, my chief of security, will be here to assist me."

"Of course, *Señora Presidente*," Diaz agreed, bowing slightly. He leaned over and whispered in Huberto's ear. "When was the last time you and your wife were alone, Huberto? You had better go before she changes her mind. Or would you rather stay here and tell jokes, comedian?"

Huberto and Griselda smiled at each other. Needing no further prompting, they followed Diaz out the door.

"I guess we should go to our room," Xavier said, morosely.

"I guess we should," Elena agreed, half-heartedly.

They reluctantly shuffled out of the room, leaving the President of Nicaragua playing with the children.

"Everybody safely tucked in?" Corona asked Diaz.

"*No problema, amigo.* They will be safe with me," Diaz assured the bodyguard. "I will guard them with my life."

"I know, Alberto. And I appreciate it. You are the only person in Nicaragua I would trust with Xavier's life."

"I thank you for your confidence, Alex," Diaz responded pleased. It was the ultimate compliment one professional could give to another.

"And what have you planned for your weekend?"

Chamorro's invitation hadn't come as a surprise to either man. Both bodyguards had known of the reunion for over a week. The security arrangements had to be planned and executed. No contingency was overlooked. Professionals hate surprises.

"The servants have been sent home and I cut the security detail to the bone."

"Sounds like you are planning a private evening alone."

"Not quite, Alberto. I've sent the limousine to pick up a young lady. She will be spending the weekend with me."

"Strictly platonic, I'm sure."

"Of course, my friend. Just someone to keep me company in that huge house."

"Don't forget the swimming pool."

"And the swimming pool, Alberto. I mustn't forget the swimming pool."

They laughed and clapped each other on the back. Diaz escorted the sniper to the entrance hall where two men waited. Corona checked their appearance and nodded, satisfied.

"Ever the professional," Diaz approved. "From a distance you couldn't tell the difference."

"You can never be too careful, *mi amigo.*"

They shook hands and Corona escorted his charges to the waiting jeep. The guards at the gate passed them through and the three men began their journey back to the Daniels' mansion.

A man of few words, Diaz thought, watching the jeep drive off. He appreciated Corona's professionalism and enjoyed his dry sense of humor, yet he often wondered what motivated the man. Why, despite his loner mentality, had Corona attached himself to Xavier's crew? Diaz knew that the sniper's obligation to Don Busambra had long been paid.

He must like us, Diaz smiled. He watched a moment longer before continuing on with his duties.

A *refresco* vendor situated across the square from the Presidential Palace watched the jeep roar down the avenue. After serving several customers, he spoke into a small radio he kept hidden in his cart. The man dutifully reported the assistant Minister of Finance, his chief aid, and his bodyguard, leaving the Palace on a possible return trip to his estate. A taxi driver stationed on the highway a few miles out of Managua confirmed the report fifteen minutes later. The quarry was headed back to its hole.

Xavier sat on a small settee staring out the window. Elena lay on the bed with her back to her husband. Their attempt at lovemaking had been disastrous. At length Elena chose to break the uncomfortable silence.

"What are you thinking about?" she asked.

"If I wanted you to know what I was thinking, we'd be having a conversation," he answered coldly.

Elena kept silent for a minute before continuing. She refused to be put off.

"How was your trip to Europe?" she asked, trying to make small talk as a pretext to draw her husband out.

"Disastrous. I was a complete failure with the IMF."

"I am sorry." Silence.

"How about the EurTel deal?"

"Disaster number two. I failed to get them to invest in Nicaragua." More silence.

"Would you like to talk about it?"

"No!" he snapped. Instantly, he was full of remorse for his temper. "I'm sorry, Elena. Snapping at my friends has become a bad habit lately."

"You are forgiven," she said, sitting up. "I just want to know what is wrong so I can help. Can you tell me?"

"What's not wrong," he started, shaking his head. "The country's going down the tubes and nothing I do seems to help. Hell, I keep busting my head against the wall but nothing comes of it. It gets entirely too frustrating."

"I understand. But the country will survive, Xavier. It always has. Something will happen."

"Like a miracle? Because that is what it's going to take."

"So then it will be a miracle."

"Sounds pretty hopeful."

"In Nicaragua, that is all that we have, hope."

"Well, I have yet to see hope feed children and create jobs for their parents," Xavier remarked angrily. "We need more cash and less hope. Chamorro is living in a fantasy world if she thinks this situation will just work itself out. It won't. What's more, it could cost her the presidency, maybe her life, if the Sandinistas or the PNA seize this opportunity to make a play for power. God knows, in the chaos they will have a good chance."

"Chamorro will see us through. She always has."

Xavier turned to face his wife. "Are you as blind as Chamorro? I just told you this country is on the brink of economic chaos. The dark abyss, Elena. We are staring into it. The end of democracy and any hope of prosperity for our friends and all you can do is shrug your shoulders and say something will happen. That's crazy."

"Yes. It might be crazy. But what is more crazy is your attempt to control a situation that is out of control. It is killing you, Xavier. You aren't Jesus Christ. You can't feed the masses single-handedly."

"Even if I were Jesus Christ, loaves and fish wouldn't help. What we need is cash. And lots of it. But there's none to be had. I am the Assistant Minister of Finance, tasked with the industrial and economic development for Nicaragua. But I can't do my job. Not without capital. Instead of a builder, I've turned into a beggar. Or something. Hell, I don't know what I've turned into. I don't even know who I am anymore, Elena. Can you tell me who I am?"

"I don't know, Xavier," she answered, speaking to the wall. "Only you can answer that question."

"We were so in love once," he sighed. "Could any two people have ever been more in love than we were? It can't have all disappeared."

"Remember Mexico?" Elena asked, thinking of their honeymoon.

"How could I forget. It was the first time I saw you in a bikini. For a stodgy old doctor, you cut one hell of a fine figure."

"You built me the house on Lake Managua. I haven't had a home since I was a little girl," she said, wistfully. "It was so big."

"A castle for my princess. I wanted you to have the best of everything."

Elena sat up in bed and looked at her husband. "We used to have so many parties," she reminisced, smiling as she continued. "Our first anniversary."

"I thought you would be sick for the rest of your life," Xavier laughed at the memory.

"So did I," she grimaced. "At least the christenings for Huberto and Griselda's children were milder."

"Not by much. Huberto spent most of his time in the pool with his best suit on telling jokes. I thought Griselda would kill him. Both times."

"And now they have a third child on the way. Time flies."

"It sure does, Elena. Whatever happened to those days?"

"I guess rest became more important than socializing."

"And when did work become more important than our marriage, Elena?" he asked, as much for himself as for her.

Elena did not answer. She rested her chin on her knees and clutched her legs. The smile was gone.

"We can still work this thing out, you know," he said doubtfully.

"How, Xavier? You have your work and I have mine. We are responsible to so many people."

He sighed. "I thought our dreams for Nicaragua would keep us together," he remarked. "Instead, they seem to be pulling us apart. But we still have each other, Elena. Our love for each other. Isn't that enough?"

"We need more than that, Xavier. And you know it. *Doña* Violeta is right. We need a family."

Xavier stood and began to pace. "I don't want to go in to this again. Let's just try to enjoy our weekend. We haven't been together in weeks."

"Xavier, we haven't been together in years."

Xavier gave her an icy look and made his way to the door.

"If we don't talk about this thing between us, it will destroy our marriage. Please, Xavier," she pleaded.

Xavier paused at the door. He had run long enough. His wife was right. If he kept on running, he would eventually lose her. Knowing it would kill him if she left, he joined her on the bed.

"I don't want children, Elena. You married me knowing that. You told me it didn't matter. And now suddenly this desire of yours to have kids has come between us."

"My desire to raise a family is not the issue. You know that. I don't love you any less for your decision because I am your wife. All that I am asking for is an explanation that will help me to understand your feelings about being a father. Help me to understand, Xavier?"

"This country could explode at any moment. A helluva place to have a family."

"I'm not buying it, Xavier. You have too much hope to be that kind of cynic."

"Oh, really?" he asked.

"Yes, really."

"I'm glad you think you know me so well."

"I do. And what's more, I know you'd make a great father."

"I don't have time to be a father," Xavier stated adamantly.

"You'd make time, Xavier."

"Like I've made time for you? For our marriage?"

"That is different, Xavier. But for the children you'd make time," Elena restated her belief.

"Like my father made time for me?"

Elena held her breath.

"You are not your father," she offered.

"And how the hell can you be so sure?"

"Because I love you. And I know what I love. The good and the bad."

"Well, there was a lot of bad in my father and I'm afraid I might have inherited some of it," Xavier conceded.

"There was also a lot of good in your father, too. I should know."

"Yeah, but what you don't know is what happened to me."

"My love, I know everything about you. I know all the pain of your childhood. But what has your father's abuse got to do with our child?"

"You want me to say it, Elena? You really want me to say it?"

"Yes, Xavier. What are you afraid of?"

His face contorted in desperation. "I might beat the hell out of our children just like my father used to beat the hell out of me. Now. I've said it. Are you satisfied? Are you happy?" he raged. "And I won't let that happen. Ever," he said with steel in his voice.

"That is right," Elena agreed. "Because you will protect your children for all the times you weren't protected. And you will love your children for all those times you were abandoned. You will be an incredible father because you know what kind of father you don't want to be. Ever."

A tear fell down Xavier's cheek. Elena cupped his face in her hands and touched his head to hers.

"I don't want to lose you, Elena. God knows, I don't. But I am so afraid of being a father. Of being my father. Help me," he pleaded.

"Shh, my darling. It is all right. I'm here."

After a time, they made love with a tenderness neither had known before. And for a while, their fears for the future were put to rest.

25

Daniels' Estate, Lake Managua, Nicaragua, August 23, 1994

Xavier Daniels' personal limousine stopped in front of the wrought iron gate blocking the drive to the Minister's estate. The two guards, standing post in front of the entrance, held their weapons at the ready. The captain of the watch emerged from the guard shack with a clipboard.

The window of the limousine lowered and the guard checked the occupants of the vehicle against the roster in his left hand. His right hand hovered over his sidearm. Satisfied, he signaled a fourth guard in the blockhouse and the electric motors began to whir as the gates swung slowly back. The limousine passed through and the gates immediately swung back into place.

The captain of the guard scanned the road and the opposing hills before returning to the shack. His master might take unnecessary risks during his journeys, but here at home he was quite safe. The men employed here would die to assure that safety.

The binoculars followed the black car as it pulled in front of the mansion. Alex Corona, Daniels' chief bodyguard, met the limousine and opened the back door. A woman emerged and scaled the steps to the house followed by the bodyguard. The limousine drove to the back of the house.

The binoculars dropped to the viewer's chest. About time, he thought. I'm tired of being in this damned tree.

"Paolo," he hissed. "Paolo! Wake up, damn you."

Paolo, snoozing at the base of the tree, jerked up and rubbed his eyes.

"*Que pasa, cabrón*," he said, looking up the tree.

"Report in. Daniels' *puta* just arrived. The list is complete."

Paolo grabbed the radio and did as he was ordered. Similar reports were made from across the country as government officials, military officers, political opponents, and anyone else deemed a threat to the Sandinista party were tracked to their homes, offices, or businesses. The trackers were assassins. The victims, ignorant of their fates, went about their tasks unaware that their surroundings, familiar as they were, would turn into killing grounds in a matter of hours.

In a walled off mansion in the heart of Managua, the plotters listened to the reports, drank wine, and waited for night to fall.

Presidential Palace, August 23, 1994

The celebrants gathered in the dining room of Chamorro's private quarters. It was a festive occasion as friends and family relaxed in each others' company. Even Huberto loosened up enough to tell a few jokes, much to the delight of the President of Nicaragua. As dessert was served, Chamorro tapped her knife on a glass to get everyone's attention.

"I have a small announcement to make," she began smiling. "Six years ago, Xavier Daniels blessed us with his presence during a very difficult time. In the ensuing years, he has worked diligently to better Nicaragua and its citizens. As a reward for his services, the country has decided to grant him full citizenship. Retroactive from the date of his entry in 1988."

Chamorro lifted a document from her lap and handed it to Xavier. He looked at it with concern.

"I don't understand. This, this..." he stammered.

"This document means that you may hold elected office, among other things, Xavier," Chamorro explained, a mischievous grin dancing across her face.

"But I already hold office, *Señora Presidente.*"

"You have a presidential appointment," Chamorro explained. "Now, should you choose, you may take a more active part in Nicaraguan politics. This country needs you, Xavier."

"I have a feeling you might want me to take advantage of my new privileges, *Señora.*"

"Most definitely, Xavier. The people trust you. Your sole allegiance is to them and their welfare. The *campesinos* know this. You are the perfect candidate to draw these people together."

"This is happening so fast," he said, shaking his head.

"You should be grateful, my dear," Elena said, grabbing her husband's hand. "*Doña* Violeta worked hard to bring this about."

"Exactly, Javi. Congratulations," Huberto offered. "Now you can work us even harder."

"But we are overlooking one thing," Xavier said. "I am still a citizen of the United States. It is against the laws of both countries to hold dual citizenship once past the age of eighteen."

Chamorro handed him another piece of paper. "This is a notification to your government that you have accepted the offer of Nicaraguan citizenship. Sign it and you will no longer be a citizen of the United States."

"You are asking me to give up the country of my birth," he stated. "That is not an easy thing to do."

"Come on, Javi. Your country shit all over you," said Diaz. "They tried to kill you and your wife. And that's just the beginning of the list. We might not be wealthy and powerful like the United States, but we take care of our own."

"I understand and appreciate that, Alberto. I really do. But this is a decision I cannot make lightly. On one hand, I am flattered and on the other, I am horrified at the thought of turning my back on my country," said Xavier troubled.

"This is your country, Javi," Griselda broke in. "It has been for years. You are just acknowledging reality."

"You're right, Griselda. Nicaragua is my country. I love this country with my heart and soul and I would give my life to defend the Nicaraguan people.

"When I was a child, Maria loved me when my mother turned her back on me. Years later, she took me in and sheltered me in a time of danger. The people of Tuapi guarded my secret, saving my life. It is here that I met my wife and here that I healed my heart. Everyone in this room has become my family. But I have another family, too. My godfathers. And they are in the United States. Those men raised and protected me. I cannot turn my back on them so easily." Xavier sighed. "I am sorry. But I need some time to think."

"Before you make your decision, Xavier, realize your effectiveness in your present position has come to an end. Your skills, your head and your heart are needed for something much more important," Chamorro spoke earnestly. Her eyes bored into Xavier.

"And when you get right down to it, Javi. What other choice do you have?" Diaz asked. As usual, Diaz cut to the heart of the matter.

Xavier looked at Elena. She nodded her head. *Do it.*

Xavier left the dinner table realizing he'd already made his decision.

Daniels' Estate, Lake Managua, Nicaragua, nightfall

Corona lay on a hammock with his date. It rocked slightly in the gentle lake breeze drifting through the open windows of the sun room. The lake glimmered in the moonlight beyond the terraced gardens of the mansion. The girl moved in his arms as she slept, and then was still. Not a bad way to spend an evening, he thought.

The sniper had accepted his new life as he would have accepted a change in the wind when he was trying to get off a perfect shot. He adjusted his sights and moved ahead. That he was now part of a family didn't disturb the habitual loner. He rather enjoyed certain aspects of it.

The lights in the swimming pool shimmered as the wind moved the water. Shadows from swaying trees danced across the flagstones. The effect was hypnotic.

Corona noticed a shadow move against the rhythm of the wind. In his relaxed state, he hesitated. As he jerked up, the windows blew in, spraying him and the girl with glass. Gunfire ripped up the room tossing the two bloody bodies to the floor.

The Minister of the Interior, Jorgé Sepulveda, was walking his dog when a car pulled up alongside. He smiled and turned to wave and was cut down by a shotgun blast. The dog was still tied to his wrist, whimpering, when neighbors discovered the body moments later.

The Vice President of Nicaragua, Tomàs Gachas, blew out the candles on his birthday cake as his family sang the traditional "*Feliz Cumpleaños.*" To the squeals of delight from the gathered children, his wife cut into the cake and the bomb hidden inside exploded. Hours later, rescuers had dug out seventeen bodies including three children and seven grandchildren. Somewhere inside the rubble an infant cried for help.

The assembled Miskito Indians stood up and cheered as their leader, Brooklyn Rivera, walked to the podium. The crowd had gathered at the Plaza in Bluefields to hear the man responsible for leading them through the dark years of Sandinista rule. The Miskitos had been singled out for a campaign of brutal ethnic cleansing and had survived, largely due to the courageous man they now applauded. He had championed their cause at the risk of his life and the detriment of the government. The Sandinistas had a long overdue score to settle.

As his speech began, twenty gunmen raced into the crowd and opened fire at point-blank range. Dozens were trampled in the ensuing panic. Rivera survived unscathed as he had survived three other attempted assassinations during the "Red Christmas" of 1981. One hundred thirteen of his fellow Indians weren't as lucky. Their corpses lay where they had fallen until well after dawn.

In Matagalpa, Major General Lèon Coasas stopped at a roadside café to have a beer with his adjutant. The chief of staff of the small Nicaraguan army had ended a day of conferences and needed some relaxation. An hour later, Coasas watched in the bathroom mirror as the same adjutant drew a knife across his throat. The body was never found.

The editor of *La Prensa* hurriedly stripped off his clothes as his mistress begged him to join her on the bed. During the height of their lovemaking, she rolled him over and mounted him in a passionate frenzy. At her peak she shouted her love for him and blew his brains out. Her duty to the Sandinistas finished, she rested her head on the blood-soaked chest, placed the revolver against her head and pulled the trigger, joining her lover in death.

"Xavier," his wife yelled. "Your phone is ringing."

Xavier cursed under his breath and spit the toothpaste out of his mouth. He emerged from the bathroom wiping his face with a towel.

"Damn him," Xavier grumbled, taking the phone from his wife's extended hand. "You think the son of a bitch would enjoy a day off without having to think about me."

Xavier took the remote and fumbled with it trying to turn it on. The remote was part of a system Corona had installed in Nicaragua at great expense. There were no commercial users and only a few available lines. The system had been installed at Corona's request. The money was obtained from *Il Padrino*, who gave it happily. Corona knew Xavier's safety was of utmost importance to the don and he tapped the resource to satisfy his paranoia.

"What the hell do you want, Corona?" Xavier snapped.

There was a momentary pause before he received a response.

"This isn't Corona, Daniels," a strange voice answered.

"Then who the hell is it?" he asked.

"Mark Kinlan, and I don't have much time," came the urgent reply from the former CIA operative.

A chill traveled up Xavier's spine. "How did you get this number?"

"Never mind—"

"Nobody has this number," Xavier interrupted.

"Shut up and listen, you fool," Kinlan demanded. "The Sandinistas are staging a coup right now. Alert your guards and get your wife to safety."

"Who is it?" Elena asked, concerned.

"I have no guards," he explained, motioning for his wife to be quiet. "We're in the Presidential Palace."

"My God! There still might be time. Get to the president immediately," Kinlan screamed in desperation.

"But—"

"No buts, asshole. Move it."

Xavier grabbed a shirt and raced to the door. "Wake up Diaz and have him meet me at Chamorro's bedroom." Without waiting for a reply, Xavier ran down the hall.

Xavier's bare feet slapped on the marble steps as he took them two at a time to the next level. There were no guards at their usual posts and Xavier's heart began to pound. He slowed to a trot as he padded down the hall. Xavier stopped at the end and peered around the corner. The two guards in front of the president's bedroom lay dead in pools of blood.

Xavier smashed into the door at a dead run, blasting it off its hinges. He hit the floor and rolled to the opposite wall as bullets whizzed over his head smacking into the wall behind him. Xavier came to a rest behind Chamorro's desk, cracking his head on the hard oak. The silenced pistol spit again and the desk lamp disintegrated, throwing the corner into semi-darkness.

Sounds of footsteps moved across the floor toward him. Xavier placed his shoulder under the desk chair and heaved himself off the floor, hurling the heavy piece of furniture at the assassin. The pistol spit again, hitting the chair twice before it crashed into the attacker. Xavier followed the chair over the desk as Diaz burst into the room.

"*Alto!*" Diaz shouted. "Put the gun on the floor."

The assassin, a beautiful woman, smiled and turned the pistol toward the bed. Diaz emptied his automatic into her before she got off a shot. Before the body had hit the floor, Elena ran into the room and straight to Chamorro's bedside. Xavier and Diaz joined her. The president was soaked in blood.

"Medical team's on the way," Diaz said. "How is she?"

"She took a round in the chest. She's still alive, but the pulse is barely registering and her breathing is shallow. Where's the damn stretcher," Elena demanded.

Diaz went to the door. "It's coming down the hall." He returned to the bedside and touched Xavier's left arm. "You're bleeding."

Xavier looked at his arm, noticing the wound for the first time. "Bullet grazed me. It's nothing." He clamped down on the tear in his skin with his right hand, oblivious to the pain.

Elena tore up some bedding and held the makeshift bandage to the wound. "You saved her life, Xavier. Thank you."

"But will she be all right?" he asked.

"I set up the medical facilities in the Presidential Palace myself. We have a full operating theater here, Xavier. And Dr. Martinez is very good with trauma cases. We have a chance."

A paramedic pulled the stretcher into the room, assisted by a presidential guard. Griselda and Huberto ran in behind them.

"Where's Dr. Martinez?" Elena asked.

"He's dead," the paramedic answered, joining Elena at the President's side. "Shot in his bed."

"Bitch wasn't taking any chances," Diaz muttered.

Elena hesitated, a look of horror on her face.

"Elena," Xavier spoke softly. "Elena," he said again as he reached out and grasped her wrist. She looked at her husband. "It's up to you."

A look of determination came over her face. "All right, damnit. Let's get her on the stretcher. One, two, three, lift!" The body was placed carefully on the litter.

"Griselda. See if any of the medical team is still alive and have them prep for surgery." Griselda grabbed Huberto and they ran out of the room. "Now, let's move it," she ordered. The small group moved out of the room led by Dr. Elena Daniels in whose hands rested the fate of the president of Nicaragua.

Bishop Costas Garachas sat in the confessional listening to an astonishing confession. The man talked openly of the coup d' état that was tearing the heart out of Nicaragua. He confessed his part in the planning and his responsibility in the deaths of innocents. The bishop was stunned. A man of peace, he detested the waste of human life.

When the man finished, he asked for forgiveness. Garachas hesitated and prayed to God for guidance.

"You priests are all alike. You judge us before God has a chance," the confessor growled scornfully.

A fist crashed through the screen, ramming an ice pick into the Bishop's temple. The fist held it there until Garachas stopped twitching. Colonel Ricardo Sanchez straightened his tie and left the confessional a happier and freer man.

Ortega Mansion, Managua, Nicaragua, August 23, 1994

Across the country, assassins, individually or in groups, destroyed the spiritual, political, and military leadership of Nicaragua. As the plan unfolded, the men in Daniel Ortega's mansion nodded in satisfaction. Soon the Sandinista party would be the only cohesive, experienced group capable of running the government. They would step into the vacuum out of necessity. Nicaragua would be theirs by default.

As the evening lengthened, all thoughts turned to Panama and the operation to destroy the canal. The nuclear detonations would signal the final phase of the coup d' état. Ortega, the former dictator of Nicaragua, would then march to the Presidential Palace and officially take over the government.

"I think we should go now, Daniel," Humberto Ortega suggested. Humberto Ortega was Daniel's brother and the defense minister of Nicaragua. He was the only Sandinista of cabinet level retained by Chamorro after the election. His position had become mostly ceremonial as Coasas, Chamorro's hand-picked chief of staff, took over control of the military.

"We follow the plan, brother. Relax and have some wine. Soon the army will be yours again, now that Coasas is out of the way. "

"How can you drink wine at a time like this?"

"What else is there to do?" Daniel Ortega asked.

"Act, Daniel. Act now! Before it is too late."

"Too late for what? Everything is going according to schedule."

"I don't give a damn about the schedule. Take the TV and radio stations now. Cut off the phones. All of them! Not just the ones we've cut to the Palace. Even as we speak, the word is spreading. Before long, the people will take to the streets."

"And who will lead them, Humberto? Who? No one. They're all dead. The people will mill about for a few hours and, in the morning, we will tell them to go home. And go home they will because no one will be alive to tell them different. Until the appropriate time, we wait."

"Wait?" Humberto spat out the word. "Wait? Sandino did not wait. He waged war against the imperialist American Marines for six years. Edén Pastora did not wait. He attacked the National Palace and won the freedom of Tomàs Borge. We follow their example. If we hadn't, we'd still be in the jungles dying from dysentery while Somoza screwed his mistresses. Instead, we gained power and Somoza died. Action got us here, Daniel. Or have you gotten too used to your comforts to remember what it's like to fight?"

"Careful, my brother," Ortega said, cutting his eyes at Humberto. "You too have a mansion as grand as this one. Colonel Sanchez, pour my brother some wine. Until we hear from our friends in South Africa, we do nothing."

The people did congregate. They visited neighbors. They gathered in churches, on the squares, and in *cantinas*. Murders were reported on the radio and TV by nervous journalists. But no official word as to the terror stalking the streets.

High-ranking officials were dead or disappeared, and the Presidential Palace was quiet. Those who approached the Palace were killed or chased off by snipers. The military stayed in their barracks. And the people waited. Waited for direction. But none was given. No leader appeared to guide them out of the dark night. Ortega's coup d' état was going exactly as predicted.

Presidential Palace, August 23, 1994, 9:24 P.M.

"The phones are still dead," Diaz reported.

"That's too tight," Xavier told the medic bandaging his arm. Back to Diaz, "Tell me something I don't know."

"The television station is on the air."

"You're kidding me!" he remarked surprised.

"No. Stupid of me not to check it earlier. So I checked the radio, too. All the stations are still transmitting. Huberto is preparing the equipment in the Palace broadcast station. When we figure out what the hell is going on, we can transmit from here on our own channel. Until then, he is monitoring the events from the studio to keep us informed."

Diaz was making his report to Xavier outside the operating room. It was nearing midnight and the situation remained cloudy. The small group of guards, bureaucrats, and Palace staffers huddled nervously in the barricaded residence waiting for an attack.

"What are they reporting?"

"Chaos. The people are screaming for Chamorro. No one knows what happened here. They just know there is no news from the Palace. Assassins are roaming the streets in every major city killing anybody with a tie to Chamorro. The vice president is dead along with the rest of the cabinet. At least those they can confirm. Some are missing."

"Including the defense minister?"

"Humberto Ortega, too. Some reporters went to his mansion and were chased away by warning shots."

"What about Daniel Ortega?"

"Same as his brother. If he's in his mansion, no one knows because they can't get near it."

"How about the army net? Have you tried to get General Coasas on the radio?" Xavier asked exasperated.

"I tried it first thing. All I get is static."

"Jamming?"

"If it were being jammed then why are the radio stations able to transmit? I don't know. It's strange, I admit."

"So there might be loyal troops waiting to come to Chamorro's aid but they can't get orders?"

"Correct. Except for Humberto Ortega and a handful of officers and soldiers, most of the Sandinistas were weeded from the armed services by Coasas during the cutbacks. I can't see this as an army coup just because they're not racing to the rescue. I just don't know."

"Have you sent anybody to find out what's going on? Maybe make it to the army base outside the city?"

"I have some volunteers from the guard detail ready to go on a recon."

"What are you waiting for?"

"Your orders."

"Orders?"

"Yes, Javi. Whether you like it or not, you're in command here until Chamorro recovers or a more senior cabinet official arrives."

"That's bullshit. You're a major in the army. So be a major and make a decision."

"Our constitution is just like yours, Javi. The military takes orders from the civilian branch of the government. I'm not about to start acting any differently, especially during a crisis."

"I don't like the thought of sending men to their deaths."

"Command's a bitch, Javi," Diaz remarked, unsympathetically.

Xavier paused a moment and looked at the closed door to the surgery. Chamorro had been under the knife for over two hours. He waited anxiously for a report. They all did.

He hoped she would come to in time to take charge, but he knew it would never come to pass. Someone had to establish some form of leadership before the whole country caved in. Xavier decided to make a start until someone more qualified could be found to take his place.

"All right, Major. Give the order."

Diaz turned to an aid. "Avaristo. See to it." The sergeant saluted and left.

"That'll do for now, *gracias*," Xavier thanked the medic.

"When the doctor gets out of surgery she will need to give you stitches."

Xavier nodded, flexing his arm. It throbbed painfully.

"Have you heard from Kinlan?" Diaz asked.

"No. The bastard hasn't called back."

"How the hell did he find out about this?"

"He's still got connections, from what I understand. After Honduras, he went back to the States determined to put an end to CIA abuses. He acted as an underground watchdog reporting things to the press anonymously. It's pretty easy to get CIA agents to talk. There are a lot of disgruntled men working for the company. Anyway, I figure that's how he heard about this. Someone got fed up and gave him a call." Xavier failed to add his intuition that the man probably had connections to *Il Padrino*.

"He put his ass on the line by warning us," Diaz noted.

"I know, Alberto. That's what has me worried. I hope the opposition didn't get to him."

"And Corona? Have you heard from him?"

"No. He doesn't answer his remote."

Both men looked at each other concerned about their friend. "He's probably all right, Javi," Diaz said. The lack of conviction in Diaz's voice did nothing to comfort Xavier.

"The men are ready, Major Diaz," Sergeant Avaristo reported back.

"Then let us see them off, Minister," Diaz deferred.

They left a squad of heavily armed men at the entrance to the surgery. Another squad followed them to a window overlooking the courtyard gate. Four bodyguards stayed close to Xavier. He was, for all intents and purposes, the leader of the Nicaraguan government.

Xavier and Diaz observed the preparations below. Six men mounted a small armored fighting vehicle. Several soldiers stood by the iron gate. At a given signal, the gate swung open and the vehicle raced through. After closing the gate, the soldiers raced back to the relative safety of the Palace. Xavier watched the armored car race across the square to the city beyond.

"Come on. Come on," Xavier muttered, willing the vehicle forward. Just when he thought it would make it out of the square, a rocket flew off a rooftop and slammed into the AFV just below the turret. A second passed before the square was lit up by a bright light as the turret exploded off the body in a fountain of flame. A few feet later, the flaming wreck rolled to a stop, the turret banging to the pavement beside it.

"That does it. We're cut off," Diaz stated, turning away.

Xavier watched the funeral pyre for another minute before joining his friend.

26

Panama Canal Defense Zone, August 23, 1994, 10:11 P.M.

Cpl. James Hooker walked patrol with his Panamanian counterpart, Cpl. Miguel Gonzales. They were part of the joint canal defense forces, an integrated force of Panamanian and American troops. The area of their patrol took them to the bank above the eastern locks.

The soldiers were beginning their ascent back to the main road when Hooker held up his hand.

"Did you see a flash?" Hooker asked, pointing to some bushes down by the water.

"Dónde?"

"There, on the water."

"Sí. It looks like a boat."

The corporals unslung their rifles and approached the water cautiously. They never saw the man who killed them.

Boüldt stood over the bodies holstering his silenced pistol. "Drag the bodies behind the bushes. Make sure they're hidden well," he ordered.

"Do you think they radioed in?" his second in command asked.

"No. Lucky for us, the fools decided to investigate first. They'd still be just as dead, but our situation would be compromised."

When the bodies were concealed, Boüldt led his group of mercenaries toward the canal.

The Pentagon, Washington, D.C., August 23, 1994, 10:43 P.M.

Alan Singleton, the national security advisor, worked late into the night, as was his habit. He was sifting through a highly confidential report detailing the preparation of a South African armored brigade for a move to an unknown destination in the Western hemisphere when his military aide interrupted him.

"What's up, Captain?"

"Thought you might like to know about Nicaragua."

"Nicaragua?"

"Yes, sir. The Central American desk is monitoring what looks like a coup."

"Really? What are the indications?" he asked, setting down the South African report.

"Wide-spread assassinations, a massacre in Bluefields, isolated bloodshed for the most part. Nobody has heard from Chamorro. Either she is being held incommunicado or she has been isolated in the Presidential Palace. We're getting most of the stuff from Nicaraguan press. Their radio and TV stations are still on the air relaying the events as they happen."

"That's odd. Any well-planned coup will take out all communications as a primary objective," the NSA mumbled almost to himself. "What about the Sandinistas?"

The captain, bone-weary after an eighteen-hour day, stifled a yawn before answering. "That's another odd thing. They're conspicuously absent. No word as to whether anyone in the Sandinista leadership has been hit yet. At the same time, they haven't taken to the streets. No one knows where they stand."

"Well, you can bet it's not the PNA staging this putsch," Singleton stated, stretching. "Pezullo and his gang of fascists aren't strong enough. At least not yet. Put your money on the Sandinistas, Captain."

"Yes, sir."

"Any word from the CIA?"

"I talked with the deputy director of intelligence. He didn't have anything to add to what we're getting from our embassy and the radio and TV from inside Nicaragua."

"Well, Barton gets caught with his pants down. Again. Can't say that I mind. I think he's a self-serving asshole and a bad team player." Singleton looked at his aide. "That's not to go any further, Captain."

The captain, well aware of his superior's attitude concerning the head of the CIA, nodded his head. "Not a word, sir."

The aide, wanting to get the meeting over with so he could go home and get a few hours of sleep, brought up the last detail. "You want to wake the president?"

Singleton took off his glasses and rubbed his eyes. Nicaragua. A Third World country with no strategic value whatsoever, he thought. And coups d' état in Central and South America are nothing new. Having made up his mind, he replaced his glasses and looked at his aide.

"No, Billy. It's not a threat to our national security and the boss gets precious little sleep as it is. Just have our embassy keep trying to contact Chamorro. And get Barton's ass over here first thing in the morning. I want to know how something like this could get this far without our knowing about it. Now, go home and get some sleep."

"Thank you, sir. Good night."

Singleton gave his aide a half-wave before returning to the disturbing South African report. Now, why the hell would they be sending an armored brigade halfway around the world, he thought.

Presidential Palace, August 23, 1994, 11:08 P.M.

"Go on television and radio and let the people know what is happening, Xavier," Diaz suggested.

"You've got to be out of your mind, Diaz," Xavier replied. "The last thing the people need to know is Chamorro's condition and that the country is leaderless."

"You're forgetting yourself, Xavier."

"You're forgetting that I'm not a citizen of Nicaragua. Besides, if the power behind the assassinations gets wind of the fact that Chamorro is still alive, they might move in to finish the job. And what have we got to stop them?"

"A reinforced company. Adding the palace staff, about two hundred people."

"So, you're going to throw maids and overaged clerks into the breach?"

"If necessary, yes. At least I know they'll fight. Question is, will you fight, Xavier? Will you take the final step and join us?"

"You mean will I sign that stupid piece of paper?" Xavier asked, annoyed.

"Yes, Xavier. Will you become a fellow citizen?"

Before Xavier could reply, his remote phone rang. He answered it immediately. "Yes."

"It's Kinlan."

"Where have you been?"

"Never mind that. Did you get to the president in time?"

"Barely. She's just gotten out of surgery. I'm waiting for word on her condition as we speak."

"Who was the assassin?"

"The daughter of one of Chamorro's lifelong friends. The president helped raise the child. We would have never guessed. Can you tell me who is behind this?"

"It's the Sandinistas, Xavier. But they have backing from outside the country."

"The Russians?"

"I don't know. I do know that the Sandinistas are waiting for some event to distract the United States long enough for them to make their final play for power."

"That doesn't make any sense. The door's wide open. We wouldn't stand a chance against an organized assault."

"There are bigger things at stake. That's all I know. If I knew more, I'd tell you. Believe me."

"Can you find out what they're waiting for?" Xavier asked, hopefully. "That might tell us how much time we have. Give us a chance to prepare."

"No can do, Xavier. My informant was killed at our last meet. I barely escaped. That's what took me so long to get back to you."

"I appreciate your efforts, Mark. What else can you do?"

"Nothing. I'm out. Sorry. But if I don't disappear quickly, I'm a dead man. They are on to me."

"Who's on to you?"

"I have the feeling it's the same organization that has been trying to destroy you, Xavier. Nameless, faceless, omnipotent. And scary as hell. Got to go, Xavier. Good luck to you."

"And you too, Mark," he offered. "One more thing. Tell my godfather I said hello."

Silence from the other end. Finally, "I will, Xavier," and the line went dead.

Xavier returned the phone to his pocket. "Well, at least we know who the enemy is. That's a start," he said to Diaz.

"She'll live, I think," Elena spoke from the doorway. Diaz and Xavier turned to see her smiling faintly in blood-spattered scrubs. Xavier walked to his wife and hugged her gently.

"Thank you, Elena," Diaz said. "All of Nicaragua will thank you."

Elena nodded in his direction acknowledging his gratitude. "I had a lot of help, Alberto. But thanks just the same."

"How soon will she be able to talk to the country?" Xavier asked.

"We will settle that now. Alberto. Get *Señor* Garcia and Huberto and have them join us in the surgery. Xavier, follow me," she said taking his hand, leading him into the surgery. "*Doña* Violeta wants to talk with you. But, we must finish this quickly because she is very weak."

Xavier approached the bed where Chamorro lay. Her color was ashen and her breathing shallow. She appeared so tiny and frail, like a small child instead of a grown adult. He took her hand and patted it slightly. Her eyes fluttered open and she smiled weakly.

"Xavier. We don't have much time," she spoke in a hushed voice. Xavier bent closer to hear better. "You must lead the people. You are the only one left," she gasped. Chamorro closed her eyes and tried to catch her breath.

"Is this necessary?" he asked his wife, concerned.

"Yes," she answered simply. "She won't rest until this is resolved."

"*Doña* Violeta. What is it that you wish me to do?"

"Succeed me, as the president."

"But—" he started to argue but she lifted her hand and touched his lips.

"It is the only way. The people need a leader. They trust you." Her hand dropped to the bed. She was too weak to continue talking but her eyes pleaded with him.

"There must be somebody else," he despaired. Chamorro, unable to speak, shook her head from side to side. No. Xavier looked to his wife for help.

"Elena, I can't do this. I'm not capable."

"Of course you are, Xavier. Do you love this country?"

"Of course I do. I'd lay down my life for these people. But I'm no politician. I'd just fuck things up."

"We don't need a politician. We need a leader," Elena stated.

Xavier looked at Diaz. "Get us through this and we'll find another bureaucrat to take your place when we're safe."

Xavier looked back at Chamorro. "Are you sure this is the best way I can serve you, *Doña* Violeta?"

"*Sí,* Javi," she whispered. "It is the best way you can serve Nicaragua."

"Then I will serve what I love, *mi Presidente*."

"*Gracias,* Javi," she said as she closed her eyes.

Xavier looked at his wife. "Okay, now that I'm going to do this, I'd like to know how many laws I'm breaking."

Someone coughed politely behind Xavier. He turned to see a small, balding man in spectacles.

"Minister Daniels, I assure you it is quite legal."

"Who are you?"

"This is *Señor* Vasquez of the Interior Ministry. He has the appropriate documents for you to sign," Elena said, making the introduction.

The bureaucrat stepped forward and opened a folder containing a sheaf of papers. The documents were stamped with the Nicaraguan Presidential seal. Adjusting his glasses, he referred to the folder.

"Our Congress enacted the law of succession in 1992," Vasquez explained. "If, for any reason, the president is incapacitated and unable to continue in office, she may pass the power of her office to the vice president. When the president regains full health, she may again resume her office after passing a physical. If at the end of thirty days she is unable to resume office, the vice president officially assumes the mantle. This law is similar to the one in your country. But there are differences.

"If the vice president is unable to assume the office, then the president may name her successor as long as that successor is of ministerial rank. Open elections are then scheduled for one month following the taking of the oath. This safeguards against anyone naming himself or herself president and declaring a state of emergency during which elections are suspended. The constitution guarantees elections. Granted these are just words, but anyone assuming power any other way will be defying the constitution and his fellow Nicaraguans."

"So if we survive, open elections will take the responsibility off my shoulders?" Xavier inquired.

"Correct, Minister. Assuming you do not wish to run for office yourself."

"I do not and will not," he said and turned back to Chamorro. He grasped her hand in both of his. "Are you sure this is what you want, *Doña* Violeta?"

"We all know where your loyalty lies," she replied. "It is now time for you to acknowledge it."

Xavier thought for a moment. Evil men were tearing Nicaragua to pieces. By taking the oath, he would have a chance to protect the country he loved and defeat its enemies.

"*Sí*, Javi," she whispered. "It is the only way."

"Then may God protect us," he said, patting her hand. She smiled back at him and closed her eyes.

"All right, *Señor* Vasquez. Let's get on with it."

Huberto came into the room followed by a cameraman. "When do you want him to start shooting?" he asked.

"Immediately," Diaz ordered. The cameraman turned on his light and began filming.

Vasquez held out the first document. "Please sign this to make your citizenship official." Xavier fumbled for a pen until one was produced by the efficient functionary.

As the proceedings continued, Vasquez knew what Walter Wagner must have felt like inside the Fürherbunker during the final days of the Third Reich. Wagner, a minor functionary in the Berlin bureaucracy had been brought to the Reichschancellery to marry Eva Braun to Adolf Hitler. With the Russians a few hundred yards from the entrance to the bunker and death around the corner, Wagner was amazed that his leader even bothered with such formalities.

As Vasquez administered the oath of office, he realized it was a waste of time. In a few hours they would all be dead and a new dictator would be in power. The constitution and the law be damned. Vasquez did not voice his opinions. He was, after all, a bureaucrat who was doing his job. At least, that part he understood.

The succession document was signed by Xavier, Elena, Chamorro, and Diaz before it was handed to Vasquez. He bent over and affixed his signature to the paper. He handed the document back to Xavier. It was now official. For what it was worth, Xavier Daniels was the President of Nicaragua. He took the oath from *Señor* Vasquez and paused.

No one congratulated him. They stood in silence waiting for the new president to issue his first order.

"Any suggestions?" Xavier asked. "It's not like I've done this before."

The assembled group laughed, breaking the tension.

"I guess it's time to make the announcement. At least while the radio and TV stations are still functioning," Diaz suggested.

"And what the hell do I say?"

"Tell them that the situation is under control and that all armed forces commanders should report to you at the Palace. Chamorro is ill, and that is why you have succeeded her."

"They won't buy it, Alberto. If I have the country stabilized, then why do I need to see the army commanders? Why did Chamorro suddenly fall ill at this time while the rest of her constituents are being ruthlessly hunted down and killed? I would look like a provocateur. The people are smarter than you think. They will know a lie if I tell it and I love this country and the people too much to do that. No, if I am to gain their trust then I must tell them the truth."

"You are taking a very great risk, *Señor Presidente*," Diaz warned his friend. "The Sandinistas will know their job isn't done and how weak we really are. They will come to finish the job. You had the same thought earlier."

"Not if we act first and with integrity."

"What do you mean?" Diaz asked.

"I hope we will live to see. Now, let's get to the studio and see if Huberto has things ready."

Fewer than three hundred people knew who was the real president of Nicaragua. That was about to change.

Rigoberto López sat in the basement of the Ortega mansion drinking beer and watching television. He scanned the monitors for additional news of the Sandinista uprising. Three radios played softly in the background, the programming alternating between news reports and music.

Rigoberto yawned and stretched his arms. He had been at his post since early in the morning. The heady excitement with which the day had begun had dwindled into monotony. The same reports over and over. He hadn't had any new developments to take to his superiors in over an hour. He yawned again and had another drink of beer. Slowly his eyelids closed and his head fell to his chest.

The test pattern on the TV dedicated to the emergency station abruptly disappeared. In its place a tired-looking man with a bandaged arm and bruised forehead adjusted his microphone and began to speak. Rigoberto was snoring minutes later when Humberto Ortega ran into the room. The man never heard the pistol shot that killed him.

Manuel Vilchez, a technician for Channel 3 in Managua, was not sleeping when the image popped onto his screen. He hit the record button on his VCR and ran screaming to the news editor.

Xavier cleared his throat and waited for the signal from Huberto. Sweat greased his palms and rode down his forehead more from his anxiety than the hot lights. Behind the cameras, his wife smiled at him reassuringly. He smiled, but somehow her presence increased his anxiety level.

Xavier didn't consider himself a great speaker, but he knew that his next words could decide the fate of Nicaragua. He rubbed his palms on his pants legs and cleared his throat again.

"We've got the feed, *Señor Presidente*," an unfamiliar voice cried out. "Three, two, one...you are on the air."

Xavier cleared his voice again and began to speak.

"My fellow Nicaraguans," the man on the TV said. "I am here, reluctantly, to inform you of the events that have transpired here at the Presidential Palace in the last few hours."

"Who is it?" the technician asked.

Freddy Calero, news editor for the Nicaraguan national affiliate, searched his memory to put a name to the face. Finally it came to him. "Xavier Daniels."

"The hero of Bilwaskarma?"

"Yes. And a minister in Chamorro's cabinet." People were crowding around the monitor to get a look. "Give me some room and quiet down, damnit!" Calero barked. The crowd immediately went still.

"You did remember to record this?" Calero asked, hoping the question was as stupid as it sounded.

"Yes, sir."

"Good. Lidia, pull the file on Daniels," he ordered. She hesitated, not wanting to miss the momentous occasion. "Now, Goddamnit!"

"...As of 12:03 this morning, I assumed the office of the presidency in accordance with the Act of Succession agreed upon by the Nicaraguan Congress..."

Before anyone could react to the incredible news, Calero began issuing orders. "Damaso, get on the phone to the other stations and see if they are recording this thing. Agree upon a time to air the speech simultaneously. Cisneros, contact the Managuan army base and get their reaction to their new commander-in-chief. Meléndez, you and Lidia work up the first story on Daniels."

"How do we play it, Chief? Is he legitimate or not?"

Calero watched the man on the monitor. He was sweating and nervous. At the same time he came across honest and humble. Calero knew appearances could be deceiving and most often were, especially in the political world.

He had learned that lesson the hard way when he began his journalism career as a stringer for *La Prensa* in the early seventies. The lesson continued to serve him when he moved to television in the eighties. And now it was the nineties, and Calero, practicing what he learned, questioned the validity of the new president. But something told him this man's appearance matched his character. Calero hoped he was right. He was about to stake his career and his life on his hunch.

"We play this one legitimate all the way. This guy is a hero. He fought for our country, spent his fortune bettering it, and now it appears he is our new president. We back him to the hilt," Calero declared.

Meléndez hurried off. Calero watched the finish of the speech.

"All right, Vilchez. Make a bunch of copies. Keep one here and send runners out to hide the rest. Clean up these two and get them ready to go with Meléndez' story." He turned to the television studio and shouted, "Hurry it up, damnit. As soon as the Sandinistas get wind of this, they'll try to shut us down. This story goes out as soon as I hear from Damaso. The fate of our country could rest on what you do in the next few minutes."

Pressure applied, Calero went to his office and got his revolver out of the drawer. His gut told him he was on the hit list. He could not guess why he was still alive, but Calero did know that when they came he would be ready.

Not many people saw the original live broadcast that began just after midnight. The majority of the country was tuned into the live reports coming from the radio and TV and not the test pattern on the emergency station. Those who saw it would never forget it.

At 12:25 A.M., August 24, 1994, the three national networks interrupted their programming and broadcast Xavier's speech. At 12:27 A.M., the radio stations followed suit. The speech ran continuously for three hours on the emergency station for those who missed the early reports. But it did not take that long for a reaction.

The hero who rescued our men from Honduras.

The man who built the school in our village.

The person responsible for the new harvesting combine in the fields.

The saint who gave us a new sewage system so our children would not get sick from the water.

He took a bullet meant for *Doña* Violeta.

His wife saved her life.

This man needs our help, our blood, our lives.

People took to the streets across the country. In Matagalpa, the Sandinista headquarters were burned to the ground. In Chinandega, the local Sandinista party boss was lynched by a crowd of several thousand. In Managua, ten thousand people took to the streets in the early morning and marched to the Palace. They were joined by local police units. A brutal firefight followed and dozens were killed and hundreds wounded as the well-armed Sandinista gunmen, reinforced by armored cars and a few tanks, outfought the police and prevented the citizens from getting to the Palace. But still they came, bearing torches and banners.

Similar incidents took place outside the national headquarters of the Sandinista Party and the Ortega mansion. No ground was gained. The people, save for a few police, were without weapons, but new leaders emerged and new assaults were tried. Stones and Molotov cocktails against assault rifles and grenades. The streets of Managua ran red with blood as the citizens paid with their lives to keep their freedom.

The counter coup had begun.

27

Ortega Mansion, Managa, Nicaragua, August 24, 1994, 1:38 A.M.

"I told you, Daniel," Humberto yelled. "Now it is too late."

"It is not too late, brother," Daniel Ortega responded. His casual demeanor was gone, replaced with a nervous nonchalance as he tried to stay calm. "Our troops are still intact waiting for our signal. They are numerous enough to overwhelm any mob. No matter how large."

"So we are to start our salvation of Nicaragua by killing thousands of her defenseless population?"

Gunfire erupted outside the compound and was returned with ferocity. "Does it sound like they are unarmed, Humberto?" Daniel yelled, pointing his finger in the direction of the battle. "They resist. And anyone who resists is not a true member of the revolution. We would have to deal with them sooner or later. If they want it sooner, then they shall get what they want."

"So is that how you will justify this slaughter?" Humberto asked, not believing what he was hearing.

"If they attack us, Humberto, it will be self-defense. We will make Daniels out to be a liar. He was the one behind the killings. The Sandinistas responded to defend the people. This could be a blessing in disguise. The truth is what we make it, Humberto. Or had you forgot?"

"I do not forget anything. But have you forgotten the army? How do you know they will not react like the people?" Humberto reminded his brother.

"The colonel in command is worshiped by his men. If he will not lead them to the Palace, then they won't leave the barracks," Ortega said, sure of himself. "You know him. He is one of our most reliable supporters."

"A supporter who has a price. Chief of the general staff. I do not trust such men."

"You approved of him. It's a little late to be rethinking your decision now," Daniel Ortega stated the obvious.

"I know this. The longer we wait, the more blood will be spilled. So I say again, go now, Daniel. Go while we still have a little time. The men at the Palace cannot hold out forever."

"We cannot go before the canal is destroyed. If the South Africans fail and we are out in the open, the United States, with nothing to distract them, will concentrate on keeping Chamorro and her lackeys in power. That would mean our destruction. It is not too much longer to wait, Humberto. Please have patience."

An explosion shook the building, causing Daniel to jump out of his chair. Fire rained down into the courtyard and debris pelted the windows. Sanchez ran into the room with a wild look in his eyes.

"What happened?" Humberto demanded.

"Some maniac tried to ram the wall with a fuel truck," he panted. "One of our soldiers destroyed it with an RPG just before it hit. Several of our men were burnt badly."

"I have a feeling we will soon be returning to the jungle," Humberto muttered disgustedly. His brother gave him a hard look, but said nothing.

Barracks, 21st Mechanized Infantry Regiment, Managua, August 24, 1994, 1:38 A.M.

"Who will go with me? Who will go to the president's rescue?"

The question was asked by Lt. Colonel Jaime Malianos, executive officer of the Nicaraguan 21st Mechanized Infantry Regiment. He had called a clandestine meeting in the officers' *cantina* to pose the question to selected officers and NCOs of the 21st. The meeting was being held in secret because their commanding officer, Colonel Fernando Pedroza y Villa, had closed the base, confined the enlisted men to barracks, and forbidden any discussion of a rescue operation until he could discover the validity of the man proclaiming himself to be the new president. So far, Maliaños hadn't convinced anyone to disobey Pedroza's orders.

"I will follow Colonel Pedroza to hell and back," a young captain from the recon company stated. "And until he orders me to go to the Palace, I will stay here."

Others murmured their approval. "All we have is rumors and a few scattered reports from the radio," the captain continued. "Most of us haven't heard the speech, but the colonel has, and if he's not convinced, then neither am I."

"But I did hear the speech," Maliaños explained. "The man was passionate and honest and humble. He is a true Nicaraguan."

"More likely a charlatan," the captain retorted. "At least that is what the colonel thinks. He told me so."

"If he's a charlatan, then I'll take him as my president any day," a large master-sergeant rumbled, breaking into the debate. "His money bought the clinic that stands in my village. His engineers built it. And his wife trained the staff that saved my child's life. A man like that cares more about this country than all the politicians in the capital."

"That may be true. But until we can prove his claim valid, then we wait for orders just like everyone else."

"Maybe this will help," a lieutenant. said entering the cantina. He waved a VCR tape in the air. "I taped this at my mother's house. Watch it and then make up your minds."

The room remained silent as the lieutenant put the tape in the VCR behind the bar. The TV flickered into life and the lieutenant turned the lights off. Xavier's image came into focus.

"My fellow Nicaraguans. I am here, reluctantly, to inform you of the events that have transpired here at the Presidential Palace in the last few hours. This evening, at approximately fifteen minutes past the hour of nine o'clock, an assassin tried to murder our president, Violeta Barrios de Chamorro. The president suffered a single bullet wound to the chest. My wife, Dr.

Elena Daniels, saved the president's life after two hours of heroic surgery. Her condition is still grave.

"When the president came out of the anesthetic, she requested a conference with me, Dr. Daniels, Major Alberto Diaz, her head of security, and *Señor* Miguel Vasquez, an attorney, formerly a circuit judge in Matagalpa presently serving in the Interior Ministry. She then invoked the Act of Succession. As of 12:03 this morning, I assumed the office of the presidency in accordance with the Act of Succession ratified by the Congress of Nicaragua.

"My first act upon gaining the presidency is to inform my fellow citizens immediately of what has happened and to let you know exactly what our position is. The Palace telephones are not operational. The army radio is either being jammed or ignored. I ordered some volunteers from the presidential guard to try to contact our army base outside Managua. Shortly after they left the Palace grounds in an armored car, they were fired upon and the vehicle was destroyed. Six men died in the attempt. I can only assume that we are cut off.

"What I know, you know. Priests, military officers, government officials, people from the press, and other prominent citizens have been systematically murdered. Hundreds of innocents, including many children, have been killed in the shootings and bombings. These events have two common threads that I can see. The first is that no Sandinista officials have been killed. The second, all people killed have either been strong supporters of Chamorro's administration, extreme critics of the Sandinista regime, or both. They are the enemy. The Sandinistas. They want our country. Will we let them have it without a fight? That remains to be seen.

"As to my qualifications for this job, I have none. I did not ask for this job, nor do I want it. I have never been a politician nor do I plan on becoming one. The future of this country is better left to people more qualified than I. Unfortunately, Chamorro will not be able to resume her office for several weeks. And, until then, you are stuck with me. With your patience and support, we will muddle through.

"I will carry out my term for one reason. Chamorro asked me to make a sacrifice for my country. I have done so, willingly.

Now I must ask you to make a sacrifice as well. The price could mean your life.

"Take to the streets. Man the barricades. Raise the banners of democracy and keep our Nicaragua free. Any armed forces personnel, regardless of rank, report to the highest local civilian authority to render assistance. For any citizen in Managua who can hear my voice, come to the Palace and surround *Doña* Violeta with a human shield. Protect the leader of your country as she has fought to protect you in the past. Hurry, before it is too late! The enemy is at the gate. We expect an assault at any time. I do not know how long we can keep him at bay. But we will all die to protect *Doña* Violeta and our constitution. I can assure you of that.

"Many of you may die before the new day dawns. Know that we here inside the Palace are ready to lay down our lives alongside yours to keep Nicaragua free. God Bless You and God Bless Nicaragua!"

Xavier disappeared from the screen followed by the tape of the ceremony of succession. Several soldiers came to their feet in anger at the sight of the wounded former head of state. Before the anger could be expressed in words, the lights came on and a voice bellowed, "What the hell is going on here?"

The men jumped to attention at the sound of Colonel Pedroza's voice. "I confined the enlisted men to barracks and forbade any discussion of this travesty. Both those orders have been blatantly defied. Who is responsible for this?"

After a second of hesitation, Lt. Colonel Malianos stepped forward. "I called the meeting, Colonel. These men are here on my orders."

"Well, Malianos. Willing to take the fall for them all? Very well. Captain," he said, turning to the recon commander. "Arrest Lt. Colonel Malianos and charge him with gross insubordination."

The captain did not move. He stood at rigid attention, eyes straight ahead. The colonel's eyes became flinty at the show of disrespect. He scanned the room and found the supply major. "Major. Take these two officers and place them under arrest. Immediately!"

"But Colonel, the tape—"

"To hell with the goddamn tape. I gave you a direct order. Now move it."

"I'm sorry, Colonel," intoned the major. He came to rigid attention and stared straight ahead. Maliaños walked to the colonel, whose face was red with rage.

"It seems we have arrived at an impasse, Colonel Pedroza. You saw the tape. It looked legitimate to me. I am an army officer. My president has ordered me to report to him. Now either stand out of my way, or I will move you, sir."

Pedroza pulled out his pistol and stuck the automatic in Maliaños face. "You mutinous bastard. I'll have you shot. I'll have you all shot. Stay here and you are safe under my protection. Leave here and you will be throwing away your careers and maybe your lives. Think before you act. Think about what you are doing. Not only to yourselves but your families."

"Who will follow me?" Maliaños asked, staring at Pedroza.

The men wavered, faced with a Catch 22.

"I will follow you."

The soldiers turned to see a figure holding a rifle standing in the doorway. His clothes were shredded and covered with dark stains. Blood crusted his arms and his face. But his eyes were steady holding the room in his gaze.

"I am Alex Corona. I followed Xavier Daniels into Honduras and I will follow Lt. Colonel Maliaños to his aid," he said, lowering his sniper rifle. The barrel pointed straight at Pedroza's belly. "And I will kill any man who stands in our way."

"And *who* the fuck are you to be threatening *me*?" Pedroza yelled, refusing to be intimidated.

"A freedom fighter, Colonel. But the question should be 'who the fuck are you?' I see you in the uniform of the Nicaraguan army, but I have a feeling under your fingernails we'll find Sandinista dirt. Colonel Maliaños, in his quarters I think you'll find a hidden transmitter that he has been using to communicate with the Sandinistas."

"Major," Maliaños said to the supply officer. "Place the colonel under arrest and search his quarters."

The major motioned to two sergeants who grabbed the colonel.

"There is no transmitter, asshole!" Pedroza boomed. "And when they don't find one, I'll be back for you myself."

The major led Pedroza out of the *cantina*.

"What if they don't find a radio?" Maliaños asked. "You know you're a dead man."

"Oh, they'll find one all right," Corona assured him.

"How can you be so sure?"

"I planted it myself," Corona said with a sly smile.

Maliaños nodded his head, "I understand. But I wouldn't be too liberal with that information if I were you."

"What information, Colonel?"

"Exactly," Maliaños agreed. "Sergeant. Call the men out and get the vehicles warmed up. We leave in fifteen minutes. Captain, you are our eyes and ears. I don't want any surprises before we get to Managua."

"Yes, sir!" the recon commander responded.

"Well, let's hope we're in time, Corona."

"Yes. I hate to be late for a party."

Maliaños shook his head. He did not understand American humor.

A single shot rang out. "I guess they found the radio," Maliaños sighed.

"Pity," Corona said without remorse. The two men left the *cantina* for the journey to the Palace.

Ortega Mansion, August 24, 1994, 3:26 A.M.

"Our men are engaging the 21st as we speak, brother."

"You told me Pedroza would hold them at the barracks," Daniel Ortega answered. For the first time his voice betrayed a hint of fear.

"So now it is I who said we could trust Pedroza." Humberto shook his head in disgust at his brother's weakness. "Regardless of the blame, they are on the move. The recon company is fully engaged with my men. More soldiers are bringing up the rear. We can't possibly hold them all!"

"We must, Humberto!" Daniel said, pounding on the table. "Your men must hold until we hear from the South Africans."

"Daniel. You are a politician. I am a soldier," Humberto said, lowering his voice. He changed tactics and tried to reason with his brother. "Listen to me. My men are courageous and well trained. But they are simply outnumbered. In the end, they will be crushed. The police are arming the populace. We are facing annihilation. Release our troops now while we still have a chance."

"I cannot do that," Daniel said timidly.

"Then we are through," Humberto said, surrendering to the inevitable. "Sanchez, prepare to evacuate the grounds. We will use the tunnel to escape."

"Yes, General Ortega."

"Daniel. Your South Africans have one hour," Humberto dictated. "If we haven't heard from them or been overrun by then, we are leaving here. Do you understand?"

"They will contact us," Daniel replied weakly. "You will see."

Humberto ignored his brother and left to save what he could.

Panama Canal, August 24, 1994, 4:58 A.M.

The sky glowed red as thousands of fires raged out of control on the eastern coast of Panama. Radioactive ash began to fall on the sea above the South African submarine. The boat glided silently underwater, the crew unaware of the hell raining down above them.

Kruger stood in the control room smoking a cigarette. He toweled his face and waited for the submarine commander to finish a conference with his executive officer. When he was done, he approached the mercenary.

"Congratulations on your mission, Kruger."

Kruger merely nodded his head.

"Sonar reports no contacts of any possible threat in the vicinity. Should we raise the satellite antenna and report to Managua?"

Kruger thought for a moment and glanced at his watch. "Negative. We will continue on the present heading for forty-five minutes. I don't want to take any chances. By then they probably will have heard anyway."

Kruger left the control room without another word.

Presidential Palace, August 24, 1994, 5:01 A.M.

Xavier stood at a window and listened to the sounds of battle across the Plaza. Tracers stitched patterns across the night sky. Flares illuminated buildings briefly before dying out. Concussions, reverberating like thunder, rattled window panes. Xavier was reminded of the first time he celebrated *la Griteria*. But this was not a holy day. People were dying a few hundred yards away.

"*Con permiso, Señor Presidente.*"

"Yes, Alberto. What is it?"

"It appears the Sandinistas are massing across the Plaza for an attack."

Xavier turned to his friend. Diaz was dressed in full combat gear. He held two AK-47s. The man was all business.

"I take it one of those is for me?"

"*Sí, Señor Presidente.* You must be able to protect yourself."

"Very well, then," Xavier relented, taking the rifle.

"Is there no way to get my wife and *Doña* Violeta to safety?"

"*Lo siento*, Javier," Diaz apologized. "I'm sorry. There is no way."

Xavier yanked the charging bolt on his weapon. "Then we'll make the bastards pay."

Diaz smiled. "That we will, *Señor Presidente*. That we will."

Xavier took a position with his bodyguards on the bottom floor in the foyer. Diaz was not too far away to his left. Mingled in with the Presidential Guard were servants, secretaries, and other civilians. Each one had a weapon and appeared ready to use it. The *campesinos* were nervous but determined.

I haven't even had a chance to say goodbye to my wife, he thought. God bless you, Elena, and keep you safe.

With this simple prayer, Xavier turned to his bodyguards.

"When they break into the Palace, you are to make your way to the surgery. Defend *Doña* Violeta to the last."

"But sir…" one man began to protest.

"No buts. Just do as I say," Xavier ordered. "Understood?"

"*Sí, jefe.*"

"Here they come!" Diaz shouted. Flares popped overhead illuminating the Plaza in a green glow. Men raced into the open and began shooting at the Palace.

"Hold your fire!" Diaz ordered.

The men reached the wrought iron fence and blew holes in the barricade with C-4 and anti-tank grenades. Sandinista gunners fired anti-tank rockets at the large, ornamental Palace doors, blasting them off their hinges. A brief pause, then Xavier heard a whistle signaling the Sandinista attack and stood up. "*Viva Nicaragua!*" he shouted, and emptied a full magazine into the men pouring through the gaps in the fence. Others picked up the battle cry and began shooting.

Then everyone was firing. The first waves were mowed down in sheets of fire as the defenders unleashed their weapons. The Sandinistas returned fire from behind the fence and defenders started collapsing.

"Vehicles coming up behind!" Diaz yelled, trying to be heard above the roar of the battle.

A few trucks, packed with soldiers and peasants, appeared in the square and sped across the Plaza, guns blazing. But the fire wasn't directed at the Palace. Instead, the rifles and machine guns fired into the Sandinistas taking cover behind the fence. The men were caught in the open and gunned down. The slaughter was over quickly.

A huge harvesting tractor crashed through the gate followed by more soldiers and citizens, peasants, shop clerks, and a few women. The tractor drove up the steps of the Palace, a platoon of heavily armed men immediately behind. Xavier ran to the door and stepped through the blasted frame. A door on the tractor popped open and a familiar face appeared.

"Hello, boss."

Xavier smiled from ear to ear. "Hello, Corona. What kept you?"

"Had a little get-together at your place. Unfortunately, some uninvited guests showed up. Took a while to teach them a lesson."

Corona climbed down from the car stiffly. Xavier scrambled to help him. "You okay?" he asked, offering him a hand.

"Nothing that a little R & R wouldn't cure," Corona grimaced. "Oh, by the way, congratulations. Do I need to bow, or what?" Corona leaned a little too heavily on Xavier's arm.

"Take him to the aid station," he ordered his bodyguards. "And tell the doctor I am all right."

They carried Corona off as another tractor drove through the gate. A captain jumped out of the cab and ran up to Xavier.

"Captain Sevilla, commander of the recon company, 21st mech infantry. Reporting as ordered, *Señor Presidente*," Sevilla declared, saluting.

"Thank you for coming, Captain Sevilla," Xavier said, shaking his hand. "Where's your armor?"

"Had to leave it on the outskirts, *Señor Presidente*. The Sandinistas have the corridors leading to the Palace covered by tanks and anti-tank weapons. I brought some men through on foot to reinforce you. These civilians volunteered to bring us across," he said, motioning to the people helping the soldiers reinforce the barricade surrounding the Palace. "I expect more to join us as soon as they can fight their way across."

"And where's Colonel Pedroza?" Diaz asked, coming up behind Xavier.

"He was executed for conspiring with the Sandinistas, Major Diaz," Captain Sevilla said, a sinister smile on his lips.

"I see, Captain. Never would have guessed myself. Oh, well... looks like the 21st will need a new commander, *Señor Presidente*."

"Can I do that?" Xavier asked.

"You are the commander-in-chief of the armed forces of Nicaragua," Diaz offered by way of explanation. "Is Maliaños still the executive officer of the 21st?" Diaz asked the captain.

"*Sí*, Major," Sevilla replied. "He is two miles off organizing attacks on the Sandinistas as well as organizing the civilian support. You should see them. Thousands of Nicaraguans have flocked to your banner, *Señor Presidente*. They are all willing to give their lives to keep Nicaragua free. Your speech has galvanized the whole country."

Xavier smiled, but Diaz ignored the tribute. "Is there any way to get ahold of this Colonel Maliaños, Captain?" he asked. "The president needs to talk to him."

"*Sí*, Major. On the radio net. Sergeant Robelo!" Sevilla turned, shouting. "Get the lieutenant colonel on the radio and tell him *El Presidente* wants to speak to him," Sevilla ordered.

A moment later, Xavier was speaking with the lieutenant colonel. "Lt. Colonel Malianos," he began. "I am promoting you to Colonel Malianos and giving you command of the 21st."

"*Gracias, Señor Presidente*," he said, respectfully.

"That done, Colonel, can you give me an update?"

"*Sí, Señor Presidente*. We are forming up for an all out attack to relieve you. I know you are in a desperate situation, but the Sandinistas have armor and I must plan this attack carefully. I am confident we can destroy them if you will allow me time to coordinate a proper attack. For that, I need all the available trained troops that I have at my disposal. I'm sorry. I wish I could send more units to help you, but that would weaken my attack and we only have one shot."

"Why only one shot, Colonel?" Xavier inquired.

"If I waited for the rest of the army to arrive, it would be too late. If I attack too soon, the effort could end in disaster."

Xavier turned to Diaz. "He speaks the truth, *Presidente*," Diaz agreed. "We must hold until he can relieve us."

Xavier nodded and spoke into the radio. "Understood, Colonel. Is there anything, anything at all, you can do for us?"

"I think so, *Señor Presidente*. The civilian support is overwhelming. I am arming several detachments of militiamen. They'll be joining you as they break through or find holes in the Sandinista lines. They will help plug the gaps in your defenses."

Xavier felt suddenly squeamish. His pride in the response to his call to arms could end up causing thousands of civilian deaths. "Are you sure about sending in an untrained militia, Colonel? They could be slaughtered."

"I couldn't stop them if I wanted to, *Señor Presidente*," Malianos answered. "They were going to fight with pitchforks, Molotov cocktails, and axes. At least by arming them and placing them under the command of a few officers and NCOs they might stand a chance." Explosions sounded across the Plaza. "Don't worry, *Señor Presidente*. We'll see you soon. Malianos out."

Xavier handed the radio back to the sergeant. "I thought it was over," Xavier said, pointing to the carnage at the fence.

"We're not out of the woods yet, *Señor Presidente*," Sevilla spoke. "The Sandinistas have been beaten back. But they are numerous and well armed. We can expect another attack at any time."

"I agree, *Señor Presidente*," Diaz concurred. "Let's get you inside now where you will be safer."

Sevilla ordered a dozen of his men to form a ring around the president and the group ascended the steps to the Palace. They met Huberto at the entrance way. He was staring open-mouthed across the Plaza.

"What are you looking at, Huberto?" Xavier inquired.

"See for yourself, Xavier," he replied, pointing.

Xavier turned and gazed upon the sight of hundreds of people advancing on the Presidential Palace in small groups. They came from all walks of life armed for a fight to the death. They bore rifles, farm tools, and torches. Upon reaching the fence, Diaz and Sevilla assigned the small groups to NCOs who immediately put them to work.

The citizens began to reinforce the fence with furniture from the Palace and bricks torn up from the Plaza. Others busied themselves making Molotov cocktails in any container that could be found, including empty *refresco* bags. Diaz sent still another group twenty meters beyond the fence line where they began to dig up the square and form an outer defense barricade of bricks, dirt, and stone. The Nicaraguans worked fast, encouraging each other to work harder.

The most amazing thing was the children. Incredibly, dozens of boys and girls had made the dangerous trek to the Palace. They raised banners on the Palace walls and propped bodies of dead Sandinsitas against the fence as a warning to those who would dare to attack. Xavier was struck dumb by the patriotism he was witnessing.

Elena joined them on the steps and took her husband's hand. "I have asked some of the women to help get an aid station ready. They're tearing sheets to make bandages and boiling water. It's incredible."

More explosions echoed across the Plaza as another round of tracers tore up the night sky. Huberto winced at the sounds of battle echoing across the square.

"Don't worry, Huberto. With the kind of courage I see here, we will most surely survive."

Xavier's theory was about to be tested to the limit.

"Colonel Maliaños, the armor has been withdrawn," an exuberant lieutenant reported.

Maliaños grimaced at the news surprising the officer who thought the colonel would be pleased. "Get me the Palace on the radio now!" Maliaños snapped.

"I have Major Diaz, Colonel," the communications officer announced. Maliaños snatched the mike from his hand.

"Diaz, I regret to inform you that the Sandinistas have withdrawn their armor from our front. You understand the consequences?"

"What's so bad about that?" Xavier asked, listening in.

Diaz looked at the president, but paused before answering. "It means that they are going to throw the armor against us in a last-ditch effort to capture the Palace. And we don't have a damn thing to stop them with." Diaz lifted the radio and spoke, "Understood, Colonel. Make the best time you can. Diaz out."

"What about anti-tank rockets, Diaz?" Xavier asked, concerned.

"Our cache was sabotaged. We have a few from Sevilla's detachment. But after those are gone..." Diaz held his arms out in the air, "...nothing. We can't stop armor."

A shell slammed into the Palace, followed quickly by three more. Plaster and masonry showered the defenders.

"Here they come!" Diaz shouted, exiting the Palace and racing to the fence. Xavier tried to run after him but was tackled by two soldiers.

"*Lo siento, Señor Presidente*, but we have our orders."

They hustled Xavier to the second floor and placed him behind a sandbagged emplacement. At least Xavier could see the battle as it developed.

The powerful armor appeared, crossing the Plaza in the light of flares thrown up by the Palace defenders. The tanks fired as they came, blasting the Palace grounds into rubble. The armor, several T-72 tanks and armored cars, was followed by heavily armed infantry protected for the most part by the steel of the fighting vehicles. The defenders returned fire with their small arms, but with little effect.

The Sandinistas rolled over the outer wall with little trouble. The defenders, those lucky enough not to be killed at their posts, spilled behind the Palace fence. Sevilla's men answered the loss of the outer perimeter with a volley of light anti-tank rockets, destroying two armored cars and damaging a T-72. Immediately, the armored force returned the volley with one of its own, and in a deafening roar of cannon fire, paralyzed the remaining defenders.

The tanks continued firing point blank into the crowd of defenders. The defenders never lost their courage, small groups charging the tanks only to be ripped apart, but the attackers' firepower was overwhelming. Inevitably the tide of battle swung to the Sandinistas.

Elena joined her husband nestling close to him. "No!" Elena cried, seeing the carnage.

Xavier pulled his wife close to him, trying in vain to comfort her.

The tanks started up and ground forward, firing at the Palace while the Sandinista infantry poured out from behind the behemoths and into the Palace grounds. They slaughtered the retreating defenders as they tried to seek sanctuary in the Palace.

The tanks crashed through the remaining barricade and followed the infantry into the courtyard. One T-72 blasted the tractors barricading the entrance and rolled over the charred wrecks. Any second, the Sandinistas would break into the Palace.

Xavier picked up his rifle, determined to die fighting. He raised it to his shoulder and aimed into the courtyard. He saw a boy race into the fight and toss a Molotov cocktail at an approaching tank. The gasoline bomb burst into flames, but the tank continued unimpeded. The boy shouted his defiance and prepared to throw another one as a machine gun cut him in half. The child was smashed to the ground as Xavier heard someone shout, "They're in the Palace!"

"Motherfuckers!" Xavier screamed dropping his rifle. He jumped up and hefted a Molotov cocktail, lit it and hurled it down onto the burning T-72. Corona joined him and did the same. "Die you sons of bitches!" Xavier raged as he pelted the tank with fire bombs. Soon others took up the bombs and began hurling them down into the courtyard.

Plastic *refresco* bags, full of gasoline, burst on the armor skins adding fuel to the raging fires. Soon the vehicles ground to a halt as their crews threw open hatches to try to escape the heat and smoke only to be cut down by small arms fire from what remained of the second and third stories of the Palace. Fire bombs continued to rain down into the courtyard aimed now at the defenseless Sandinista soldiers. They screamed and frantically tried to put out the flames engulfing them.

"Viva Nicaragua! Viva El Presidente!" The battle cry raised spirits to a fever pitch as the defenders, led by their president, counterattacked, maniacally driving the Sandinistas back in a hail of grenades and bullets. The fighting quickly degenerated into hand-to-hand combat with the defenders achieving the upper hand.

The raiding force, badly mauled, retreated to the fence while the Sandinistas left inside had no choice but to surrender or face certain death. Most died anyway. After the massacre endured by the palace defenders, sympathy was in short supply. After a few minutes, the only Sandinistas remaining alive huddled behind the shattered fence unable to attack and unable to retreat.

When the firing died down, an old woman walked into the open, unarmed. Xavier watched, amazed at the woman's courage as she asked for the Sandinistas to surrender, begging them to stop the killing. At length a young man stood up, his uniform in tatters.

"We cannot surrender, *vieja*. Not so long as the spirit of Sandino runs through our veins."

"Is that you, Adolfo?" the old woman asked.

The young man hesitated. *"Madre? Madre*, is that you?" he asked haltingly.

"Sí, Adolfo. It is me."

"My, God," Xavier whispered, standing on the Palace steps. "Mother and son."

"Civil war, Xavier," Corona said. He'd seen it far too often in his CIA career. "Brother against brother. Families torn apart. Now you know why these people suffer so much."

Xavier's rage was replaced with hope. He raced down the steps and across the courtyard as Corona tried to keep up. The new president of Nicaragua joined the old woman and placed an arm around her shoulder. "I will grant immunity to any man or woman who surrenders and joins us!" he shouted. "It is time we healed our country! Let it begin here!"

"*Por favor*, Adolfo," his mother pleaded, hands clenched in prayer. She knelt on the bricks and began to pray.

Adolfo stood for a long time. The vanguard of Maliaños' force advanced behind the Sandinistas and took up positions behind the outer barrier. And still he stood. Huberto had their television camera turned on the lone Sandinista soldier.

"Oh, Mother," he said taking a small step forward as tears welled up in his eyes.

A Sandinista stood and leveled his rifle at Adolfo. "No, Adolfo!" he shouted. "Not like this!"

Corona shot the man through the heart. Everyone took cover, raising their weapons as they prepared for the final bloodbath. The old woman screamed as Xavier ran forward and knocked Adolfo to the ground covering him with his body. "*Bastantè!*" Xavier yelled. "Enough, goddamnit!"

Silence descended over the Plaza. Eventually, two Sandinistas stood up and dropped their weapons. They walked cautiously to Xavier and Adolfo and helped them up. The four proceeded to the Palace grounds. Others followed suit and cheers resounded across the Plaza as the last Sandinistas laid down their arms.

Xavier led the group to the top of the steps and raised Adolfo's arm in victory to the cheering of the small crowd.

From the far side of the Plaza, thousands of Nicaraguans marched to the Palace. They carried banners declaring their love of Nicaragua, freedom, Chamorro, and the new president. By torchlight they marched on, singing the national anthem. When the crowd reached the Palace, the sea of humanity seemed to stretch as far as the eye could see. An impenetrable wall of Nicaraguans.

Xavier handed the AK-47 to Diaz. "I don't think I'll be needing this anymore."

"Good. Then maybe you'll quit running around and I can get some rest," Corona grimaced, holding his ribs in pain. Diaz put an arm under his friend's shoulder and supported him.

Xavier, Diaz, Huberto, and Corona stood together and watched the spectacle in awe. Flares flew into the sky illuminating the celebration below. It was an amazing sight.

Xavier felt fingers intertwine in his and looked to see his wife standing by his side.

"What does it mean, Xavier?" Elena asked.

Xavier looked at the crowd, fierce in its determination to resist any attack. "For the moment, freedom, Elena," he said squeezing her hand. "Freedom for all of us."

The Pentagon, August 24, 1994, 5:08 A.M.

Singleton was sleeping in his chair when the duty officer woke him up. He sat up and wiped the grit from his eyes.

"What is it, Lieutenant?" he rasped.

"Panama, sir. Someone has blown up the canal with nuclear bombs," the lieutenant responded excitedly.

"What?" he cried. Singleton ripped the message from the officer's hand and scanned it quickly.

"I'll be goddamned," he said incredulously. "Get the White House on the line and have my car pulled up out in front."

As he got his things together, all thoughts of South African tank brigades and Nicaraguan coups left his mind.

Ortega Mansion, August 24, 1994, 5:32 A.M.

Daniel and Humberto Ortega took one last look at the living room. Sanchez and other staffers were busy burning documents. Several Sandinistas smashed and disabled equipment. The battle outside had reached a crescendo as Nicaraguan army troops joined the police and civilians. Time was running short. Soon they would be heading to exile in the jungle.

"It was a good life. Eh, brother?" Daniel asked.

Humberto stared at his brother in stony silence.

"We will be back, Humberto. Trust me."

Humberto gave his brother a look of utter contempt, abruptly turned on his heel and left the room.

"Make sure you burn everything, Colonel Sanchez. Especially the plans for the canal."

"I will, *Señor Presidente*," Sanchez said, coming to attention.

"Almost, Sanchez. I was almost a president again. And some day in the future I will be the president. But for now, I am a simple revolutionary. Good bye, my friend."

"*Adios, Señor* Ortega."

Ortega descended to the basement and the tunnel leading under the mansion.

Sanchez was frantically fulfilling his task when Nicaraguan army troops burst into the mansion minutes later. He threw the last blueprint in the fire as soldiers invaded the living room. Sanchez went for his pistol and was shot, his dead body falling on the glowing ashes of the coup d' état.

Troops fanned out through the mansion searching for the ex-president and his brother, the minister of defense. In the basement, they discovered the tunnel. The soldiers followed the tunnel to a garage nearby. The garage was empty and the doors stood wide open. The Ortegas had vanished without a trace.

Landringham Estate, Virginia, August 24, 1994, 5:44 A.M.

Senator Marion Hammersmith paced the Landringham grounds deep in thought. What next, he asked himself repeatedly. What next?

The coup had failed and along with it the chance to make untold tens of millions with his South African partners. Xavier survived and prospered. Busambra and the Jew Rabinowitz grew old in comfort. "They mock me, Father," he spoke aloud.

With all the damage he'd done to Busambra's organization in years past and all the wealth and power he'd accrued, he still felt empty, unfulfilled.

"What next, Father?" he asked, looking at the stars in the sky. "How else could I have succeeded?" Hammersmith lowered his head at the silence and continued with his walk.

Financial support wasn't the problem. Hammersmith had money. Staggering amounts. And he had the group. His father had seen to all his needs.

The disenfranchised Lord Hammersmythe had taken the family wealth to California and invested it in the fledgling movie industry in the early twenties. He made millions and branched out.

For every dollar Lord Hammersmythe invested in California oil and real estate, he syphoned an equal amount into numbered accounts in Swiss banks, buried under layers of false corporate fronts. He used these funds to establish and finance the group.

Hammersmythe had originally created the anonymous organization to bribe or blackmail politicians, judges, and police to increase his power base. As the organization grew in size and power, the former lord began to steer it toward darker ends. The first contract murders were carried out. When depression and prohibition descended on the land, Hammersmythe quietly positioned himself in the illegal liquor trade and made another fortune. The Swiss bank accounts grew and with the money he further expanded the group. And through it all, Hammersmythe remained virtually anonymous.

"Unlike you, Busambra, you fucking wop," Hammersmith snorted.

Hammersmythe never named the group, so no notoriety was ever attached to its misdeeds. He worked through blinds and drops to contact his people. All worked as mercenaries without specific knowledge of their employer. The two to three lieutenants he had direct contact with at any given time did not know of the existence of the others. No alliances could be formed to challenge his primacy. And if anyone in the group was compromised, death quickly followed. This was the organization of granite and stone that Busambra warred against.

And now to what ends do I use my wealth and power, Hammersmith thought. He looked at the evening sky again and saw a meteor descend from the heavens. Is that you, Father? he thought. What are you trying to tell me?

Hammersmith thought about his father. The man's philosophy had been simple. Accumulate wealth. Use the wealth to gain power and then use that power to crush his enemies. He had bequeathed everthing to his son along with his dying wish. And so far Hammersmith had failed.

"What kind of power do I need, Father?" he asked aloud.

A voice as clear as a bell answered the question. Startled, the senator stopped in his tracks and looked behind him. He was alone.

Then he realized the voice he'd heard came from within. It was the voice of his father. The former lord answered his son's question with two words.

Absolute power.

Nicaragua, August 24, 1994, dawn

Nicaraguans awoke after the attempted coup and took stock. As far as revolutions went, the overall cost was mild in comparison; under four thousand dead and light destruction of property, most of it in Managua. But many of the dead were the people who held Nicaragua together. This was the greatest damage.

28

Presidential Palace, Managua, Nicaragua, September 1, 1994

Xavier sat at his desk, eyes closed, resting his head on his arms. He had chased his staff out of the office, demanding fifteen minutes of privacy. He knew he'd have to add a quarter of an hour's work onto the end of an eighteen-hour day, but he didn't care.

Two minutes into his break there was a knock at the door.

"What!" Xavier barked, raising his head from the desk.

Corona and Diaz entered the room carrying several cardboard tubes. "Sorry to disturb you, *Señor Presidente*," Diaz apologized.

"This had better be damned important," Xavier threatened.

"It is, sir."

"Maliaños found the Ortegas?" Xavier asked, hopefully.

"No, sir. As a matter of fact, he has temporarily halted the search," Diaz answered.

"Goddamnit! On whose authority did he stop the search, Diaz?"

"Maliaños made the decision based on his knowledge of the situation. His troops are disorganized and the search is being conducted haphazardly."

"I'll cashier him, Diaz!"

"That would be a mistake, Mr. President," Corona said, defending Diaz. "He is the commander on the scene and in his judgment the search would be better conducted after a refit and a look at the latest intelligence. His troops are careening around like Boy Scouts without a compass and the colonel wants to narrow the search," Corona said, pointing at a large map of the country tacked to the wall. "Give him a break. He's doing what we would do in his place."

"All right," Xavier relented. "But I want those bastards. I want them to hang after what they did to this country."

"No one would disagree with you, *Señor Presidente*," Diaz added.

"Dispense with the formalities, please." Xavier said, waving them closer. "I don't need any more ass kissers, I've got plenty already. What is so fucking important?"

Diaz placed a cardboard cylinder on Xavier's cluttered desk. "In our search of Daniel Ortega's mansion we found nothing—no information about the attempted coup. All his documents, including those from his presidency, had been destroyed. But we hit the jackpot at Humberto's. No one got the word of their defeat in time to burn their evidence and we captured his papers intact."

"We got everything," Corona continued, placing a sheaf of papers on the desk. "Assassination lists, recorded conversations between conspirators, timetables. It's all here."

"Good job, my friends," Xavier smiled. "Outstanding. As soon as this is catalogued and duplicated, let the press research it to their heart's content. Anything else?"

"This, Javier," Diaz said, lifting the tube. "Come here and I'll show you."

Diaz walked to the conference table and shoved a mound of papers aside. He unfurled a sheaf of papers from the tube and laid them on the table, using books to keep the ends from curling up.

"We found a fireproof, waterproof, and airtight chamber in Humberto's basement—like a walk-in safe. The room was full of these tubes, each containing a different set of plans. Hundreds of them. The fact that they were so well protected made me think.

Sanchez died burning a massive set of blueprints. Corona and I figured they were important so we brought them here."

"Great, but do you have any idea what they're for?"

"No idea. Could be anything from an airfield to a nuclear reactor. The writing's foreign and I'm not a technician."

"Well, I know someone who is," Xavier said, walking to his desk. He punched his intercom and yelled, "Huberto! Get your ass in here."

Huberto entered the room. "You rang?"

Xavier ignored the sarcasm and pointed at the blueprints. "What are those, smart ass?"

Huberto walked to the table and bent over the paper. He studied them for a minute and replied, "Engineering blueprints."

Xavier, Diaz, and Corona shared a look that said "no shit," but kept quiet. "I'd say construction diagrams. Get Tito in here. He'd know better than I."

"Tito?" Xavier asked.

"Yeah, your minister of industry and procurement. You appointed him a few days ago. The guy only worked for you for six years."

"Big bear of a guy," Corona said, holding his arms out.

"Always chewing a foul cigar," Diaz added straight faced.

"I could see how you would forget him, Javier. He's only the best construction engineer in Nicaragua's history."

"Finished?" Xavier grimaced. "Get him for me, Huberto? If it's not too much trouble?"

"No problem, *jefe*," Huberto smiled.

Xavier rubbed his forehead. He'd made hundreds of appointments in the last six days on three hours of sleep a day. His memory was faltering.

Tito came into the room and rumbled, "Where are they?" nodding at the president as a formality. The construction engineer wasn't much on protocol.

Huberto pointed to the conference table. Tito bent over the plans and traced them with his fingers. His eyes narrowed in concentration as he scanned the blueprints. He opened all the containers and examined every blueprint before he straightened up and smiled.

"I'll be damned," he remarked and took a large draw off his cigar. The smoke drifted out of his mouth as he continued, "It's a canal."

The cloud of smoke descended on Huberto and he coughed. "A canal?"

He looked at Huberto as if the man were stupid. "Yeah, a canal. I should know. I just finished working on an irrigation canal outside Chinandega."

"What's so important about plans for an irrigation canal?" Xavier asked.

"Men died to protect these plans, Tito," Diaz added.

"Well, this isn't an ordinary canal. This is designed to carry the largest ships in the world from the west coast of Nicaragua to the east coast and back again."

"You mean like the Panama Canal?" Diaz asked.

"Only bigger and better. State of the art," Tito paused, realizing what he was saying.

"A new canal would take decades to build, this can't be right," Xavier said.

"Actually the original Central American canal was supposed to have been built here in Nicaragua. That's why the Bryan-Chamorro treaty was signed with America in 1914," Tito explained. "We've got numerous lakes and rivers crisscrossing our country. At the turn of the century, Cornelius Vanderbilt connected the lakes by railroad and used ships and trains to ferry people from the eastern seaboard up the San Juan River to California. Take it a step further and replace the railroads with earth cuts and there's your canal. The Panama Canal took ten years to build. A Nicaraguan canal would take less time than that and be much wider, allowing passage of the largest ships in the world."

"Holy Mother," Huberto gasped.

"You don't think they would go this far?" Diaz asked, astonished.

"That far, and maybe further," Corona answered.

"Who designed these?" Diaz demanded, bending over the plans. "What kind of language is this? German? Dutch?"

"What kind of language do South Africans speak?" Tito asked.

"English and Afrikaans," Corona answered. "Why?"

"Then it is Afrikaans."

"How the hell do you know that?" Xavier asked, disbelieving.

"It makes sense," he said to himself. Tito took another draw on his cigar and explained. "I've been all over Nicaragua working on dozens of projects. Several times in the past few years I've run into South African surveyors and engineers. As I see it now, they were in places directly related to the building of this canal.

"Didn't pay much attention to them at the time. We've got East Germans, Russians, and others as our guests. They didn't seem to be much different. But they were funny as far as construction engineers went.

"Most engineers are pretty gregarious, but these guys wouldn't so much as look at you, much less carry on a conversation or let you buy them a beer. I marked it up to *gringo* superiority, no offense. Now I can see why they didn't talk."

"Jesus, Javi," Huberto said, panic in his voice. "If anyone in the United States finds out about this they'll scream for revenge. They won't care that it was the Sandinistas. They'll think we're all Nicaraguan terrorists and they'll take our country by force." He grabbed Xavier's arm. "We need to burn these plans now. Before it's too late."

But Xavier wasn't thinking about the Americans or the canal. He was thinking about the South Africans. And Kruger.

"*Un milagro,*" Xavier muttered. A miracle.

"What?" Diaz asked.

"Never mind," Xavier said. He bent over the plans. "No. We don't burn anything. Nothing that has been said here leaves this room. Understood?" he asked, looking each man in the eye.

"Now, to business. Diaz. Get the rest of these plans. Don't make a big show of it, but take enough security to make sure there are no problems. Bring the plans to my office here and keep them under armed guard."

"No place safer in Nicaragua than right here, Xavier. I'll make sure of that."

"Good. Corona, I assume you can get in touch with Rizzi?"

"Twenty-four hours a day, Xavier," Corona intoned.

"I thought so. Get him here tomorrow. Incognito. I don't want his presence known to anyone not in this room. And Corona, have him bring an expert in construction engineering. No offense, Tito, but I want these plans verified as authentic by an outside source."

Tito gestured that he understood.

"And, Tito, go to the interior immediately and find out if they started any construction. Take whatever air assets you need. Diaz'll handle the military. I need that information now!" Xavier exclaimed, slapping his palm on the table.

"You'll have a preliminary report before the end of the day, *Señor Presidente*," Tito said, confidently.

"Okay then. Get to it!"

"What are you going to be doing?" Corona asked, as he rolled up the plans.

"I'm going to see Chamorro. The miracle she's been waiting for may have just fallen in our laps." He slapped Corona on the back and left his office, wide awake for the first time in a week.

29

Busambra Estate, Palermo, Sicily, September 10, 1994

Xavier flew the helicopter west, away from Palermo. It had been months since he'd flown, so he decided a small joy ride was in order before heading to Busambra's estate. It was a joy ride with a purpose.

The pilot had protested at first, but eventually allowed Xavier to take the controls. He was, after all, the godson of *Il Padrino*. The pilot rode in the copilot's seat while the copilot remained behind in Palermo wondering how he would explain his presence if Don Busambra called.

"Beautiful country," Diaz remarked from the passenger compartment. "When will we be arriving at your godfather's estate?"

"We've been flying over it for the last ten minutes."

"My God. It's huge," Huberto exclaimed.

"You have no idea, Huberto. You can travel on Busambra land south to Monreale, west to Carini, or north to Capo Gallo without once crossing another landowner's property."

"And those vineyards?" Elena asked. "He makes wine?"

"Yes, Elena," Xavier explained, passing over the well-tended groves. "My godfather produces some of the finest grapes in Sicily. And most anything else you eat. At dinner you will quench your thirst with vintage Busambra Lambrusco, dip your bread baked from Busambra wheat in olive oil bottled in one of my godfather's factories. And it will be one of the best meals you can remember."

"I thought your godfather was chased out of Sicily by the mafia?" Huberto asked, curious.

The pilot looked nervously at Xavier. "It's best never to use that word in the presence of the godfather or one of his employees," Corona broke in quickly. "They are a tight-knit family and easily take offense to outsiders."

"Listen to Corona," Xavier said, emphasizing the point. "Although you are here under my godfather's protection, be aware that Sicilians have notoriously long memories."

"I didn't mean to offend anyone," Huberto apologized, sounding hurt. "I was just interested."

"It's okay, Huberto," Xavier said, trying to put his friend at ease. "But to satisfy your curiosity, it wasn't my godfather who escaped from Sicily, but his father, Antoni Busambra. He fled in 1917 with his family and friends. In 1925, after becoming a successful businessman in America, he returned and contacted an old friend, Don Giacomo Nicotera. Together, they built the estate and numerous other businesses. My godfather has holdings all across Sicily and the mainland. But it all began here in these hills."

Abruptly the helicopter dropped over a huge precipice. The move startled the pilot, who reached for his controls. Xavier barked at him in Italian and the man placed his hands back in his lap.

The helicopter was rocked by turbulence, but under Xavier's maneuvering the Sikorsky flared and came to a rest on a narrow ledge beneath the huge rock. Xavier said something to the pilot and turned to the passenger compartment.

"We're stopping here for a few minutes," he said without further explanation and climbed out of the cockpit. Elena, Diaz, Corona, and Huberto followed him. They trailed him up a small path that opened onto a clearing. Openings in the rock face overlooked the clearing. The place had a deserted, primitive air about it.

"*Rocca* Busambra," Xavier said, breaking the silence. "Antoni Busambra was born in those caves. His tribe lived here for centuries raiding the valley below. For my godfather, this is where it all began. He treats this place as a holy shrine.

"When I was a boy, we trekked up here every summer and spent a night in the caves. Bennedetto would tell me stories of his father, the famous bandit chieftain, by the light of the campfire. Don Busambra also told me of the time he and my father hid out here from the Nazis during the war when they were forced to bail out of their bomber. He made those people and those times come alive for me."

Elena walked to Xavier, placed her arm around him and rested her head on his shoulder. "My godfather is too old these days to make the journey," Xavier said sadly. "I make it for him today out of respect. You are with me because you are the closest friends I have in the world. You are with me out of a sense of respect and loyalty. Please treat him with the same respect. When you meet him and see his power and opulence, remember where he came from and what kind of man it takes to rise as far as he has."

Xavier left them to walk on Rocca Busambra. He did not want them to see him wipe the tears from his eyes. After a time they returned to the helicopter and lifted off for the final leg of the flight.

Xavier flew east over the valley floor. He flew up a gently rising hill until the Sikorsky shot over a massive Mediterranean mansion. Xavier pointed the nose down and the sea burst into view, leaving the passengers breathless.

Xavier landed the helicopter and cut the engines. Bodyguards and servants rushed to greet them.

"Huberto, you and Diaz take the plans and the luggage to the house. Servants will show you the way. One more thing before we go." Xavier shifted in his seat to face his friends. They could sense a change in attitude come over him.

"You have entered a different world. The citizens of *Estato Busambra* are born in the small hospital outside Carini, named for Don Busambra, educated in the schools built by my godfather, and buried in cemeteries on his land. Generations of Sicilians have known no other life. And for this reason, they give sole allegiance to the man they call *Il Padrino*.

"And I am his godson. To these people that is a title of extreme importance and respect. If I treat you differently, it is not because I want to, I do it because it is expected of the godson of Don Bennedetto Busambra."

Xavier left them to sort things out and walked to the house.

He had spent the summers of his youth here with Don Busambra. The memories were legion—his first fishing trip, learning to hunt, camping, his first kiss. She was his first love—the daughter of one of Busambra's house servants. They had spent the whole summer in each other's arms. When he returned the next summer, his heart broke. Bennedetto informed him she had married another man.

The memories flooded back as he stood on the steps of what the don referred to as his country house. The three-story mansion was designed in the Mediterranean style and luxuriously appointed.

"Xavier," Elena gasped, joining him. "What a view."

To the south, Palermo lay glistening in the sun. To the east, the ocean spread to the horizon, a deep, dark blue. To the west, the green and brown hills of northern Sicily stretched as far as the eye could see.

"Yes. It takes my breath away." He turned and smiled at his wife. "Ready?"

They held hands and were escorted into a parlor. Two old men were seated in the room. Elena noticed their eyes light up when they saw Xavier. Both men came to their feet and took turns hugging him.

"Zavi," Don Busambra whispered tears in his eyes. "Zavi, my boy." He held Xavier's face in both hands and kissed his cheeks.

"Hello, Papa. I have missed you," he said, returning the kisses. "And Uncle Jake," he said, turning to the doctor. "I've missed you, too."

Jacob hugged Xavier and scolded him. "Missed me? You couldn't tell it by how often you write. Take pity on me. Your letters help keep this old man alive."

"I will try to write more, Uncle Jake. I promise."

Jacob turned to Busambra complaining. "He promises. Again he promises."

"Calm down, Jacob. Enough of our selfish interests. I am waiting to meet this amazing woman," Busambra said, expectantly.

Xavier held out his hand to Elena who stepped forward. "Bennedetto, Uncle Jake. My wife, Dr. Elena Daniels."

Neither man made a move toward her. They stared at her for a moment before Jacob spoke. "What do you think, Benjamin?"

Busambra tapped his chin with his forefinger. "I don't know, Jacob. She is pretty enough. But can she cook?"

"If she's a decent doctor, then she doesn't have time to cook. Is she a decent doctor, Xavier?" Jacob asked.

"The best, Uncle Jacob. Next to you, of course."

Jacob smiled at the compliment. "Then she is good enough for us." He opened his arms to her. "Welcome to our family."

Elena gave Jacob a hug. "Thank you, Jacob."

"Now me, young lady," Busambra said. He hugged Elena and then held her at arm's length. "So you can't cook. That is all right. By the look in Zavi's eyes, I can see that he loves you very much and that is good enough for me." A serious expression came over his face and he looked into her eyes. "You are a member of our family. Protected by our family. Remember that. If you ever need anything, anything at all. Ask. Nothing is too big. Do you understand?"

"Yes," Elena answered, not sure whether or not she did. She stared into his eyes. They were dark and, for a moment, exceedingly sinister. Busambra felt the goosebumps on her arms and his eyes changed, lighting up in a smile. The moment passed.

"Sit down. Please. And tell us about your trip."

They sat and Xavier spoke of their journey. The old men hung on every word no matter how trivial. It was obvious they had missed the sound of his voice, the look on his face, the presence of his company. These men loved her husband very much.

Several retainers moved about the room serving coffee and tea. Busambra acted as though they weren't there. Corona stood behind Xavier's chair, but was not acknowledged in any way.

Elena was surprised. Surely Don Busambra was aware the man had saved her husband's life. Corona did not act slighted in the least. Observing the rituals, Elena became aware she had entered another culture, one with rules strikingly different from her own. It was as Xavier had said, a different world.

Jacob asked Elena to join him for a walk while Xavier conferred with Bennedetto. They walked arm in arm through the beautiful gardens overlooking the ocean talking as they went. She felt at ease in his presence and quickly warmed to the old man. He was kind, intelligent, and had a quick wit. He was also in good shape for a man in his eighties. His pace was quick and purposeful.

"It is so nice to finally meet Xavier's favorite godfather," Elena said to Jacob.

"What makes you think I'm his favorite?"

"Well, he talks about you much more than Bennedetto."

"Don't let that fool you. He loves Bennedetto as much as me. I am just easier to talk about."

"Why is that?"

"I don't kill people as a way of life, Elena." He paused to look at her and continued. "It is hard to talk about a man you love who you believe in your heart lives a life of sin. I, on the other hand, try to live a life based on the teachings of the Torah. I am not perfect. But I am most assuredly easier for Xavier to stomach."

They continued their walk. "You are so kind. I can see why he loves you. He is like you in so many ways."

"Thank you, Elena. But the kindness comes from his mother."

"Really? I rarely hear him speak of her. And when he does, it is not with fond words."

"It is because she is not his real mother."

"What?" Elena reacted, dumbfounded.

"It is time someone knows," he sighed. "Here let us sit and watch the sun set and I will tell you a small tale."

They sat on a stone bench and looked over the ocean at the explosion of colors in the sky.

"I swore an oath to keep this secret. But as I grow older and closer to death, I wonder how important that oath is. To deny my godson his true heritage, I think, would be a crime greater than breaking the oath to his father, my best friend. But to deny it to his children would be an even greater sin. I am sure of that," he said, looking at Elena closely.

"You know?" she whispered.

"That you are with child? Yes. I am a very good doctor," he laughed, pleased.

"But how could you? I only have an intuition. No proof. It hasn't been that long since—" she stopped, blushing.

"You glow, my child. It is like an aura I learned to read. Sometimes I knew it before my patients did."

"My, God. You really can tell."

He smiled knowingly. "I have very good instincts. Most doctors do. We come to trust them as we do our surgical skills."

"You are right. So right," she agreed. "So who is my child's grandmother?"

"Ah. But that would spoil the story. And old men do like to tell stories."

"Then I'd love to hear it," she encouraged him.

"Good, then I'll begin. Xavier's father moved to Dallas after the war. Victor was a handsome man who enjoyed his bachelor life. Many beautiful women vied for his attention and he was only too happy to oblige them. That is until he met a southern belle and they fell in love. He gave up all his old romances except for one. A secret one that he treasured above all the rest.

"He kept her secret because she wasn't white, and in the south, an interracial relationship was taboo. But he loved her and couldn't leave her, so he supported her and continued to see her. During this time, he became engaged to, and finally married, his southern belle.

"His mistress was jealous and, in retaliation, she conceived a baby to try to trap him. It didn't work, and Victor cut her off. Destitute and pregnant, she pondered suicide. But she realized her act would kill the baby. She had come to love the object of her revenge. She wanted a good life for the child even if she could not have one for herself. In a fit of desperation, she threatened to expose him if he didn't take the baby and raise it.

"Victor panicked and went to his friend Bennedetto. He contemplated having the woman killed, but Bennedetto would have none of it. He ordered the woman brought before him. She was lovely and kind and, oh, so loyal to the unborn child. In a small way, Bennedetto fell in love with her. He forced Victor to agree to certain conditions and, when the baby was born, Victor adopted him into his family. Trust funds were set up for the mother and the child."

"A couple of years after Xavier was born, the real mother moved into the house with them as a nanny—"

"—Maria Escalante," Elena interrupted in a rush. "Maria Escalante is his mother."

"You spoiled my ending, Elena," he chided her. "That is what telling a good story is all about. But you are correct. The woman who always loved him and nurtured him as a child and raised him to a young man was actually his mother. Not just a servant doing her job."

"Amazing. Now I see where his love and loyalty come from. Maria Escalante."

"And when the time is right, we will tell him together. And he will know his heritage."

"But it is more than Maria," she said. "It is all of you. His intelligence and morality come from you, Jacob. His anger and rage from his father."

"And from Bennedetto?"

"From Bennedetto he gets his cunning and the will to survive. I know that after looking into his eyes today. I saw that look in Xavier's eyes the night I met him," she answered, remembering that evening on Maria's porch. "It was cold and relentless and very frightening."

"You are correct, Elena. He is a product of us all. And our gifts to him, both good and bad, have helped him to survive in the toughest times. You might despise what his father did. You might fear Bennedetto. But what he learned from them saved your life in Honduras. Never forget that."

She knew he was right. And here in Sicily, she was faced with a sinister part of his past and a murderer Xavier would die to protect. She held her belly as if she could protect her baby from these thoughts.

"Enough time for stories tomorrow," he said, pulling her head to his shoulder. "Come now. Let us go in. It is time to drink and eat."

Jacob held her a little longer before leading her inside.

Xavier watched Jacob and Elena walking in the garden. He longed to be with them but business came first. With a sigh, he dropped the curtain and took his chair.

"The meeting day after tomorrow will be tough, Zavi," Busambra said. "These men are negotiators of the highest capability. Don't let them fool you. They did not become the wealthiest and most powerful men in Europe and Japan for their generosity. We have a code. We have honor. They know only greed. And they would sell their mothers for a profit.

"They will try to squeeze every concession out of you that they can. And then some. In the end, if you are strong and incorruptible, they will threaten you. Their threats are real. You must be very careful."

"I've dealt with these men before, Bennedetto. I agree that they are ruthless and my footing precarious. My position is not helped by the fact that my country is broke and in chaos after the attempted coup. I have very little to bargain with. If I'm not careful, as you say, they can suck Nicaragua dry."

"Then throw caution to the wind, Zavi," Busambra declared. He leaned forward in his chair and clenched his fist. "Be ruthless. Be the president of what has become the most strategic piece of earth in the western hemisphere. Do not forget that they need you as much as you need them."

"But if they stall, Nicaragua collapses."

"Good. Let them stall and then force their hand."

"How?"

"Tell them the United States has a deal on the table."

"But that would be a lie. Besides, I sense CIA complicity here. I won't deal with a government that had anything to do with the coup."

"I understand. So don't deal with the United States. You don't have to. All you have to do is lie. Make them think you do have a deal with President Davis and the American industrialists. When they panic, you can name your price."

"It's a ballsy move, Papa. These men have sources everywhere. A few phone calls and they will uncover my deception. If they call my bluff, then we are dead in the water."

"Trust me, Xavier. Just do as I say."

"You treat this like a game," Xavier said, wonderingly.

"Oh, yes, Zavi. The oldest game for the biggest stakes in the world. The gamble for power. Only the strongest, most cunning survive. But to survive is to win, because when you're the only one left, everything is yours. Everything."

"I will trust your judgment, godfather. You have never failed me."

"How could I fail what I love? It is impossible. Unthinkable. We will win, Zavi, and you will go down in history."

I hope you are right, Papa, Xavier thought. Because if you are wrong...

"But first you must formulate your plan. I have extensive dossiers on every individual who will be at the meeting. I also have a list of assets available on a moment's notice."

"What do you suggest?" Xavier asked, needing guidance.

"Beyond what I have already told you? Nothing. You must decide your course of action. Only then can I be of assistance."

"But why?"

"I know how far I would go to protect my family and the things I hold dear, Zavi. How far would you got to protect Elena, Maria, and Nicaragua? Only you know. Only you can decide," Busambra explained.

They talked for another hour and studied Bennedetto's files before joining the others for dinner. Xavier was understandably distracted during the meal. The fate of his nation rested on the actions he would be taking during the next forty-eight hours.

How far am I willing to go, he asked himself repeatedly. How far?

He looked at his wife who smiled at him lovingly. For some reason she was more radiant than he could remember her being.

How far?

Huberto told an off-color joke at which Bennedetto politely smiled and Jacob laughed out loud. Diaz grimaced and kicked Huberto under the table.

What would I do to protect my friends?

He thought of Dario making his last stand in Honduras. He remembered the cold clutch of Chamorro's hand when he stood by her hospital bed. Abruptly Xavier stood up, interrupting the conversation.

"*Scusi*, godfather. Corona, Diaz. Meet me in my godfather's study. Papa. When is Rizzi arriving?"

"Tonight. In an hour or so," Busambra answered.

"Good. I will need his services."

"He is at your disposal, Xavier."

"Thank you. Huberto, when he arrives, would you ask him to join us?"

"Of course, *Señor Presidente*."

"Let's get going. We don't have much time," Xavier said, understating the obvious.

When the three had left the table, Bennedetto turned to Elena and asked, "More wine, my dear?" as if these kinds of intrusions were commonplace.

After midnight, Rizzi and Diaz went by helicopter to Palermo and there were met by a team of bodyguards. They split up and boarded separate private jets bound for the mainland. Diaz flew to Barcelona with Luca Baracca and two Busambra soldiers. Rizzi flew to Bonn and a rendezvous with a well-placed Busambra supporter. Corona visited with Don Busambra's chief armorer and security specialist and spent the rest of the early morning hours in the ballroom. And Xavier placed a scrambled call to Managua. It was the most difficult phone call he could remember making.

On the estate, Xavier revealed his plot to Don Busambra. The *capo di tuti capi* smiled, pleased with his godson's preparations. Xavier had decided how far he would go.

Starting with the sunrise, helicopters began arriving from Palermo carrying the participants of the secret summit. Don Busambra greeted the men at the door and offered them his hospitality, as was the custom. The industrialists, financiers, and politicians mingled in the quiet, elegant music room, eating pastries and drinking coffee. Several last-minute meetings were held in private rooms provided by Don Busambra. Upstairs, Xavier paced nervously while Elena and Jacob shared breakfast and light conversation.

Security teams patrolled the estate grounds and a hand-picked team of detection specialists and bodyguards swept the banquet hall, site of the summit, for bombs and surveillance bugs. Satisfied that the room was clean, the doors were sealed and guards placed to prevent access by anyone including *Il Padrino's* personnel. A short while later, the grounds were declared secure by the assembled bodyguards.

Promptly at eleven A.M., the doors were opened and the participants ushered in. They took their seats and waited for the arrival of the Nicaraguan president.

At a quarter after eleven, Xavier Daniels entered the banquet hall. Conversation stopped as the men stood and looked at the president of Nicaragua for the first time. In contrast to the conservatively tailored participants, the president wore a pair of khaki pants, a dark green button-down shirt open at the collar and a gray linen blazer. His long hair was pulled behind his head in a ponytail and a pair of glasses hung at his chest. The men smiled in deference while they counted their lucky stars. This man would be a pushover.

Xavier nodded at the participants and observed the banquet hall. The room was a giant rectangle with vaulted ceilings from which hung two giant crystal chandeliers. Tall sets of slender French doors opened onto the gardens from three sides of the hall. The floor was laid with huge tiles of pink and white marble. In the middle of the floor stood a long mahogany dining table and high-backed chairs which were upholstered in a dark green and taupe striped silk fabric. A large crystal vase containing a beautiful spray of flowers rested in the center of the table.

Xavier walked the length of the hall and opened the French doors set in the opposite wall. He took several breaths of fresh air and turned to take his seat at the head of the table. After a moment, he held out both arms.

"Gentlemen, please take your seats."

When everyone was settled, Xavier began. "I would like to thank everyone here on behalf of the Nicaraguan people. You have traveled a long way to offer us your assistance in building a trans-isthmian canal. Also, I would like to thank our host Don

Bennedetto Busambra for graciously allowing us to use his home for our purposes."

The men turned and nodded at the don sitting at the far end of the table. The don smiled at them and said, "Thank you for coming. And may God bless our efforts."

"I am sure he will, Don Busambra. And now to the business at hand, gentlemen—the construction of the largest canal in the history of the world. You have had a week to study the proposals presented to you by me on behalf of our country. The contracts are fair and benefit everyone present." Xavier smiled, "But I am open to suggestions on anything I might have missed."

There was polite laughter. The Nicaraguan proposal was one of the most well thought out and detailed documents ever set in front of them. No contingency had been overlooked. But this was business and, as with all business deals, everything was negotiable.

For the next two hours, Xavier listened as the men, one by one, took an immensely fair business proposal and turned it inside out. Every advantage for the Nicaraguan people was taken away. Every opportunity for Nicaraguan business was bypassed in favor of European and Japanese interests. In the end, Nicaragua was left with a large ditch bisecting their country from which they would receive minuscule benefits and over which they would have no control. There would be, in effect, two Nicaraguas separated by a strip of land owned and ruled by outside governments.

When they were through, Xavier paused in thought. Finally, he suggested a recess to confer with his aides before making a final decision. When he was gone, the negotiators quietly congratulated themselves on a successful mission. They had worn the president down and would now move in for the kill.

"The bastards gloat over your corpse, Xavier," Busambra spat, as they listened to the transmission. "They have earned what they will get."

"Corona did a good job on these bugs, Xavier," Huberto said. He adjusted his headphones and tuned the equipment. "The Japanese chairman of MITI is telling the Spanish vice-minister of the European common market about his golf game he has scheduled for tomorrow."

"Of course," Busambra remarked. "They feel the deal is already done. And I invited these men here in good faith. Bastards!"

"You said yourself, Papa, that these men are ruthless. Good faith or no. They are doing exactly what you or I would do in their place. They are going for the kill. And that is their downfall. They are too predictable and overconfident. So much so that they failed to cover their flanks. And their arrogance will be their undoing."

Elena sat and listened to her husband. He was a much different man from the one she had held on Rocca Busambra. He was confident and cunning. His eyes were cold as ice. This Xavier frightened her. Jacob sensed her feelings and patted her hand.

"Corona. It is time for you to take your position. Huberto, signal Rizzi and Diaz and have them ready," Xavier ordered.

Corona left the room by a side door. Huberto made two short phone calls. When he was done, Xavier helped his godfather up and escorted him to the door.

"Good luck, Xavier," Elena said, standing up.

Xavier looked at her and smiled. But the smile wasn't genuine. It was plastic and his face was a mask that hid his true feelings. He turned and left the room without responding.

"Gentlemen. I am sorry. We offered you a fair contract and you have rewritten it without regard for my country's welfare," Xavier began, when he had taken his seat. "As it stands, we will not accept your changes to the original Nicaraguan proposal."

Alejandro Fabio Mondragòn lit a cigarette and blew out the match. The Spaniard was the Minister of EURCOM and the wealthiest industrialist in his country. He measured the silence before speaking.

"*Señor Presidente*. What is it you find so disturbing about the proposed amendments to our deal?"

"Everything. To begin with, you suggest that my country cede a vast piece of our territory to your consortium which you will run autonomously. You wish to place a military force inside our borders that will not be under Nicaraguan authority, but under yours. And you want us to pay for the force out of the proceeds we receive from our share of the tolls. Preposterous!"

"Is that all?" Mondragòn asked smugly.

"You mean that's not enough? The fact that you choose to import a foreign work force instead of employing and training Nicaraguan labor is grossly prejudicial. You want to ship all the necessary tools, equipment, and supplies from abroad instead of stimulating the regional economy. What other kind of reaction did you expect?"

"Mister President," Taketsu, the chairman of MITI interrupted. "We in Japan, along with our European counterparts, will be putting up tens of billions of dollars to complete this project. We are taking a giant risk. We will not begin to make money on this project for over a decade. We are simply trying to make this as economical as possible. As for yourself, you will become a very wealthy man."

"You think a bribe to me will garner my support? Frankly, Mr. Taketsu, I thought you were more cosmopolitan than stooping to payoffs. Or is your position the consortium bagman?"

Taketsu colored, but did not respond.

"*Con permiso, Señor Presidente*. It is a fair proposal."

"No, *Señor* Mondragòn. I don't think it is, and neither will my countrymen. It won't happen. I won't let it."

"And what other choice do you have, *Herr* President?" asked Helmut von Keisling, owner of the German electronics giant BETA.

"The Americans, *Herr* von Keisling," Xavier answered.

There was a moment of silence. Several men coughed nervously. Mondragòn crushed his cigarette butt in an ashtray and looked at Xavier. "And what Americans would those be?"

"None of your business, *Señor* Mondragòn."

"I see," he replied. "And what if I told you that we know of no American attempt to put together a deal to build the canal, *Señor Presidente*? What would your response be then?"

"I'd call you a liar."

"Well *Señor Presidente*, liar or not, our assets inside the United States government and business community report no such activity. We are smart businessmen. Did you not think we would check out that possibility?"

"You think I am bluffing?"

"We don't think it. We know it," Mondragón said, lighting another cigarette.

"And if things are as you believe, what then?"

"Deal with us and your continued existence as *presidente* is assured."

"And if I don't?" Xavier asked, warily.

"Then we simply wait another few days and Chamorro will be back in power. Your thirty days will be up. Or had your forgotten?"

Xavier ignored the question. "What makes you think she'll deal with you?"

"She'll have no other choice," Taketsu answered. "Her country is in chaos. The treasury is nonexistent. Chamorro will grab at anything to keep the country from disintegrating."

"You underestimate *Doña* Violeta. She is stronger than I am. I don't think she will deal with you."

"I would hate to think of what would happen to her if another coup broke out," von Keisling mused. "She might not survive the next time. A lot of people might not survive the next time, *Herr Presidente*," Keisling said coldly, staring straight at Xavier.

The gauntlet had been thrown down. The men waited expectantly for Xavier's response. The Nicaraguan president got out of his chair and went to the window. After a moment's thought, he returned to his chair and stood beside it.

"You dare to threaten me. Threaten my family and my country!" Xavier slammed his hand on the table. A split second later, a hole blew through his chair and the vase exploded in a cloud of dust and crystal. The flowers fell to the table and water splashed the men nearest the shattered vase.

"Shut up and keep your seats," Xavier yelled. They sat down and anxiously looked at the door waiting for their bodyguards to come rushing in. Nothing happened. Xavier kicked the chair out of his way and leaned on the table holding the men in a gaze of withering contempt.

"I offered you a fair deal and you shunned it in favor of your selfish interests. Now I offer you a new deal."

The door to the banquet hall opened and Rizzi walked in, followed by Huberto and a man everyone in the room recognized. Richard I. Thorncross III stood next to Don Busambra. Mondragòn and von Keisling had conferred with him the past week during an economic conference in Bern, Switzerland. Thorncross was the wealthiest man in America, a kingmaker who had access to the inner sanctum of the White House.

"Good day. It is nice to see men of such wealth and prominence here to assist a small country in so great an undertaking. You should know that I have been invited by the president of Nicaragua to begin work immediately on construction of the canal. That is, assuming you are unable to come to terms. I will wait to hear from you, *Señor Presidente*."

"Thank you for coming, Mr. Thorncross," Xavier said.

"Godfather," Thorncross said, greeting Busambra warmly. He shook Busambra's hand in both of his. "I am looking forward to dinner this evening."

"As am I, Richard."

"Good day, my friends," Thorncross smiled and left the banquet hall.

"If the Americans build the canal, they will start with nothing," Xavier went on. "It will take them, at the very best, twice as long to complete the project as this consortium, considering you already possess the plans. Five to eight more years of shipping everything around the tip of South America. How much are you going to lose? Billions? Tens of billions? A hundred billion? It boggles the mind.

"And none of your industries will be stimulated. Just American and Nicaraguan industries. How much will that cost in the future growth of your nations? I don't think anyone in here can add that high. I know I can't. But that's just the beginning."

Rizzi handed Xavier a folder. Xavier opened it selected a document and handed it to Mondragòn.

"This is Chamorro's signed resignation. She will be unable to resume her office due to medical reasons. As we speak, the government is announcing the date for new elections to be held in a little over two months. Chamorro is also announcing my candidacy for president and urging her party and the people of Nicaragua to give me their full support. Short of my death, I am the new president of Nicaragua until the next century. But I'd better not die. I think you'll see why."

Huberto walked around the table and handed a folder to each man in the room. They stared at a file with their name embossed in bold letters on the front. The men looked at them nervously.

Xavier paced alongside the table. He had their undivided attention.

"Open your folders, please, gentlemen, and review the contents. Pictures of yourselves and your families along with other pertinent data such as your addresses, the location of your children's schools, where you fuck your mistresses, and so forth."

The men looked up in shock. "You can't be serious?" von Keisling asked.

"You know goddamn well I'm serious," he said, patting the chair with the hole in it. "I can get to you anywhere at any time. Even here surrounded by your personal security. It could have been any of you sitting in this chair..." Xavier said, pausing for effect.

"Why are you making these threats?" asked Taketsu bewildered.

"Because I am protecting myself, my family, and my country from you. Or didn't you listen to *Herr* von Keisling, Mr. Taketsu? Who the hell do you think you are to hold the lives of friends and family over my head? Did you not think I would retaliate?"

"He's bluffing, Taketsu," von Keisling said. "Anyone can shoot through an open window. Anyone can find out the information here. Hell, most of it's public knowledge. I say he's bluffing."

"Bluffing?" Xavier asked. Huberto placed a speaker phone in front of Mondragòn. "Dial your private home number, *Señor* Mondragòn. The one you have changed every three days."

Mondragòn swallowed nervously. Sweat popped out on his forehead.

"If you don't know the number, I can give it to you," Xavier said, taunting him.

Mondragòn picked up the phone. He dialed as the others looked on.

"Hello," a rough male voice echoed from the speaker.

"Luca, put on *Señora* Mondragòn."

There was no reply. Seconds later, panting emanated from the box. "Fabio? Is that you, Fabio?"

"Yes! Yes! It is me, Sylvie!"

"They have me tied to the bed—" the voice was cut off. A dial tone was the last thing he heard before Huberto pulled the plug.

"If anything happens to me, my family, or my country, you and your families will be hunted down like dogs and killed to the last person. Believe it as you've never believed anything in your lives. This is not a threat. It is a contract."

A heavy silence hung over the table. No one dared argue. No one dared move.

"Next time you make threats, be prepared to back them up. I was forced into these unpleasant actions by everyone sitting at this table. Now for the new deal..." and Xavier went on to spell it out for his new partners.

When the new contracts were passed out, everyone signed without question. Each man came and shook Xavier's hand and offered their complete support. Even von Keisling offered his compliance, though with a stiffer back than his partners.

When the room was cleared, Corona came in through the open French doors. "Good shooting, Alex," Xavier commented.

"It was pretty windy. Could have gone either way," Corona remarked, casually. He nodded at Busambra and left the room.

"You did well, Zavi," Busambra noted.

"I only hope I did nothing to harm you, Godfather."

"It is not your problem to worry about. Besides, most of those men are indebted to me in some form or another."

Xavier helped his godfather out of the chair and walked with him to the door. Busambra could sense his distress.

"You are strong, Zavi. And bold. You did what you had to do," Busambra remarked.

"If strength is cruelty, then I am the strongest man alive. If blackmailing men with the lives of their families is bold, then I am as bold as any common criminal. I manipulated...no, that's too polite. I forced my friend *Doña* Violeta to relinquish her claim to the presidency and terrorized an innocent woman for my own personal gain. Tell me, Bennedetto. Are my sins absolved because good may come out of them? Where do I draw the line in order not to become what I fight?"

"Where do the men who killed Min draw the line, Zavi?"

"I don't know."

"You don't know, because there *is no line* for men obsessed with power and greed and revenge," he said, gripping Xavier's arm tightly. "Don't forget that. It will keep you alert against your enemies."

Busambra sighed as he struggled to explain. "You cannot fight this war with words and understanding and morality. Not when your enemies use bullets and bombs, deceit and treachery. Men like that understand one thing. Force. You used force today. You showed these men, these pigs, that you will stop at nothing to protect what is yours. Today, they learned to fear you. And out of that fear comes the greatest respect. You are now a man to be reckoned with. Enjoy your new position, Xavier. But remember the responsibilities that position brings."

"I did not ask for it, Papa. I don't know if I want it," Xavier spoke, arms flopping at his side.

"Then, hopefully, you won't let the power go to your head."

"And if it does?"

"Then you will become one of them. You will become your father, Zavi. You will end up like poor Victor."

A flash memory of a disease-riddled man, full of despair and lost hope in an oxygen tent. Xavier stopped at the door and looked at his godfather. "How do you live with it, Papa?"

Busambra smirked. "It is a good question, Zavi. You remind me of myself in the old days."

That's what I'm afraid of, Xavier thought. I am afraid I am becoming like you.

Xavier ushered his godfather through the door. As soon as the banquet hall was empty, servants entered the room and cleaned up the vase and replaced the chair with an exact copy. The last servant to leave closed the French doors, shutting off the ocean breeze, and pulled the heavy drapes, leaving the banquet hall dark and still.

The young man led his mother up the hill to a small plateau covered by a grove of olive trees. Nestled in the middle of the grove was a small fountain used to irrigate the trees and to provide water for the workers. At a table beside the fountain, two men sat and ate from a picnic basket.

"Is that him?" the son asked.

"Yes," answered his mother. "I recognize him even from this distance."

"Would you like to move closer?"

"No," she sighed. "It would not be appropriate."

"Then we should leave?"

"No. Please," she grasped her son's arm. "Let me look at him just a while longer."

Her son patted her hand and nodded in understanding. "We will stay as long as you like, Mama."

She stared at the two figures for several minutes. Eventually two bodyguards appeared from behind the fountain and headed in their direction. Their walk was casual but their purpose wasn't, she knew.

"Now we must go, my son."

His back stiffened. "Why? We work this land for Don Bennedetto. It is our home as much as the *soldati*."

"It would not be appropriate to draw attention to ourselves. Please understand, my son. It is a difficult situation."

He knew she spoke the truth. He wanted to avenge his mother's honor, but she forbade it because of the feelings she still held for the man seated at the table, the same man who had taken her honor. Honor and loyalty. The Sicilian's code. The two were in conflict and it left him uneasy.

"Good bye, my friend, my lover," she muttered. Through her tears, she failed to see his gaze fall upon her. She might have stayed and the world would most certainly have been different had she seen his look. As it was, she turned and followed the dusty trail down the hill, painful memories clutching at her heart.

"What are you looking at?" Jacob asked.

Xavier blinked his eyes at the figures shuffling down the hill. "Nothing, Uncle Jacob. A memory from the past. For a moment I thought..."

"Thought what?"

Xavier blinked his eyes again and reconciled in his mind that the impossible could not, in fact, be reality.

"My eyes playing tricks, Jacob. Never mind."

"Wait till you get to be my age. The eyes. Ach, how I wish for the vision of my youth."

"Your vision's not that bad, Jacob. You shouldn't complain."

"I'm old, Zavi. It's my right to complain. It's one of the few pleasures I have left in life. You'll see someday."

Xavier conceded the point with a smile. "If complaining makes you happy, then bitch all you want, Uncle Jacob. Happy men live longer. And I want you around for a long time to come."

"Ha. You don't know what you're asking for."

The men laughed and ate. The early morning picnic had been Xavier's idea. He wanted to spend some time alone with his godfather away from the house and the constant intrusions. Alone, in this case, meant only four bodyguards. *Il Padrino's* rules were strict and he would not be swayed on this point. Xavier accepted it as a fact of life.

"Just breathe that fresh air," Jacob suggested, inhaling deeply. "I'm glad we came out before the heat set in."

"Fortunately for us, we don't have a problem getting up early. Although, I do worry about you getting your rest."

"Don't know how to sleep late, Zavi. Can't remember the last time I did. Can you?"

"No, I can't."

It was true. Early rising was a habit for both—Xavier from his days in the Corps and Jacob from decades spent making early rounds at the hospital. Normally, Elena rose with Xavier, but the past few days she had stayed in bed late and napped often during the day. Xavier knew she was not sick and his mind was too occupied with other matters to give her change in behavior more than a fleeting thought. He stretched and yawned, stirring sugar into his espresso.

"These olive groves remind me of Israel. Mount Hebron. You should visit sometime."

"Maybe, when I get time, Uncle Jacob."

"You should make time. You'd be surprised what you might find."

"We'll see. So when are you leaving for the U. S.?" Xavier responded, steering Jacob away from discussing his spiritual well-being. Jacob knew he was being dodged, but let it go for the moment.

"In a few days. When will you be going home?"

"Tomorrow. I've got an election to run."

Jacob hid his disappointment. "Yes, you do. But can you win?"

"I think so. I'm bringing home a multi-billion dollar project that will make Nicaragua prosperous and powerful. The people will be grateful. At least long enough for me to win."

"And what of the United States?"

"We've already been receiving entreaties from the State Department. They're scared to death of being left out of the project altogether."

"Are you going to leave them out?"

"It's possible. My heart says yes. But my head says no."

"Listen to your head, Zavi. The United States would be an unbelievably powerful enemy. Throw them a few bones to keep them happy."

"You sound like Papa," Xavier remarked. "If I do that, then they might try to eat the whole carcass."

"President Davis is too good a man to overstep his bounds. But he is also stubborn," Jacob warned. "Try not to alienate him."

"Uncle Jacob. I find it hard to trust him. We have solid evidence that shows direct CIA involvement in the attempted coup. Furthermore, that involvement was aimed at keeping a drug pipeline open from the South American drug cartels through Nicaragua to the United States. The CIA used the profits to finance black ops around the world that Congress would not approve of."

Xavier sipped his espresso and continued.

"Barton, the CIA director, is in it up to his neck. As for Davis, I can only hope it was done under his nose without his sanction. If Davis will agree to extradition of the offending parties to Nicaragua to stand trial, then I will entertain his ideas. If not, then I will have no choice but to alienate him. Nicaragua won't stand for that kind of interference. And neither will I."

"You are as stubborn as President Davis," Jacob said disconcerted. "Sooner or later, you must come to terms with the fact, however uncomfortable, that the United States rules your part of the world. As difficult as it is, you must forgive and move on."

"Have you forgiven the Germans for killing six million Jews during the war?"

Jacob's silence was his answer.

"That's what I thought, Jacob. I can't forgive the thousands we lost in the coup. The United States must be held accountable for its crimes.

"The British called it colonialism. The Nazis called it *lebensraum*. The United States called it Manifest Destiny. Either way it means the same thing. The deaths of innocent people due to the will of a foreign government. Other countries in Latin America might not be able to stop it, but I will use all my power in Nicaragua to make sure it stays at our borders."

"All this talk of freedom and justice is very noble. But are you sure your personal feelings aren't fueling your desire for a confrontation with America?"

Xavier dropped his head and stared at the table. "That was a long time ago, Jacob."

"So were my experiences on my journey to America. But the pain is always there."

Xavier stood in the living room of the Davis mansion looking at a picture of a mighty man-of-war hanging over the fireplace. He waited for his friend John Jr. to come down the stairs to play. When the door opened it wasn't John Jr. who entered the room, but his father.

"Hello, Xavier. I'm afraid John can't come down to play at the moment."

"Is he sick, Mr. Davis?" the small boy asked.

"No, Xavier. He's not sick."

"Then can I come by later?"

"No, Xavier you can't." Mr. Davis looked very sad. "I don't think it is a good idea for you to play with John anymore."

Xavier's heartbeat raced the way it did when he was in trouble. "Are you mad at me?"

Mr. Davis tried to smile. "No, Xavier. You've done nothing wrong. It's just…better this way."

Xavier opened his mouth but nothing came out—his throat felt thick and closed. As he started to cry, he ran past Mr. Davis and out of the house into the cold autumn air.

"President Davis wasn't the only parent who kept me from children," Xavier stated.

"No, but he was the first, wasn't he?"

Xavier's face became hard. "It changes nothing, Uncle Jacob."

Jacob smirked. "Why do you always choose the difficult path?"

Xavier shrugged. "Unfortunately, in my life, the difficult path has been the right path. I wish it were not so, Jacob. But I cannot deny my destiny."

"Benjamin told me the president has sent an emissary. Will you meet with him?"

"Yes. Of course I will. The president has called for a summit in Mexico City as soon as possible."

Jacob paused. "He sent John Jr., didn't he?"

"Yes, he sent my lost friend. How thoughtful," Xavier answered sarcastically.

The men were silent for a moment. At length, Jacob looked at Xavier with moist eyes. "I fear for you, Zavi; you take so many chances."

Xavier reached across the table and grasped Jacob's hand in his. "Do not worry, Uncle Jacob. Things always seem to work out."

The two men spent the rest of the morning drinking espresso and talking about happier times. When the heat began to rise, Xavier summoned the car and took Jacob back to the house.

Busambra Brownstone, Manhattan, New York, September 13, 1994

"No news?"

"Nothing, Anthony," Bruno Patagali, Anthony Busambra's bodyguard, answered.

"When was the last time you called?"

"A few minutes ago. I call every hour, like you said," Patagali confirmed, confidently. He hesitated, then offered, "If you called, they'd put you through to the don right away."

"You're calling for me, Bruno! It's the same goddamned thing, you moron!"

"Sorry, boss."

Anthony waved him off. "Forget it. Just get me something to drink. And keep calling!"

Truth be told, Anthony was afraid to contact the estate. He would be humiliated if his father wouldn't take the call.

"Goddamned Rizzi," Anthony mumbled.

His father had turned control of the family over to Anthony while he was on vacation in Sicily. Anthony's moment had finally arrived and he was determined to use this chance to earn his father's full trust. Rizzi had even left him with the impression that more power could be conferred on him when they returned. The keys to the kingdom had been within his grasp.

Then he'd discovered the vacation in Sicily was a ruse. Rizzi and his father had gone on important family business which might well affect the economy of the whole world.

"And I'm stuck here counting beans. What bullshit." Anthony huffed and stood up.

Once again Rizzi has maneuvered me right out of the picture. Why does he always shield my father from me? What does he think I'll do?

Anthony leaned on his father's desk, looking at Rizzi's chair. "Maybe it is not what I'll do but what I'll find out."

With this troubling thought in his head, Anthony Busambra went in search of his bodyguard.

Sicily, September 15, 1994

"It's been a long time, John."

"Yes it has, *Señor Presidente*."

The president of Nicaragua shook hands with the chief of staff to the president of the United States in the foyer of the Busambra house.

"What brings you here, my old friend?"

"As you know, the president would like to hold a summit in Mexico City concerning the disposition of the canal. He's asked me to come here and secure your agreement, *Señor Presidente*."

"I remember a time when you called me 'Xavier' and President Davis, 'Dad'."

John Davis Jr. flushed slightly. He was unsure what protocol would dictate in this situation. "I guess I'm going by the old marine adage 'if you can't kill it, paint it, or blow it up, then salute it'."

"I was a marine once," Xavier said quietly.

"Could we speak privately, please?"

Xavier took pity on his former friend. "This way, Mr. Davis. My family welcomes you."

He led the COS into his godfather's study and offered him a chair. Davis stared at his former schoolmate settling behind the imposing desk. Xavier caught his eye and John looked away.

"What are you staring at, Mr. Davis?" Xavier asked.

"I'm sorry. It's been a long time since I've seen you."

"Having a hard time relating me to the kid you grew up with? Or can't you believe the godson of a gangster, cashiered from the U.S. military, is now the president of a foreign country?"

Davis was flustered now and looked it. "I...meant..."

Xavier held up his hand. "Forgive me, John. Seeing you brought up a lot of difficult memories—none of which are your fault. I'm sorry if I've made you feel ill at ease. If you'll call me Xavier, I think it would be easier for both of us."

"Thank you, Xavier," Davis sighed in relief. "I know this is hard for you. It's not exactly easy for me."

"Then let's get on with it," Xavier smiled. "What did your father send you here for?"

Davis came to the point quickly. "He is afraid that what happened in the past might color your thinking. He wants to meet with you to make sure our countries can coexist peacefully."

"I understand his concern. But I wouldn't allow the past to jeopardize the relationship between our two countries."

"He will be greatly relieved to hear that, Xavier. My father still struggles with the decision he made years ago."

"It must have been a difficult one. I know your father is not a cruel man; he had his reasons for breaking off our friendship."

"I watched you leave our house that afternoon from my window upstairs. I cried for days," Davis admitted. "But father was adamant. He wanted nothing to harm our family. And he was afraid of your father's connections to the—er—other side."

"You mean the mafia? It's all right, John. It is no secret that my father was heavily connected to *La Cosa Nostra,* or that Bennedetto Busambra is my godfather," Xavier said matter-of-factly. "It took courage for you to come to Sicily, even in secrecy. I wonder what the press would make of your visit to this house?"

"Dear God, Xavier. Let's hope they don't find out. Your connection to Don Busambra has already gotten quite a lot of play on the news back home," Davis disclosed.

"I can imagine. What's the consensus?"

"There's only speculation. The canal will be under mafia control. Nicaragua concocted the bombing of Panama to get their own canal. Quite a few Americans think you're a traitor and should be shot. It's unbelievable. Conspiracy theories are everywhere and getting more unreal by the minute."

"And what does that mean to us?"

"We need to come to some sort of accommodation," Davis insisted. "And the quicker, the better."

"I'm going to ask for terms before I accept an invitation to a summit in Mexico City."

"Such as?" Davis asked, anxious to know.

"A written guarantee, signed by the president, specifically stating that no overt or covert operations will be targeted at Nicaragua for an indefinite period."

"That's asking a lot, considering the political climate," Davis expressed, vacillating. "Americans look on your country as an enemy. That document would tie my father's hands and I don't think the voters would cotton to that. A verbal statement would be a lot easier for the public to swallow."

"Your father's word is good. I know that. Nonetheless, if I can get it in writing, then I will attend the summit in Mexico City. U. S. cooperation will be a lot easier for me to sell to my people with that piece of paper. You understand, they don't trust your government worth a damn. Not with all the rumors about CIA complicity in the deaths of several thousand Nicaraguans."

Davis wondered how close Xavier was to discovering the truth behind the rumors. His office's investigation of the coup had uncovered several unsavory facts about Barton. Enough to scare the president. If they came to light, the negotiations would be finished. As soon as the summit was through, the president planned to sack the CIA director.

"I see your point," Davis conceded. "I'll get it in writing."

"Good," Xavier smiled, encouraged. "As soon as the document is in my possession, then we can begin discussion of more serious matters at this summit your father has called."

Davis took Xavier's statement to mean talks on American involvement in the canal could begin. He didn't know how wrong he was.

"Now that we have that settled, tell me how your family is," Xavier said as he relaxed.

For the next hour they exchanged news on family, former classmates, and exploits. Davis told the stories of his helicopter flight around the world and the exciting presidential campaign. Xavier told Davis about *his* presidential campaign and the trials of running a government. On a somber note, they talked about the nuclear terrorist attack in Panama and Russia's return to dictatorship.

"What we do here and in Mexico City could have a great impact on the world stage."

"I know, John. Let us pray for guidance."

Xavier walked his former classmate to his car.

"Who could have guessed that we would become so powerful, John?"

"Your godfather?" Davis guessed with a sly smile.

"You could be right. He has been the power behind many. Now, Godspeed and good luck."

"*Buen suerte, Señor Presidente,*" the COS replied formally, shaking Xavier's hand. "*Hasta luego.*"

"Until then, my friend."

"So you leave on the morrow?" Bennedetto Busambra asked. He sat with his godson in the study sipping Sambuca.

"Yes, Papa. I have so much to do."

"I know," Busambra yielded. "I just never know when I will see you again."

"Soon, Papa. I promise."

"And next time you will have a family."

Xavier smiled proudly. "Yes, Papa. Elena told me the news this afternoon. Can you believe it? I am going to be a father."

"I am so happy for you, Zavi. It is about time." Busambra smiled slightly. "And now that you are finally settling down, I have a present for you."

The door to the study opened and Luca Baracca appeared carrying a small dog. He handed it to Xavier.

"That will be all, Luca," Busambra said. The bodyguard left the study.

"A dog, Papa? What am I going to do with a dog?"

"Not just any dog, Zavi," Busambra explained. "It is an Italian Greyhound, what you call a whippet. Strong, fast, loyal, and very smart. Just the thing for an old married man with children. I have several myself."

Xavier stared at the small bundle. It was all legs and ears. "Thank you, Papa." At the sound of Xavier's voice the dog looked at him and raised his ears.

"You see he already knows the voice of his master. It is a good start," said Busambra, satisfied that the dog and the man were taking to one another.

The dog climbed onto Xavier's chest and licked him in the face. "Well, what a loving fellow you are," Xavier laughed surprised. The puppy wagged his tail and looked at Xavier curiously. "And what will I call you?" The pup's ears stood straight up at the question. "Such big ears. How about Radar," Xavier decided. The puppy seemed satisfied with Xavier's choice. "You like that, huh, boy. How would you like to be the First Dog of Nicaragua?"

The news of the Nicaraguan Canal burst upon an unsuspecting world. Latin America, the European Commonwealth, and Japan celebrated the new pact. The United States was furious, while Krikalev and his marshals looked on with suspicion.

Xavier returned to Nicaragua victorious. The hero of Honduras was swept into office as the president of a rejuvenated Nicaragua. Millions of dollars poured into the country's treasury and the president began to rebuild his country.

President Davis, reeling from the Panamanian disaster, was vilified in the press for not anticipating the Nicaraguan move. One U.S. canal had been destroyed with the loss of thousands of American lives. The country demanded the new canal be built, at least in part, by the United States. Some suggested that the bombs were a plot hatched by the Nicaraguans to bring them the canal, and too many people listened to the conspiracy despite all the evidence pointing to a Libyan plot.

Under immense pressure, Davis authorized limited air strikes against Libya to punish them for their transgressions. Libya responded by pouring billions into Russian arms production, upsetting the military balance and starting a new arms race. The hope and peace of only two years evaporated as the Cold War was revived. In the midst of these events, President Davis traveled to Mexico City for a summit with the Nicaraguan president.

Public opinion favored a U.S. invasion if the summit was a failure. Many Americans felt Nicaragua had pushed them aside for Japanese and European interests.

Politicians in Congress revived the long-dead spirit of Manifest Destiny and the Monroe Doctrine and whipped the country into an anti-Latin frenzy. The State Department blew the dust off the 1914 Bryan-Chamorro treaty to demonstrate the Unites States' legal right to intercede in Nicaragua. Race riots broke out in East L.A. and Spanish Harlem. The Latin world retaliated with attacks on U.S. embassies throughout Central and South America. The world watched and waited, praying for level heads to take charge and calm things down before the situation came unhinged.

30

Mexico City, Mexico, December 17, 1994

The president of Mexico arrived at 11:45 and was greeted by Xavier Daniels and his ambassador to Mexico. At noon, President Davis was greeted by the president of Mexico who, as the host for the summit, introduced him to President Daniels. After a brief photo session, the men entered the embassy and disappeared from sight.

The summit was held in the embassy reception room. The three presidents took their seats at a circular table that dominated the hall and waited for their various aides to settle in. After a cue, the president of Mexico gave his opening remarks. When he was done, the proceedings were blessed by Cardinal Marquez d' Aqina. Following the blessing, the men got down to business.

"I believe you have something for me, President Davis," Xavier opened.

"No formalities, just straight to it President Daniels? I can do that," President Davis responded.

Davis handed a document to his son, who passed it to Xavier with a smile.

"Signed, sealed, and delivered, President Daniels. My written pledge not to interfere with Nicaraguan autonomy in any way for the length of your presidency. I hope you understand how difficult this will make it for me back home," Davis queried.

430

"I appreciate your position, President Davis. It took courage to sign this. My country thanks you."

Xavier handed the pledge to an aide who left the room to make copies and present them to the media immediately.

"And now, Mr. President I have something for you."

Huberto laid a stack of documents in front of President Davis. Davis looked questioningly at his secretary of state, Milton Tremont.

"What is this, President Daniels?" he inquired unsurely.

"Proof for a man of justice such as yourself, President Davis. The signed confessions of two CIA agents captured recently at a contra camp in northern Nicaragua. They were captured in a raid planned to find the Ortega brothers who, unfortunately, got away. Included in the material before you are Swiss bank account statements tracing payments made to the director of the CIA from members of the Cali drug cartels. Other documents concern operation orders detailing CIA participation in the August coup on the side of the Contras and a recent campaign aimed at destabilizing *my* government."

The president was stunned. He quickly conferred with his Secretary of State while the room waited anxiously for a response.

"We appreciate your concern, President Daniels," Tremont began. "We'll look into these allegations at the earliest possible date."

"We will look at them now, Mr. Secretary," Xavier replied sternly.

"President Daniels," Davis snapped, barely containing his temper. "We had a deal. You told my chief of staff that we would discuss the canal if I signed that damned pledge. I did so. Now let's get on to the business at hand."

"I told your son that when I had this written guarantee of non-interference, we could discuss more important matters," Xavier said, clarifying his comment. "To my country, this is far more important than your desire to participate in the building of the Nicaraguan canal, which, I might add, is already under construction. As soon as this issue is resolved, I promise we can open discussions on American involvement in the canal."

"President Daniels," Tremont broke in. "President Davis already plans to dismiss Barton as soon as he arrives back home. This evidence will only speed up the process. But we came to Mexico City to make an agreement concerning the construction and defense of the Nicaraguan Canal. Surely this matter can wait."

"I will be happy to discuss your desire to participate in the canal," Xavier reiterated. "But only after the criminals named in those papers are extradited to Nicaragua to stand trial for murder."

"Impossible!" Davis shouted, throwing his hands up in frustration. The Mexican president suggested a recess to calm things down, but Davis and Daniels refused.

"If you want a fight, then we'll fight, President Daniels," Davis continued. "The Bryan-Chamorro treaty of 1914 gave the United States the sole right to construct and defend the Nicaraguan Canal. That treaty is still in effect and is being used by a growing number of congressmen as the basis for military action. I'm trying to save lives here, Mr. President. Let's sign an agreement before things get ugly and out of control."

"The United States has broken dozens of treaties with its Native American population. The only time you honor a treaty is when it is convenient and serves your purposes. Like now, Mr. President. I would like to help you, President Davis, but my hands are tied on this matter. My vice president, Brooklyn Rivera, is a Miskito Indian. He suggests that we should honor the Bryan-Chamorro treaty after you honor all your treaties with Native Americans."

Davis jumped to his feet and pounded on the table. "What the hell do American Indians have to do with the damned canal in Nicaragua?"

The assembled bureaucrats jumped at Davis' unexpected outburst. Milton Tremont pulled at the president's arm trying to get him to take his seat. Davis wasn't having any of it.

"I'll bet if I dig deep enough I can find Nicaraguan complicity in the Panama debacle," Davis threatened, shaking a finger at Xavier. "And if so, I'll have a mandate to take Nicaragua by force. Don't push me, young man."

Xavier lifted a copy of Davis' pledge. "You know, as well as I, that Nicaragua had nothing to do with Panama," Xavier lied. "Your name is on this piece of paper, Mr. President. Right now it is being read to the world press. Either you are a man of your word or you are not."

Davis' face was red with rage, but he fought to get himself under control. "My word is good, President Daniels. If I am known for one thing it is that. But please do not let the crimes of a few men stand in the way of mutual cooperation," he begged.

"Those few men are responsible for the deaths of thousands of my countrymen, President Davis. Why do you protect them?"

"They will be tried under due process. Do you remember what that is?" Davis asked, thinking quickly. News of Barton's involvement would be a disaster. The CIA director would be treated as a hero for having tried to do what he just threatened—take Nicaragua for the benefit of the United States. The drug connection would be overlooked. If Davis had Barton extradited to Nicaragua, a fate he deserved, the president would be crucified back home. The Ollie North affair loomed in his mind. "Our justice department works slowly, but it works."

"Tell that to the families of the people killed in the coup!" Xavier voiced with righteous indignation. "All they comprehend is their grief."

"Trust me, President Daniels, if they are guilty, then you will get them," Davis promised.

"Their guilt will be decided by a Nicaraguan court. Enough evidence has been presented to hand down indictments. Nicaragua and the U.S. have an extradition agreement, Mr. President. If you follow it, the talks can continue."

"I can't do that, Mr. President. I am sorry," Davis said as he resignedly sat down.

"You are a man of justice, President Davis," Xavier spoke quietly. "Why do you not seek it now?"

"Why are you so damn insistent on having it?" Davis countered. "I didn't know about Barton. I swear. Will you make both our countries pay for the sins of one man?"

"It has to stop somewhere," Xavier propounded. "The abuses of power; the forgotten innocents trampled underneath the boots of selective memory and partial justice. You have to be held accountable. It's time to pay the piper for years of doing whatever you wished in our part of the world."

"You wish me to pay for the transgressions of countless previous administrations when all I've tried to do since taking office is change the way things are done in Washington?"

"Sometimes, President Davis, we must pay for the sins of our fathers," Xavier uttered without mercy.

President Davis slumped in his chair defeated, visions of a young boy standing on his porch with tears in his eyes swimming in his memory.

"Why, Xavier? Why?" Davis asked dejectedly.

"All I want is the chance for Nicaragua to prosper. Let her go, Mr. President. She doesn't need a father anymore. It is time she learned to walk by herself."

"And if I don't?" he asked, not meaning it.

"If you break your word, we will go to war to protect our right of self-determination."

"Then we are done here," Davis said, standing. "I would have protected you, President Daniels. Now you have tied my hands. Proceed carefully. The world is a dangerous place."

"Thank you for the advice, President Davis. But I already know how dangerous the world can be."

No, you don't, Davis thought as he led his entourage out of the reception hall.

Daniels returned to Nicaragua to another hero's welcome. Construction on the canal began while the world waited for the American's response. The quiet closing of the American Embassy was the only retaliation for Nicaragua's stubborn behavior. No embargoes were launched. No economic measures sanctioned. They wouldn't have done any good. Not with the money pouring in from Europe and Japan.

Davis' welcome was less enthusiastic but far from the nightmare he expected. The situation in the Balkans, the new arms race, and a cataclysmic earthquake in California diverted the public eye from what had taken place in Mexico City. The country was, once again, happy to have a strong president at the helm.

Barton was dismissed and replaced by Admiral Chace Haynes. The new director of the CIA frantically tried to discover

Barton's co-conspirators, but the trail had long since grown cold. The conspirators, undiscovered and unpunished, were left to hatch new plots on an unaware planet.

Landringham Estate, December 24, 1994

"So what do we do now?" the Sicilian asked as he sipped on a glass of red wine.

"You can do what you want. My plans won't include any more imbeciles," Hammersmith answered. He warmed his hands by the fire and examined the Man Ray original hanging above the mantle. It was his second purchase of a painting by the artist and, as such, he referred to it simply as Man Ray 2. When he was done examining the work, he walked to the window. Outside, heavy snow fell on the Virginia countryside.

"I understand. How you feel, that is," the Sicilian responded after a moment.

Hammersmith half-turned to look at his guest before turning back to watch the snowfall.

"May I ask what your plans might be?" the Sicilian asked.

Hammersmith didn't respond.

"I can assure you I'm not one of the imbeciles responsible for what happened," the Sicilian guaranteed.

"I had him, again," Hammersmith spoke softly. "And again he slipped away. Next time it will not happen."

"What will happen next time?" the Sicilian asked more than curious.

Hammersmith turned and faced the Sicilian. "Everything." Hammersmith said smiling.

"Everything?"

"Everything, my friend. We fulfill all our destinies in one move," Hammersmith spelled out. "President Davis dies. President Daniels dies. Bennedetto Busambra dies. The Jew Rabinowitz dies. I become the most powerful man on earth. You assume the mantle of *il capo di tuti capi*. And my father can finally rest in peace."

"And how do you propose we do that, Senator?"

So Hammersmith told him. "It will take years to plan. But, for once, time is on our side. First, Marshal Krikalev and the Russians will..."

The Sicilian listened patiently. The senator was a diabolical genius.

When he was done, the senator asked, "Well, what do you think?"

"Brilliant. I am impressed with your plan, but it's missing one thing."

"And what is that?" the senator asked surprised.

"Daniels' pain. Or had you forgotten?"

"No, I hadn't. But this time I will have to be satisfied with his death."

"No, you won't," the Sicilian smiled. "Consider this gift a Christmas present."

The Sicilian lit a cigarette and expounded on his newly discovered secret.

Hearing of his gift, the senator laughed and clapped his hands in childlike glee. "I can't believe it! I don't know how to thank you."

"Oh, I don't think you have to worry about that, Senator. I'm sure I'll think of something," he chuckled.

Christmas Eve passed into Christmas Day, but neither man seemed to notice. On the holiest day of the year the most unholy of plans was given life.

Lago de Nicaragua, Managua, Nicaragua, December 25, 1994

The shores of the Lago de Nicaragua were packed as thousands of Nicaraguans celebrated the groundbreaking of the trans-isthmian canal. The president declared a national fiesta and, across the country, people were gathering to celebrate. Daniels timed the ceremony to coincide with Christmas and its malleable symbolism. The birth of the Savior and the birth of a new Nicaragua.

The canal would take years to complete instead of the decade it had taken in Panama, partially due to Nicaragua's unique topography. A series of lakes and rivers were scattered across the narrowest section of the country. Every mile of existing waterway cut months off construction time. The Panamanian canal had required workers to cut a ditch across an entire country. Although the construction would continue well into the new millennium, the first ships were scheduled to pass through the canal in only six years.

The celebrants danced and sang as they waited for the emergence of their hero, Xavier Daniels. Many had traveled across the country on foot, sleeping in the fields and waiting for days to be a part of their hero's celebration. At noon, Xavier Daniels exited his limousine with his pregnant wife and their dog Radar and mounted the steps of a small stage on shore. At the sight of him, the crowd erupted in a spine-tingling shout that rushed over the water.

Xavier smiled at the crowd and put an arm around his wife. He felt goose bumps rise on his arms as he enjoyed the adulation of the people. Radar barked energetically, startled by the noise, and Elena waved to the masses with her husband.

Finally, Xavier approached a podium centered on the stage. He turned to the packed dais and acknowledged the international dignitaries who had been invited to join in the celebration. After shaking several hands, he turned to face his people. He held up his hand and a hush fell across the shore.

Xavier began simply. *"Nuestro milagro."* A burst of applause came from the Plaza. Our miracle. Nicaraguans had christened their canal with this phrase.

"Nuestro milagro empezó contigos!" Our miracle began with you.

The cheering that followed was the loudest sound Xavier had ever heard. When the roar of the crowd subsided, Xavier motioned for Huberto to hand him a detonator. The crowd noise diminished dramatically as Xavier turned the arming key.

An explosion blew an enormous cloud of dirt into the sky. As the dust settled, a huge depression appeared in the dry river bed close to shore. The citizens of Nicaragua raised their voices in celebration as the construction of the canal officially began.

The fresh-water sharks of the Lago de Nicaragua darted about in the dark nervously snapping at one another. Noises had reverberated through their previously silent domain for the past few weeks, upsetting the predators. They waited anxiously for the new threat to appear, ready to strike at anything.

The explosion slapped across the water and reverberated throughout their domain. The sharks scattered, trying to flee the unseen horror. When nothing happened, the wary sharks, the only fresh-water genus of their species, gathered again and swam in a defensive circular formation.

When the sound had subsided, the sharks investigated their dark realm, realizing with some primitive sense that the lake in which they lived, secure and unchanged for millions of years, had somehow been transformed forever.

EPILOGUE

Busambra Estate, Palermo, Sicily, December 31, 1994

The sun dipped low as the young peasant hurried back to his house, hoping his mother would not be upset with him. He was taking her to a New Year's party in Palermo, but had been delayed by his job at the local olive press.

Although he had put in a full day of labor, he was not fatigued. His eighteen-year-old frame was sturdy and lined with muscles. He played soccer whenever he got the chance and enjoyed hiking the hills of the estate.

His mother, amazed at his stamina, had often worried that her son's constant activity would exhaust him. Whenever she complained, he would lift her off her feet and twirl her around the room. Thinking of this, he smiled and quickened his pace, anxious to see her.

Reaching the crest of the hill, he paused. Their front door was open and light spilled onto the porch as the sky darkened. Realizing something was wrong, he broke into a run.

The peasant leaped through the doorway and stopped in his tracks. Blood was splashed on the walls of the living room. His mother's body lay half-in and half-out of the fireplace smoldering in the dying embers. With an animal scream, he jumped to her side and dragged her corpse from the fire.

He held her for a long time, examining the charred flesh, smelling the horrible stench. He forced himself to take in the nightmarish sight so that he would remember every detail.

A sound at the doorway drew his attention. His long hair flew and blue eyes flashed as his head whipped around and he saw the stranger standing in the doorway. The peasant laid his mother on the ground and snarled, ready to attack. The man held up his hands and said, "I am not the one who did this. But I know who did."

The peasant crouched ready to commence his assault, but held back for one question. "Who was it then? And quick before I kill you," he screamed, barely containing himself.

"Bennedetto Busambra's godson. Your father, Xavier Daniels."

My father? he thought. My father?

The boy became dizzy and collapsed. When he regained his equilibrium, he noticed the house was dark. He saw the stranger in the twilight, kneeling next to his mother's body.

"Who are you?" the orphan asked.

"A friend," the stranger said reassuringly as he clicked on a small flashlight. The stranger shined the light on his face and the boy noticed the scar for the first time. It ran up one side of the man's face and glowed white in the light from the electric torch.

"If you are a friend," the peasant said through gritting teeth, "you will lead me to my father so that I may kill him and avenge my mother."

Kruger clicked off the flashlight and smiled. Phase One of Man Ray 2 was complete.